Havoc Peaks

Havoc Peaks

A Havoc in Wyoming Story

Millie Copper

Written by Millie Copper

Edited by Ameryn Tucker

Proofread by Light Hand Proofreading

Cover Design by Dauntless Cover Design

Also by Millie Copper

The Havoc in Wyoming Series

When a series of coordinated attacks devastate the United States, the people of Bakerville, Wyoming, must come together to survive. Unfortunately, not everyone has the town's best interest at heart. Some are striving for personal gain during the apocalypse.

The Montana Mayhem Series

A group from Bakerville, Wyoming strikes out on their own while searching for the desires of their heart. Unfortunately, the road will not be easy, and sometimes the heart is hardened and deceitful. When things don't work out as they hoped, will they become stranded in the wilderness? Or will each be able to find their way home?

The Dakota Destruction Series

After a series of coordinated attacks devastate the United States, Katie and Leo sacrifice everything to help their country. But some things aren't as they seem. Is it time to go home and start fresh, or can something good come out of this terrible situation?

The Lights of the Collapse Series

As martial law descends and society crumbles, families must band together to survive, finding strength in their unity amidst the chaos. But with danger lurking around every corner and the very fabric of reality seeming to unravel, they discover that the greatest threats might be closer than they ever imagined.

In The October Fall World

In the blink of an eye, an EMP changed everything for Lauren and her family. Now they are in a fight for survival, trying to keep their loved ones alive as society collapses around them. Their once peaceful town of Cody, Wyoming has turned into a powder keg. And with law enforcement a thing of the past, evil lurks around every corner.

In The As The Light Dies World

Lisa Bentley thought having her daughter attacked and left for dead was the worst thing that could happen. She was wrong. She and her family lived an ideal life operating a bed and breakfast in the perfect Wyoming town. That world came crashing down when her daughter was attacked.

The Code Umbra Series

When Dr. Tessa Courtland is called in on a top-secret government project, she knows it's something big. But the truth is far more terrifying than she ever could've imagined. A massive asteroid is on course to skim past Earth, close enough to throw the world off balance and change life forever.

Nonfiction Books

Millie has penned seven nonfiction, traditional food focused books, sharing how, with a little creativity, anyone can transition to a real foods diet without overwhelming their food budget. Many of her books also include preparedness and food storage tips.

Find these titles at MillieCopper.com

Join My Reader's Club!

Receive a complimentary copy of *Wyoming Refuge: A Havoc in Wyoming Prequel*. As part of my reader's club, you'll be the first to know about new releases and specials. I also share info on books I'm reading, preparedness tips, and more. Please sign up on my website:

MillieCopper.com

Chapter 1

Day 1

Mollie tosses an oversized suitcase into the trunk of her rental car, taking her sweet time to mess with the mass amount of stuff she has. I do my best to keep an even look on my face. Part of me wants to tell her what I think of her plans and how ridiculous she's being. The other part of me just wants her gone. We're in the middle of a crisis, and she's the last person I want to have around.

As my husband's employee, she visits the business several times a year. Because our small community doesn't have a hotel, Mollie stays with us. I dread her visits. The first few days aren't terrible, but it's the old adage of fish and houseguests both starting to stink after three days. She's been here since Sunday and is now way past her prime. And tonight, I saw a part of her that really makes me wonder if she might not be mentally ill. That would explain many of the strange things I've noticed about her over the years.

After she finally finishes fiddling, she turns to us and hurriedly—almost frantically—says, "I worry it's not safe here. Maybe it's too close to Portland. Do you think you guys should come with me? We can get your dad, of course."

I meet Ben's eyes, assuming he knows what I'm thinking. Finally, he says, "We worry it's not safe here either."

Nope, that wasn't it.

He continues with, "I think, if things go bad in Portland, people will start heading this way."

What? He's sounding almost as loony as Mollie! I give him a hard look, but he keeps talking.

"Some will probably think they can survive in the forest, and when they can't, well, we're the next populated area. But I'd like to think that isn't going to happen. Remember the comradery after 9/11? Most likely, it will be the same now. There's no reason to think otherwise . . . as long as nothing else happens. If it does, we could combine forces with the neighbors here, then we can increase our chances of safety."

He gives me a look, and I nod. Not because I agree. I'm not sure exactly *why* I nodded. Maybe just so this conversation can finish and Mollie will leave.

"I think that's a good plan," Mollie says with a slow nod. "I have to admit, I wasn't even thinking long term, but I'm concerned, if there's another attack, Portland could be affected and whatever happens there would directly affect you."

"Also possible," Ben says. "We're going into town first thing in the morning. We'll be there when the store opens and buy a few things."

We are? First I've heard of this.

He gives me a nod and says, "I think getting what we need just in case is a good idea."

"Good plan, Ben. Maybe get your camping gear in order too. You know, just in case you have to leave your place in a hurry," Mollie says, looking like a bobble head.

I'm sure I make a face, but Mollie chooses to ignore it. There's no way we're leaving our home. That would be nothing short of ridiculous. I barely listen as she drones on about wanting to have paychecks handed out early. I'm sure Ben will put his foot down and remind her payday is Monday and there's no reason to provide checks sooner. Then she tells him she wants to suggest the employees get cash and buy extra food. What a nut she is!

I want to smack Ben when he says, "Sure, Mollie. Checks tomorrow are no problem. I suspect a few of the guys are already planning their purchases for tomorrow."

Mollie gives a solemn nod and then turns back to the rental, fiddling with things a bit more. I'm just about to tell them I'm going inside when she turns and wraps Ben in a hug. "Be safe, Ben. I'll check in with you soon."

"Yeah, Mollie," he says. "Call tomorrow and tell us where you are. Use your company card for fuel. You're still on the clock until you get home."

"Okay, thanks, Ben."

She turns to embrace me, stretching up slightly on her toes.

She's so short, I have to hunch over to keep it from being awkward. "Take care of yourself," I say woodenly.

"Oh, hey, did you happen to look and see if your rental car includes an emergency kit?" Ben asks. "Pop the trunk and let me look. I doubt it does."

I roll my eyes. *Is she ever going to leave?*

Mollie pops open the trunk. Ben reports there isn't one and tells Mollie to hold on a minute. I stand awkwardly while he goes inside the house, then returns with a premade roadside kit.

"I get these things as gifts but never need them," he says, bouncing down the front steps. "You take this one, just in case."

"Thanks, Ben. I appreciate it." Mollie finally climbs in her car and heads down our driveway, giving a wave as she goes.

"Well . . . " I say. "That was weird."

"In what way?"

"All the garbage she had stored here. The mass amount of junk food she bought at the mini-mart. Her paranoia. All of it. I've always thought she was strange, especially these last few years after she *found Jesus again.*" I pause long enough to make sure he knows what I think of that. "But this . . . this seriously takes the cake."

He narrows his brilliant blue eyes at me. "You don't think she might be right about this? That things might be worse tomorrow and getting home is smart?"

"I think she's a nut. And I think you should've put your foot down about her taking the rental car. Do you know how much it's going to cost for her to not drop it off where she rented it? And what is with telling her to use the company fuel card?"

"Seriously? Five planes were just shot out of the sky, and from the sounds of it, there's no way to prevent it from happening again. Air travel will be nonexistent for who knows how long. And with what happened at the airports after the first responders arrived, with things being blown to kingdom come, I think she may be right. This could be the beginning of World War III."

"Oh, puh-leeze. You're sounding as loony as she is."

"You even agreed!" Ben throws his hands in the air. "When we were still in the house and talking about whether or not we'd be safe here, you asked if we'd be safe anywhere."

"I didn't really mean it! I just—I was caught up in the moment. Maybe reason left me for a minute or two, but seriously. This is awful and terrible, even *more* than awful and terrible, but it's not going to be the end of the world."

Ben gives me a look, a cross between anger and pity. He pushes a tuft of thinning blond hair out of his eyes before giving me a curt nod. "I hope you're right, because I'm leaning toward Mollie's thoughts."

"Remember 9/11? You thought that was going to be more too. It wasn't. The country came together for a few days and then we got on with our lives."

"9/11 changed things, Clarice. It changed how we fly, and it started a war. You and I may not have been affected by it, but others were. It's naive to think things won't change after these attacks."

"I'm not an idiot, Ben," I say with disgust. "I know things will change. I just don't think Mollie needs to be so dramatic with her survival supplies and rushing out in the middle of the night. And I think you should make her pay for the car rental. It's not a business expense when she just wants to go home and be with her family."

Ben shakes his head and sighs. "If it was you, if you were the one away on work for your company, wouldn't you want to get home to us as quickly as possible?"

"Totally different. I'm co-owner of my company. Mollie is nothing but an employee—an employee who's paid way too much and still takes advantage of you."

"Enough," Ben practically bellows. I shrink back slightly at his anger. "She's paid an appropriate amount for the work she does. Not that it's any of your concern."

"Not true. Every pay increase and bonus you give her is taking away from our retirement."

"And how does she get bonuses? By bringing in business. If she weren't bringing in the business, we wouldn't be building our retirement. I'm not making her pay for the rental car, and I don't want to hear another word about it. What I *am* doing is going back inside and going to bed. I'll be leaving early to fill up all of our gas tanks and buy extra food."

"Fine. But plan on using your own money for those things because I'm not on board and will not contribute to such lunacy."

"Give it a rest, Clarice," he says between gritted teeth. "You don't need to be so uptight."

"Uptight? You think this is about me being uptight?"

"No, I think it's about your ridiculous and unsubstantiated hatred of Mollie Caldwell."

"My dislike of her is neither ridiculous nor unsubstantiated. She's annoying and . . . and this is it, Ben. Next time she's here for work, she stays in Alto."

"Fine," he hisses.

"And another thing, tonight *is* terrible and tragic. I'm not denying that. Most likely this will change things for us, for the United States, but I refuse to believe it's anything more than what it is."

"And exactly *what* is it?" Ben crosses his arms and glares at me. "What is it you think you know?"

"A terrorist attack! What else? Not some major conspiracy requiring packing up and driving home in the middle of the night—though, I'm glad she's gone! You can look like a fool if you want. It won't be the first time." He narrows his eyes at me and opens his mouth, but I hold up my hand and rush on. "But I refuse. I refuse to get swept up in some ridiculous conspiracy theory." I stomp away, beating him to the front door and slamming it hard behind me.

Every time Mollie visits, which is two or three times a year so she can catch up on things she *thinks* she can't do from Wyoming, we end up in an argument after she leaves. While she's here, I keep my mouth shut and try to make her stay as comfortable for both of us as possible. But it never fails. Ben and I always end up in some sort of argument after she leaves. Usually, his complaint is that I'm too snotty to her. That may be true, but she doesn't notice. She actually thinks we're friends. *Ha!*

Even though I'm not a part of Ben and his dad Bart's machine shop business, I still contribute to the plans and ideas. I know more about marketing than Mollie will ever hope to know, so it's important I give my input.

Tonight, after a delicious dinner out, as expected, Mollie made me crazy when she went on and on and on about how delicious the nasty oysters she ordered were. Seriously. Every single time she visits, we go out to eat, and she always orders those things. She knows I hate them and find them disgusting, but it doesn't matter to her. She'll order the slimy, raw shooters or oysters on a half shell or—like tonight—baked oysters. I'm positive she does it just to irritate me.

Of course, I smile and pretend like it's no big deal, gushing over how wonderful it is she can always have oysters when she visits. It's not like she can get fresh oysters very often in Wyoming.

Anyway, after dinner, we were working on plans for a marketing event at the Portland Convention Center to be held in October. As usual, she had some crazy ideas, so it was up to me to keep things under control.

I was counting the minutes until her flight tomorrow and when she'd be out of my hair for a few more months, when the television announced the attacks: five planes at five different airports were purposely crashed as they were landing. As first responders showed up, multiple bombs were detonated, causing mass casualties. I hate to admit, one of my first thoughts was fear. Fear Mollie could be stuck here for days, or even weeks, while waiting for air travel to restart. I guess I should just be happy she's gone and out of my hair.

Ben's dad thinks Mollie walks on water and can do no wrong. At least Ben is slightly more realistic. Usually, a few days after she leaves, Ben and I laugh over how her visit went and the crazy things she said while she was here. We'd probably talk about how ridiculous this whole thing was—not the crashes, those are terrible, but Mollie's overreaction to them. That's likely what we'd do. Let things calm down, then we'd have a couple of drinks and poke fun at her.

Of course, that's not going to happen. I have no intention of being here in a couple of days. I've made other plans and have just been waiting to execute them until after Mollie's visit. I'm finally going to do what I want to do with my life.

I stifle a sigh. I know I'm too hard on her. Mollie means well and most certainly wants Ben and Bart's business to succeed. And I should thank her for that. We've built up a tidy nest egg over the last couple of years from their business alone. But she's so annoying, even more so in the past year or two since she's started—as she calls it—becoming reacquainted with God and Jesus. At least before then she had a sense of humor and wasn't such a stick in the mud.

Before going to bed, I check in on Liam. Our thirteen-year-old son was terribly upset about the attacks. I poke my head into his second-floor bedroom; his lamp is still on, but he's sound asleep. I can't help but smile at the innocent little boy face. Tonight's tragic events hit him hard. And he's not going to like the changes coming up. But he'll be fine. We'll all be sad in the beginning—change is always hard—but then things will be fine. Great, even. I'm confident of it.

Chapter 2

Day 3

"You were supposed to call me an hour ago," I say, not even bothering with hello, thanks to caller ID, as I quickly move from the living room to my office. Instead of an answer, I hear a strange noise. "Mark? Are you okay?"

"N-no. Not really," Mark says with a sniff." I don't . . . things aren't good here." He sucks in a loud breath. "I know we made plans yesterday, but you shouldn't come here."

"Mark," I say in a near hiss. "I thought . . . you said— "

"I know, Clarice. It's not that. I *do* want us to be together."

A smile crosses my face, and my heart does a flip. "I want us to be together too."

Mark is my business partner. I brought him on a few years ago when I wanted to expand but needed not only more capital but someone who had more business knowledge than me. We've made a great professional team for four years.

The last couple of months, things have changed. Completely out of the blue, his wife left him last fall. He had a terrible time of it, and I've tried to be there for him. I didn't expect our work relationship to change into something different, something more, but it has. We've grown closer than just business partners. Closer than friends, even. And with my own marriage on the rocks . . .

"We *can* be together," I say.

"I don't think it's smart. The cyberattacks the news has been talking about, it's hit Alto."

"Oh. That's not good. We still have power here. Maybe it won't affect us." I bite my lip and think about the last couple of days. The plane crashes were only the beginning. Yesterday, there were bridges destroyed across the United States. Today, the news has been all about a cyberattack taking out electricity and closing all banking. Even social media went down. It's so bad, they're talking about taking the internet offline completely.

"Well, the power went out about half an hour ago," Mark says. "I was packing things up at the office, like we talked about."

I bite my lip. He thought it was a good idea to grab the important stuff out of our riverfront office. I thought it unnecessary, but I figured, if he wanted to waste his time, I'd let him.

"That's why I'm late," Mark says. "The packing went fine. But you won't believe the things happening around here."

I wait for him to continue. When he doesn't, I prod, "Like what?"

"I'll, uh . . . gosh. It's hard to talk about. Let me—I need to back up."

I roll my eyes. Mark is great, but he has a flair for the dramatic. His wife, Patty, always said he loved to build up to things. He can't just give the facts; he has to paint a picture. Usually, I like that about him since his attention to detail is helpful in business and in the new relationship we're developing. He notices everything. Ben never pays attention to me, but if I even try a new shade of lipstick, Mark will notice and comment.

"Take your time," I say, knowing he will anyway.

"When the power went out, it was so strange. Not like just a flicker and it was off. It kept flickering, like a dozen times, then I swear there was a loud *pop* and that was it. I was at the office then, and the phones there stopped working too. Of course they would, since they're a VoIP and it's all hooked through not only the electric company but also the internet. What else would I expect, right?"

"Right. Every time the power goes out, the phones go down. We still have power here," I say again.

"And at least our cells are still working. Clarice, I want you here with me. I really do. And you aren't going to like hearing this— "

"Just tell me."

In barely a whisper, Mark says, "Ben's right. We're not safe here."

"You think Alto is unsafe?"

"I know it is. There are too many refugees. You know how I told you yesterday all the hotels are full?"

"Yes, you told me. Plus, it's all over the news how hotels are filled everywhere."

"Yeah. Within a few hours of the bridges in Portland exploding, we were slammed. It's like super tourist season, with people everywhere, but it was still controlled, you know? Sort of, anyway. But now, that's fading fast. There were three separate house fires last night and a business. The guy renting the office next to ours, he said each fire is arson."

"And he knows this how?"

"His brother-in-law is with the sheriff's department. Or maybe it's his sister. I can't remember. One of his relatives."

That's another thing about Mark. While he likes to tell a good story, he often gets the details wrong. "Arson? That doesn't make any sense."

"None of this makes any sense! Why are all these people even here? It's like everyone has lost their ever-loving minds. There was even some sort of protest last night right outside the city police station."

"Protesting what?"

"The lack of hotel rooms and fuel. With everything full, people are sleeping outside. Their demands are to get either lodging or fuel so they can move on to the next town."

"How do they think the police can provide those?"

"Beats me. Last night was nothing compared to today. The protests are still happening and look to be turning violent."

"I'm sure the police will get it under control."

"That's just it, though. They're not even trying. Rumor is, some of the police aren't even showing up."

"Really? Do you think that's why no one came out here? You know the car wreck I told you about? Ben said the cars are still blocking the highway. He said it's completely unpassable."

"I think so, especially since I've witnessed their slow response with my own eyes."

"Did something happen to you?"

"Yes. Well, not to me directly, but . . . oh, Clarice. It's terrible."

"You're not hurt, right?"

"I'm . . . I'm traumatized," he says with a whine.

I roll my eyes and shake my head.

"You see—oh, Clarice, it's so terrible."

I let out a slow, patient breath. "Just tell me."

"Okay, I will. The parking lot of our office has people sleeping in their cars. One guy asked me if I had any fuel. He was nice enough but seemed almost desperate. His wife's family lives in Seaside, and they just want to get there."

Mark and his dramatics. "Did you ask him why he was in Alto? Why he left his house and ignored the shelter-in-place orders being given?"

"They live close enough to the Sellwood Bridge they could *feel* the explosion. With the airports being targeted after the planes crashed, they were afraid something similar would happen, like maybe the neighborhood would be blown to bits when first responders showed up. Thought a few days at the beach was a good idea. They didn't realize half of Portland had the same idea."

"Oh. I guess that makes sense."

"Yeah." Mark lets out a large breath. There's a long pause. I'm just about to ask if he's still there, when he says, "But he won't be going to the beach."

"Why's that?"

"Because . . . I can't even believe this happened. After I finished up in the office and went back outside, there he was. Dead! Someone stabbed him. The wife was holding him in her lap as she sat on the ground rocking back and forth."

"Dead?" I gasp, putting my hand to my mouth.

"Very dead and blood everywhere. That's why—you can see why I'm so upset, right?"

"I can't even imagine how awful it must have been," I agree with a nod he can't see.

"It really was. There was quite a crowd gathered. I never could quite figure out what happened, and the police still hadn't shown up when I left. I'm back home now, but . . . see what I mean? Alto isn't safe."

"Why was he stabbed?"

"Who knows! That's what I'm saying. It's all gone crazy."

"It's okay, Mark."

"It's not okay, at all. Nothing is okay."

"Calm down. You're ranting."

"Of course I am! You didn't see him. You'd be ranting, too, if you saw a dead man, if you were here and saw the craziness."

I take a breath before saying, as calmly as I can, "What do you think we should do?"

"I was thinking, maybe—I hate to even say this because you won't like it. But you said Ben has a plan to combine forces with the neighbors, right?"

What's he getting at? He isn't thinking about . . . I take a deep breath. For the past several weeks, I've been planning to run away with Mark. I was just waiting to get past Mollie's visit so we could take our relationship from an emotional affair to the next step. The plane crashes and bridge explosions are terrible, but they really shouldn't affect my happiness. But now it sounds as if he's suggesting he should come to my home—where my husband is. "You're not saying you should come here, right?"

"What? Oh, no. That isn't what I'm thinking. But I do think *you* should stay there. Nemont must be safer than Alto is now. You're not overrun with refugees."

"Uh, we are, remember? I told you yesterday how they're everywhere."

"But they're just passing through, right? Walking on to Alto?"

"Some, yes. But there's people camped, at least that's what Ben and Bart say. I haven't gone out much."

"I still think you're safer there. And I'm . . . you see, I talked with Patty. She's scared."

The anger courses through my body as I realize what this is really about. In a totally snippy voice, I ask, "What are you telling me?"

He responds in a whisper, "She needs me."

"She needs you? She left you, Mark."

"That was before. Everything is a mess now. I'm going down to Seaside. I'm going to help her through this. After all this craziness is over, you and me, we can— "

"Are you seriously going to say we can get together later?"

"Don't you think that would be smart? After all, you have Ben. He'll take care of you. And you made a point of saying you'd be bringing Liam with you."

"He's my son."

"Right. But I just don't . . . I'm not sure I have it in me to take care of Liam, you, and myself. Patty—she's all alone."

Tears are stinging my eyes, partly from anger, partly from hurt. Mostly from feeling like an idiot. "Goodbye, Mark. When this is all over, we'll be dissolving our business relationship."

"Don't be like that, Clarice. Surely, you can see how my wife— "

"Your *ex-wife*."

"I care about you, I really do. B— " The phone makes a weird screeching sound and is completely silent. I pull it away from my ear and stare at it. There's no call-drop notice or anything, but he's not there.

I sink into the chair at my desk and lay my head on my arms. The tears come hard and strong. Years of friendship followed by months of flirting, and now, when we make a decision to be together, he chooses to go crawling to his ex-wife instead. Where does that leave me? Stuck. Stuck in a loveless marriage. This was my chance. My chance to feel loved and desirable again, to be able to model an affectionate relationship for Liam instead of a cold and dispassionate marriage.

Sure, Liam would've been upset about it at first, but once he saw how happy I was—and I'm sure Ben would be happy, too, once he was also free—Liam would be happy for me. He'd thrive. Now, I've not only lost a chance at romantic happiness, but my business will suffer.

When there's a knock at the door, I straighten and wipe my eyes. "Yes?" I call out.

"Clarice?"

Ben. Of course it is.

"What?" I snap as he cracks the door open.

"Dad called a few minutes ago. The phone went dead while we were talking, and I can't get it to work. Does yours work?"

"I don't know."

"Let me try calling you." After a minute, he says, "Doesn't work. You try me."

With a loud huff, I pull up his number and swipe to connect. It says it's calling but never rings. After several seconds, I give up. "No."

"That's what I thought. I guess our phones are getting the cyberattack. At least we still have electricity—for now. Dad said I should fill up containers with water in case it does go out. We'll lose our well. I've been working on that, but I was thinking lunch sounded good. Can I make you a grilled cheese sandwich?"

I shake my head. He knows I'm not eating bread, not because I need to lose weight—I'm too skinny as it is—but because bread and similar foods give me a gut ache. "No thank you," I answer, clipping my words.

"Okay, let me know if you change your mind."

I remain in my office, wallowing in my pity. The rich smell of butter, bread, and cheese wafts into the room. My stomach lets out a growl in response. Even though grilled cheese is a bad idea, I need to eat something. As I stand, the lights go out.

Chapter 3

Day 6

"Clarice? Clarice?"

"Mm-hmm?"

"I'm going over to my dad's place to help finish moving his stuff here," Ben says. "Are you going to get up?"

"No," I say, covering my head with the pillow.

"It's almost nine. You should eat. You didn't have dinner last night, and not much for lunch either."

"I'm not hungry. I just want to sleep." I roll over, putting my back to him. "And I'd appreciate you not telling me what to do."

He lets out a large, over-the-top sigh. "All right. Do what you want then. We'll be back in a few hours. When we get back, we're going to talk. There are things . . . things you don't know. Things that, well, things that change everything."

I can hear him standing there, breathing way too loud, while he waits for me to respond. He finally leaves, closing the door with a decided thump.

I roll onto my back and stare at the ceiling. Yesterday, Ben talked with a few of our neighbors. He and my father-in-law want to start putting together a group to secure the neighborhood. I guess, since I'm stuck here, I'll be part of the group too. Funny how they didn't ask for my opinion or include me in visiting people. Par for the course as far as my marriage is concerned. Ben does what he wants, unless there's something Bart wants more, and then Ben will go along with Bart. Me and my needs or wants are an afterthought.

At least our neighborhood is somewhat secure. Our immediate area is composed of two cul-de-sacs connected by a road off the main road, and each dead-end street has four homes on it. We're the last house on the north end of this semi-new development.

Seven years ago, when we found this treed five-acre property, we knew it'd be perfect for our dream house. The shop he and his dad

14

own is also in the unincorporated community of Nemont, giving him a short daily commute. My office is half an hour west in the town of Alto, but I can work from home.

We started building the house before I'd brought Mark into my business. He'd only been with me a short while when the house was completed, and I'd often work from home and let him run things. But as Ben and I grew apart and Mark and I grew closer, I found myself preferring to go to the office. Most days I stay home, but I do look for excuses to go to town.

In some ways, Nemont is a great place to live. With around 2,500 people and a wonderful school just up the road, it has a small-town feel. When Ben first told me about this new building lot, I wasn't sure I'd want to be so far from Alto where the grocery stores and restaurants were within an easy walk of our old house. But it's been great, and the easy drive into town works well. But now I'm not so sure about Nemont. At least it isn't as bad as Alto.

Though Ben and Bart are making plans with the neighbors, they both talk about Wyoming and how we should take Mollie up on her offer. They have this wild idea we should leave our homes and go to Bakerville. Bart has said many times we should've gone when she did, when there was still a way to get fuel. When the bridges were destroyed on the day following the plane crashes, thousands were killed. And like the man Mark met who was tragically killed, people in the affected cities fled their homes, resulting in highways and interstates turning into nothing but parking lots.

The next day the power went out, killing the internet, telephones, and more. We can't use our credit cards, and most gas stations are either not working because of the power outage or because they ran out of fuel. Though the electricity is out, we can still listen to the news on a battery-operated radio belonging to my father-in-law, Bart. Sunday and Monday saw additional terrorist attacks, with oil refineries destroyed in the Gulf and other areas and trains sabotaged. Monday, many of our elected officials were assassinated. We don't know who was killed or exactly how many.

I don't even know if I'm that sad about it. I know I should be, but with everything else happening, it doesn't seem to be something that directly affects me. I've decided I don't even care about Mark. I'll miss the attention he gave me, how he listened to me and made me feel important. It's been so long—years—since Ben gave me a second glance, since he paid attention to me. So Mark chooses to go crawling to his ex-wife. Fine. Let him. I don't need him or any man to make me complete.

As soon as the roads clear up and the power comes back on, I'm leaving Ben. Liam and I will move into Alto. I'll buy Mark out of the business and make a fresh start. Maybe . . . maybe we won't even go to Alto. Maybe I'll make Mark buy me out. With that and my half of the value of this house, plus money I've tucked into a private account, Liam and I could have a fresh start almost anywhere.

I chew on my lip, thinking of where we could move. As much as I'd like to be able to go anywhere, I couldn't take Liam too far from Ben. That wouldn't be fair to either of them. Truthfully, we only have Liam because of Ben. Not in the usual *it takes a man and woman to make a child* way, but in the *I didn't want any children and Ben hounded me until I gave in* way. We'd been married five years before I agreed. It took another year before I got pregnant.

Now, twenty years into our marriage, the only thing we have in common is our son. And even though I may not have wanted a child, I can no longer imagine my life without Liam. When Liam was two, Ben suggested we try for a second. That was a hard no from me. Liam is amazing, but I couldn't go through that again. One child is more than enough.

I sit up and decide I may as well get out of bed. My sleep has been fitful for days and is often interrupted. Early this morning we were awoken by the sound of shooting—lots of shooting.

After it stopped, Ben and Bart left to check it out. I tried to go back to sleep but was awake until Ben returned an hour or so later. He looked terrible, but when I asked him about it, he brushed it off and said someone was shooting at the resident elk herd.

It's not elk season, but I guess those who don't have a very full pantry may already be running low on food. And we do have a neighbor who's been arrested for poaching before. I asked Ben if Rick Burdock, the poacher, was involved, but he just shrugged.

I lift my arm and give myself a sniff. I'm starting to stink and am desperately in need of a shower. I'm grateful Bart told Ben to load up on water; otherwise, we'd be getting water out of the creek that runs along the edge of our property. Being without electricity is hard enough. I can't imagine having to haul water.

In the bathroom, I dip a washcloth in the three-quarters full tub. My large soaking tub was the first thing Ben filled. We're using this water for washing up and flushing the toilet. I need to wash my hair. Other than running a wide-tooth comb through it, I've totally neglected it since the power went out. Why bother? Ben stopped looking at me long ago. He doesn't care what my hair looks like. Even so, he did put a small bucket next to the tub to use for hair washing. That works fine for his short, thinning hair, but with my long, thick mane, I'll never get the soap out. After cleaning up with the washcloth, I spend several minutes combing my hair. Once it's smooth, I put it on top of my head.

In the living room, Liam is sitting on the couch playing a battery-operated handheld video game. He briefly lifts his head. "Hey, Mom. You feeling better?"

I answer with a shrug. "Did you eat breakfast?"

"Dad made eggs and pancakes on the grill. We saved you pancakes, but he said you wouldn't want cold eggs. He left coffee in the thermos."

"He's right. I don't particularly like cold pancakes either," I mutter. At least there's coffee.

I choke down the cardboard pancakes after slathering them in peanut butter and washing them down with the coffee. I'm using my stash of emergency powdered creamer—not my favorite but better than straight black. Ben was right; I didn't eat much yesterday and am starving.

I glance around the dining room. My house is a mess. Ben and Bart have junk strung out everywhere as they organize our supplies and what was brought over from Bart's house. Ben invited Bart to move in with us on Sunday morning, after we found out the owner of the mini-mart up the road was brutally murdered.

While I'm not terribly happy about him staying with us, it's best this way. At seventy-five, he's still a force to be reckoned with, but Ben worries. Especially after the mini-mart owner's murder. While that's fine for now, I know it won't be long until Bart starts getting on my nerves. I love my father-in-law, but some of his ideas and mannerisms annoy me to no end.

Plopping onto the couch next to Liam, I say, "Did your dad tell you when he expects to be back?"

He doesn't even look up from his game as he gives a shrug. He seems carefree and unconcerned about everything happening. While he was upset the night of the plane crashes, now his concern seems focused on the lack of electricity and not being able to play games or watch TV. I'm glad he's not letting it get to him. Even though it's concerning, I'm sure things will be fine in a few days. Ben and Bart might think our world is crashing to an end, but I think they're overreacting. And I see no reason to worry our son about any of it.

I can't help but smile as I look at him. From the side, he looks a little like me. His brown eyes are slightly lighter than mine, but we have the same shaped nose. From the front, his face matches his dad's. His blond hair is several shades darker than Ben's, but they're still incredibly similar. Bart, too, though his facial shape is harder to make out, thanks to his full beard and mustache. But the resemblance is still there. Ben and Bart share the same piercing blue eyes. I think both were disappointed Liam got my brown eyes.

"Are you winning?"

"It's lame," Liam says, stretching out his long leg to prop it on the coffee table.

"The game? I thought you were happy when Dad found it in his dresser and said you could play it."

Liam shrugs again. "It's better than nothing, but it's still lame."

"Well, maybe— " A knock at the door interrupts my response.

I get up from the couch, as Liam casually says, "Dad said not to answer the door."

"He probably meant that only for you." I move toward the front door, then lean to the right and peer out the side window. A man a few years older than my forty years, but likely younger than Ben's fifty years, is staring back at me. He lifts a hand in a slight wave.

"Yes?" I ask through the windowpane.

"Yes, hello." The man gives me a kind smile. "I'm out of gas. Thought maybe you might have some? And maybe some food and water?"

"I, uh . . . no. Sorry."

His kind smile fades as he furrows his brow. "You can't spare any food or water?"

"Mom?" Liam asks, only a few feet behind me.

I motion with my hand for him to stay back and keep quiet. "Sorry," I say to the man. "I can't help you."

"Can't or won't?" he demands. His smile's now completely gone, and an angry scowl covers his face.

Instead of answering, I pull the curtain closed.

"You're going to be sorry!" he yells.

Moving to the window on the other side of the door, I pull that curtain closed also. I've just removed my hand from the curtain when the entire door shakes.

"Mom!" Liam cries. "Can he get in?"

"N–no," I stutter, as the door gives another rattle. "Your dad put those extra-long screws in. It should hold."

"You sure?" Liam asks as the guy pounds on the door.

"Go away!" I yell. "We can't help you!"

I breathe a sigh of relief when the shaking and pounding stops. I turn to give Liam a smile when there's a loud crash. The window to the right of the door blows in. Liam and I both jump back as we scream. The curtain contains most of the mess, but I quickly see a hand coming in, looking for the deadbolt. Liam grabs a decorative pewter vase from a nearby side table and strikes at the hand. The guy lets out a yell, along with a string of obscenities.

Deterred for only a moment, the hand reaches inside again. Liam gives it another whack. "Mom? What do we do?" he hisses.

If our power wasn't out, the security system would be going nuts right now. All the windows are set up to sound an audible alarm if broken, in hopes of scaring away any intruders. That gives me an idea. I run to the kitchen counter and grab my SUV key fob out of the small wicker box it's kept in. I push the panic button, and my BMW emits a high-pitched siren noise from its place in the garage.

Liam gives me a nod and says, "Do Dad's too. They took Grandpa's truck."

Ben's keys are right next to mine. Pressing his button, a series of alarms begin to sound. Both keys in hand, I run to the office. It's location next to the front door gives me a view of the porch. The guy's not there. I scan the driveway and see him moving away, his eyes still on the house as he steps into the trees lining our driveway. Is he leaving, or is he waiting for a new opportunity?

I plop both keys on the office desk, leaving the panic alarms to continue their ruckus. Taking a deep breath, I say, "He's still out there but has stepped into the trees."

"We should get a gun. Do you want me to do it?"

Biting my lip, I shake my head. "I'll do it. Can you clean up the glass? Don't cut yourself. I'll holler down and let you know what's happening."

He gives me a nod as I start up the stairs. Ben's an avid big game hunter, and when we designed our house—my dream house—he added a locked room to keep his gear in. The hunting room overlooks the driveway, so I should be able to see the guy.

Once inside, I take a quick look out the window, trying to find the intruder. Not seeing him, I turn to the well-organized array of weapons, locating the hunting rifle Ben gave me a couple of years ago when he took me on a weeklong hunt in Montana. I haven't shot it since then, but I know it better than any of the other large guns available, though I could take one of the .22 rifles. I've shot them plenty of times. I give a quick glance over my options, then turn again to the window and search for the guy.

"Liam?" I shout.

"Yeah, Mom?"

"I don't see him. I'm going to stay up here and watch. I'll let you know."

"Okay. I'll finish cleaning the glass, then I'm going to tape some cardboard over the window."

"Good idea. Can you silence the cars?"

I leave the gun in place as I settle in to watch for the guy.

Chapter 4

Day 7

"Do you really think they're dead?" Liam asks, his voice cracking as his eyes fill with tears.

Ben looks up from what he is doing. With a grim face, he says, "We don't know for sure. It just seems suspicious so many families would disappear."

"Humph," Bart says. "All the families we planned to coordinate with are gone. Everyone in your loop!"

"I know, Dad."

"And the next loop over, only those two crazy guys and their wives are there." Bart's eyes glare as he spits out his words. "I'd be surprised if your other neighbors really left on their own accord. We need to take off before we find ourselves in the same situation."

"I don't know, Dad," Ben says. "Rick Burdock has done some questionable things, but I'm not sure if he'd be capable of— " Ben stops himself, glancing toward Liam and giving a slight lift of his chin.

"Murder?" Liam asks in a croak.

"Your dad didn't say that," I answer, giving Ben a hard look. I'm beyond angry at Ben and Bart for even suggesting these things in front of Liam. "Ben, can I see you in the bedroom?"

"Clarice," Bart growls, "I appreciate you wanting to protect our boy, but the time for that has passed. We're all facing something we've never experienced. Liam needs to know what's going on. That's the best way he can protect himself."

I spin toward Bart. "I didn't ask for your opinion. Liam is my son. *I* will decide what he needs to know and what he doesn't."

"Dad's right," Ben says. "The time for secrets is over. If we're going to . . . to survive this, we all need to be on the same page. Liam will be fourteen in a few months. He's old enough to be included in our plans and decisions."

"You mean like you've included me in the decisions?" I yell. "You stopped consulting me long ago. And these past few days, it's been you and your dad deciding everything. I have zero say in it."

Ben smacks both hands on the counter and yells, "If we left it up to you, we'd be dead in a matter of days! You do nothing but mope and pout."

I narrow my eyes at him. "You can just— "

"Stop it," Liam says with a cry. "Stop fighting."

I shift my gaze toward Liam. His hands are clenched as tears stream down his face.

"Mom's scared," he whispers. "I'm scared too."

Bart puts a hand on Liam's shoulder. He starts to shrug away but gives up and collapses into his grandpa. Bart purposely avoids my eyes.

Ben walks around the counter. Mimicking his dad's actions, he places a hand on my shoulder.

I glare at him and grit my teeth. "Don't touch me."

He reluctantly removes his hand. "Liam's right. You're scared. He's scared. Dad and me too. We don't . . . we don't know what the right, or I should say *best*, thing to do is. But it is what it is."

I narrow my eyes at him and his cop out cliché. "No. I don't have to just accept what is happening. There's something we can do about it."

"Like what? This is all new, but one thing I do know is we're not safe here. I talked with a few others in different neighborhoods, thought maybe we could move over to one of those."

"Why didn't you tell me?" I snap. Taking a deep breath, I try to remove the venom from my voice. I give him a small nod. "Let's do that. Or go into Alto. We could stay at my office."

"Alto's not safe," Bart says. "They've got it worse than here. You heard the radio announcements. That protest turned into a riot. How many are dead?"

I shake my head. The radio stopped broadcasting yesterday. But the day before, they talked about the group who wanted food and fuel to move on. Dozens were killed: protestors, police, and Alto residents. "Then how about your shop? That would put some distance between us and whatever is happening here with the disappearances."

"The whole community has gone mad," Bart says in a low voice.

Liam, still safe in his grandpa's embrace, lifts his head. "What do you mean?"

With a pained look at Ben, Bart shakes his head. "Son?"

Ben closes his eyes and gives a shake of his head. "Let's move to the couches. There's things happening that we haven't . . . there's more than you know."

He reaches for my hand, but I yank mine away and stomp toward the couch. I try to get Liam's attention, to indicate for him to sit on the couch next to me, but he takes a spot on the loveseat with Bart. When we're all sitting, I say, "Okay, spill it."

"Staying here in Nemont could be dangerous," Ben says softly. When I start to speak, he gently raises his hand. "Just let me get it all out and then you can say whatever you want. But you need to understand one thing. We will be leaving our home and community."

I purse my lips and raise my eyebrows. "Well if your mind is already made up, then why the pretense of this conversation?"

"Mom," Liam says softly. "I want to know what's happening. Don't you?"

I look to my son, who's so much like a man in his height and body structure. His voice has even started to change. But right now, with tears staining his face, he reminds me of the toddler I remember. When he'd fall and scrape his knee, he wanted to be held and rocked until the pain subsided.

I give a slow nod before saying, "Tell us."

Bart and Ben share a look before Bart flicks a hand toward his son.

"Uh, yeah, so you know yesterday morning, when we said someone was shooting elk?" Ben says.

"Yeah, Dad. I still don't know why you didn't get us some meat," Liam says. "An elk steak would've been great cooked on the grill, especially since you didn't get one last year and we're almost out of deer."

Liam doesn't mention how the meat in the freezer is being kept frozen with the help of a generator while we cook up what we can. But because of the time of year, our freezer doesn't have much left. Ben got two deer last year, one in eastern Oregon and the other in Montana. We had the Montana deer turned into jerky, summer sausage, and pepperoni sticks; there's still a fair amount left. But the Oregon deer, which was steaks, roasts, and burger, is mostly gone.

A look passes over Ben's face. I can't quite decipher it, but think it's a combination of disgust and grief. "We lied," he says quietly. "They weren't shooting elk."

"They weren't shooting elk?" I ask. "Then what?"

"People," Bart says.

"What!" I cry.

"People?" Liam asks, confusion painting his face.

"They were massacred," Bart says. "The refugees camped by the creek—all of them."

"All of them?" I ask, my eyes wide. "Who?"

"We don't know," Ben says. "Seems no one saw who did it."

"Did you bury them?" Liam asks.

"That Burdock character was digging a trench with his backhoe," Bart says. "You ask me, he's the ringleader of the slaughter."

"We don't know it was him," Ben says evenly.

"Maybe it wouldn't stand up in a court of law, but I'm telling you, that good-for-nothing man is guilty."

"Why did they do it?" Liam asks.

"Don't know," Bart says. "Some people just have evil inside them, and with the way things are, they figure they can let it out. There's no police, no law, nothing. Those are the people we need to avoid. Whatever it takes, we stay out of their way. But Burdock—he knows we're here. He knows we have things he wants."

"Dad's right," Ben says. "While I'm not convinced Burdock is the killer, either of our neighbors or the refugees, he's a threat to us. And we have no way to defend ourselves."

Chapter 5

Day 8

"Let's get those totes packed up so we can put them on the trailer." Bart motions to the plastic container I'm filling with Liam's clothes. Mine and Ben's clothes are already in there. "What do you think about adding a second tote with winter clothes?" Bart asks Ben, who's pulling things out of the pantry.

"What? No," I say. "We have no need for winter stuff."

Ben looks up from his work and makes a face. "Clarice is probably right. We shouldn't need to be gone that long. But it might not be a bad idea to take light jackets. Evenings could be chilly."

"Hoodies?" I ask.

"Yeah, probably fine," Ben says with a nod before returning to the pantry.

"Well, whatever we're taking, let's get it done," Bart says in a gruff voice. "I want to leave right at daylight. I'd leave sooner, but I agree with you, son. We should take the logging road that cuts over to the main highway, and we need to do that in the daylight. From there, we can hop on the other small road, then make our way south and then east. Escape and evade—that's the plan. Won't make good time, but we should avoid most of the refugees. Of course, we're assuming all the roads are in the same condition as this one near us."

I shake my head. The way Bart's been talking, he sounds like some kind of survivalist instead of a machinist. Mollie must have shared some of her crazy thoughts with him. We're even planning a similar route as she did, heading south first instead of east. Mollie was dumb not to just drive on the interstates to Wyoming. I think we're dumb, too, but with the highway by us jammed, we don't really have a choice.

"I think it's a safe assumption," Ben says. "Those roads to the coast are always busier than ours anyway. You should get some rest, Dad. I'll need you to stand guard for a while again tonight."

"Yeah, and we need as much rest as we can get before we take off. Not sure how well any of us will sleep in the truck while we're bouncing around those logging roads. Some are barely more than goat trails. But staying one more night here, with this place turning into a powder keg, doesn't seem that smart either."

I stare at Bart with blank eyes. The last thing I want to do is leave my beautiful home. Last night, after the revelation of the massacre, I immediately agreed we needed to leave. But then, the more I thought about it, I wanted to stay. This is our home, with our things. I was willing to give it up to be with Mark, but I'm not willing to leave it for Burdock and his cronies to have.

But Bart and Ben put up a good argument. It's too dangerous to stay. The guy trying to break in yesterday was frightening. I stayed on watch from the gun room and had Liam watch from his bedroom, which faces the backside of the house, until Ben and Bart returned several hours later.

But with the other families on our streets disappearing and the killing of the refugees, we don't know what to do. With only the four of us, we can't maintain security of our place for an extended length of time.

I asked again about going to a different neighborhood and banding together with them. Ben said we just don't know anyone well enough to feel comfortable with putting our lives in their hands. And so far, we've heard nothing about when we can expect help from the state or federal government. There's no FEMA response, no National Guard, nothing. There's not even any clue as to when the electricity will come back. I think having electricity might lessen some of the fear people are feeling. It would certainly alleviate some of mine!

Now, even Liam thinks the best thing to do is head to Wyoming. Ben says the best chance we have is Bakerville, where Mollie and her family lives. Ben really sold the idea, saying it's such a remote area there shouldn't be any troubles.

I tried to convince Ben that going to Mollie's place isn't the best choice. We'd be better off finding a spot in the woods, setting up camp, and hunkering down. We have plenty of food to last several weeks, and Ben could always kill a deer if we needed.

But he insists we wouldn't be the only ones in the woods. With the number of people around, he suspects many others will have the same idea: stay in the woods and survive off the land until everything blows over. There are just too many people in Portland, Salem, and the immediate area to make living in the wilderness sustainable.

At least in Wyoming the population of the entire state is less than Portland alone. Less people could mean more resources. Living off the land in Wyoming may be somewhat possible in comparison to here.

I shake my head and stifle a sigh. "Liam, go get your hoody. Grab a pair of sweatpants, too, and another pair of socks. Get those nice thick ones I bought for you for our last camping trip."

Leaving our home and all of our possessions is not something I want to do. The car I bought last fall, family heirlooms—everything stays. I put up a stink about leaving the car, saying since my tank is full, I should at least drive it. Ben wouldn't even consider it, said he and Bart already discussed it and we're taking only the semitruck. They've made it ready for the trip and have fuel to get us all the way there.

I briefly considered telling Ben to leave without me. If he wants to go to Wyoming so badly, he should go right ahead. Liam and I can stay here. But just as the words were on the tip of my tongue, I bit them back. I'm not completely foolish. And part of me is afraid, if I really did say that, he'd be more than happy to take Liam with him and leave me here to manage on my own.

A few hours later, we've got everything packed and ready to go. Ben's at the table looking over his map book, plotting our way out of Oregon. I'm in the recliner playing on my phone, while Liam is stretched out on the couch playing the handheld game.

Even though he said it's a boring game, he's still using it to help pass the time and alleviate some of the grief he feels for his friends. I understand. I've been playing puzzle games on my phone. I'm glad the charger in my car still works so I can keep the battery full.

With the games and a book app on my phone, I still have things to do, which helps with my stress level. Even with those, I'm still overextended and tense. Maybe, when we get to Mollie's place, she can pamper me for a change!

Bart's had a nap and is pacing around the house. He's not particularly good at sitting still. If things weren't so serious, I might laugh at the way he goes from window to window, wringing his hands or playing with his wristwatch.

As always, he's dressed in his daily attire. I used to laugh at his clothing choices: heavy-duty black pants with multiple tool and utility pockets—even patches at the knees for sliding in kneepads—a heavy denim button-up shirt, which he wears even in the summer, and steel-toed work boots. On occasion, he'll change up his uniform by switching to a leather work shoe, but that's only for special occasions.

I once asked him why he didn't have more clothing choices, and he said, "I have no desire to spend any more time than necessary thinking about what I'm going to wear." Okay then.

On about his fiftieth lap around the room, Bart says, "You know, son, I think we should just go, put some space between us and here. We can drive until dark and then set up camp. Wouldn't make much more of a difference than staying another night."

"You think so, Dad?" Ben asks.

I glare at him and give a small shake of my head.

He narrows his eyes before saying, "What? You don't want to leave?"

Bart is staring at me when I say, "You know I don't *want* to leave. You both know that. I'm resigned with having to go but think we should stick with the original plan. Why go today? How about we get another night's sleep in the comfort of our own beds?"

"I have a bad feeling about it," Bart says. "With the neighbors missing and the guy breaking in— "

"He didn't break in," I argue. "He tried, but Liam and I scared him off."

"Even so, we haven't even left the house today. What happened since yesterday that we don't know about? We all heard the shooting last night, so something was definitely going on."

"Maybe it was nothing. Staying another night won't hurt."

"Just like leaving today won't hurt either," Bart snaps back. "We're going to go, so let's just go."

"Might as well," Ben says. "Clarice, what do you need to do?"

I close my eyes while shaking my head. "I can see my opinion, once again, means nothing."

In his most condescending voice, Ben says, "Must you be so dramatic?"

"Yes," I snap. "I must."

After many awkward minutes of silence, I shake my head. "I'll need to grab my toiletries bag and use the bathroom."

"Okay, let's get to it," Bart says, rubbing his hands together. I shoot him a look. He's way too excited about this.

Within half an hour, we're loading up. On the day after the bridge attacks, Bart came up with an idea to turn their work's semitruck into a car pusher. Ben says Bart Mad-Maxed it by adding a wicked-looking brush guard to the front of it. They've also added cables and a winch.

They put one of the shop's smaller flatbed trailers on the back, and we have our totes full of supplies, two side-by-side UTVs, and two dirt bikes, along with extra fuel for both the semi and the recreation vehicles. A third dirt bike is mounted on the back of the trailer, and the fourth is on a carrier welded to the front of it.

Ben and Bart both assure me we have plenty of fuel to take the semitruck the entire way to Mollie's place—the UTVs and dirt bikes are insurance. Seems Mollie stopped the morning after leaving our place and bought a bicycle as her own insurance policy for making it home. Bart thought her brilliant—of course he did!—and suggested we add bikes too. Ben decided the UTVs and dirt bikes made more sense.

Ben's driving, and I'm in the passenger's seat. Bart and Liam are on the small bunk. At one time, this truck was a source of contention between Ben and Bart. When their old semi needed more repairs than it was worth, they started shopping. Ben wanted to replace it with a similar model, preferring to buy something used. Bart wanted to get a new truck with a sleeper cab. Once or twice a year, they'll use the truck to transport materials several states away. Bart, who hates hotels, decided the sleeper truck made sense. Ben didn't want the cost or additional size.

They compromised with a newer model slim sleeper. The bed's only two feet wide but is enough for Bart to use on those longer trips, and the size of the cab isn't too much larger than the model without a sleeper. I still think they spent way too much money for it—another dig at our retirement account—but my opinion wasn't considered. Right now, I'm glad we have it so we can all fit in this crazy looking semitruck.

The neighborhood roads between our place and the logging road are mostly clear of vehicles. There's a considerable number of people walking around, including Burdock, one of the guys Ben said was first on the scene of the massacre, and who Bart considers a person of interest in the cul-de-sac disappearances. When he sees us, he gives us a hard look, his hand going to the gun on his hip.

"What's he doing?" Bart mumbles, as Burdock smirks at us before turning and walking away.

I glance at Bart, who has his own gun resting on the seat as he peers out the small rear window. Where my husband has a love of all things hunting, Bart has a handgun fetish.

In some ways, Ben has taken after his dad, always upgrading to new hunting rifles or archery equipment and then selling his obsolete items. Where Ben's firearms each have a purpose, including the sidearm he carries when hunting in Montana, Bart buys guns just to buy them. According to Ben, Bart's always been like that. It used to drive Ben's mom crazy when Bart would come home with a new pistol. In those days, he was always looking for a deal, often trading up.

These days, now that he's a widower and has a successful business, money is no longer a concern. He buys what he wants. His most recent purchase is the one sitting on the seat: a Springfield Armory 1911 in .40 caliber. And knowing Bart, he has a gun on his ankle and possibly another under his arm, having a necessary Oregon concealed carry permit.

I swipe at my eyes as we leave our little town. I'm going under protest. I understand the need to keep Liam safe. With the massacre and people disappearing, I'm not sure we can do that in Nemont. But I don't like it.

Ben expertly guides the truck through the neighborhoods to the logging road. He's very familiar with this area since it's a favorite place for archery elk hunting. It's no longer actively logged; it's been replanted and is now prime elk habitat. The main reason he's chosen this road is it goes over a small mountain and connects with a state highway, which will then allow us to get on another logging road as we make our journey south.

Once we're far enough south—and hopefully in an area with fewer people escaping from Portland—we'll head east and continue to use logging roads or other small county roads. Bakerville, where Mollie and her family live, is in the northern part of Wyoming, so we'll have to snake our way north at some point. Ben and Bart have looked over multiple maps plus Ben's detailed map books he uses for hunting to try to find the best routes.

Ben is driving terribly slow on the bumpy logging road. Even at this speed, it's a rough ride. Thankfully, we seem to be the only ones on this narrow road.

It's almost two hours before we reach the county highway and once again see people. Lots of people. There are dozens of men, women, and children walking along the road. There are also dozens of stalled cars. We need to drive about half a mile on this highway before reaching the next logging road.

As Ben turns onto the road, people point at our truck, almost like they've never seen a semitruck before. A few people even holler at us, asking for a ride. At least there aren't any cars in the middle of the road that need to be pushed out of the way.

We finally reach the logging road and, once again, set out through the wilderness. This road, which leads to an active commercial logging site, is slightly smoother than the previous. Ben still minds his speed, but with it not being as rough, I'm able to lean back and relax.

I'm almost asleep when I hear Liam say, "Dad, there's a guy in the road. Dad!"

I open my eyes to see a man standing smack in the middle of the dirt road, holding his hand in front of him in a *stop* motion.

"Ben?" I say.

In response, he gives a long, continuous blast of the airhorn. The man stands firm, continuing his stop signal. Even at the slow speed we're traveling, we're quickly eating up the space between us and him.

"Ben! You're going to hit him! Stop!" I yell.

Without slowing, Ben continues to blow the horn.

Liam screams again.

I scream.

But Bart calmly says, "Do what you have to do, son."

At the last moment, the guy dives out of the way and we narrowly avoid having him as a grill ornament. I'm crying and shaking terribly as I glance in the side mirror. The man rolls over and gives us a one-fingered salute.

Taking a deep breath through my tears, I say, "Why didn't you stop?"

Ben's pale and shaking so badly he can barely hold onto the steering wheel. He shakes his head. "I c-couldn't. Dad and I, we talked about this. Too risky to stop."

"Too risky?" I shriek. "You almost hit him!"

"We can't risk stopping and letting someone take our truck," Bart says frankly. "If we lose the truck and the all-terrain vehicles, we won't make it to Wyoming."

Chapter 6

Day 11

That first night, we camped several miles farther into the forest from where the guy jumped out of our way. There was a locked gate between him and us. Ben and Bart used bolt cutters to snap the lock. These barriers are common on the logging roads, so the men came prepared, not only to open them but to replace the lock they broke. Bart put his own large lock on the gate, leaving it loose and hanging the key in a visible spot nearby. He said it just felt wrong to destroy the locks without replacing them. We only have four locks, so hopefully we won't encounter too many gates.

The last three days have been full days of travel. Even though we've been on the road from dawn until nearly dusk, with only short breaks for eating and taking care of our bodily needs, we haven't traveled nearly as far as any of us thought we would. We're still in Oregon, still using forest roads. But finally, instead of bumping along on the unimproved logging roads, we're on one of the many paved forest service roads in the Mount Hood National Forest.

We ended up going much farther south than we expected, past Eugene, before we were able to cut across I-5 and make our way east. The souped-up brush guard has come in handy on several occasions as we gently nudged cars out of the way. Even so, avoiding cars and people has been our main goal. Any outsiders following our route would think we had no idea how to read a map.

While we know the best way to get from Alto to Bakerville, having visited Mollie twice in the past couple of years, we're avoiding all major roads, which leaves us with limited options and lots of extra mileage. We've now been on a mostly northeast trajectory, but Ben says today we're going to start heading due east. Both Ben and Bart think we'll make better time today than any other day since starting this prolonged journey.

Visiting Mollie in the past was never my idea. The first time was three years ago, when we were on a trip to Michigan for Ben's work. We made a detour to go to Mollie and Jake's. We were only there for a day before heading home.

Ben was enamored with Wyoming, specifically with Bakerville. He's been hunting in Montana and Idaho for years, and when he can get the draw, he also hunts around Jackson, Wyoming. But this was his first visit to Prospector County. I'll admit, it's beautiful. Not green and lush like Oregon, but the mountains were amazing. And the lack of trees allows you to see forever.

We spent a week there last summer. During that time, Ben was looking for property, saying we need a retirement home. He's thinking he'll be ready to sell the machine shop within ten years and wants to move to Wyoming. At forty, I'm ten years younger than Ben. Will I be ready to retire in ten years? I don't think so, but he didn't care.

When I look back, I think that was when I started to realize we want different things in life. Retiring in Wyoming is not what I want. I like the beach. I like living a short drive from the city. I like warm weather. Wyoming has none of those things.

Before we left, Ben said I should consider this trip a vacation. We'll get there, and Mollie will pamper me like I always do to her when she visits. Bart quickly ruined that image by reminding us that things are currently a mess and there will likely be little time for pampering.

"I know that, Bart," I said irritably.

"Just reminding you. That's why we brought all those clothes for working in instead of your evening gowns."

Evening gowns. *Ha.* It's not like Nemont, or even Alto, gives me opportunities for evening gowns. Even the one time I talked Ben into taking me to the opera in Portland, there wasn't a need for an evening gown. It's Portland after all, and many people think going formal means wearing socks.

We're making decent time this morning. Bart's driving with Liam in the passenger's seat. Ben and I are on the bunk. I've been napping on and off, the best way to pass the time. I'm between wake and sleep as I lean with the truck as it takes a slight bend in the road. I'm startled fully awake when Liam cries out, "Grandpa! What's that?"

With the alarm in his voice, I immediately look in his direction. He's pointing into the rearview mirror. I let out my own cry as I see it too—a mushroom cloud rising high above the trees. Bart and Ben both say several choice words as Bart brings the semitruck to a stop along the narrow road. He hops out and the rest of us quickly join him.

"Are we safe here?" I ask, tears running down my cheeks.

"Is . . . Is that . . . Portland?" Liam asks. "Was it nuked?"

"I think it is," Bart says quietly. "What do you think, son? Portland?"

Ben clears his throat. "Yeah, it must be. I don't think we'd see it if it were as far north as Seattle. And I'm not sure if we're safe. Let's get back in the truck and keep moving, put as much distance between us and that as we can. Dad, do you want me to drive?"

"Nope. I've got it."

Once we're back inside the truck and again on the move, Bart is driving much more cautiously and slightly slower than before.

"Go faster, Grandpa!" Liam orders.

"Better to keep an even pace," Bart says, his voice surprisingly calm.

I look to Ben, eyebrows raised.

In a whisper, he says, "I think he's right. We don't want to wreck."

Liam is crying softly in the front seat; I'm crying in the back. Ben and Bart are completely silent. Bart's focusing on driving, as Ben occasionally glances through the back window. I do my best to avoid looking but can't help peeking on occasion. A nuclear bomb detonated on US soil. All the things happening up to now pale in comparison.

Part of me wonders why we're even bothering to put more distance between us and the bomb. Can we survive a nuclear attack? What if this is happening everywhere? Will we have to drive through places that have been nuked? And what about radiation? I gasp as I think about the effects of radiation on us.

About half an hour has passed and I'm finally somewhat pulling myself together. I lean into Ben, putting my mouth near his ear so Liam can't hear us. "We'll be okay, right? The radiation— "

He pats my hand and gives me a nod, then moves close to me and says, "If there's only the one, it's nothing to worry about."

"Why do you say that?"

"I think, with the direction of the wind, we're fine."

"And if not?"

He gives me a sad smile. He leans in again, but the truck suddenly shuts down.

"Not fair!" Bart yells.

"What's going on?" I ask.

"Probably caused by the nuke," Bart grumbles as he wrestles the now useless truck to a stop.

"What? Why?" Liam asks, holding onto the door, bracing himself for a crash. Ben puts his arm around me, pulling me close as Bart muscles the truck to a stop.

"Nuclear weapons put out a pulse," Ben says, trepidation evident in his voice. "The pulse can affect electronics. This truck is mainly running by computers. I would've thought the pulse would've happened the same time as the blast."

"Must have been another one," Bart says.

Ben takes his phone out of his pocket. After a moment, he says, "Clarice, Liam, try your phones. Are they working?"

"Mine's shut off, Dad. I can't get it to turn on."

I take mine out of my purse and tell him I can't get it to work either. "Will the phones come back?" I ask.

"Don't know," Ben says.

"But . . . I need it," I say, tears filling my eyes.

"You'll be fine without your games," he chides.

"Not just my games. All of our pictures. I— " I take a deep breath. "You're right. I backed them all up to the cloud." The thought of losing pictures is horrible. I keep photos of Ben and me from our wedding and a few baby pics of Liam in my wallet, but it's been years since I've had anything but digital photos.

"Let's worry about pictures later," Bart says as he turns the key on. Banging the steering wheel, he says. "Guess that's it. Not sure we can do anything about it."

"You can't fix the truck?" Liam asks, eyes wide. "How do you know?"

"What about the UTVs?" I ask as my tears start up again.

"We'll see," Ben answers, giving my arm a squeeze.

"I watched a TV show about an EMP a few years back," Bart says. "Did some research on what might happen after that. Nothing good, I'll tell you."

Ben clears his throat. "Um, Dad. Let's talk about it later. Clarice, you and Liam wait in here while we figure out what we're dealing with. Then we can plan our next step."

"I should help," Liam says, his voice cracking.

"No," Ben says firmly. "We don't know exactly what's happening. I think we're far enough away from the blast to not have any trouble right now, but stay in here just in case."

"Grandpa just said he thought there was another bomb. Where was it? It must have been close, right?"

Bart is looking in all directions as he says, "I don't see anything. Not like before."

"What's your plan?" I ask as I pull a tissue out of my purse to blow my nose.

"We'll check out the truck first, in hopes I'm wrong," Bart says, turning so he and Ben can have eye contact. I catch something as it passes between them. "Then we'll try the UTVs."

"We'll figure it out," Ben says.

As soon as they're out of the truck, Liam says, "We're okay. Dad and Grandpa will take care of things." He wipes his nose on the tail of his shirt.

I hand him a tissue. "Blow," I say. "They'll figure it out." Ben and Bart are at the front of the truck and opening the large hood. After a few minutes, Bart returns to the truck, leaving the driver's door open as he crawls back inside.

"Did you fix it?" Liam asks.

Bart answers with a noncommittal shrug.

"Give it a try, Dad," Ben shouts.

I hold my breath as Bart turns the key. Nothing happens. He tries again before saying, "No good."

"Yeah," Ben says as he appears by the door. "It was a long shot."

"Sit tight," Bart says to Liam, then turns to me. "You holding up okay?"

I shake my head and drop my eyes to the floor.

"We'll be just a few minutes," he says before leaving us again.

"How will we take all our stuff?" Liam asks.

I answer with a combination shrug and headshake. How will we haul our stuff?

"Good thing Dad had you load up those backpacks for us. I'm glad you were helping Mollie when she packed hers, so you knew what to put in them."

I roll my eyes in response. My main contribution to preparing for this trip was putting together bags of essentials, modeled after what I could remember from Mollie's bag. I thought it was silly since we have several boxes of must-have items. But Ben and Bart both insisted that having the essentials ready-made to carry was smart.

Where Mollie had a backpack designed for spending several days on the trail, we're using Liam's schoolbag and camouflage-patterned daypacks Ben has for hunting. Ben also brought his large aluminum pack frame, what he uses to haul out elk or deer quarters from the wilderness.

"You sure they don't need my help?" Liam asks after several minutes.

"They'll come get you if they do," I say as we both look out the rear window. I can't see either Ben or Bart. "Do you see them in the side mirror?"

"No. I did until just a few minutes ago when they were on the trailer. But now they're off. Maybe they're behind it and out of sight."

He's barely finished speaking when the rumble of an engine carries through the quiet forest.

"All right!" Liam says, giving an arm pump before his smile falters. "It's not one of the side-by-sides. Must be a dirt bike."

I close my eyes. I hate riding those things. I was really hoping the UTVs would be fine and we could ride in semi-comfort. The dirt bikes are miserable in comparison. At least my new Husqvarna is considerably more comfortable than my old bike. Ben bought it for me last spring, along with a new Honda for himself, after saying he was tired of hearing me complain. It's considerably better, but only in small doses. He sold my old bike but kept his old Honda, declaring it a classic. We brought it along on this trip for his dad.

I can still see the old Honda attached to the front of the trailer, as well as my Husqvarna and Ben's bike on top of the trailer, so it must be Liam's Kawasaki they have running.

"Can we get out now?" Liam asks.

"Wait for your dad and grandpa to come back for us."

"They're getting Dad's old bike off now." Liam lifts his head to indicate I should look out the back window.

"Okay, good."

After a few minutes, a second engine is running, then Ben opens the driver's side door and crawls in with us.

"So, you can hear the bikes running."

"That's good, Dad," Liam says with a smile. "Should we get the backpacks?" He motions above my head where we've stashed the packs in the cubbies.

"Yeah, but here's the thing. Only the two bikes are running. We couldn't get my new Honda or the Husqvarna going."

"What?" I gasp. "How will that work?"

"We'll ride double. We'll have to take some things out of the backpacks, at least for the front person. We'll do what we can. Liam, you and Grandpa will have your bike. Clarice, you'll ride with me."

"I'm riding behind Grandpa?" Liam asks.

"You'll ride in front. He doesn't have the experience you do."

Liam gives a solemn nod. "I need to take stuff out of my backpack?"

"Right. Clarice, can you take care of that for both his and mine? I'm going to have Dad wear my pack frame with the larger backpack attached to it."

"Why are you bringing the hunting frame?" Liam asks.

"We might need it. Put extra stuff in my dad's bag, but don't go too crazy. We don't want to get off balance. Same with yours. Concentrate on food and other survival items. Dad's going to bungee a couple of small bags on the front of each bike so we have a little extra space for things."

"What bag?" Liam asks.

"The one he's using for toiletries plus a small overnight bag."

"My overnight bag?" I ask, wondering how he plans on attaching it. He'd better not ruin it. It's part of a set. I shake my head at the idiocy of my thinking. I'm worried about ruining my luggage when a nuclear bomb just killed who knows how many people?

He gives me a slight shrug in response. "I'll bring you the things that are in it so you can figure out what you want in your backpack."

"What about the rest of our stuff?" Liam asks.

"We'll have to leave it. That was the purpose of the backpacks, making sure they are packed with our essentials. Is there anything you need in your suitcase?"

I shake my head. I knew about this. Ben and I had a rather heated discussion before leaving the house. It's an absolute no-win thing. Ben and Bart both felt our house could be vandalized if we left, but we could be hurt—or killed—if we stayed. A few heirlooms passed on to me from my parents were buried in the treed area behind our home.

My suitcases only have work clothes for helping on Mollie's farm. After Bart made it clear we'd be working and not on vacation, we packed accordingly. While I'm not afraid of hard work, that was nearly a deal breaker for me. The idea Mollie might try to boss me around turns my stomach.

The backpacks, which seemed excessive until the moment the truck and phones died, have only absolute essentials: a change of clothes, fire starters, small bottles of bleach to purify water, no-cook foods—such as energy bars, dried fruit, nuts, and jerky—and other crucial items to help us reach Wyoming.

Liam furrows his brow and says, "I gave Mom everything I didn't want to leave behind so she could put it in my backpack."

"Great. We'll need a few minutes and then we want to get going. We're still not sure we're a safe enough distance to avoid radiation."

"Can we take the extra gasoline on the dirt bikes?" I ask.

"We haven't figured out a way to do it. We'll just have to get fuel as we go."

"You think there will be gas stations open?" I ask snarkily.

He gives a slight shrug. "Not likely. We have a plan."

I shake my head. "The rifles?"

"We're going to take them. We'll need them. I think, with the slings, we can make it work. We'll figure it out."

"I've worn my .22 on the three-point sling before. Remember?" Liam asks.

"Yeah, I'll have you use that one. When we snugged it up tight, it wasn't in your way when riding."

Liam gives a nod. "Can you wear yours that way?"

"I will. Your mom is wearing the backpack with the sling attached to it."

I make a face. I've worn the pack with the sling on it before. I didn't like it. It's a roomie daypack with a sleeve holding the rifle against it, with a pouch at the bottom of the sleeve for the stock. While walking with it, the rifle flopped around more than I felt it should. It was better once the weather warmed up enough for me to stick my jacket in the bag.

Back at the house, Ben told me he wanted me to put my stuff in it. I'd removed the sleeve sling when packing, but he insisted I put it back on and said, if we needed to wear backpacks, we'd certainly need the sling. With a variety of slings in the gun room, we did have options.

Most were what Ben refers to as Elmer Fudd slings, the type you'd wear over one shoulder, but he did have a few other choices that I can now see better fit our needs.

As Liam said, we've taken our .22s on the bikes before to reach a remote area Ben wanted to use for plinking. Before Ben gave one of our nice .22 rifles away to Mollie, we had two of them, each with a high-capacity magazine. Ben and Liam always used those for target practice, liking how they could shoot and shoot without needing to reload. While I'd go along with them, shooting wasn't nearly as fun for me.

I have my own five-round .22 Ben bought me one year as a Christmas gift. Yeah, not my favorite gift—and believe me, he knew about it. A few days later, he came slinking home with a beautiful pair of sapphire stud earrings. Definitely a much better gift choice. I'm carrying the Christmas rifle and Bart is carrying a similar .22 Ben has owned forever. We also brought Ben's 7mm Magnum in case he needs more firepower than a .22 can provide. Bringing only two calibers means we only need two types of ammo. Thankfully, .22 ammo is light, and we can carry a lot.

While I do understand the general thought process behind Ben's choice of rifles, I would've liked to have a say in it. I'd prefer my hunting rifle over the light rifle. When I brought this up, Ben said he thought the .22 would be a better choice since I've shot it more often. Target practice and plinking with it is something we do on a semiregular basis. Or at least we used to.

Ben bought the hunting rifle for me specifically for the Montana hunting trip we all went on two years ago. He made all the arrangements and didn't even discuss his plans with me in advance.

One day, he came home carrying two new gun cases. He'd bought me and Liam each a rifle. He then told us about the trip he'd planned. Liam, who turned twelve just before the hunt, had been shooting the small-caliber rifles for years but had said on numerous occasions he wasn't interested in hunting. He'd never even gone with Ben before, since Ben would hunt solo or with a friend.

For the actual hunt, I was the only one who got my deer. None were big enough for Ben, and Liam missed the one and only shot he took. I half expected we'd go again last year, but Ben never mentioned it. Neither did I.

Even though I used the hunting rifle only a few times—when sighting it in and getting familiar with it, then when harvesting the deer—I was comfortable with it. And the large caliber 30.06 seemed a smarter choice for self-defense.

When I mentioned that, Ben poo-pooed my argument, saying he didn't want to hear me whine about lugging the larger rifle around. I started to argue until I recalled just how heavy it was. While walking for miles in search of my deer, I did moan quite a bit about the weight. The smaller rifles are much lighter, and Ben has a couple of interesting slings for them that make them hang better.

Giving Mollie the gun to take home was a mistake, and Ben says we also made a mistake not buying a larger high-capacity weapon when we were able to. He's lamented on it several times in the last few days, saying he never had a need and preferred to focus on weapons he could use for hunting as opposed to something to have just in case. If we had more firepower, maybe we could've stayed in our home. But, as Ben says, it is what it is.

"And I know you won't be too happy about this," Ben says, touching my arm, "but each of us will carry a sidearm."

"Liam too?" I can feel my eyes widen at the thought. "Do you have enough?"

I see a small smile on Liam's face as Ben says, "Yes, each of us. He's practiced with Dad enough. He knows what to do. Dad made sure to bring a sidearm for each of us. And I brought the one I usually use."

"I can do it." Liam nods vigorously.

I shake my head. A tear makes its way down my cheek.

Chapter 7

Day 14

"Tomorrow's Independence Day," Bart says as he stretches out on the ground. He's leaning up against a log, using it as a backrest.

"Is it?" Ben asks.

"Guess we won't be watching any fireworks this year," Liam says, lifting his head from the log he's using as a pillow.

I'm reclining on one of our tarps. Even after three days on the bikes, we've yet to leave Oregon. The first day, out of fear of radiation, we rode as hard and as fast as we could for four hours to put more distance between us and the mushroom cloud we saw. When we finally stepped off the bikes, we each stumbled.

That night, we stayed in a rickety shack, which would've had zero chance of protecting us from anything falling from the sky, since most of the roof was gone. I expected to wake up the next morning without any hair. Ben and Bart both insist we're safe from the bomb we saw because of the wind patterns. I keep reminding them they're machinists, not meteorologists, but it does little good.

The next morning, Ben talked Bart into going against the original plans that called for us to avoid towns and even people as best we could.

"I know we agreed," Ben said emphatically. "But this is important. I want to know if others had the same troubles. Maybe things are better here. Maybe we were just too close to the nuke."

"It's a bad idea, son. Putting us in harm's way for a little information that doesn't really matter—I don't like it."

In the end, Bart conceded. But instead of all of us going into the nearby town, Ben went alone. And, so we didn't risk losing the bikes, he walked while we waited in the broken-down shack. He returned over four hours later, looking pale and drawn.

As soon as I saw his face, I asked, "Did you have trouble?"

"No, not exactly. But, wow, what a mess. They're in the process of setting up roadblocks on the major road through town. I talked with one of the guys, after I convinced him I wasn't a threat and I wasn't staying. When I told him we're trying to get to Wyoming, he laughed in my face. 'Good luck. That's a long walk.' I didn't mention the bikes. Anyway, they're dead in the water too. They were already having issues because of the cyberattack. It's not good."

"Welp, so now you know," Bart said.

So far, that was a onetime thing. We're now back to the original plan of what Bart calls escape and evade, which means our travel is painfully slow. The dirt bikes don't go terribly fast, and we find ourselves needing to backtrack too often.

We're avoiding towns and trying to take roads in unpopulated areas. With major highways and the interstate littered with dead vehicles, from not only the fuel shortage but now the EMP, we have little choice. And learning our lesson from the first day on the dirt bikes, we ride for no more than two hours before we get off and stretch. These bikes were not built for comfort. Add in the fact we're riding double with packs on, and it's pretty close to miserable.

We're in the Wallowa-Whitman Forest now, on the northeastern edge of the state. Today's route, the Hells Canyon Scenic Byway, was a risk. Usually heavily traveled during tourist season, we thought it might be congested as people ran out of fuel. Fortunately, it seems as soon as the attacks started, people were smart enough to stop their vacations and head home. We only saw a few stranded cars and zero people before we left the main road for another forest service road.

Tomorrow we'll cross over into Idaho, continuing to use the smaller roads as we're able to. There's a state highway we haven't found an alternate for that we'll take for several miles—not only to get where we need to be, but so we can steal fuel from any abandoned vehicles. We stop at every gasoline-powered car or truck we find so we can pop a hole in the fuel tank and take what we need to keep our dirt bikes going, plus to check for stuff we can use.

Food and water are the main items we scrounge. While the actual food is limited, we do find bottled water on occasion and, surprisingly, a lot of condiments. I guess throwing extra packets of ketchup, mustard, salt, and pepper in gloveboxes is a thing. We've even found a few packages of soy sauce and a couple of fortune cookies. And any time we find napkins, I grab those. The one roll of toilet paper we have for the four of us is rapidly diminishing.

At first, I thought sticking with the logging roads and lesser traveled paved roads was dumb. Let's just get where we need to go as quickly as possible. But yesterday, we were on a busier road when someone started shooting at us. I don't even know where the shots were coming from, but luckily they weren't accurate and we escaped without harm.

While yesterday was the first time we'd been shot at, from the beginning of riding the bikes it became obvious Ben and Bart were right about carrying a pistol. We've often had people flash their weapons at us in a threatening manner.

Each night after we stop riding for the day, we practice drawing our guns and dry firing. When we were in the Oregon desert, well away from any towns or signs of people, we had a quick shooting practice. Out of fear for being found, Liam ran through the drawing and dry firing sequence he'd practice and then shot five times at the target. As soon as he was done, we quickly got back on the bikes and left the area.

At a later suitable spot, we repeated the process for me. Liam was a considerably better shot than I was. He hit the target—a water bottle we'd picked up from the side of the road—four out of five times. I hit only once, jumping each time the gun barked in my hand. The one time I was on target, it barely nipped the edge. As we were getting back on the bike to make our getaway, Ben said I was jerking the trigger. I snarled, "I was trying to hurry, just like you said I needed to do."

He gave me a patient nod. "We'll practice the dry firing more to make sure you're gently squeezing the trigger, then we'll find another spot for you to live fire again."

Ben and Bart, both having shot their handguns many times, didn't do live fire practice, but they dry fire and draw each night with us. Bart also makes a point of drilling in little sayings and tips when we practice. Things like, "Guns have only two enemies: rust and politicians." He says we don't need to worry about the politicians now, but we do need to keep the weapons clean. He showed Liam and I how to use the little cleaning kit he has in his bag.

"Remember, if you're not shooting," he said, "you should be loading. If you're not loading, get moving. And if you're not doing either, welp, you could end up dead. The key is to do something. It might be wrong, but if it's life or death, it's better than nothing."

While I appreciate his knowledge, I'm not sure, if it really came down to it, what I would do. Could I shoot someone? Or would I stand there like a deer in the headlights waiting to be shot?

One advantage to our backwoods travel is the ability to add to our meager food supplies. The bags Bart bungeed to the front of the bikes were loaded with our jerky, summer sausage, and pepperoni sticks from last year's deer. We finished the last of the summer sausage yesterday and are working on the pepperoni now, deciding the jerky is the most shelf stable. It won't be nearly enough to get us to Wyoming, not at the pace we're traveling.

Bart, having grown up poor in a small West Virginian mountain town and learning many skills, sets multiple snares at each new camp. The experiences of his childhood have been supplementing what we brought along. The first thing he caught was a ground squirrel, which none of us wanted to eat.

"Aren't these things like rats?" I asked.

"Yeah," Bart agreed. "They're in the rodent family."

"I'll pass," I said, shaking my head. Not wanting to waste it, Bart cleaned it and then simmered it in some water. He and Ben picked at it, while Liam and I made disgusting faces. I'm confident they found it disgusting, too, but didn't want to let on.

When we were in the desert area of Oregon, he caught a chukar. The single bird was an obscenely small amount of meat, but he found a few wild onions to add to the pot. The simmering dish smelled so good, I gave in and tried it.

Ben and Bart talked about using one of the .22s to shoot a rabbit—another meat I plan to avoid—but they decided even the small-caliber report would carry too far in our now silent world and could give away our location.

Tonight's meal—a marmot Bart snared last night, then cleaned and stewed before we left this morning's camp—is reheating over a low fire in plenty of water and a handful of dried prunes chopped ridiculously small. I'll be passing on the meat part of the dish, but I'll eat some of the prunes, which are desperately needed in our diet.

We're all suffering from the effects of too little food and not the right variety. My stomach started hurting this morning. The salty pepperoni we eat on the road seems to be making it worse.

A huge worry for me is food poisoning from the meat being unrefrigerated all day. At this elevation, it's cooler than when we were in the arid areas of Oregon but not as cool as it should be for keeping meat fresh. It's bad enough we're eating rodents—which is nothing short of disgusting—but to think it might cause us illness makes my stomach turn. And it makes me angry. Angry Ben and Bart insisted we leave our home, where the food was plentiful and would not kill us, to be out here in the wilderness where we have too few options for staying healthy.

Thinking of home reminds me of the deaths of our nearby neighbors and the missing people in the adjacent cul-de-sac. Just because it happened to others doesn't mean it would've happened to us. We could've banded together with a few of the extended community members to make it work.

Ben, sitting next to the stew pot, adds a few small twigs to the fire. He's made what he calls a Dakota fire hole for the cooking. One of his hunting friends taught him about these a few years ago. It's two holes, one holding the fire and the second acting as a draft to keep the fire going. Having camped extensively during hunting expeditions over the years, Ben had the forethought to bring a small grate and cooking pot along with us. When we were rearranging our gear, the pot went in the bottom of Bart's pack and the grate was attached with a small bungee cord to the outside.

Ben must feel me staring at him. He looks up and gives me a small smile. My stomach gives an unfamiliar flip flop. Taking a deep breath, I cautiously return his smile.

I've been awful to him these last two weeks—these past several months, really. I was done with our marriage and wanted out. Then, when I realized the attacks were not just a single event, I freaked out and decided taking Liam and going to Mark's was the better choice. Being forced from my home to go to Mollie's has taken its toll. I've been hateful to Ben—to Bart also—and I've made it clear I'm going against my will.

After giving the stew a stir, Ben walks over to where I'm lounging. "Hey," he says with a grin.

"Hey yourself." I feel a wave of nostalgia for what we used to have. "Want to sit with me?"

"Our dinner seems to be doing fine. I can sit for a minute." He plops on the tarp. Ben only had one tent small enough to fit into a backpack, and it only sleeps one person. Even though it's small, Liam and I both stay in it. Bart and Ben take turns using two tarps as a tent—one as a ground covering, and the other over the top if the weather warrants. One of them is always on watch while the other sleeps.

I've thought about offering to help with the overnight watch, but I've been so exhausted I'm not sure I can do it, that I can even stay awake.

"We made good miles today," I say.

Ben nods. "Not bad. If we can keep making forward progress and not always have to backtrack, we'll be fine."

"Have you thought any more about using the main roads? Maybe things are settling down and it would make sense."

"Yeah. Dad and I were thinking that too."

"You think we've been safe enough—as far as radiation is concerned?"

He gives a slight shrug and whispers, "We can only assume. I think we were far enough from Portland not to be affected immediately after the blast."

I let out a deep breath. We've had this conversation before, or some variation of it, since the radiation is something I worry about. Not for me, Ben, or Bart as much as for Liam. Can even a small dose cause him issues? I'd like to think we'd know if we were receiving fallout. Maybe there'd be some clue. Bart calls it a silent killer; says we could be dosed right now and not know. He and Ben also say there's nothing we can do about it, so there's no reason to worry. If our hair starts falling out or we get sores on our bodies, I guess we'll know then.

"Hello in the camp," a deep voice calls from out of view.

We all sit up immediately, and Ben and Bart move their hands to the guns on their hips. I took mine off earlier, and it's sitting at the edge of the tarp.

"Find cover," Ben hisses.

I grab my pistol before quickly duckwalking to where Liam is. I motion to him as we both move behind the log he was using as a pillow. Ben and Bart have also found trees to hide behind.

"Move along," Bart says in a gruff voice.

"Please," a new, wobbly female voice says. "Please, we have children. We can smell your food. Can you help us?"

Bart repeats his move along phrase.

"Ben," I whisper.

When he looks at me, he shakes his head.

I straighten my shoulders and very loudly say, "Step out where we can see you."

"Clarice," Ben says, voice full of anger.

Bart turns to me and shakes his head.

I give them each a hard look before continuing, "We won't harm you, and we expect the same from you."

Bart and Ben, weapons at the ready, both make a noise of disgust. A second later, with hands held high in the air, a small woman steps out from the trees. She's followed by two children that are a few years younger than Liam and a scrawny, disheveled man.

The woman gives a small smile. "We're unarmed."

"Turn so we can see," Bart says gruffly. "The man first."

With his hands still in the air, the man gives a slow spin. He has a soda bottle hanging off his waist. Several strips of duct tape are bound around it, forming something like a water bottle holster.

After he's turned around, Bart says, "Use one hand to lift up your shirt so I can see your waistband."

The man complies, then Bart has each of the others repeat the process. Each has a similar water bottle setup but nothing suspicious. I almost say something when he has the children spin and lift their shirts, but I manage to hold my tongue.

"All right. My son's going to pat you down now." Bart motions toward the man. "You, step toward him. The rest of you, stay where you are."

Once Ben checks all four of them, Bart asks, "Anyone else with you?"

"No, sir," the woman says.

"Why are you out here?" Ben asks.

"Trying to get home." She shrugs. "I'm Leanne. This is my brother, Wes, and my children, Sadie and Sebastian. We were in La Grande when the attacks started. We thought we could wait it out—you know, wait for the roads to clear and gas to become available again. But when the announcement came over our phones about the missiles, we freaked."

"What announcement?" I ask.

"The emergency alert? Didn't you get it? Do you know about the bombs?"

"We saw the mushroom cloud," Liam says. "But our phones—they haven't worked right since the cyberattack."

"You saw the bomb?" the boy asks in awe.

"Yeah," Liam answers. "But we were far away."

The man, Wes, gives a nod. "Our phones stopped working after the cyberattack, too, but a few days later, we occasionally got reception. We were able to talk to our mom and stepdad. We all live outside of Spokane. That's where we're going."

Ben and I share a look. Our phones never worked after the cyberattacks. Or if they did, we didn't know they were working. I never tried calling anyone, and no one tried calling me. I did test the lights several times a day, and those never worked. Could they be lying to us? And if so, why?

"How many bombs?" Bart asks.

"Don't know for sure," Leanne says. "We were in a shelter with a few others. There are rumors Portland and Seattle were both bombed, but I have no idea how people would know this. And a high-altitude nuke was detonated, which took out the power and phones."

"Probably for good," Sebastian says. "We haven't eaten yet today." He looks longingly at our stew pot.

Straightening my shoulders and avoiding looking at any of my men, I say, "Would you like to join us?"

"Clarice," Bart says in a low voice.

I turn on Bart. "So far, I've followed your lead, Dad. I allowed you and Ben to drive by people—people in obvious need of help. No more. We will invite them to eat with us."

He gives me a hard look before shaking his head and muttering under his breath.

"Sharing one meal will be fine," Ben says stiffly.

"Thank you for your kindness," Leanne says. "You're an answer to our prayers."

Prayer, huh? I give a nod in response and motion to them. "Have a seat . . . anywhere. I think it's still a few minutes until the food will be ready, but we don't have any extra bowls."

"We have mugs," the girl says, as her mom beckons her toward the tarp. "In our backpacks."

"What backpacks?" Ben asks, a hint of alarm in his voice.

"We left our supplies in the woods," Wes says. "We weren't—we didn't want to lose anything."

"Smart," I say. "Go ahead and grab your things. We won't steal from you."

"Um, how about I go with you," Ben says.

"I'll join you," Bart says, his voice harsher than usual. "Liam, you watch over your mom."

I can see Leanne visibly pale at the suggestion she might mean me harm. I give Bart a pointed look before saying, "I *won't* need watching over."

Leanne, the three children, and I sit in silence while we wait for the men to return. It's only a few minutes before Bart reappears, shaking his head.

"Why didn't you say you're on bikes?" he asks.

"I didn't— " Leanne shakes her head. "Bicycles are a commodity. It was a risk reaching out to you. We prayed that you'd be friendly and . . . and help us because of the children. But the bikes— " She gives a shrug. "We have to have them in order to reach our home."

Ben steps out from the woods, pushing a mountain bike with a trailer behind it. Wes follows with a second bike and trailer.

"We searched the trailers and backpacks," Ben says. "We'll keep the bikes here while they eat."

"Thank you," Leanne says. "The place we were sheltering at in La Grande gave us what they could and helped us find the bikes and trailers. They were good to us. We've seen God's hand in so much of this." Tears fill her eyes. "Like with the water. We were there when the rule to purify water came out—you know, because of the suspected contamination of our food and water supply."

I nod that I do know. It all blends together, but it seems those orders came out the morning of the cyberattacks, or maybe the day before. We were advised to drink bottled water or somehow purify municipal water. Several people were sick or died from typhoid fever. At the same time, we were warned of possible E. coli contamination happening with fresh vegetables. Since we had a private well for water, we didn't worry about it being contaminated, but I tossed all our produce.

Now, I'd give anything to have a fresh salad. I don't care if I do get sick from it. I almost smile at my thinking. I'm concerned about food poisoning from carrying around unrefrigerated cooked meat all day but willing to risk E. coli for a fresh salad. Ben did insist we bring several small glass containers of bleach for the trip—containers I kept after emptying essential oils from them, thinking I'd find a future use for them—saying we needed to be sure we could clean our water.

"Anyway," Leanne says, "we bought one of the last bottles of bleach at the store. We've been using it to clean water we find." She motions to a soda bottle hanging from her waist.

"That's a smart idea for carrying water," Liam says. "How'd you think of that?"

"It was Sebastian's idea," Wes says. "He's quite the inventor."

"I wish I knew how to invent food," the boy says.

"We did!" Sadie exclaims. "We prayed for it, and we found these nice people." She gives me a beaming smile.

Leanne pats her on the arm before saying, "Praise the Lord."

Just great. Jesus freaks. We'll feed them and then they can be on their way. I had my fill with Mollie and her *Thank God this, praise Jesus that* while she was visiting. I'm in no mood for it now.

Chapter 8

Day 18

As badly as I wanted to get rid of Leanne and her Bible-thumping family, Bart seemed to like them more and more once they started spouting their nonsense. He added more water to our already thin stew to make it stretch for everyone. Then, when they bowed their heads to thank their imaginary God for their food, he joined them.

Over twenty years ago, when I first met Bart and his wife Jessa—Ben's mom—they were both what I would call Holy Rollers. After Ben explained my beliefs to them, they toned it down around me. When we'd go to dinner at their place, they'd still pray but didn't object to my nonparticipation. Jessa died when I was pregnant with Liam. Bart was devastated but still clung to his make-believe religion during his grief. I believe, as I believed when my dad was taken from me when I was only seventeen by a massive heart attack, and my mom two years later from excruciatingly painful pancreatic cancer, there's no such thing as God.

I remember when a pastor stopped by my mom's hospital room and tried to convince her that if she'd only accept Jesus as her Lord and Savior, she'd go to heaven. When he said that was the only way into heaven, I knew for a fact he was a liar. My dad was the kindest, friendliest man I've ever known. For the pastor to suggest he was not allowed into heaven because he'd never believed in some fairytale was wrong.

So wrong that I didn't let him get away with saying it. I gave him a tongue lashing I'm sure he remembers to this day before promptly booting him from my mom's room.

In her drugged and slightly delirious state, she actually entertained the idea—the idea he might be right. She calmly said, "Clarice, you know your dad was a good man. He didn't completely reject the idea of God or of Jesus."

"What he said, Mom, it's fine for other people," I patiently explained. "But Dad chose to live life by his own bootstraps instead of placing faith in something he couldn't see or prove."

She gave me a smile and a nod before saying, "But many times, he also entertained the truth of the idea. Pastor Robert has visited me before— "

"Mom!" I cried. "You shouldn't have let that man in here. He'll fill your head with nonsense."

She gave a slight lift of her hand. "We've had good chats. One thing he said has stuck with me. Neither I nor you know what your dad's final thoughts might have been. I think he may have chosen heaven. I think I should do the same."

"Mom. I don't know what lies that man was putting in your head, but I don't want to hear any more about it. Dad would be—he'd be disgusted with both of us for talking this way."

She gave me a small smile and said, "I don't think he would be. I think he'd probably agree with me. But I'm too tired right now. We'll talk more later." She closed her eyes and, with a peaceful smile on her face, promptly fell asleep. We never did talk more. That night, she slipped into a coma and died two days later. Did she actually believe that nonsense? I don't know for sure, but I think she may have. Not that it matters. It's not real anyway.

After the night of sharing marmot and prune stew—no marmot meat for me, but I did sip some of the nasty broth and ate a few prunes—Bart invited the family to travel with us. He said it made sense to stay together if we were all heading in the same direction. The trouble with traveling together: they're on pedal bikes and we're on dirt bikes. Our motored bikes travel more than twice as fast as theirs.

Bart wasn't discouraged by this. Somehow, he convinced Ben it was smart to join forces. We could use Wes and Leanne for extra guards at night. According to Ben, they had a minor disagreement about it before he finally agreed. I wasn't consulted. I'm still miffed. My opinion should count as much as each of theirs.

They devised a plan to start off together each morning and then have a rendezvous spot somewhere ahead. The dirt bikes will arrive much sooner than the mountain bikes. Then, when the mountain bikes arrive, we'll swap riders so those on the bicycles can "rest" while riding the motorbikes. The former dirt bikers will then be fresh for pedaling.

The first morning, Ben and Wes were on the bicycles. I rode behind Liam, and Bart drove the larger dirt bike with Leanne riding behind him. Leanne's children rode in the too-small-for-them bike trailers attached to the bicycles, as they had been before.

When we arrived at the rendezvous spot, Bart immediately set up a couple of snares. He had a rabbit snared, cleaned, and stewed—and a second caught and cleaned—before Ben and Wes showed up. I'd never seen Bart so happy. He went on and on about how catching two rabbits in such a short amount of time was nothing short of a miracle.

And now that's become our norm, the short time we're stopped doesn't always result in successfully trapping food, but it's still worth the small amount of effort. Head out together, meet up later, motorbike riders set up snares and prepare any food, and so forth.

Liam and I never ride the mountain bikes. I'm good with that. I don't think I'm physically up for riding a bike while towing a trailer. Liam has taken the lead on setting up the snares, even when Bart's on a dirt bike. After the first day, Leanne introduced us to pine water. She heats water, then steeps pine needles in it. She says it will give us some vitamins we're missing, especially vitamin C. I don't mind it, and I like having a new flavor experience. While she does have some usefulness, like with the pine needle drink, she still annoys me.

We're now camped near a creek, not far from a small town, after our day of riding. While I would've preferred to camp right next to the creek, Ben and Bart wanted to stay in the trees to provide us some concealment. We're also not cooking tonight. They decided we're too close to town and the food odors could attract unwanted company. We have rabbit and partridge from our earlier snares braising to eat cold.

Though I'm still disgusted by the food we've been snaring, I've started picking at a few of the meats out of necessity. The lack of vegetables is really taking a toll on me. I need those prunes more than ever. We're down to the last of our dried fruit and now handing them out like medicine. It's not enough. My digestive system is an absolute wreck, and my stomach has been aching since yesterday.

Because of my discomfort, I'm cross with everyone. As soon as we found our campsite, Ben and Bart pulled out the maps and started going over the plans for tomorrow. I'm so glad we only have another day, two at the most, before we head east and Leanne and her group will continue north.

I've, again, tried to convince Ben and Bart it's time to return to the major roads so we can start making better time. These side roads may seem safer, but our rapidly dwindling supplies—especially the food—is becoming a problem. Again, they shot me down, this time with Wes and Leanne joining in on how smart it is to stay hidden and avoid people.

I'm barely listening as Ben marks out a spot for the first rendezvous in the morning. Because we have only the one detailed map book for each state we'll be traveling in, I've been tasked with writing down the directions to our rendezvous spots on two pieces of paper from a small notebook I stashed in my pack. Each group of bikers gets a piece of paper. When those of us on the motorbikes stop at the first rendezvous, we'll repeat the process of picking out the next stop. I'm so quick-tempered that when Leanne asks what something on one of the notes says, I snap at her.

Instead of snapping back, she gives me a small smile and says, "Thank you for clarifying what you wrote, Clarice. I appreciate it."

I feel like a heel. But instead of admitting it, I give a dirty look.

A few minutes ago, Leanne took her children by the hands and motioned to her brother, saying they were going to go for a walk along the creek.

"Good riddance," I mutter under my breath, even though I'd really like to see them stay here and help set up camp. I start storming around, unzipping the big backpack and removing the tent.

"Why don't you sit for a bit?" Ben says. "Have some water and— "

"And what? And everything will be fine?"

"No, probably not. But you don't look very well. We have plenty of daylight, so there's no hurry putting camp together. Rest, and you might feel better."

"Doubtful," I say, my voice dripping with contempt.

"I think I'll walk with the others," Bart says. "Liam, you want to come?"

"He's staying here," I say abruptly.

"Let him go," Ben whispers.

I shoot daggers at him. "Liam is staying here." I pretend not to notice the look Bart gives Liam as he shakes his head while walking away.

"Clarice," Ben says softly. "I know you don't feel well—none of us do. But you're acting like a child."

"Thanks for that. I really appreciate my husband telling me I'm a child."

"Well, you are."

"Can you just once try and see things from my point of view?"

"Your point of view?"

"You and your dad forced us to leave our home. Then you make stupid decisions like taking the most ridiculous roundabout way to get to Wyoming. Do you not see how insane this is? You should just once try and look at things from my point of view."

"Your point of view?" he hisses. "Your point of view would've already got us killed." I flare my eyes at him, but he lifts a hand. "That's right, Clarice. We'd be dead if we had to rely on you. At least Dad and I are trying to keep us alive. But how about this, how about— "

"No," I say. "How about you— "

Bart comes rushing through the trees. "Go! We've got to go now," he says in a rushed, low voice.

"What's happening, Dad?" Ben asks, immediately ending our argument and jumping into action as he hands me the large backpack. He then grabs for the next pack while Liam picks his up.

A voice calls out through the woods, "Hey, man, we've already seen you. Why don't you come on out here and join your family?"

I feel myself pale as Bart's shoulders slump. "They don't know about you," he whispers. "Take the bags and the motorbikes. Go!"

"You go, Dad." Ben hands both backpacks to him.

"They saw me, son."

"Full on or just a glimpse?"

"I don't know. I think just a glimpse."

"No, Ben." I grab his arm.

"Take them, Dad," Ben says, as the voice calls out again. "Take care of my family. I'll see you at the rendezvous spot."

With my whole body shaking, I hand him the note I wrote.

"No," he says. "I can remember. If I'm not there by tomorrow night, go on to Mollie's. I'll find you. Now get them out of here." He pulls Liam into a quick hug, whispers he loves me, and then says, "Go, Dad. Go." He turns and walks into the forest. I reach to pull him back, my fingers just brushing his T-shirt.

He walks several yards into the woods before yelling out, "Okay. No problem. I'm coming out."

"Go with God, son," Bart says, barely audible. He hands me the second backpack and a rifle before putting on his own pack and grabbing two more rifles.

"Are we taking Dad's things?" Liam asks.

Bart puts his fingers to his lips and nods. He hands the fourth rifle to Liam, then motions to the small dirt bike while he starts pushing the larger one. Carrying both backpacks and a rifle, I stay close behind. With tears streaming down my face, I look back often to see if we're being followed. We're going deeper into the forest, finding a spot to hide. We move quickly and quietly into the dense forest.

After a considerable amount of time, Bart has us move into a thicket. "We'll wait here," he says.

"Should we try and rescue Dad?" Liam whispers, his face also stained with tears.

I nod as Bart shakes his head. "We can't do it. None of us would know the first thing about staging a rescue. Your dad's smart. He'll get out of it and meet us tomorrow or, worst case scenario, at Mollie and Jake's place. I'm sure of it."

As we sit quietly in our hiding spot, I strain to listen. Did they realize there were more of us? Are they looking? Is Ben okay?

It's nearly dark when Bart says, "I'm going to take a look. You two wait here. I'll be back within the hour—unless they grab me. If that happens, stay hidden. Don't leave until it's safe."

"How will we know when it's safe?" Liam asks.

Bart shakes his head. "Wish I knew. Clarice? You got this?"

Even though everything inside of me is screaming, *No, I don't have this*, I give a slight acknowledgement. He meets my eyes. "We're okay," I say, attempting a more convincing nod.

He's been gone about fifteen minutes when we hear rustling in the brush. "Grandpa," Liam says, starting to stand.

With a pounding heart, I grab his arm and put my finger over my lips. "Wait," I mouth.

His eyes widen as he shrinks back down into our hiding place.

"Clarice," Bart says in a soft voice. "You and Liam come on out. They're gone."

Tears flood my eyes again. They're gone. Ben's gone.

"Dad?" Liam asks, his voice cracking on the word as he stands up. He offers me his hand. My legs are like spaghetti from staying in the same position for so long. Combined with the extreme emotions I've been experiencing since Ben left us, I can barely stand. As soon as I see the look on Bart's face, I crumble to the ground.

Chapter 9

Day 20

We've been at the rendezvous spot since about 10:00 yesterday morning. After Bart returned from our original camp, which had been stripped clean of everything left behind, we set up about a hundred yards away, taking turns at fitful sleep until daylight.

Leanne's family and Ben were gone. Bart tried to stay positive by saying he thought they'd be okay. If the intent were harm, he thinks it would've been done right then and there. Without directly saying so, he meant since there were no bodies left behind, there was still hope. My hope is fading as each minute passes without Ben showing up, my last angry words to him replaying on a loop in my head.

"We should probably get a move on," Bart says, as the rising sun begins to peek over the mountains.

"We should stay here another day," Liam replies.

"Clarice, you ready to go?" Bart asks.

I drop my eyes to the ground. Like Liam, I want to stay—stay here until Ben shows up. I may have been looking for a way out of my shaky marriage, but this wasn't it. Sadly, Bart's right. We should go. Ben said to only stay until last night and then head to Mollie's. Knowing him, he'll follow the plan to the letter and will expect the same from us. He may not even show up at this rendezvous spot since it's beyond the designated time. Provided he's even still alive. I know Bart thinks it's a good sign they were taken and not killed on the spot. But an ache in my gut tells me he's not safe—maybe still alive, but not safe.

"We should go," I say quietly. "Ben will do exactly what he said. Since he didn't arrive here last night, he'll go to Mollie and Jake's—if he can."

"Of course he can!" Liam shouts. "Dad's fine and . . . and we should wait here for him."

"Your mom's right," Bart says calmly. "He'll go on to Bakerville. We'll see him there."

Liam shakes his head before stomping off. I watch as he leans one hand against a tree, shoulders slumped and quivering on occasion. I leave him to his emotions as Bart and I begin to pack up. Like Liam, I'd like to just cry, to curl up in a ball somewhere and bawl my eyes out. There are so many things I wish I could say to Ben. And even more things I wish I could take back. I bite my lip to try and stop a new onslaught of emotion.

After many minutes, Liam returns and helps us finish loading everything. We lost one of the tarps and the tent when Ben was taken. The tarp was already spread on the ground so we could do our map work; I'd taken the tent out of the backpack. Had I been thinking, I'd have grabbed it. The addition of Ben's backpack gave us a few additional supplies, which we distributed among the other three packs.

The extra rifle has turned into a hindrance as we try to figure out how to transport it. We've decided to leave it behind, burying it along with anything else from Ben's backpack we won't need. Bart and I went back and forth over leaving behind Ben's hunting rifle or one of the .22s. We finally decided to leave the second, smaller .22, using the exact logic Ben used when bringing the hunting rifle: we might need the extra firepower. A .22 is fine for small game, but not so much for large game. And while a well-placed shot can take a man down, the larger caliber may be needed. Leaving these things felt very final. How long will it take us to get to Bakerville? And is it possible Ben will survive his capture and meet us there?

Another change Bart made to our routine was removing the pages from the map books we will need to reach Mollie's place. Bart said it doesn't make sense to continue carrying items we may not need. We tore out the far eastern pages of Oregon, the northern parts of Idaho, the southwestern pages for Montana, and the areas surrounding Bakerville, Wyoming. The rest of the books were buried with the rifle and clothes.

I asked Bart why we were burying them, and he said it just seemed like the right thing to do instead of leaving them for someone else to find. I watched as he folded up the page we're currently using and stuffed it in his pocket. By way of explanation he said, "Thought it'd be easier to have it in my pocket as opposed to dragging it out of the backpack multiple times a day. Don't know why we didn't think of this before."

Right before we're ready to climb on the bikes, Bart says, "Clarice, Liam, I'd like you to pray with me."

I don't bother to keep the surprise off my face before shaking my head.

Liam quickly says, "I'll pray with you, Grandpa." With a nod, he looks to me. "Mom? Let's do it. Let's pray."

"You two go right ahead," I say stiffly. "I need—I'll go into the brush before we go." I take a moment to dig some toilet paper out of my pack before turning stiffly on my heel. Bart wants to pray. Fine. Let him. If it makes Liam feel better, he's welcome to do so too. But not me.

Twenty minutes later, we're on the road. I'm riding behind Liam on the smaller bike while Bart, still wearing the pack frame, now with both his and Ben's backpacks attached to it, is on the larger bike. My tears continue to fall on and off throughout the day. Many times, I want to scream at Bart to stop, to turn around and we'll go back to wait for Ben to show up. While it's what my heart wants, my mind knows it's futile. Ben would've already been there if he were able to be. Is he still alive?

Chapter 10

Day 24

With the ability to now ride full days, we should be much closer to Wyoming than we are. But it's been one thing after another. We had another day where we had to do some backtracking after seeing what looked like a roadblock ahead, plus something was wrong with the big bike one morning, and it wouldn't start.

Bart fiddled with it for hours, finally giving up on it and saying it looked like one of us would be on foot. As he started making plans for a similar setup to what we used with Leanne and her family by making rendezvous spots, Liam suggested trying it again. It started right up. We still have no idea what the problem was. Yesterday, I woke up with such a gut ache I couldn't go anywhere. The constipation that's been troubling me for so long left me curled up and withering in pain.

"I think we'll need to go into a town and find you a doctor," Bart says. "Or at least a pharmacy so you can get some laxatives."

I nod my agreement. "I should've thought of packing those."

"We need more fat and fiber in our diet," he says. "We saw those elk yesterday. Maybe we should camp a few days, see if we can find a fat elk or deer. Might make a world of difference."

"Too bad the berries we found weren't ripe yet," Liam says. Yesterday, shortly after seeing the elk, we found a bunch of chokecherry trees. Bart told us they weren't ripe and that they'd still be bitter. Liam tried one anyway, quickly spitting it out.

What plagues us the most is our massive grief over Ben. We all spend a lot of time looking over our shoulders, thinking he'll find us and we'll be together again. Ben and Bart spent so much time pouring over the route. Of course, with the backtracking and changes to our route, running into each other would be like a needle in a haystack. I think back to a time when Ben and I were on vacation in Southern California. Liam was around four at the time and staying with a neighbor while we took some much-needed couple's time.

We were making our way along Hollywood Boulevard, holding hands and taking our time as we examined the Walk of Fame amongst the throng of others doing the same thing, when a voice called out, "Clarice Cervelli? CC? Is that you?"

Spinning my head, I sought out the person referring to me by my long-forgotten nickname. Waving wildly was a short, plump woman with a brilliant smile. "It's me!" she cried. "Whitney Barrister from David Douglas."

"Oh," I gushed. "Of course, Whitney, you haven't changed a bit," I lied. She'd changed a ton. She used to be petite and adorable when we served as co-captains of the cheer squad in our senior year of high school. Now, though her face was still pretty, she'd obviously let herself go. I haven't seen her since graduation—and truly, I barely remember the event. My dad had died only two weeks prior. I wanted to skip the whole thing, but my mom insisted I go. I was so wracked with grief, I was a shell of my usual self.

But there, in Southern California, I knew the years had been much kinder to me than they'd been to Whitney. Feeling a smug satisfaction that I'd kept my svelte figure even after the birth of my son, I made a point of standing even taller, towering over Whitney—almost posing so she could admire my beauty.

"It's so amazing to see you," she said, not even commenting on how good I still looked. "I can't believe I'm running into you here." She made a motion and a handsome man standing near her stepped forward. "My husband, Alistair Fisher. That's my last name now, too, of course." She let out a childish giggle. "Whitney Fisher. Are you married?" she asked, looking pointedly at Ben standing next to me.

"Yes, this is my husband, Ben Ferguson. I still use my maiden name, especially for business." I gave her a sweet smile as I made sure she knew I was an independent woman with a successful business.

Thinking back on the chance encounter with Whitney—the odds of meeting someone I hadn't seen in over a decade in a tourist trap of an area with thousands of people walking the same space—the idea of Ben finding us seems more realistic.

When we set out this morning, Bart said it was only to find a better camping spot, a remote location where we can live off the land for a few days in hopes of improving my health. He's going to kill an elk or deer. Unlike Ben, Bart's not a hunter, but he used to be when he was younger. Then, hunting was part of their survival. It was how his family was fed. While we always eat the meat Ben brings home, it's not like we must have it to survive. We can buy anything we need. Bart assures me he'll remember what to do.

He'd looked over the map last night and found a spot he thought would be perfect. But as we pull off onto a small road well before where I think we should turn, I'm not sure what's going on.

"Bart?" I ask, raising my eyebrows.

"Why don't you two go on ahead, up to the cluster of trees. I'll catch up in a bit."

"What are you doing, Grandpa?" Liam asks.

"I think . . . it looks like the house back there is vacant. I thought I'd check and see if they might have something to help your mom's stomach."

"A vacant house probably didn't leave medicine behind when they moved out," I say.

"No, I don't think it's vacant as in empty. I mean, no one is home."

"You're going to steal from them?" Liam asks aghast.

I give Liam a look. We've been stealing from cars this entire trip. Does he think stealing from a house is different?

Bart gives a slow, sad nod. "Yeah. But I don't think they'll be needing it."

I feel my eyes widen. "Why do you say that?"

"There's a horse lying dead in the pasture."

I close my eyes, glad I missed seeing it.

Liam whips his head around. "I don't see it."

"Better that way. You two take both bikes and stay hidden. I'll be there shortly."

"Why would we take both bikes?" Liam asks.

"I don't want to make noise driving up the driveway. I can quietly check it out before going in."

"I could just wait here for you, Grandpa."

"No, we'll do what he says," I say, as I start to climb on the bigger bike.

"You got this, Clarice?" Bart asks, motioning toward the bike.

"I've got it."

With a nod, he turns and darts across the road to a line of trees. I watch for a moment as he weaves through the brush and foliage. Liam and I move to where he asked us to wait. His version of *shortly* turns out to be closer to an hour. I'm just starting to worry when I see him in the distance, laden with several reusable grocery bags tied onto the pack frame.

"Wow, looks like Grandpa found lots of stuff."

I give a nod as Bart lifts his hand in a wave. When he reaches us, he says, "Got something that's going to help you, Clarice."

"Food?" Liam asks, his mouth practically watering at the thought.

"Some. There wasn't much. I wasn't the first one there."

"The people?" I ask. I notice a slight odor on his clothing as he steps closer.

He gives a grim shake of his head. "Let's get on to camp, get you rested and well. I want to get this trip over with."

We set up camp in a well-forested and well-hidden area near a creek. Liam and Bart put out their snares, then head out. They plan to just walk and see if they can find a game trail. They tell me they'll be back before too long. Once they have an idea of the area, they'll plan tomorrow's hunt.

I've stayed at camp and am sipping peppermint tea Bart found in the farmhouse. It's not exactly what I thought he'd produce to help me feel better, but it does seem to be helping. I don't know if it's psychological or actual, but I swear I can almost feel the cramps in my stomach release a little with each sip. Of course, I did have a dose of magnesium citrate, which should start it's work soon. I've put the wad of napkins within easy reach so I have them when I need them. While we're here resting, I'm going to make sure I get enough water. Maybe dehydration is part of the reason I'm having so much trouble.

After finishing my tea, I stretch out on the tarp. We're in a buggy place, and even though I've generously doused myself with the mosquito killer Bart found at the farmhouse, they still won't leave me alone. Once again, I wish for the tent we recklessly left behind. Because our backpacks aren't much larger than schoolbags, we didn't have room for sleeping bags. With the warm weather, we decided sheets and light blankets would be substantial enough and take up only a small amount of space.

It's colder at these higher elevations, and I've been chilled the past couple of nights. Bart found a couple more sheets and a throw blanket. I give one of the new sheets a sniff. It smells of lavender and reminds me of my mom. She always kept a lavender sachet in the linen closet. She kept a second in her underwear drawer.

How would she handle the disaster we're now living in? How would she handle losing her husband in such a way? I slowly let out my breath. She'd hold her head high. She would've been strong from the beginning. She wouldn't have pouted and moped or chosen to stay in bed instead of facing the troubles. She most certainly wouldn't have made plans to run away with another man in the midst of a disaster. She would've been right there, right with my dad, doing what needed to be done.

I straighten my back. With Ben gone, Liam is depending on me. Depending on me and Bart to keep him safe until we can get to Bakerville. While I still have zero desire to live in Wyoming with Mollie and her family, I know it's the best thing for Liam. It'll give him the best chance of a normal life. The best for Bart and me, too, though now I wonder if I can have a normal life without Ben.

It seemed so right to leave him, to throw away twenty years, since we'd grown apart. But there were times in those days after we escaped from Nemont when I saw a glimpse of our old love, of the way things used to be. I'd give anything to take back those last awful words, the terrible way I treated him.

I spread the sheet in hopes of covering my body to help with the bug issue. As I smooth out the cover, a shot rings out. It's so close, I immediately throw myself back on the tarp. On my belly, I scoot to the edge of the tarp where I've left the Sig Sauer 9-millimeter pistol I've been using and training on. Bart calls this gun the big brother to the one he carries on his ankle. Other than the one time when I shot at a bottle and only hit it once—and jumping each time it went off—I haven't fired with ammunition in it.

With my heart beating in my ears and my mouth dry, I stay low as I move toward a large tree, pistol beside my thigh. I'm almost there when my stomach cramps, causing me to double over in pain. I bite my lip to avoid yelling out. Crouched behind the tree, I take a few deep breaths to control both my fear and the agony in my gut. Time seems to stand still as I hear a rustling in the woods.

I hold my breath and make myself as small as possible. Seconds later, Liam steps out from the trees, a huge smile on his face. The smile quickly turns to confusion as his eyes dart around camp, trying to find me.

"Mom?" he says in a near whisper.

"I'm here." I motion him to the ground. "Get down. Someone's shooting."

"It's Grandpa. He got one. Got a fat deer."

"He did?" I stand up and quickly realize my mistake. I'm again doubled over from the pain.

Liam rushes toward me. "Are you hurt?"

"Just the stomach pain."

He helps me back to the tarp. "Are you sure it's not something more? Like an appendicitis or something?"

"Not my appendix. I had it removed when I was a child. You know I've had digestive issues for years. This is the same—just more."

"Grandpa says this is going to help you. I need to go back and help him get it taken care of. He wanted me to tell you so you didn't worry."

"Okay, should I go with you?"

"No. Stay. Rest. We're going to make you better."

Chapter 11

Day 26

The last two days have been almost luxurious—at least as luxurious as camping in the middle of nowhere can be. Bart was right; he didn't have any trouble taking care of the deer. Once he had it skinned and quartered, he took the meat off the bone. To preserve the venison, he's been drying it over a smoky fire that he keeps stoking with green wood in a shallow trench. The thin strips of meat are spread out on rocks. He also made a smokehouse using an old tarp he found at the farmhouse. I question how well any of it will keep; we'll probably all die of food poisoning.

In addition to the venison, he's been foraging the woods for other edibles. He found a spot along the creek where cattails are growing. He brought back a few roots of the cigar-shaped plant, along with small green leaves. He had a small partial jar of olive oil—also found at the farmhouse—and cooked the cattail leaves with the venison in it, resulting in something like a stir-fry.

As Bart was preparing it, he said, "These are really too old for this use. I won't get much yield from it, but we'll make do. Think of it as a leek." He gave me a nod as he worked on peeling it. "Some of it's definitely too tough."

He finally got to the part of the cattail he said would work in our dish. While it wasn't very flavorful, the feeling of a real meal was a marked improvement over the limited foods we've been eating. We've been making our dwindling supply of pepperoni and jerky stretch. As things have been turning bleak, I've even resorted to eating the things Bart snares.

For breakfast this morning, he peeled the rhizomes from the cattail, then boiled them. He'd found a small bag of cornmeal at the farmhouse and breaded the venison before cooking it this morning. In addition to the cornmeal, he found flour, salt, garlic powder, and pepper—all things I wish I would've thought to pack.

I'm not sure if it was the boiled cattail root, the venison, the peppermint tea, or the half bottle of magnesium citrate I've chugged, but my stomach finally agrees with me. The cramping has stopped, and things seem to be working as they should. Bart warned me not to go too crazy with the laxatives, for fear of things going in the other direction. That would certainly be bad. While he did find a partial box of Kleenex, our roll of TP is long gone, and the stash of fast-food napkins we've found in cars is dwindling.

"I think I might take a drive today," Bart says quietly.

"A drive? Where?" I ask.

"Back to the farmhouse. Maybe see if there might be another place to check out."

I glance at Liam; he's using a flat stick to turn the meat strips.

"Why?" I ask.

"See if we can find additional supplies. I'll get a proper turner so we don't need to use a stick. There's a few other things I've thought of, and I didn't go through the barn and only gave a cursory glance in the bedrooms, spending most of my time in the bathrooms, kitchen, and garage."

"Too bad there wasn't more food."

"Yeah, we're not the only ones looking for it."

"What happened to the people living there?" I ask, even though I'm not sure I really want to hear his answer.

"Nothing good."

"You found them?"

"They were there. My guess is, whoever originally ransacked the house murdered them."

"Did you just . . . leave them?"

"I covered them with blankets. I'll take care of them when I go back today."

"Take care of them? You mean bury them?"

"If I can."

"Do you think that's what happened to our neighbors? Burdock killed them so he could have their things?"

He gives me a long look. "It's the only thing that makes sense. I know you didn't want to make this trip, but I believe—Ben believed—our best place to ride out this disaster is Wyoming. He said, with the small population, it'd be safe, or *safer* at least."

I can't prevent the tears that well up at the mention of Ben's name. "Did you and Ben discuss the danger between here and there? Did it occur to you he might be . . . be taken?"

Bart doesn't even attempt to hide his grief. With a drop of his shoulders, his voice turns husky. "Some, yes. We thought we were being paranoid. When the things we talked about, starting with the guy who wouldn't get out of the way on that first logging road, started coming true . . . " He shakes his head as his voice fades away. "I know it should've been me, Clarice."

I draw circles in the dirt with my finger while thinking of my response. Part of me agrees. It should've been him. He should've been the one to give himself up. "You know that wouldn't happen. You know Ben never would've let them take you. He would have fought them. Shot them. Something. You taking Liam and me away, it was the safe thing to do. Now, we need to get Liam to Bakerville. We must, or Ben's— " I choke back a sob. "Ben's sacrifice would've been for nothing."

"We'll do it. We'll get Liam to Bakerville. I know you don't exactly like Mollie." When I open my mouth to argue, he lifts a hand. "You've made enough comments over the years. I get that you and she are too much alike and it bothers you."

"What? We're not at all alike," I say, making motions with my hands, almost trying to shoo the thought away.

Bart lets out a hearty laugh. "Seriously? You don't see it?"

"No, absolutely not. She's annoying and always has to be right. She's always researching things to death just to prove her point."

"And you don't do the same?"

"Well, no. It's not the same! I do it for my business so it's successful."

"She does the same, for our business so we're *all* successful."

"But she's just an employee! There's no reason for her to be so . . . so intense all the time."

"She's an employee with a vested interest in our success. And I don't think she's that intense. When she's here, she's cramming a lot in during a short time."

"Maybe so, but you have to admit, it's going to be hard living in the same house. Haven't you thought about it? She's your employee, but we're going crawling to them to save us."

"And you think she's going to, what? Hold it over us? Decide she's been wronged all these years and make us clean out the chicken coop as punishment?" He gives me a small smile.

"Well . . . no. Not exactly. I just—I can barely handle the five days she stays at my house. How will I not go crazy around her all the time? And her new religion stuff, I'm not sure I can handle being immersed in that."

"Her religion stuff isn't new. She was a Christian when she started working for us."

"Really? She kept it well hidden then."

"I'm not sure she kept it hidden. It's just, something happened a few years ago. She realized she needed to put God first and have Jesus as a focus. I think it's been a good thing. After that happened, things changed for our business too."

"Oh? So you're crediting her wacky religious beliefs with the success of your company?"

"God has always been a part of my business. When Jessa and I first started thinking about hanging out our own shingle, we prayed about it before moving forward. It was scary to quit a paying job with decent benefits. Ben was only a couple years older than Liam then. God's hand was definitely in it. Somehow, even in those early days, we made it. Jessa was a prayer warrior, and I'm convinced that's the only way we stayed afloat."

"Or . . . " I say with as gracious of a smile I can manage, "your hard work kept things going."

"We did work hard, no doubt about it, but some months it took a miracle to pay our bills."

"I thought the Bible teaches money is evil. Shouldn't God be against successful businesses?"

"The love of money is the root of evil, not money itself. Money is a tool, but if we put the desire for money above other things, *then* it becomes a problem. Jessa used our new business to glorify God. She'd share the amazing things God was doing with anyone who'd listen. She'd help those less fortunate, and she'd use our miracles to tell them about the love of Jesus. She was on fire for the Lord, and it showed."

"I bet she drove people crazy." I quickly cover my mouth out of embarrassment for being so blunt.

With a smile, Bart says, "Oh, I'm sure some found it annoying. Just like how you find Mollie annoying. But when Jesus gets ahold of a person, it's hard to keep it quiet. The fire Jessa had was something I always wanted. I had more of a simmer. But these last few days, while we've been so focused on our survival, I find a new desire to get to know Him better."

"Know who?"

"God. And His son, Jesus. Since Jessa passed, my simmer has faded. God has become more of an afterthought in my life. I see now what I've been missing. I see what Liam is missing too."

"No." I shake my head. "You can believe all the fairytales you want, but you will not share that . . . that hogwash with my son."

A look passes over his face. He nods. "I won't start the conversation, but I won't lie to our boy either. He has questions, and he deserves answers."

"He doesn't need you filling his mind with rubbish. He needs reality-based answers."

"And when he asks you what happens when someone dies, what is your reality-based answer?"

"It's just the end." I shrug. "Before, at least we had the option of donating our organs and could live on by helping others. But now, it's just the end. We become fertilizer."

Bart closes his eyes and drops his head. I'm not exactly sure what he's doing, but it's several moments before he looks at me again. "I'd better get going. I don't plan to be gone long. I'll go to the farmhouse from before and then see if there are other places around. But I'm not sure if I'll actually enter any of them."

"When do you think we'll hit the road again?"

"Let's see how you are tomorrow. If you're still good, how about the next day?"

"Yeah, okay. Don't go nuts bringing stuff back. Our space is too limited."

"I'll keep that in mind."

Chapter 12

Day 29

The other day, when Bart returned from scouring the farmhouse and outbuildings, it *was* with way too much stuff. He's always been a bit of a packrat, so I wasn't entirely surprised. He said he wasn't sure what all we'd need and wanted me to make the final decision. I must admit, I appreciated being included in the choices.

The best thing he brought back was a second pack frame used for hunting. It's very plain, without the extra straps Ben's nicer one has, but I think it's also a little lighter. For this I'm grateful, since I'm wearing it now. With this addition, we're able to attach a second backpack to it, which Bart also found at the farmhouse. Good thing! With our newly smoked meat, along with the goods Bart found on his two trips there, we need the extra space.

Putting the backpacks side-by-side and keeping the weight close to even, it shouldn't mess up our balance on the bikes. I'm still riding behind Liam on the small bike while Bart handles the big bike, wearing the other heavily laden pack frame with the two backpacks—his original one and Ben's—almost bursting at the seams.

While he had already brought back all the food in the kitchen and most of the medicine, he managed to find many other useful things: several toiletry items, another tarp—slightly rattier than the one we're using as a smoker—hand towels, a few candles, and two big surprises.

The first was several pounds of cracked corn he found in the barn. I know I turned up my nose at eating livestock food, but Liam was so excited, I quickly shed my aversion and put a smile on my face.

"We can toast the corn in our little pot," Bart said. "It'll turn out fine. Give you a little more bulk to keep your system regular too."

"Thanks, Bart," I said. "It was good thinking."

He reached his hand back in the bag, pausing before he pulled out the next treasure. "Not sure if this will help your digestion, but I think you'll like it." With a flourish, he presented a box of cream-filled cakes.

"Grandpa!" Liam gushed, as I broke out in tears.

"Found these in the bedroom dresser. There's only four left, but we'll have a treat."

"You found them in the bedroom?" Liam asked, shaking his head.

"Yep. Don't know who keeps dessert in their dresser, but I'm glad they did."

After our dinner of smoked venison and sautéed cattail leaves, we each savored one for dessert. Bart told Liam and me to share the fourth. I gave it to Liam, who had it as part of his breakfast this morning.

"Let's take it slow, Liam, get a feel for the extra weight your mom is carrying," Bart says as we get ready to roll.

We mapped out our plan for today and think we can make good time. As always, we're keeping to the less-traveled roads and staying out of towns. Without the terrible ache in my stomach, riding is almost pleasant. We've been on the road for about two hours when Bart finds a wide spot along a densely forested section for us to pull off and stretch.

"Whew," he says after we stop. "The little bit of extra weight on my back is talking to me." He slides the straps of the pack off. "You two doing okay?"

I take off my helmet. I'd love to run my fingers through my damp hair, but I put it in a French braid today after giving it a good washing last night. Even though it's slightly sodden now, it feels so much better.

"No problems," Liam says. "I don't notice anything different."

Like Bart, I'm feeling the larger, heavier pack. "It sits weird on my hips," I say as I shimmy out of the pack. I do a few waist twists and notice several sore spots.

"Maybe we can shorten the straps," Bart says, setting his helmet on the ground next to his pack.

"That won't be necessary," a voice booms from the edge of the trees.

"Mom?" Liam cries out as he gestures toward a man pointing a shotgun at us. My knees go weak and tears immediately fill my eyes. On shaky legs, I step between the gunman and Liam, shielding him as best as I can with my body.

"Hold still," the man says, as two more similarly armed guys step out. One's a boy barely older than Liam. The other man is around the same age as the first one. All three look so much alike they must be related, each husky with puffy faces and a bulbous nose.

"We don't want any trouble," Bart says cautiously.

"Well, friend, that's great to hear," the second man says before letting loose a brown stream of phlegm. Wiping the back of his hand across his mouth, he says, "Let's just make this easy then."

The first guy snorts out a laugh. "Yeah, easy."

I give a quick glance at the boy; a look of fear covers his face. "Pauly? What's going on?" he asks.

The first guy waves a hand at him and mutters, "Don't worry about it. Everything's going to be fine. Lady, you don't need to cry. We'll take your packs, bikes, and everything else off your hands and then let you be on your way."

With my heart pounding in my ears, I brush the back of my hand against my eyes.

The spitting guy says, "Quite the setup you folks have. Good way to carry the rifles." He motions to the backpack attached to my frame with the rifle holder built in. "Boy, you need to put your rifle on the ground—the backpack too."

"And throw those pistols down," the first guy says.

Bart's shoulders drop as he says, "Our boy will slowly remove his. Okay?"

"Yep," the spitter says. "That's what we want. And no funny business. Lady, step aside so we can see him."

Bart turns slightly and gives a single nod.

"Take a couple of steps toward me."

At some point, Liam grabbed my hand, or I grabbed his. I keep ahold of him as I move. I'm so upset, I wobble as I walk.

Liam doesn't let go of me as he removes his backpack with one hand. He gives my hand a squeeze before releasing it to take off the rifle, sling and all.

"Your helmet," Pauly says, motioning to the pile.

Liam lets out a loud sigh.

"Now the pistols," Spitter says. "And like Pauly said, no funny business."

After the pistols are away from us, the boy says, "Holsters too. Handguns aren't much good without them." He looks at me. "Ma'am, you'll be okay."

I give a weak nod as I toss my holster near the pistol.

"That everything?" the spitter asks.

"Should we check their pockets?" Pauly asks.

"No!" the boy says forcefully. "Just let them . . . let them be on their way. And let them take their water jugs."

I feel my eyes widen as my heart rate speeds up even faster. They're letting us go?

"All right. I suppose it's the right thing to do," Spitter says. "But you grab the water for them. And only one each. We can use the rest."

As the boy grabs three of our water flasks, Liam says, "How about our small bottle of bleach?"

"Liam," I say quietly, voice full of warning.

Liam ignores me and continues, "Can we have the bleach? And my mom, she's been sick. Can she have her medicine?"

"What kind of medicine," Pauly asks.

"Laxatives," I say quietly.

He makes a face and a shooing motion with his hand. "Let her have 'em."

"Where?" the boy asks.

"The bleach is in the front pocket of the blue backpack," Liam says. I'm glad he told him about that one; it's the largest bottle and is still completely full. Liam looks to me. "Mom?"

"There's a container in the top of the smaller camo pack," I quietly say, "and a package of tablets next to it."

The boy hands all the water jugs, meds, and bleach container to Liam and whispers, "Sorry about this. We're just trying to survive."

"So are we," Liam replies. "And you've just made it harder for us."

The boy gives Liam a nod. "It's the way things are now."

"It doesn't have to be."

My eyes dart to Liam, willing him to be quiet.

He either doesn't see me or chooses to ignore me as he says, "People could work together, make things better."

"We are working together. We've got a group— "

"Enough," the spitter says.

The boy gives a nod as Liam asks, "Have you heard anything about help? Are they working on fixing things?"

"Who's this *they* you speak of?" Pauly asks with a rueful laugh.

Spitter also laughs. "There's no help coming."

"You haven't heard from anyone then?" Liam persists, directing his question toward the boy. "No government people? Nothing like that?"

"Nothing like that," the boy answers, sadness oozing from him. "We're alone in this."

"Okay, that's it," the spitter bellows. "Start walking. There's a town in about thirty miles. Stay on this road until you hit the intersection, then head east. Don't bother mentioning this to them. They're spineless, so it won't do you any good anyway."

Bart gives a solemn nod and reaches for my hand. I grab onto Liam. We've taken several steps when Bart quietly says, "Get in front of us, Liam. Be ready to move. Clarice, pay attention."

I give a nod and again wipe at my eyes.

"You need to toughen up, Clarice, and stop crying. We're going to get through this."

"How do you figure?" I ask in a whisper. "We're as good as dead now." I jump when the big Honda fires up.

"Don't look back," Bart says. "Pick up the pace, but don't run. And I won't hear another word like that. We're going to be fine."

I shake my head. There's no way we'll be okay. Without our things and the bikes, we're doomed.

Two hundred yards farther and the road curves. As soon as we go around the bend, Bart says, "Now we run. Stay with me."

Seventy-five-year-old Bart sets the pace. It's not a sprint, but it's also not a leisurely jog. I'm starting to lose my breath when he motions to the right and heads off through the trees. He slows slightly as he navigates the timber.

Just when I'm about to call for a rest, he takes us behind a fallen log, telling us to get down. It's then I notice he has the micro compact Sig Sauer 9-millimeter in his hand, the one he carries at his ankle. I never even saw him take it out of the holster.

"Stay quiet," Bart says.

I'm breathing as loud as a freight train and feel a cough coming on. I give a solemn nod as I try to get myself under control.

"Are they following us?" Liam asks.

"I don't think so. Seems they really did just let us go."

"After stealing all our stuff," Liam says with disgust. "What'll we do, Grandpa?"

"Make sure they're gone and then get moving again."

Chapter 13

Middle of August

It's been several weeks since we lost the bikes and most of our gear. Exactly how long, I'm not sure. I've stopped keeping track of the days. I've stopped keeping track of most things. We walk and stop. Walk and stop. We eat when we can find food. Nothing else matters. I feel myself sinking, barely able to put one foot in front of the other. Bart thinks it's the middle of August. I don't know, so I just agree. A trickle of sweat runs down my back. Yeah, August feels about right.

We've been even more careful, staying out of sight as much as possible, avoiding towns by going around them. Several days ago, Bart broke our rules. He set our camp up a couple miles outside of a small town, then said he was going scouting. We've found that houses on the edges of towns seem to be empty. We assume many of the people chose to move into town, deciding there's safety in numbers. It was long after dark before he returned. While he did do some salvaging, he also went into town.

"Thought I'd see if we could buy some food," he said when I asked why in the world he would do that—why he'd risk it.

My eyes went wide. "Did you?"

"Nope. Talked with a nice guy who got a good laugh out of me offering money, though. He said money has been useless since the EMP. Once everyone realized they were on their own, currency changed."

"What are they using for currency?"

"There was some trading for a few weeks, but nothing now. They're just trying to survive."

And so are we, though sometimes I wonder why we're even bothering. Is this what we have to look forward to? Scrounging up each meal? Will it be better when we get to Wyoming? Can we even reach Mollie and Jake's place?

We've seen a few other groups hiking. When we can, we disappear and wait for them to pass. One time, we came around a corner and ran right into a family. I was instantly scared. So scared, I wet my pants. Thankfully, we'd found replacement clothing by then.

I'm beginning to think there's something wrong with me. Not only am I a nervous wreck, but I'm having trouble with my hearing. Liam or Bart will be talking to me, and I don't hear them. I've hurt Liam's feelings several times when he thinks I'm ignoring him. It's not that, I'm just . . . I don't know. Either I'm going deaf, or I'm so deep in my own head I don't pay attention to what's happening. I think it started when Ben was taken, but I was able to hold things together until we were robbed. Now . . . somedays I wonder if it even matters.

We've tried hiking at night to be stealthier, but that was dangerous, too, because we found ourselves tripping over things. Now we hike early in the morning as soon as there's enough light, while most people are sleeping. Then we rest during the day and hike the last few hours before it's completely dark. Even with the reduced amount of time we hike, we're still getting in many miles each day.

Thanks to the page from the map book Bart had in his back pocket, we've been able to keep on track to Bakerville. Sadly, the map page we had is no longer accurate. We've moved beyond the parameters of the page and are now winging it, heading in the general direction of Wyoming. I have no idea how we'll ever find Mollie's place. I have no idea if it even matters if we do. We never should've left our home. At least if we would have stayed there, we'd all be together. We might all be dead, but at least we'd be together.

As it is, Ben died alone and my son is slowly withering away, starving to death as we walk, expending more calories than we can take in. Before the attacks, he was a healthy weight for his almost six-foot lanky body, but he's now unhealthily thin. Bart may be in even worse condition, his skin hanging from his frame. I'm a skeleton.

Unlike most women, who struggle to keep the weight off, I have trouble keeping weight on. And the older I get, the harder it is. Now it's nearly impossible. My collar bones are sticking out, and my hips hurt when I lie down. There's just no padding. Bart and Liam are concerned about me, but there's nothing that can be done. As Ben was fond of saying, it is what it is. At least I haven't had the terrible stomach pains again. Without putting food in it, constipation isn't an issue. And with all the walking, I suspect the exercise is also helping things.

After losing everything but the few items we had in our pockets—the now useless map, a few pieces of jerky we each had for nibbling as we traveled, a ChapStick I had, and Liam and Bart's pocketknives, along with the water bottles, bleach, and laxatives they let us keep, and Bart's hidden pistol and wristwatch, which they thankfully didn't notice or didn't want—we've slowly built up our supplies. Bart was most upset about losing his snare-making stuff. He replaced the wire at the first car we came to, saying since the EMP fried everything and the car would never run again anyway, we might as well take what we need.

A few cars later, he found an empty soda box in the trunk. Someone before us had already broken the lock and taken the drinks, leaving the box behind. They also left the lug wrench; Bart thought we may be able to use it.

When we camped the first night, he set up the new snares and box trap. Our dinner was the jerky from our pockets. The next morning, the snares were empty, leaving our stomachs in the same condition as when we started our walk. That day, Bart found a house that still had a small amount of food in it. That food kept us going until we reached the outskirts of the town the thieves told us about. While we didn't go into town, Bart found us a deserted house to stay in that night. He even managed to snare food for us.

Since then, it's been one foot after the other day-to-day, walking in a fog. Most days, our snares and box trap are empty. We often go several days without catching anything, without eating anything. We've slowly found backpacks for Liam and me, while Bart carries a large duffle bag across his shoulder—the kind with multiple carrying options, including wheels for dragging. We pick up anything we think we may be able to use.

While we haven't resorted to outright stealing, like what was done to us, we are continually checking cars and houses that appear to be empty. Bart made a mistake one day, walking up on a house he thought was abandoned, and he was shot at. They barely missed him. Would being killed by a bullet have been better than slowly starving to death? I'm beginning to think it might be.

Liam and I are now waiting in a small clump of trees. When we saw a house on the road, Bart said he'd check it out and see if it's abandoned.

"What do you think Grandpa will find today?" Liam asks me.

"Don't know." I wipe my forehead. Even with the shade this tree provides, the heat is miserable, and it's only midmorning. We should be looking for a spot to camp and rest until evening.

We sit quietly for a few more minutes, when Liam says, "He's coming back already. That was quick—too quick."

"Hey," Bart says when he's close enough for talking. "Let's stay here tonight. The house is empty, hasn't even been pillaged."

"Is there food?" Liam asks. I can almost see the saliva forming as he thinks about a meal.

"There's food," Bart says with a twinkle in his eye. "And there's fresh tracks all around the dirt from the last rain. Elk or cattle."

"You going to kill one with your pistol?" I ask, raising my eyebrows.

"I was thinking of using the hunting rifle I found in the house." Bart wiggles his wild mustache at me. His beard and mustache, worn as long as I've known him, used to be kept trim and neat. Now it's an untamed mess.

Liam and I are similarly savage with our own scraggly manes. His hair is well past his ears and often shooting off at odd angles. When I lost my wide-tooth comb and the few products I had for keeping my tresses under control, it all went downhill.

Bart found me a brush within the first few days, but it did little more than smooth the top layer. It took several weeks to even find a comb I could get through my hair. By then, I already had several matted areas. I considered just letting it go and forming dreadlocks, but I have no idea what the process might be to keep it from becoming a mess. I painstakingly worked my way through the snarls until it was smooth. Without regular washing, conditioning, and special smoothing products, my heavy, curly hair is out of control. With my skinny body and crazy big hair, I'm beginning to resemble a cartoon character.

"Really? No way," Liam says as he starts walking toward the building.

"Wait. You're sure it's safe?" I ask.

"As safe as anywhere," Bart answers.

"Great," I mumble, feeling less than confident.

The house is a single-level dwelling, a modular home as opposed to stick built, with a thick coat of dust over most surfaces.

"Don't open the fridge," Bart says. "I'm sure whatever's in there is rotted and will stink the whole place up."

"Is there water?" Liam asks, walking toward the sink.

"The faucets don't work."

Liam opens a cabinet and is greeted by several cans of soup, pasta, and other goods. "Wow! It's—it's amazing." He turns to me with a sheen of tears in his eyes.

"There's more down the hall, a large pantry."

"Full of food?" Liam's voice is full of wonder as he starts walking in the direction Bart indicated.

"No, they use it for storage too. But quite a bit of food—bottles and jugs of water too. Living this far from civilization, they probably needed to keep stocked up. There's a garden also, but it's wilted. Not sure if anything survived without being tended. I'll take a better look at it later."

"Where do you think the people who live here are?" Liam asks as he reaches the pantry. "Mom! You need to see this."

When I get to the hall pantry, he wraps me in a hug. "We can eat until we're fat again."

I give him a squeeze on the shoulder as an unfamiliar feeling washes through me. *Hope?*

Turning toward Bart, who's now standing in the doorway watching our shenanigans, Liam asks, "Can we cook?"

"The propane's still on. There's matches in a drawer next to the stove to light the burner. Don't know how much is in the tank, but I'll check when I go out."

"I hope the people that lived here are okay," Liam says with a quiver in his voice.

He's staring at a tub of infant formula, two large boxes of size one diapers next to it, and several containers of wipes.

"Yeah," Bart says. "When I first came in, I saw their pictures." He motions to the photos lining the hallway. "Then I saw the room full of baby stuff." Bart shakes his head. "It's a sad thing. I'm praying they're okay."

Bart doesn't tell Liam about the bodies he finds in the houses he salvages. He doesn't talk to me much about it either. Unless it's something he just can't get past in his own head, then he'll give me limited details of the carnage. Murders are the norm, but there's also suicides and murder-suicides. The worst was an entire family.

He glosses over the details, but often tells me how happy he was to find a jar of vapor rub; he uses it under his nose to help with the smells. I appreciate how Bart tries to protect Liam and me from the worst of it. I don't think I could handle it, going into the houses and finding the carnage he finds. I'm barely holding on now. Seeing those things, I'd go over the edge for sure.

"You two get settled," Bart says. "I'm going to check out the barn and outbuildings. Already looked in the garage, no car or anything."

"Want me to go with you?" Liam asks.

"No, stay with me," I say.

Bart's checked out many barns and buildings on this journey, often finding the livestock perished. Locked up for their safety, they rely on their owners for food and water. With the owners away or somehow meeting their ends, so did the animals. Many times, where there should be livestock, they'd been taken, along with anything else useful as the house and buildings are ransacked.

After Bart leaves, Liam asks, "What do you think we should eat? It's close enough to suppertime we can make something to have when Grandpa gets back inside."

"Definitely close enough. And maybe we'll even eat again later. We should stick with small amounts at a time since we haven't been eating nearly what we should." He gives me a strange look. "Our stomachs have probably shrunk. If we eat too much at once, we'll get sick."

"Really? You think so?"

I give a shrug. I don't really know if it can happen, but it sounds legit. "We'll try for several small meals a day."

"How long do you think we'll stay here?"

Instead of answering, I say, "How about pasta tonight? There's several choices of shapes and different jars of sauce. Even a few boxes of mac and cheese. What sounds good?"

We decide on macaroni with alfredo sauce. While it's cooking, Liam and I spend many minutes looking over the calendar on the wall as we try to sort out what day it might be. We're not certain but decide it's probably around the twentieth or twenty-first of August. We go with the twenty-first, marking it on the calendar so we can start keeping track. Our meal is almost ready when Bart comes back inside. I give him a questioning look.

"I think there's chickens out there. They have a coop with a fenced-in area. The gate, along with the coop door, were both wide open. I didn't see any birds, but there's tracks everywhere with some leading into the forest. They probably spend their day there. Cows too. I'm convinced the tracks I saw are cow. They have a water trough with a small solar panel on it. It's pumping away, so much that the water is running out and there's chicken and cow tracks in the mud. Deer tracks too."

"Did you find eggs?" I ask.

"No, but we'll look for them. Smells good in here. About time to eat?"

During our meal, Bart shares more of his findings. "With the forest and the watering trough, the livestock were able to survive. Good thing they left the chicken coop open so the birds could wander."

"Did they leave the cow pen open too?" Liam asks.

"No, I found a place where it must have been weak. Looks like they just pushed it over. Probably got hungry and could see food."

"How many cows?" I ask.

"Not sure. I didn't see them. Quite a few, I'd guess."

"Did you find water for us?" I ask.

He chews on his mustache, then makes several faces before saying, "I was thinking we could clean the trough and then we'd have water."

"Clean the trough?"

"Yeah, right now it's not looking like anything we'd want to drink from. But if we empty it and clean it up, we'll be able to see where the water's coming in. We can figure something out so the animals have their water and we can get fresh water too. We can use what they have in the pantry while we work on it."

"You think we'll be here for a while?" Liam asks.

I meet Bart's eyes. Personally, I'd like to stay here. It's fairly hidden, and with the cattle and chickens, we'd have food. If we can get water out of the trough, then we could stay for a long time. That sounds much better than walking however many hundreds of miles we still must go. And it sounds better than living at Mollie's house. Much better.

Chapter 14

August 23rd

"How many is that, Liam?"

Liam looks in the bucket. "At least two dozen—maybe even closer to three."

We've been at the house for two days now. We were awoken the first morning by the crow of a rooster. Or I should say, Liam and I were awoken. Bart was on watch and already awake. He hustled outside to see a good-sized flock being led out of the coop by the rooster.

Yesterday, Bart made sure the coop and pen were both sound, then cleaned up the nest boxes and put fresh straw from the barn in them. He then filled up a feeder and waterer in the coop. Last night, as soon as it was fully dark, Bart went out to the coop and locked it up. This morning, we were still awoken by crowing, but the rooster and ten more chickens were inside the coop—all ready to be let out. Bart kept the pen gate shut so they can be outside, but they are no longer roaming free.

Bart found the herd of cows. There's a dozen of them, and none are very large. He says they're all steers, possibly bought in the spring with plans to fatten them up during the good weather and then sell before winter. With the size of them, he thinks we could easily butcher one to smoke and make more jerky for our trip.

As expected, the garden is a near fail. With only rainwater to sustain it, the aboveground plants are dismal. There are a few potatoes growing under the sad-looking leaves and also some small onions, even though the tops are brown. Harvesting them gave enough tiny potatoes and onions for several meals. Fried potatoes for dinner last night! What a treat.

The regular meals are helping immensely. Liam is much more energetic, and Bart has a bounce in his step. I've noticed my attention span has improved. I'm able to better follow conversations Liam and

Bart have, and I'm even participating more. I caught myself laughing over something Liam said at dinner last night. This house is good for us.

Today we're looking for eggs. Bart thought it strange there weren't any eggs in the nest boxes; he thinks snakes or skunks might have been taking them. We didn't really expect to find eggs out in the forest, but we have. I totally turned up my nose when Bart said we could eat most of the ones we collect. He says they should have a fairly long shelf life since they were freshly laid and not washed. But to prevent eating bad ones, we'll do a float test by putting the eggs in a bowl of water. Any floaters are old, and we won't keep them.

"What's that noise?" Liam asks.

"What noise?" I ask.

"Sounds like a waterfall."

"I can't hear anything," Bart says. Not surprising. His hearing has been deteriorating for years, but he's been too stubborn to check into hearing aids.

"It stopped." Liam shrugs.

"I think there's something behind this brush," Bart says as he reaches into a bush to retrieve an egg.

"There it is again," Liam says. "You can't hear it?"

Bart starts to shake his head but quickly jumps back and yells out, clutching his hand against his chest.

"What's going on?" I ask, rushing toward him.

"Stay back! Liam, you take a step back too. It's a snake. I think it's gone, but let's give it some space."

"A snake!" I cry out. "Did it . . . did it bite you?"

Bart is walking backwards, away from the bush he was just attacked in. He gives a solemn nod. "We best get back to the house and clean it up." I try to ask him more, but he shakes his head. "We'll talk in a bit. Bring the bucket of eggs, Liam. You can get those taken care of while your mom helps me with my hand."

Our pace to the house is brisk. Once inside, Bart tells Liam to place a towel on the counter and lay the eggs out. He needs to sort them and check to make sure there aren't any cracks.

"Clarice, there's medical supplies in the master bathroom. Will you help me?" He doesn't wait for my response. Once we're in the master bedroom, he says, "Close the door. I don't want our boy to hear this."

"Is it bad?" I ask after clicking the door shut.

"Did you hear anything? Like the waterfall noise Liam mentioned?"

"I heard something, but it sounded— " I close my eyes as my breath leaves my body. "It was a slight rattle."

Bart shakes his head. "Should've listened to our boy. I remember a woman back home when I was just a boy saying she thought rattlesnakes sounded like rushing water."

Tears run down my face. "What do we do?"

"Not much *to* do. Let's clean it up and see what happens."

"Are they . . . is it— " I throw my hands up, not wanting to ask the question.

"Will I die?" He raises his eyebrows. "I guess it depends on the amount of venom—if there was venom. It could've been a dry strike."

"A dry strike?"

"No venom released. Happens sometimes. Not sure how common, but sometimes."

"Should we suck it out?"

He gives a slight laugh. "I think that's just in the movies. Let's get it cleaned up."

Yesterday, in addition to getting the chicken coop ready for the birds, we also cleaned the water trough. We skimmed the layer of algae from the top, then pulled a plug near the bottom of the round water container. As it drained, we could see where fresh water was pumping in.

Once the old water was out, we used scrub brushes and the homeowners' well-stocked cleaning supplies to tidy up the tank. Originally, we wanted to figure out a way to have clean water for us while keeping the water trough filled for the livestock. We couldn't come up with a way to make it work, so we filled every container we could find with the fresh, clear water gurgling into the now somewhat clean trough. Using a jug that we have in the bathroom for washing up, I clean his bite. It's already swelling up and reddening.

"It doesn't look too bad," Bart says unconvincingly.

After the soapy water, I pour hydrogen peroxide over it and cover it with a large bandage. I'm impressed at the mass amount of medical supplies under the sink in the master bathroom. There's a wide assortment of bandages and over-the-counter medicines.

"You want a pain reliever?" I ask.

"Yeah, I'll take one, the kind that reduces inflammation."

I give him three ibuprofen.

"Looks good," he says, making a loose fist. As he does so, he grimaces. "Probably best to keep it immobilized for a few days. Did you see anything around to make a sling with?"

"There's some large dishtowels in the kitchen, the flour sack kind. I'll grab one and see if it'll work."

In the kitchen, Liam looks at me with wide eyes. "Is he okay?"

I avoid meeting Liam's eyes as I open the drawer of dish towels. "You know your grandpa. He's tough."

"Mom, please. Tell me how he is."

I lift a hand. "We cleaned it up and bandaged it. I'm going to use this towel to make a sling. We'll go from there."

Once we have his arm secured against his chest, Bart says, "Clarice, I don't want you worrying Liam about this. Not yet anyway. If it seems it's . . . that it's going bad, we'll tell him then and make a plan."

I give a grim nod. "We planned on staying here a few days so we could rest, maybe that's all you'll need."

"Sure, yeah. But we'll need to get going before too long. As it is, we won't make it to Jake and Mollie's before winter hits."

"Maybe we should stay here—spend the winter and then leave in the spring."

"I've thought the same thing. But we have the same problem as before, the reason we couldn't stay in Nemont. We can't keep watch indefinitely. Besides, Ben will be waiting for us in Bakerville."

As my eyes once again fill up, I pull my lips tight. Ben's dead. I'm sure of it. I can even feel it.

"Now, now," Bart says. "I know you doubt it, but I'm convinced Ben's alive and he's doing all he can to be with you and Liam again. My son doesn't give up."

I give him a weak nod. We've had similar conversations before. Like Bart, Liam is confident Ben's fine and will be waiting for us in Wyoming if we don't find him somewhere along the way. But I know the truth: Ben is dead.

In the kitchen, Liam is sitting at the table. As soon as he sees us, he asks, "Is it bad?"

"Not too bad," Bart answers. "Hurts a little, but not anymore than a bite from one of the machines." He gives Liam a wink. Owning and working in a machine shop, Bart and Ben are no stranger to sharp objects. Though they do engage in many safety features, there's still the occasional cut, bump, or bruise.

"So, it's . . . it's okay? You'll be okay?"

"I'm fit as a fiddle. Now, how'd we do with the eggs?"

With a doubtful look, Liam shakes his head, straightens his shoulders, and stands up. "Let me show you. I just got them in the water when I heard you coming down the hallway. More than half already had some sort of crack, so those are back in the bucket. From what was left, a good number of those are floating."

"All right," Bart says. "We'll add the floaters to the bucket. If we hard boil them, we can feed them back to the chickens."

"Isn't that— " I make a face. "You know, something like cannibalism?"

"Nah. Feeding the eggs back will be good. Remember the egg I picked up and it broke as soon as I touched it? The chickens have been finding their own food, and they're probably short the calcium needed to form a strong shell. They'll love the eggs and eat it all, including the shell, which will help them."

I give a shake of my head. "Whatever you think."

"What will we do with the chickens when we leave?" Liam asks.

"Open the pen up and let them roam again. My guess is their owners were gone when the attacks started around two months ago. They've done fine this long on their own."

"When will we leave?"

"Well, your mom and I were talking and think maybe we should stay here until this hand of mine heals up. With it being my right hand, I'm not a hundred percent. It'll be safer just staying here."

Liam nods. "So the eggs on the bottom of the bowl are still good?"

"Yep, should be fine. But just to be sure, we'll crack each egg separately to make sure it smells and looks good so we don't ruin whatever we're adding it to. One time, when I was a boy, I cracked an egg and there was a chick in it. That's not something I'll ever forget."

"Gross!" Liam says with a disgusted look on his face.

"Indeed," Bart agrees, making his own face. "Ruined eggs for me for weeks."

"Can we have fried eggs and pancakes for lunch?" Liam asks. "There's a bag of buttermilk mix in the pantry, the just-add-water kind."

"Sounds good to me," Bart says, while I nod my agreement.

Pancakes and eggs for lunch. Something so simple and ordinary in our previous world, but in today's world, it's nothing short of a delicacy.

Chapter 15

August 29th

Our last few days have been almost normal. Well, normal if you consider the lights are out, most cars won't run, and we're forced to keep watch. Oh, and Bart was bitten by a snake. Yeah, that all sounds normal. His hand swelled up more than the first day, looking like a balloon on his wrist. He says he thinks it was a dry bite, or else he'd be having other troubles. Of course, we know so little about what to expect when bitten by a rattlesnake, so it's all just a guess. The swelling has decreased slightly from its worst and is still noticeable, but not nearly what it was.

It's been six days since Bart was bitten by the snake. Each morning, Liam takes a minute to mark off the new day on the wall calendar. He found a small pocket-sized calendar he also marks, keeping this one in his backpack.

With his arm in a sling, Bart's still doing what he thinks needs to be done. Even though I've encouraged him to rest—in hopes if there was venom released, resting will keep it from spreading—he keeps working.

At his advanced age of seventy-five, you'd think at thirty-five years younger I'd have no problem keeping up with him. Wrong. Ever since our dirt bikes were stolen, he's been the one setting the pace for us, walking fast in our shortened time frame of hiking only in the early mornings and evenings, allowing us to hike up to twelve miles a day. Liam said he read that people hiking long trails for fun will walk twenty or even thirty miles a day. I can't even imagine!

The first few days, we barely made five miles. Our bodies hurt so much, and we all had blisters on our feet. Bart found us bandages and mole skin during the early salvaging trips. One by one, we've even managed to replace our shoes. It amazes me how quickly our shoes break down with the walking.

I still believe staying here would be the smart thing to do. It's obviously safe, since in the time since the attacks it's been left alone. The food supply, while it won't last through the winter, will keep us going for several months. Plus, we have the chickens and the cattle.

I didn't tell Bart or Liam, but I'm so comfortable here I've been sleeping during my night watch. The first time, I didn't intend to fall asleep. There's such a sense of security here, I couldn't help it. It's the first time since we started this ordeal of trying to get to Wyoming that I was relaxed enough on my watch to let myself go.

I'm debating about talking to Bart about eliminating our overnight watch. It'd be wonderful if all three of us could get a full night's sleep. Liam especially needs more sleep than he's getting. He usually takes the first watch, which ends at midnight, then Bart or I will watch from midnight to 3:00 am, with the last one watching from 3:00 to 6:00 am. I had the last watch this morning, falling asleep in the chair, waking up only when the blasted rooster sounded his alarm.

The rooster drives me crazy, crowing and carrying on at all hours of the day. The first day after locking them up, he was mad. He spent most of his time pacing along the fence, looking for a place to escape. The hens settled in quicker and seemed almost content. They've adjusted well to being locked up again, giving us several fresh eggs each day.

I'm surprised at how interesting the chickens are. I've never been around them, having always lived in town until we moved out to Nemont. And raising chickens is something I'd never want to do—way too much time involved. We didn't even have dogs or cats; our life was just too busy for any added hassle.

Weirdly, I often find myself migrating toward the chicken pen. I take the duty of gathering the eggs each morning, afternoon, and again in the evening. Bart said the chickens should only lay in the morning and be done with it. Apparently, no one told these birds that. There's usually at least one egg each time I check.

Two of the chickens are super friendly, almost begging for me to pet them and pay attention to them. One, a small black bird with a poof on its head, seems to be just a chick. Bart calls her a juvenile and thinks she's only a couple of months old, not even laying yet. The other is brown with black tips on her tailfeathers. She'll often be in the nest box when I go out to check midday. When she sees me, she jumps up and runs toward me, then walks back to the nest box with me, almost proud to show me the egg she's left behind.

A few days ago, I got brave and gave her a pet. She leaned into my hand. After a few strokes, I carefully picked her up. She didn't mind at all! The little black one saw what was happening and moved right next to me too. I wonder if the homeowners paid extra attention to these two birds and they've missed the contact. Is that something chickens do? Can they become attached to humans like dogs or cats do?

Spending time with the chickens has been surprisingly enjoyable. At the coop, I feel myself relax. Sometimes, I even put a folding camp chair in the pen. I sit and watch them as they do their stuff. The crazy rooster seems a little calmer than he did at first, but he keeps his distance from me. The little black chick and brown hen are the friendliest, but several others seem comfortable coming closer to me now. I don't pet them or pick them up, that's reserved for my two favorites.

While the chickens are adjusting to being back in their pen, the cattle are a different story. They're completely wild. With Bart's guidance, Liam repaired the spot where the cows went through the fence. Then, the two of them tried luring them back into the corral with a trail of hay. They completely ignored the trail until Liam and Bart had given up and went inside. At one point, Liam looked out the window and said, "Hey, I think they're in the corral!"

Before they could get out there and close the gate, the herd took off for the trees. Bart spent many minutes chewing on his scraggly mustache while deep in thought. As I watched him, I decided today he's getting his mustache, beard, and hair trimmed. Liam is also getting a haircut. Maybe I'll even take off my split ends and see if I can do anything to make my mangy mane a little lighter. I don't want to cut it, but it's heavy and miserable.

As I'm trimming Liam's hair, he asks, "Do you know their names?"

"Who's names?"

"The people who own this house. I know the baby's name is Sidney since it says that on the nursery wall, but what are the parents' names? The only piece of mail I found said *Resident* on it. I thought they'd have a stack lying around like we do, but I haven't found it."

"They keep the mail and other things on a desk in the master bedroom," I answer. "His name is Levi. She's Amelia. Their last name is Delgado."

"I think, when this is all over, we should send them something. You should get their address so we have it."

"Like money for the food we've eaten?"

"Yes. I know we've taken a lot of things, and I haven't felt bad about it before, but this is different. I feel like they're counting on having these things here when they return. And we're taking their rifle and all the ammo we've found."

I make a noncommittal noise in response. I don't imagine they'll be returning to this house at any point in the future. But, like Liam, I'm profoundly grateful for the things we've found, including both a partial and full box of cartridges for the rifle.

Bart says the lever-action gun is based on the model that won the west. Bart showed Liam and I how to use the old Winchester .30-30. I'd never used anything like it before. While we didn't shoot it, due to not wanting to draw any attention to ourselves, he did have each of us load it and work the lever several times. And we've practiced dry firing many times so we could get a feel for it. I'm not exactly comfortable with it, but I know I'll be able to shoot it if I must. Liam loved it, relishing in the action and the noise it made.

We also found an almost full box of 9-millimeter shells but never did find a handgun to go with them, assuming they had it on them when they left. Bart happily took the ammo. His Sig is still fully loaded, with ten in the magazine and one in the chamber, plus a second twelve-round magazine in a slot on his ankle holster.

After a few minutes, Liam says, "Do you remember the show we watched with Dad? The one about the man and his little girl traveling around after most of the women died?"

I pause midcut to consider his question. "It sounds familiar, but I'm not sure."

"Yeah. The mom died when the girl was a baby. I think she had a virus or something that only affected females. For some reason, the baby was okay. The dad pretended she was a boy, and they'd travel around, salvaging food, trying to survive."

I give a shrug. "Maybe. Why are you asking?"

"One thing they did was, whenever they stopped someplace, they always figured out how to escape. They'd make sure they kept one of their backpacks stashed away from where they were staying so, if they had to make a run for it, they'd have supplies. They'd even put holes in walls and figure out how to get out windows in advance. It kept them alive several times."

"In the movie."

"What?"

"It kept them alive *in the movie*. Do you think it'd work the same in real life?"

"I've been thinking a lot about it. Seems like it'd be smart for us to do too."

"We have the backpacks and the duffle bag at the mudroom door ready to go. Even the rifle is there."

"What if we were outside taking care of the chickens and couldn't get back to the house?"

I close my eyes and suck in a deep breath. "Liam, you shouldn't be worrying about things like that."

"Why not, Mom? You still think I'm too young? I've been," his voice cracks on *been*, "keeping watch and helping. I'm— " The cracking voice recurs. At first, I think he's upset, but I realize it's still his voice changing with puberty. "With Dad gone, me and Grandpa are . . . " He gives a shrug. "I do think about these things, Mom. You should be too."

"Are you mouthing off to me?" I ask with plenty of grit in my voice.

"No. I wasn't mouthing off, Mom. I just think you don't seem too concerned about things. It seems you think we're safe here."

"We *are* safe here, Liam."

"We're not, Mom. Not really. And even when we get to the Caldwells', I don't think we'll be safe there either."

"Of course we will!"

He lifts one shoulder a fraction. "Things are different now, Mom. I think deep down you realize it, but your actions don't show it. You seem to think— "

"Liam, that's enough," I say warningly. "You *are* mouthing off to me, and I won't stand for it."

"I'm not, Mom. I'm trying to tell you, to make you realize, you can't just mourn for the life we used to have. Things are different now. I know you think Dad's dead." Liam swallows hard, and this time his voice does crack with emotion. "I don't think he is. But we're still alive, and we need to pay attention to stay that way. We need to work hard and have plans."

I clench my jaw as the anger washes over me. In a low, quiet voice, I say, "Is that what you think? I'm not, what, pulling my weight?"

"I'm not trying to make you mad, Mom."

"Really?" I snap. "You think it's okay to call me *lazy*?" I feel the spittle come out of my mouth on the word lazy.

"I don't think that, and it's not what I meant." Liam attempts to keep his voice even, but his body betrays him as the sentence travels over several octaves. "I know you're having a hard time with Dad not here and the walking and not eating. You seem better these last few days. I was getting really worried about you."

I soften my shoulders and take a deep breath. He's right. I was a mess. Still am in some ways, but at least I'm physically better. My face reddens thinking of the multiple times Liam thought I was ignoring him or when he'd have to help me as we made our way. One time, I was so confused I started walking in the wrong direction. Liam had to hold my hand to keep me going the way I should've been. We stopped shortly afterward when Bart found us an easy-to-reach, yet still hidden, camping spot. He had a little sugar and salt he'd salvaged, which he added to a partial bottle of water found under the seat of a pickup truck.

I squeeze Liam's shoulder.

He twists to look at me and says, "It's good you're better, but now it seems you're almost too relaxed. I know about— " He lets out a loud breath. "I was up early this morning and saw you sleeping in the chair. I was just about to wake you when the rooster crowed and you jumped up."

"Oh," I say softly.

He nods. "We have to be diligent. Even though it seems safe, it's not. Every day is dangerous, even here. I mean, look at Grandpa. He got bit by a snake, and there's nothing we can do about it. We're not safe, Mom. We're not safe anywhere. We always need to be on alert. Even when those guys took our stuff, I know you were scared, but there was something—I don't know, Mom. Carelessness?"

"Carelessness? What do you mean?" I feel myself getting snappy again. The fact my son is talking to me in this manner, I should shut it down and remind him that I'm the parent and he's the child.

"Maybe careless is not the right word. You stepped in front of me. I know you were protecting me. But you were crying and happy to let them take our stuff."

"Happy? No, not even."

"Happy isn't the right word. I can't think of the word."

"We had no choice in the matter. What did you want to do? Fight our way out of it?"

"No, and I understand. We were out gunned. But you seemed to give up then. You've always been so strong, Mom, a leader at everything. What did my friend's mom call you? Type A?"

I give a small smile. "She didn't mean it as a compliment."

"Well, it is. You'd never give up. And maybe it's good you weren't so Type A when they took our stuff. I know Dad not being with us has made you less . . . aggressive."

"Again, we had no choice in the matter. We were, as you said, out gunned." I give a firm nod. "And you're right. I am different now. I can't even figure out why. I just feel like a part of me is missing."

"I'm sorry, Mom. I know you're sad about Dad, and so am I. Grandpa too. He blames himself."

I don't say, *as well he should*, which is the truth. I do blame Bart for those guys taking Ben. Taking a deep breath, I say, "Back to your getaway plan, you think that's something we need?"

"I do. I'm going to start setting things up today—as soon as you finish my hair."

I wipe at my eyes. "And I'll try to do better, to keep my head in the game."

"You need to be fierce, Mom," he says softly. "Be like you used to be. I know when those guys robbed us, we didn't have any choice but to comply. But falling apart like you did . . . I hate to think what could've happened if they took advantage of your weakness. At least they just wanted our stuff."

Chapter 16

September 2nd

"Almost good as new," Bart says while flexing his still slightly swollen hand. "You've got quite the magic touch with your doctoring skills." He gives me a wink.

"I think we should still keep a bandage on it. I don't want you to knock the scab off and get dirt in it."

"Yeah, but I think I can ditch the sling and start using it as normal. I've already lost some strength in this arm."

"You'll still need to be careful. We don't know if there's any lasting effects from the bite."

"What? You think after all this time I'm going to suddenly turn into Snake Man?" He waggles his bushy eyebrows at me and attempts to flick his tongue, mimicking a reptile.

I roll my eyes in response while I replace the bandage.

"Where's our boy?" he asks.

"Outside, trying to figure out a way to trap one of those cows."

"Steers."

"Huh? Oh. Okay. Does it really matter?"

"I'm sure it does to the steer. Or we could call them bovines."

"Sure, Bart." I shake my head.

"If you're finished with me, I'll go help him. 'Course, we don't really need to get them in the corral. With my hand mostly better, we should butcher one and get the jerky made. We really need to get back on the road soon."

"I still think we should winter here," I say assertively.

"Our best bet is making it to Bakerville. They'll be better set up for the winter."

"We're set up here. With the fireplace, we can stay warm. There's the winter clothing, and we'd have food."

"And it'd still just be the three of us. We're all struggling now to stay awake during night watch." He gives me a pointed look.

While I have been staying awake after the talk Liam gave me when I was cutting his hair, Bart's right. It's not easy. We're eating good now and no longer walking miles and miles a day, but we're all exhausted.

I've been focusing on being the way I used to be, as Liam asked, but I'm completely drained. Now, instead of assertive, I'm just crabby. At least I'm closer to feeling like my old self than I did before. I'm putting on a little weight too. I still look almost skeletal, but the scale in the bathroom says I've gained four pounds since the first time I stepped on it. Even with the additional weight, I'd likely be in a hospital as they tried to fatten me up if our world were still normal.

"Maybe, once the snow starts, we won't have to keep watch. They get a lot of snow here, right?"

"Based on the snowsuits we found, I'd say it gets plenty cold."

I give a nod.

"You might be right," Bart says. "At this elevation, they should get a fair amount of snow. But we'd still want to stay on alert. The best thing is to get to where we're going. There's safety in numbers. You and Ben have visited Mollie a couple of times. Ben said their neighbors are nice."

I shrug. "Nice enough. We had a barbecue, and a couple of them joined us."

"And you visited with them?"

"A little, sure." I don't tell him how I found a couple of them to be almost as annoying as Mollie—especially the neighbor who thinks he's a preacher. Bart will probably love him, more so now since he's taken to reading his Bible whenever he sits in the recliner in the living room.

One day, I even caught him talking to Liam about what he read. I gave him a look that shut him up. Later, when we were alone, I once again made it clear he is not to fill Liam's head with that rubbish. He nodded before saying, "You know our boy is about old enough to start making his own decisions. If he wants to ask me questions, he should be able to."

I let Bart know he is never to start a conversation about God or Jesus or anything else Bible related. If Liam has questions, he should come to me. I turned on my heel and strode away before Bart could add anything else.

"That will be an advantage, you knowing people when we get there. I've been thinking, they've likely put some security measures in place. You know, like some of the roadblocks we saw."

During our travels, we've seen several roadblocks from a distance. Bart's convinced they're only doing what's best for their towns or communities. Even so, we make a point of giving them a wide berth, following our rules of staying hidden and out of sight as best as we can to avoid danger.

"They might have," I agree, thinking of Mollie's get-home bag. With the level of planning put into her supplies, I suspect they've thought of things like setting up roadblocks and other things. But I can't imagine something like that is needed in the remote area they live. Their small community is over a half hour drive from the nearest town and is somewhat hidden on the edge of the mountains. But it would be like Mollie to go over the top on this. She's done that with plenty of other things.

"You want to go out with me, help see about rounding up the steer?" Bart asks.

"I need to check the vegetables first, then I'll catch up with you," I reply, following behind him.

When Liam was lamenting over leaving so much food behind, Bart suggested we dehydrate some of it. He removed a couple of window screens and made a drying rack. Draining the canned vegetables and putting them in a sunny spot on the rack, with the second rack on top, has worked out fine. We've made several plastic zipper bags of dried veggies already.

After Liam told Bart about his idea for a stashed bag in the forest in case we had to move in a hurry, Bart got on board with the idea. Now we have the duffle bag Bart was carrying, along with a smaller bag found in the Delgados' house, hidden in the woods, hanging from trees to keep predators away. The large duffle is filled with winter gear found in the closets, plus other essentials. Both he and Bart think we'll have snow soon and we'll need the warm clothes. In the smaller bag is several days' worth of food.

Moving the duffle to the forest forced us to reload the other backpacks. We've made a point of not filling them completely so we can add the dehydrated items to them as they are completed. Keeping the dried items in zipper bags should allow them a long enough shelf life so we can eat them for a few weeks. We also have a couple of canned goods in each bag, especially tuna and sardines since they're small and have good nutrition.

When I finish drying the canned vegetables, I'm going to try cooking dry beans and then dehydrating those as well. I think it'll work out well, and it'll be more welcome food on the trail—provided we can prevent being robbed again.

I take in a deep breath, enjoying the fresh air. Being here has been good for me; doing the dehydrating has also been good. I never had time for things like this before; I was always too busy working to even think about preserving food or doing other things like this. Just keeping the house clean was more than enough. I'm in the process of using a pancake turner to flip the vegetables, trying to make sure they're drying on all sides, when the rumble of a motor reaches my ears.

I straighten up and frantically start looking around. Bart's about halfway to the corral when he turns and looks at me. "Run and grab our bags! I'll get our boy and meet you in the woods. You know the place?"

"I know it!" I'm already running. "Find Liam!"

The packs and rifle are just inside the mudroom. The roar of the engine is much louder. They've got to be getting close. Did the homeowners finally make their way back? *Please, God. Please let Bart get Liam, and let us get to safety.* I catch myself, the pseudo prayer still in my head. I put the rifle and a pack over one shoulder, grabbing the other two bags by the web handles at the top.

The roar of the vehicle eases slightly. They're slowing down. I risk a quick peak out the mudroom window. A big black Chevy pickup is turning into the driveway. Homeowners or not, I don't want to be found here. If I run out the back door and straight toward the chicken coop, I can get behind it and make my way into the forest. I waste no more time and run out the door. I cringe at the sound of the slamming screen. Hopefully, they couldn't hear it with the noise of their truck.

As I run, the pack on my shoulder slides down and makes my movements awkward. Even so, I don't stop until I'm behind the coop. Breathing hard, I look for Bart and Liam. The truck motor has turned off, and everything is silent except my ragged breath. I give a tight smile when I see the chickens have been freed from their pen, able to run free once again. If their owners are home, they'll have no problem retrieving them. If it's someone else, maybe they won't find them.

"Clarice," Bart hisses from the edge of the woods, "I have Liam. C'mon over here."

I give a nod and run to where he is. "Can you see them?" I ask, as he takes two backpacks and the rifle from me. I slip the other one on my shoulders properly.

"Haven't seen them. You?"

"A big black truck. Maybe the homeowners?"

Bart shrugs. "I'm not sure we should stick around to find out."

"But if it's them, maybe they'd let us stay. Then we'd have more people for watch."

Bart shakes his head. "We aren't staying. Ben will be waiting in Wyoming. We must keep going."

"He's dead," I hiss. "If you weren't so stubborn, you'd admit it too. Then you could grieve and get on with things."

"We're not staying here," Bart says again. This time, there's no emotion in his voice.

"And if I refuse?" I ask, crossing my arms.

Bart grabs me by the arm, pulling me down. "Does that look like the homeowner?" He points to the big man walking around the house, a large black gun at the ready.

I hold back a sigh. We've stared at the homeowners' photos for days. I know what the family looks like. The dad, Levi, is average height and slight with a ready smile. Amelia has shiny blond hair that lays smooth and flat, except in her wedding picture where it's done in spirals and piled high on her head. She seems more serious than Levi. Baby Sidney must be only a few months old, based on the newborn clothing and diapers. Her baby photos show a healthy-looking little girl with no hair and blue eyes of a newborn. In one picture, it almost looks like she has dimples on both cheeks. As I've stared at the picture, I've wondered if she'll get her mom's green eyes or if she'll end up with her dad's brown eyes.

"It's not him," I whisper, as another man comes around the corner—also not Levi.

"We need to go," Bart says. "I don't think they can see us, but stay low just in case. Liam's waiting for us farther into the forest."

"We could . . . we could fight."

"Fight? No. We agreed. We avoid people and stay out of harm's way. They don't know we're here, and we're going to keep it that way. Besides, what are you going to do? Shoot them with the .30-30 Winchester? It's no match for what they're carrying."

I reluctantly agree and we start into the forest.

A few minutes later, Liam launches himself into my arms. "Did you see who it was?" he asks in a hushed voice.

"We don't know who it is. They're at the house now."

"Should we wait? See if they leave?"

"I don't think they'll leave anything for us," Bart says. "We have enough. We should put some distance between us and them. You already got the duffle bags down?"

Liam gives a sad nod, pointing to the bags against a tree. "I put the eggs in the top."

"Eggs?" I ask.

He shrugs. "When Grandpa was trying to get me into the woods, I let the chickens out. Then— " He gives Bart a sheepish look. "Then I defied Grandpa and went in and grabbed the eggs from the nest. Even though we got them this morning, I hadn't checked for the afternoon layers. There were five."

"Five? That's a record at one time."

"We'll have eggs tonight," Bart says, opening the duffle bag and trying to sort out how to carry the eggs without breaking them. Satisfied the eggs are secure, he zips it back up and then hefts his backpack into place before hoisting the duffle across his body and shouldering the rifle on the Elmer Fudd sling. Liam and I each have our packs on when Bart says, "Let's go."

I heave out a sigh. My hopes of staying in Levi and Amelia's house for the winter are gone in an instant. We take only a few steps when I see the light brown hen with the black-tipped tailfeathers. "Hey," I say softly.

She runs over toward me in her crazy way, acting almost like a cat as she moves her back for me to stroke her feathers. Then, the small black one with the poof on her head pops out of the woods. I take a minute to pet her too. "You two stay hidden," I say, my voice choked with tears.

"Can we bring them with us?" Liam asks.

I raise my eyebrows. *What a great idea.*

"No," Bart says definitively.

"Why not?" I ask.

"You want to haul two chickens halfway across the country?" he asks skeptically.

"Our backpacks aren't full," Liam says, turning to me. "Could we open the top and then you carry one and I carry the other?"

"You want a pack full of chicken poo?" Bart asks. "We need to go, and they need to stay here."

"We'd have fresh eggs on the way," Liam says. "The brown one gives us an egg almost every day."

I slide my backpack off and open the top. "I think your grandpa is right about the poo problem. But what if we put both birds in one pack? Could we put a couple of slits in it for air?"

Bart shakes his head. "Just put your backpack on and each of you carry one of the dadgum birds under your arm. We need to get away from here before those numbskulls decide to search the forest for the cattle and chickens. We'll figure this out later."

Chapter 17

September 3rd

After fleeing the Delgados' house yesterday, we've stayed in the woods, walking parallel to the small road. The basic road maps we found in the Delgados' desk will be a huge help in making our way to Bakerville. While not the same level of detail as the gazetteer topographical maps, it's certainly better than nothing. From their mail, we discovered their address and were somewhat able to sort out where we are. We don't know exactly, because figuring out their house number on the map didn't happen, but we've got a good idea.

Bart and Liam had spent time pouring over the maps and creating a plan so, when Bart's hand was well enough, we could get back on the road. I abstained from the planning process, still hoping to convince Bart staying the winter at the Delgados' home would be the smart choice. Now that's no longer an option, and I'm resigned to months of traveling by foot.

In our days without a map, we strayed slightly from our course and are farther north than we should be. We'll start heading east and then slightly south today. Yesterday, we walked until almost dark before setting up camp. The chickens were little trouble, but we quickly learned they poo whenever they wish, even while being carried. We stocked up on baby wipes at Amelia and Levi's, so we were able to wipe up the deposits easily.

Bart was less than pleased with me when I told him one of the collapsed cardboard boxes he uses as a bird trap needed to be repurposed for housing the chickens overnight. Leaving while it was still mostly dark, we chose to keep the birds in the box for the first leg of our hike.

Liam and I have taken turns carrying the box, and occasionally carrying the rifle to give Bart's shoulders a break. With both the backpack and large duffle bag, he's carrying more than is comfortable. The smaller duffle bag, which Liam and I swap off along with the chicken box, isn't nearly as cumbersome. And we know our supplies will dwindle as we travel, lightening our load. Bart has commented and shaken his head many times over the ridiculousness of hauling chickens with us. I can't help but smile when I think of my little birds.

We've found a nice place along a creek for our extended break. The chickens were more than happy to be let out of the box and are now pecking around looking for treats. We take turns napping and keeping watch—not only for any threats but so our chickens don't take off.

As the sun begins to set, Bart says, "Let's see if we can get some miles in. Maybe we'll stumble across something better than my trap box for carrying those silly birds."

"I remember seeing pictures of chickens with harnesses on the internet," Liam says.

"You want them to walk ten miles a day?" Bart asks with a shake of his head.

"No . . . maybe not. What if we put diapers on them so we can carry them in the backpacks like we were thinking yesterday?"

"Good idea," I say. "Too bad we didn't bring some of Sidney's diapers with us."

"Surprised you didn't," Bart says. "You brought baby wipes and formula. If you think I'm drinking from a bottle, you've got another think coming."

I snort out a laugh. "I thought we'd treat it like protein powder. I would've been happy for a cup of baby formula a few short weeks ago." I shudder at the memory of how close we were to starving to death.

"I s'pose you're right," Bart says. "Things were pretty rough. But still . . . " He gives another shake of his head while muttering something as he begins to walk off. "Let's get a move on it."

It's about an hour before dark when we're crossing a field with a farmhouse a couple hundred yards off. We've been out of the trees and in the open for the last thirty minutes or so of our walk. I'm starting to wonder if we'll be able to find a well-hidden place to camp tonight, when Bart asks, "Does that place look vacant?" He's putting small binoculars he salvaged weeks ago up to his eyes.

"Should I look too?" Liam asks. "I have binoculars from Levi's house in my backpack."

I set the bird box on the ground and say, "I'll get them out. Do you know where they are?"

"The main compartment, right on top."

"No need," Bart says. "I see movement by the house. Let's get going."

I bend over to pick up the box when a puff of dirt flies into the air a few feet from me, followed by a loud repercussion.

"They're shooting at us!" Bart says in a yelp. "Let's move!"

I'm hunched over with the box, the chickens moving and squawking, as another shot comes way too close. The shots continue one after another, convincing me there's more than one person shooting at us.

Liam is almost to the barbed-wire fence when I watch him go down. "Liam!" I cry, running toward him. He's struggling to his feet when I catch up to him. "Are you hit?"

"I tripped in a hole. My ankle hurts." With the box under one arm and the other arm around Liam, I help him as he hobbles toward the fence.

Bart is right behind us as he says, "Make yourselves smaller. Stoop over."

As soon as we get to the fence, the shooting stops. "Can you get through?" I ask Liam as Bart puts his foot on the bottom string and pulls up the next string. I slide the box underneath as I help Liam through, his backpack catching on the way. When we came into the field on the other side, we took our time taking off our packs and carefully going through. Now we just want to get out of this place where we're sitting ducks. Are they taking their time to line up for a kill shot, or are they done shooting?

Once Liam is through, Bart says, "Go, Clarice. As soon as you're on the other side, get our boy out of here. I'll be right behind you."

With a nod, I shimmy through, managing to make myself small enough to not get too hung up on the barbs. I look back at Bart, who's tossing the large duffle bag over as I grab Liam and we get moving, his limp pronounced as he winces in pain. His backpack, which is still in place, and the smaller duffle slung across his body like a messenger bag aren't helping his progress. I'm still expecting another shot any moment. A few minutes later, we reach another fence. Bart's caught up with us, and we repeat the process of struggling through the barbed wire.

Once on the other side, Liam asks, "Can we stop for a minute?"

"Gotta keep going." Bart says. "We need more distance between us and them."

"Are they following us?" I ask, quickly looking around.

"Not that I've seen. But . . . " He lifts his hands in a shrugging motion.

"Let me look at his ankle," I say. "It'll just take a minute."

Bart gives a single nod. "Move over there so we're not completely out in the open." He points to a dip in the field. As we get closer to the dip, we see it's a large crevice, perfect for hiding out. Bart keeps the old rifle at the ready while I help Liam sit down and check his ankle. It's slightly bruised and already swelling.

"Are the chickens okay?" Liam asks, watching the box bounce slightly as they move within it.

"They're fine," I say.

"Grandpa tore his pants." He motions to a slit in the right leg of Bart's trousers. After losing his own clothes, except the ones he was wearing when we were robbed, he's found replacements—not his preference of thick utility pants and heavy button shirts, but he's made do. He's wearing a thin pair of hiking pants he found at a place he looted before we reached Levi and Amelia's. While some of Levi's clothes fit Liam, they were much too small for Bart. Amelia's clothes didn't fit me either. She's shorter and on the heavy side. I do have a pair of her yoga pants, which hit me midcalf. Those are what I was wearing yesterday when we had to flee.

"Quiet!" Bart whispers. "Get your heads down." With his rifle perched on the edge of the crevice, he moves his head so it's concealed. "Clarice, crawl over here and get the pistol out of my ankle holster."

"I'm not done checking Liam's ankle."

"Doesn't matter if we're dead!"

With wide eyes, Liam chews on his lip. I squeeze his shoulder before going after the small pistol. It's in my hand when the shooting starts again. I stifle a cry and scoot back toward Liam. Bart returns fire, resulting in a yelp from the shooter. Another shot from him—or *them*—quickly follows. Bart shoots again, again, and again. I know the rifle holds eight rounds, and he's used half of them in a manner of seconds, immediately working the lever after each shot.

"Get me more ammo." Bart kicks at his backpack with his foot. I dig in the backpack as the bad guys shoot again. Bart shoots his final four rounds. He ducks down as the aggressor fires again. "Give me the pistol and fill up the rifle. Be quick."

The light report of the handgun keeps the shooters at bay as I fumble with the reload.

"Take a deep breath," Liam says, as he now sits next to me. "You've done this before."

I nod and attempt to relax. Bart fires two shots in quick succession. There's another cry from the aggressors.

"Now go away," Bart says firmly, directing his order at our attackers. "About got that gun ready? They've both been hit, but I'm not sure it'll stop them. As soon as you reload, we're going out the back of this hole."

"I can't get the last one in," I whisper. Without the shooting, it's way too quiet.

"Fine. I'll remember there's only seven." He stoops down and grabs the extra magazine out of his ankle holster, then pops it in the gun as he keeps an eye out for the shooters. "Liam, you take the pistol. Clarice, you'll have to handle the big duffle and the stupid birds."

"Liam needs help walking."

"He'll have to do it on his own. We need to go."

"Are they still out there?" Liam asks.

"I don't want to stick around and find out. You two start out. I'll keep watch."

Liam is already limping toward the back of the crevice. "Don't go out without checking for them," I whisper.

I'm right behind him as he crawls up the slope, making sure to stay low. He pauses, looking in all directions. "I don't see anyone. There's another fence about . . . about as far away as the size of our backyard at home."

I jump when Bart's voice sounds right by my ear. "I'll go first. As soon as I'm at the fence, Clarice, you make a run for it. Leave the birds if you can't handle them."

"I can handle them. What about Liam?"

"Liam, you cover us. That means if you see anyone with a gun aimed at us, you shoot them. You have a good view from here. Got it?"

With wide eyes, Liam nods. "I got it."

Bart gives him a look. It's then I notice the tears glistening in his eyes.

I bite my lip to keep my own tears at bay. Now is the time, as Liam told me before, to be fierce. I straighten my shoulders and say, "Go on, Bart."

He scurries up the slope and makes a run for the fence, not stopping until he reaches a brace of two posts, using them as cover. As soon as he's set, he motions to me.

"Be careful, Liam," I say as I pop a kiss on his cheek. I'm soon at the fence, breathing hard as I try to catch my breath.

"Shove the birds and bag under. You crawl under too. As soon as you're on the other side, I'll motion for our boy to make his run."

The distance between the ground and the bottom strand is too small. I shimmy out of my backpack and crawl under, then pull the bags and box with me. I'm under and leaning against the post, trying to make myself small, as I put my pack back on.

Liam's run is more of a shuffle, his face clenched tight and determined.

Bart has the rifle at the ready, looking for anyone who's a threat to his grandson.

"C'mon, Liam," I whisper. I catch myself before I petition Bart's God for assistance again.

Liam finally reaches us, his face a mask of pain.

"Set the gun down and take your pack off. Crawl under the fence," Bart tells him. "Once you're under, quickly get yourself back together." Liam is sliding the pack off as Bart continues, "You cover me while I get under the fence and get my backpack on. Then you and your mom will make a run for the rock outcropping. Once you're there, I'll have you cover me while I run."

The rocks are about half the distance of our last run. Liam and I stay together until we reach it; the size is large enough to give us good cover, and we're able to scrunch and stay hidden. Liam motions to Bart that he's ready. Soon, we're all together again, huddled against the boulders.

The sun has started its descent as Liam and I make another scurry to cover, another dip in the ground, while Bart keeps watch. We continue in this same manner until it's almost full dark and we spot a cluster of trees. It's not a forested area we'd prefer, but it's better than anything we've had since the shooting started.

"We need to stop," I say. "Liam's ankle— "

"Yeah," Bart agrees. "This will have to do for tonight. It's getting too dark anyway. Check his injury while you still have a little light left. I don't want you turning on the flashlight."

The ankle has about the same amount of swelling as earlier, but the color has deepened. I don't think it's broken, but what do I know? My medical knowledge is limited to cuts and small bruises. "Which bag has the medical supplies?" I ask.

"The large duffle," Liam says.

I quickly rifle through it, finding ibuprofen and a wrap that sticks to itself. It's a little like an ACE bandage but a different material. Giving him the pills first, I then tightly bind the ankle.

"Can you give me a couple of those alcohol swabs, one of the gauze squares, and a length of the wrap?" Bart asks.

"What for?" I ask, finding them in the zipper bag of first aid supplies.

"Cut my leg." Bart pulls up his pant leg. "Nothing more than a scratch."

"You sure? Should I look at it?"

"No need." He waves me away.

I give him a closer look. "Where are your glasses?"

"Knocked them off somewhere along the way. It's fine."

"Will you be able to see well enough?"

"For hiking? Sure. Let's settle in. I'll take first watch. Clarice, it's just you and me tonight. I think Liam needs the rest."

Chapter 18

September 8th

It's been five days since the shootout, and Bart has yet to seem himself. He's quiet and rarely smiles. On the day of the shootout, after I took care of Liam, I was so tired I quickly fell asleep, leaning against a tree. When Bart woke me for my watch, I was shivering. To keep warm while on watch, I paced the small area. We still haven't been able to replace the tent or other items those three guys stole from us to make a comfortable camp. The Delgados, like the other houses we've pillaged, had camping gear but little for camping while hiking. It's always the kind of things to use for car camping.

We did find a folding shovel at one of the earlier places Bart salvaged, along with a small tarp. Amelia had a trowel in her gardening supplies that we picked up, and we have an additional couple of blankets. While the days are still warm, the nights are cold. At least we're at a lower elevation than we were at other times. I wonder how long it'll be until we need the heavy snow wear we grabbed from the Delgados' closet.

At Bart's request, I'm now wearing the pistol on my ankle. He kept the rifle, saying it's smarter for both of us to be armed. He also said he'll start looking for a hip holster so I can access it easier.

The morning after the gunfight, we set out as soon as the sun was beginning to rise, only going far enough to find a spot to camp that was more hidden and with better shelter. We needed a place to, as Bart put it, hunker down and let Liam's ankle heal enough he can walk comfortably. Right now, he hobbles when he must move, using a limb Bart whittled on to turn into a walking stick.

During the days we've been here, I've practiced with the pistol. I want to be competent at removing it from my ankle and comfortably firing. Of course, with needing to stay hidden and silent—and having a finite amount of ammunition—my practice is all limited to perfecting my quick draw, dry firing, and attempting to develop muscle memory.

While Liam is napping, I ask Bart how his hand is feeling.

"All good. I don't even think I need a Band-Aid now."

"You want me to look at it?"

He shrugs and thrusts it in my direction. I peel the bandage off, watching his face for any reaction. He's right; it does look good. He'll have a small scar from the two fangs, but even the scab is gone. I declare him healed. He gives a barely visible smile.

"Do you want to talk?" I ask.

He lets out a loud breath before saying, "I think I killed them both. The first one I'm sure about. He went down with the first shot and cried out. I shot him again after he was on the ground. The second one . . . " Bart shrugs. "I think it was . . . it was fatal too. If not right away, then eventually. Looked like a gut shot." I close my eyes, thinking of what to say. Before I can come up with anything, Bart says, "That was their intent, too, to kill us."

I give a nod. "You kept us safe. You protected Liam."

"And I'd do it again," he quickly replies. "I'm just feeling bad about it—about taking a life."

"They don't deserve your pity," I say with too much venom in my voice.

Without responding, he opens his backpack and pulls out his well-worn Bible. He flips through several pages, finally settling on one. I watch as he puts his finger on the page. "Glad Jessa had the forethought to buy me a Bible with the large print. I teased her then, asking her if she thought I was an old man. Who'd have thought it'd come in so handy after losing my bifocals?"

He gives me a small smile before reading aloud, "'The Lord is my Shepard, I lack nothing.'"

I want to tell him to stop, that I'm not interested in hearing about it, but I know that'd be cruel. It's part of his grieving process for the lives he took.

I'm not sad he killed them, but I wonder if I'd feel the same had I been the one who pulled the trigger. It wasn't too long ago when I was lamenting over the fact that I'd never be able to shoot someone. But now, things are different. I haven't been forced to directly defend my life, or the life of my son, but I think of it differently.

Bart continues reading, "Even though I walk through the darkest valley, I will fear no evil, for You are with me."

I've heard this reading before; it's popular at funerals. Tears stream down his face as he continues to read. When he's finished, Bart asks if I can handle things while he goes for a walk. He grabs his pack and the empty water jugs as he leaves.

By the time Bart finally returns, Liam is awake and I've started getting concerned.

"Filled up our water while I was gone. The creek seems a little higher than yesterday. I think they might have received rain somewhere upstream. Liam, did you put those rain ponchos in the duffle?"

"Yes, sir. They aren't much more than the thickness of garbage bags. We have a couple of those too."

"Let's put them at the top of the bag."

Liam uses his walking stick to gingerly make his way to the duffle.

"How's it feeling?" Bart asks.

"Doesn't hurt much."

"How about you walk around a little bit. Let's see how you're looking."

Liam takes several steps around the camp before looking inquiringly at Bart.

"Good enough," Bart says. "How's it feeling now?"

"Still fine."

"Why are you limping then?"

"I guess . . . I don't know. I just don't want to hurt it."

"Can you walk normally?" I ask. "Still use the stick for support."

He takes several steps across the campsite, turns, and walks back. "It's okay."

"Think you're ready to leave tomorrow?" Bart asks. "We'll take it easy and stop as you need."

"Yeah, I'm ready."

Later in the evening, we pack up and clean the campsite as best we can.

In the morning, we wait until there's plenty of illumination before, once again, starting on our journey. Being in camp for so many days, and with Liam injured, we don't want to risk tripping over anything in the dark.

Liam's using the walking stick and carrying his backpack, which we made lighter so it'd be easier on him. Bart has the large duffle, with the few items left from the smaller duffle along with some of Liam's gear crammed inside. Being in one place for several days really took a toll on our food supplies. The now empty smaller duffle is housing the birds. Since I can wear it against my body, it's easier to carry than the box, but the chickens don't seem to like it. I think the lack of structure makes it easier for them to slide around.

Bart's still quiet but seems a little less lost. I'm not sure how someone is supposed to feel after what happened. I'll admit, I don't really feel bad that he killed them. It was one thing for them to shoot at us from their house; I thought they were only warning shots to keep us away. But they came after us. They hunted us even after we'd fled their space.

I'm much more comfortable being back in the woods, hidden from prying eyes. We're on a slight uphill grade, making our way southeast. Using the road map for a guide as we stick to the woods, Bart estimates we still have over six hundred miles before reaching Bakerville—two months of travel, if we go ten miles each day. But I know we won't be able to travel every day. There will be times we have to stop for a rest or to take extra time salvaging from houses or cars.

I think back to Levi and Amelia's comfortable house. Undoubtedly, we would've left in a few more days, letting Bart's hand continue to heal while we dehydrated more food. We've yet to start on the veggies we dried, choosing to eat all the canned goods first, along with snared small game, foraged fruit—which is finally ripening—and any eggs Little Brown Hen gives us.

That's her official name now; the other is Poof Head. Both were incredibly happy to scrounge around the woods while Liam healed. I'd leave the box open, and they'd hop right in as the sun started to dip each night.

Our speed is much slower than previously, but we're allowing Liam to set the pace. I'm behind him, with Bart bringing up the rear. We're staying in the woods, hidden by the dense foliage, between a creek on our north and a road to our south. In a couple of spots, we've had to cross the slightly swollen stream. So far, we've managed to not get too wet in the process. I worry about Liam losing his balance in the water, but he seems steady.

We stay quiet as we walk, for fear of others. We're approaching the end of our usual morning hike time when Bart taps my shoulder to stop. I do the same for Liam. In a voice barely above a whisper, Bart says, "As isolated as it is here, think we should put in another hour or two?"

"I think Liam needs the rest," I say.

"How about we take a fifteen-minute break, then keep going?"

"We can try it, but if he still needs more, we stay longer."

After our short break, I check Liam's ankle. We have a limited amount of the sticky wrap stuff, so we switched to the reusable elastic wrap bandages. I gently unwrap it and have him flex and wiggle his toes.

"It's okay, Mom."

"I think it's swollen a little more than when we left this morning."

He shrugs. "Probably. But it doesn't hurt. And it seems less bruised."

"Not less," I clarify. "The color is changing since it's been several days. You know how bruises work."

"I'm good to walk more. We should take advantage of the trees and make up some of our missed days."

"Okay, but if you start having pain, we'll stop."

"Sure, Mom." He gives me a smile. "I'm glad you're back to your bossy self."

"Hey." I pretend to punch his bicep. I wrap him in a hug and say, "I'm working on being fierce."

Sometime later, I'm lost in thought when I see Liam fall to the ground. I start to run to him, but he turns and puts his finger to his lips while making a *get down* motion with his other hand.

I squat and turn to make sure Bart's following suit. He's also low as he moves toward me. Liam is sliding back toward us, remaining fully attached to the ground. Once we're all together, barely audible, Liam says, "There's a car."

"A car?" I mouth.

He nods, as Bart asks, "People?"

"I didn't see anything except the car."

"Did they see you?" I ask.

He answers with a shrug followed by a shake of his head. "I don't think so. But I didn't see any people."

I give Liam's arm a squeeze and motion for Bart to go back down our path. He starts to nod, then shakes his head. "I'm going to check it out."

"No," I say. "Let's just go."

"At some point," he says calmly, quietly, "we need to start salvaging again. If the car is abandoned, there might be stuff we can use."

"Abandoned? Out here? Why would it be?"

"We're not far from the road. And there's a town about ten or fifteen miles east. You two stay here. I'm going to shimmy up and take a look. Be ready to move." He takes the duffle bag off but leaves the backpack on. The rifle is in his right hand instead of on the sling. He motions to the duffle and then to me, implying that if things go sideways, I should grab it as Liam and I run.

I bite my lip to keep from lashing out at him. While there is some validity to what he's saying, we don't need to be salvaging yet. We still have enough for several days. My heart is pounding as he awkwardly crawls up the hill, moving in the direction of a clump of brush.

"Should you get your gun out?" Liam asks, motioning to my ankle.

I shake my head. "Not yet."

Liam shakes his head in return and mouths, "Fierce."

I narrow my eyes slightly before darting them toward Bart. He has binoculars up to his eyes. I watch as his head moves slightly, scanning the area. I let out a silent breath. If he's using the binoculars, he must not see any nearby threat. It's many minutes before he turns and motions for us to join him. As he begins to stand, I have a moment of panic. Is he sure this is safe?

"I think I know what's going on here," he says in a normal tone. I cringe at the sound of his voice. "Liam, I want you to stay here. Wait for your mom and me."

"Why's that?" Liam asks. Bart raises his eyebrows at him. In response, Liam gives a nod.

I grab the large duffle bag and the birds' bag, setting both on the ground next to the bush Bart was concealed behind. I can see the car—an old, faded-green Volkswagen Bug—parked in a clearing.

"You're sure?" I ask Bart as my eyes dart around.

"I am. You'll see."

I give Liam another look and say, "We'll be right back."

Bart strides toward the car, not acting nervous or cautious. When we're about fifteen feet away, I discover why. There's a man leaning against a tree with a woman lying across him, her head in his lap. Both are dead.

Chapter 19

September 8th

"Oh," I say with a gasp.

"Yeah. That's why I had our boy stay back. No reason for him to see this."

"I could've gone without seeing it too," I say quietly.

"There's a note or something pinned to the tree. Without my glasses . . . " Bart lifts his hands in a surrender motion.

As we get closer to the couple, I put a hand to my nose.

"Here." Bart hands me a jar of vapor rub. "Put it under your nose. It helps."

I dab the salve above my lip, the strong smell an improvement. I can't imagine what it was like for Bart going into the closed-up houses. I still attempt to not breathe too deeply and to not look in their direction. I've already seen enough.

"You want to wait here? I'll grab the note," Bart says.

"I could've waited back with Liam. You could've grabbed it and brought it back there."

"Oops. Didn't think of that."

I turn my body so I'm looking at the faded car. It has a large dent in the front panel and several smaller dents in various places. The paint on the roof is not only faded but also flaking off in spots.

"Here it is," Bart says. "The car keys were hanging behind it." He jiggles the chain holding four different keys.

"Really? Do you think they have fuel and it still runs?"

"They got it here somehow. They've only been here a couple of weeks or so. The EMP was over two months ago."

My heart is racing as I think about what this means. While we have seen working vehicles, they're few and far between. Bart found one old car he thought he might be able to get running, but he wasn't successful. Apparently, hot wiring is easier in the movies than in real life. With the car, we could get to Mollie's place in a matter of days instead of months.

Bart thrusts the note in my direction. I quickly scan it, my hand going to my mouth as I read.

"What?" Bart asks.

"It's . . . they're asking us to bury them. They've already dug the hole. In exchange for our help, we can take the car. And they even give the address of their home, saying we can have anything there."

"What? Why?"

"She says their little girl died. They've already buried her, right next to the place they dug their hole. They don't want to go on without her."

"Huh." Bart shakes his head. "Where's the hole?"

I give a shrug and start walking toward the woods, purposely avoiding looking toward the couple. "Over here," I say. "There's a mound of dirt. Oh—and maybe I can see where the grave they dug is. I don't think she was very old."

Bart stands by my side. "Sad stuff. The loss of a child, it eats at you. You know about the baby Jessa and I lost before Ben."

I reach out for his hand. I haven't thought of Melissa in years. Ben told me about her death when we were dating. When Jessa was still alive, they had pictures of the baby around the house. But when Bart moved to a smaller place after she died, he didn't put them out. He didn't even have their wedding pictures out after that. I wonder where those pictures are now?

The only physical photos I had with me were lost when my backpack was stolen by those three degenerates. Everything else was on my phone or is stored in some mystical cloud. Did Bart have pictures of his daughter and wife with him? Photos of Ben? I'd love a picture of Ben.

"Do you want to go tell Liam what's going on? I'll start moving them. Uh . . . did they tell us their names?"

I wipe at my eye. "Her name is Isabel. He's Jeff. Their little girl was Ava."

"Okay, I'll take care of Isabel and Jeff. You want to wait with Liam? Then we'll have a burial service for them."

"Why don't I . . . I can help you. I think there's a sheet on the front seat of the car. I'll let Liam know what's going on, then I'll grab the sheet. We can move them into the grave and then cover them. Liam can help with filling up the dirt after they're covered."

"All right. Probably a good idea."

I watch Bart for a minute. Something looks off. His color is paler than normal, and he has a sheen of sweat on his forehead. "You're sure you can do this, move them without help?"

He flexes his hand, the one with the snake bite. "Yeah. I don't want you to have to do it. And I certainly don't want Liam helping. I know . . . I know I've said he needs to grow up, that things are different. And they are—he does. But this is something I don't want him doing unless there's no other option."

I straighten my back. "You're right. I'll help. I don't want him to have to do it either, but they'll be too heavy for you to move on your own, especially the guy."

"Go tell our boy and then grab the sheet. I'll get them . . . " he pauses a moment, then says, "positioned. I may need your help, but we'll see if I can do it on my own."

Liam's eyes go wide when I tell him what we've found. "The parents . . . they must have been so sad."

"Y-yes," I say, trying to control my own emotions. "We'll get them taken care of and then I'll come back for you. We'll have a little funeral service for them."

Twenty minutes later, Liam and Bart are taking turns covering the couple with dirt. They used a handgun, a .357 loaded with .38 special rounds, according to Bart. The gun still has four rounds. The rest of the box of cartridges was on the car seat underneath the bed sheet. There's also a map to their house, several bottles of water, and a box of granola bars. I can't help but cry at their consideration.

"Ready, Clarice?" Bart asks, startling me.

"Uh, yeah." I wipe at my eyes, and Bart gives me a knowing nod.

The three of us gather around the new grave. I ask Bart about making a marker for their grave and the grave of their daughter.

He scratches his head and says, "I think they might have done that if they wanted one—you know, already had them in place. They planned everything else. Besides, with the way things are, it might be better to keep a low profile with things like graves."

"You think there could be grave robbers?"

"Wouldn't surprise me. Nothing would surprise me these days." With his Bible in hand, Bart says, "Let's bow our heads."

I stare at the mound of dirt again, struggling with tears. I avoided looking at the couple, and in my mind, they look like Levi and Amelia Delgado whose house we lived in for so long. Levi and Amelia saved me. I'm not sure how much longer I could've gone on if we didn't find their house full of food, if I wasn't able to rest and recover. I would've loved to stay there, but now, with Isabel and Jeff offering us their house, maybe we have a new safe place to live.

My mind drifts as Bart prays. I don't close my eyes; that'd be completely hypocritical of me to pretend to pray. After a couple of minutes, he says, "Amen." I look around, thinking he's done, when he opens the Bible and starts reading from it. He reads the part he was reading a few nights ago, the one I've heard before about the valley of the shadow of death.

When Bart's finished reading, he says, "I guess that's it. I know we didn't know this couple, but from the things they left—the note and other things, even leaving food and water for us to get the burying done—I suspect they were good people. I pray they knew the love of Christ and are now sitting at His feet, relishing in His glory. That's all— " He chokes back a sob. "That's what I want. To bask in the glory of our Lord and . . . and to be with my Jessa again, to hold our daughter."

After a few minutes of silence, Liam is staring at the grave as he says, "I don't know anything about the things my grandpa is talking about. I haven't read from the Bible or learned about God, but I want to. I want to learn more. And I hope all those things Grandpa said are happening for you, because it sounds pretty nice."

Liam avoids my eyes. Part of me wants to be angry at him, but another part of me understands he needs to be allowed to make his own choices. While I choose to not want to read the Bible or learn about God, I won't stop him. He'll be fourteen in a couple of weeks. I suppose he's old enough to make his own decision.

"Clarice?" Bart says softly. "Did you want to say anything?"

"Um . . . yes. Uh, I'm sorry about your little girl. I hope you are . . . are all together again. Thank you for leaving the things you did. You have no idea how much they'll help us. Thank you for your generosity."

We load up our bags and chickens into the Bug. Liam climbs in the back. I'm already in the passenger's seat when Bart is crawling behind the wheel. As he puts his leg in, he winces.

"What's that about?" I ask.
"What's what?"
"Is something hurting?"
"Oh. Yeah. The cut on my leg's bothering me some."

Chapter 20

September 8th

"The cut on your leg?" I ask as he starts the little car.

"You know, from the day we went through the barbed wire in a hurry."

I stare at him a moment while I remember the day. I was so focused on Liam, on getting him to safety and not hurting his ankle any further in the process. Bart had asked me for a bandage but said it was nothing to worry about. He didn't have me look at it, and he hasn't mentioned it since. "You should've said something."

"Didn't think about it again until last night when I was on watch and brushed it against the stump we'd been sitting on. It stung. Let's find this house and then you can do your doctoring."

"Is the clock right?" Liam asks, pointing to a little digital clock on the dash. It's the kind with sticky stuff on the back, and it looks several years old.

"Huh." Bart glances at the watch on his wrist. "I'm surprised it's working. I'd have thought the EMP would've wiped it out. But, yeah, it's pretty close. Seven minutes slower than what I have."

I act as navigator, giving Bart directions from the handwritten map. We're turning left onto the main road—the small two-lane paved highway we've been walking parallel with—when Liam asks, "Where's the town you said was nearby? Will we go through it?"

"I don't think so," I say. "Looks like the house is before the town. And we were closer to the town than we thought. Their house is only two miles this side of it."

"Don't you think we should've waited until dark?" Liam asks, furtively looking out the windows.

"Maybe so," Bart agrees. "But with the noise of the vehicle, we would've been targets anyway." He looks toward the map in my hand. "How far?"

"Three miles. The driveway will be on the left."

We ride in silence for those three miles. The driveway is somewhat hidden, and we miss it, needing to back up on the road. We haven't seen anyone or had any indication of other people around, but I'm still a nervous wreck. I can barely breathe out of fear of being discovered.

The long driveway winds through the trees until it finally opens to a modest two-story with a detached garage. I can't help but smile at the adorable place. The brown home with dark green shutters and a metal roof reminds me of a vacation cabin. Bart stops the car as soon as the home comes into view, then backs up until we're hidden behind a tree.

"Let me check it out," Bart says. "I'll take the handgun. You keep the rifle. How about you move over here in case you need to leave in a hurry. Go back to where we found them. I'll come to you. If I'm not there by tomorrow morning, get going to Mollie's."

I shake my head. "We're not doing that again."

"We are," Bart says firmly. He turns and looks to Liam. "You will get your mom to Wyoming."

"Yes, sir," Liam says.

"Understood?" Bart looks at me. "Clarice?"

"Fine," I snap.

He removes the two keys from the keyring that look like house keys and then opens the car door, crouching behind it. He has the rifle in his hands, which was nestled between him and the door. I climb over the gear shift and into the driver's seat. Once I'm in place, we exchange guns.

I touch Bart's arm. "Be careful."

"I think this will be fine. Just cautionary." He pats my hand, then moves into the trees. I quietly pull the door shut. Liam and I don't speak. With the trees blocking my view, I can only see him on occasion as he makes his way toward the house, until he's completely out of sight.

"Can you see anything?" Liam asks.

I shake my head in response. The minutes feel like hours as they tick by. He's taking so long, I start to wonder if there's something wrong—if he sees some sort of threat. Finally, he comes into view as he darts between the trees.

"There," I say breathlessly.

"Everything's probably fine, right?" Liam says with a slight quiver in his voice.

"Yes," I reply, trying to fake confidence. Within a minute, Bart is in full view and waving me forward.

"All right!" Liam says, as I start the car up and ease it into gear. It's been years since I've driven a stick shift. I pop the clutch, killing it. I start it again and ease it forward. After a couple of lurches, we're moving. Good thing I didn't have to try and get out of here in a hurry while driving this thing.

Bart meets us at the front of the house. "Everything looks good. Like the other house, this one hasn't been disturbed."

"You think we'll have to leave here in a hurry like we did at the Delgados' house?" Liam asks. "Should we plan our escape again?"

"We should." Bart nods. "That's always a good idea. And we'll keep watch too. Right now, I'm going to walk back down to the end of the driveway. Thought I'd use some brush and get rid of our tire prints in the dirt. No sense in advertising we just came up the road."

"I don't remember seeing any other prints," I say. "Do you think they did the same thing after they left?"

"Maybe." Bart shrugs. "Or they might've had a little rain to wash them away. We don't know what the weather's done in the last couple of weeks, but we do know the creek rose while we were camping along it."

"Is that how long they were there?" Liam asks.

Bart makes a motion with his entire body, something like a shrug.

I don't want to think about how long Isabel and Jeff were in the woods by the tree. "Let's check out the house, Liam," I say.

Bart turns and starts to walk away; I notice he's limping.

"Bart, is your leg okay for walking? Should I check it first?"

"I've been walking all morning, ya know. A short while longer isn't going to make a difference."

Inside the house, Liam looks around. "I think I'll check upstairs," he says.

I spend a few minutes in the living room, looking at the pictures displayed on the shelves on both sides of the fireplace. Isabel has dark hair and deep brown eyes. Jeff's a redhead with green eyes. Adorable Ava is almost identical to her mom. My favorite photo is one where Ava is kissing Jeff on one cheek while Isabel kisses the other. He has the best smile, seeming to be happy and content with his life.

Letting out a sigh, I move on to the kitchen. There's a note on the counter. I glance at it before going to the sink. I'm surprised when I turn the faucet and water gushes out. "Liam! There's water!"

"Awesome!" he yells in response. "It doesn't work up here, though."

Hmm. I don't know much about why the water would be running in the first place, let alone why it's working in the kitchen but not upstairs. I try the hot. Even after several minutes, it doesn't change temperature. I open the cabinets and find a few canned goods. The fridge is completely empty. I search for a pantry, finding nothing. Okay, so they don't have much food. Is that why their daughter died?

I go back to the note on the counter, written in what I assume to be Isabel's handwriting, to see if there's more information. The note starts with thanking us for putting them to rest. It also includes a line saying, "*If you've found our house without finding our bodies first, we implore you to follow the map on the back of this note to locate us and bury us next to our beloved daughter. As a thank you, we gladly give all our earthly possessions to you, including a still running vehicle located at the burial site.*"

After the opening paragraph, she goes on to detail where to find a few items she believes may be most helpful in our quest for survival—including items Jeff sells in his small online backpacking and camping store. After reading, I yell out for Liam. "Hey! Can you come here a minute?"

"What's up, Mom?" he asks from the top of the stairs.

"There's a building behind the house that the man used for his business. They might have some camping stuff in it."

"That's cool. Should I go check it out right now?"

"Let's wait for your grandpa to get back. It's probably best to make sure it's . . . " I let my voice fade off.

Liam finishes with, "Safe?"

"Yeah. Safe."

"The house is nice," Liam says. "Three bedrooms and two baths upstairs. Another bedroom and a half bath downstairs. I'm going back into the master bedroom. I was looking out the window when you called me down. They have a garden. Maybe there's still vegetables?"

"That'd be an amazing treat."

He gives a nod. "The clothes in the closet look like they'll fit Grandpa."

"Good. Maybe we can find him some winter things."

"I'll look."

"Okay, honey."

I return to the note. Isabel tells how they were doing okay and getting by when three-year-old Ava got sick. They took her into town, where a doctor had an office off his house. After examining her, he said he wasn't sure what was wrong and, without power, couldn't do much testing. He gave them a few suggestions but mostly told them to give it time. And he asked them to return in three days. She died before then. That was early August. On September 3rd, Isabel and Jeff decided they couldn't go on without her. I furrow my brow. Only five days ago. Bart thought they'd been there a few weeks.

A light tap at the back door causes me to jump. Bart gives me a wave. After letting him in, I ask, "Do you think what you did will help?

"Hard telling. We already know things can change in an instant."

"Look at this," I say, turning on the faucet.

"Hot diggity! Wonder how it's still working? Maybe it's gravity fed, coming off the hillside back there." He jerks his hand toward the side of the yard.

"It's only the cold water, but still . . . running water! Can you believe it?"

"A blessing from heaven for sure. I was just thinking about that. While I don't celebrate the couple taking their life— " He pauses and shakes his head. "Definitely don't at all. But it's truly an answer to our prayers that we happened upon them. The car will make a huge difference. Did you find anything else useful?"

"I haven't looked around much. There are some cans in the cabinet. I was just reading the note. They run a business for camping gear out of the backyard." I point to the shed. "We were waiting for you before we check it out."

"Where's Liam?"

"Upstairs."

"I'm here now," Liam says, causing me to jump as he enters the kitchen. "Oops. Sorry, Mom."

"You find anything interesting?" Bart asks him.

"Clothes that will fit you," Liam says with a smile. "Winter stuff too. Now we'll all have warm clothes. But I think we might not need it since we have the car, right?"

"Right. How about we load up what we need and hit the road in the morning?"

As we start walking to the shed, Liam says, "You're still limping, Grandpa. Did Mom look at your leg?"

"Not yet," I say, trying to hide the fact it slipped my mind with the excitement of the water and other things in the house.

At the same time, Bart says, "She'll do it after we check out the shed and see if they have any good camping gear."

Chapter 21

September 8th

We walk together to the shed, realizing after we get there we should've brought the keys. Liam runs back and grabs the house keys sitting on the counter by the note.

While waiting for Liam, I take a deep breath. The smell of the trees, combined with the grass of the yard, almost takes me back to our home. There's a hint of rain in the air. I close my eyes and enjoy the sensations. It's peaceful here. Will the peace continue long enough for us to get the items we need along with a good night's rest? Or will we need to leave in a hurry again? If someone came up the road and surprised us, we'd lose the car.

"Should we move the Bug?" I ask Bart.

Looking at me, he tilts his head to the right. I notice again how his pallor isn't quite right.

"Are you feeling okay?"

He puts his hand to his chin and gives his beard a slight tug. "I'm tired. Walking down to the road and back took more out of me than it should've. I guess . . . I guess I'm feeling my age today. Where do you think we should move the car to?"

"I was just thinking about how we had to leave the Delgados' house in such a hurry. Can we hide it somewhere so we can get to it if that were to happen again?"

"Not a bad idea. Let's do this first. Liam is heading back with the keys now."

Inside the shed, there are shelves lining each wall. Some of them are empty, but most are well-organized and full.

"Hey!" Liam says. "Check out the backpacks!" There are at least a dozen large backpacks on one of the shelves, each flattened and wrapped in plastic. "And look—dried food, camp stoves. Look at all this stuff!"

I'm struggling to take it all in. It's like being in a swanky camping store in downtown Portland. A much smaller version, of course, but there's just about everything we could possibly need to backpack our way to Bakerville.

"This is good stuff," Bart says, making his way to a desk chair in the corner. "You two want to pick out whatever you think we'll need? Let's load the car up, then we'll move it down the driveway and into the forest a bit, set it up for a quick getaway."

Liam nods. "Good thinking, Grandpa."

"It was your mom's idea." Bart gives me a wink.

We pick out a new backpack for each of us, then add a one-man tent and a two-man tent, both rated for winter. The one-man tent is a bivy sack that, according to the packaging, doubles as a sleeping bag. But Bart says he wants a sleeping bag, too, so we add lightweight zero-degree bags for each of us. Bart stands to help with his bag; I wave him off, telling him it's just as easy for me to fill two bags as it is to fill one. The food section of the shelves has not only packages of dehydrated backpacking food—in a brand I've never heard of but promises to be organic, all natural, and vegetarian—but also meal replacement bars of the same brand. The bars promise to be a ready-to-eat meal of over six hundred calories with no cooking required.

"These are pretty great," Liam says, reading one of the packages. "You'd probably like this one, Mom. It's dark chocolate and banana."

"I probably would," I agree. "Which ones look good to you?"

He makes a face before saying, "Before this . . . this stuff . . . I wouldn't have chosen any of them. Now, I don't think it really matters what I like. Food is fuel." I give a nod. He rushes on with, "But I might actually enjoy the caramel apple one. Hey, what's this?" He thrusts another package toward me.

"A dehydrated meal?" I ask, based on the packaging alone.

"No, I don't think—it's a milkshake or something."

"Really?" I take the package from him. "Huh. It is. Just add water. But it's more than a milkshake. It's a liquid meal replacement. Says, 'Drinkable meal so you don't need to stop hiking.' Might even be better than the baby formula." I give him a wink.

"No doubt!"

"Those are another great find." Tears suddenly fill my eyes as I think of Isabel and Jeff—who have plenty of food to get them through several months in this shed—choosing to end their lives. My heart breaks thinking of the hurt they must have felt after losing their daughter.

"This is a huge blessing," Bart says. "With these things and the car, we're going to make it now. I'm sure of it."

I give a solemn nod as I go back to the packing, adding food, water filters, camp stoves, lanterns, and everything else. Like Bart, I'm immensely grateful and also feel like this is it; we're going to make it.

"Should we take more than what will fit in the packs?" Liam asks. "You know, since we have the car? Maybe stuff we think the Caldwells might need?"

"Not a bad idea," Bart says with a nod.

"How much can we fit?" I ask.

"Whatever will fit in the trunk . . . or, uh, the hood," Bart says. "Let's put the backpacks we'll need in the backseat. Think you can fit all three next to you, Liam?"

Liam shrugs his answer as he begins filling a fourth backpack.

"That way we have them if we need to get them in a hurry. Did you happen to find any firearms in the house?" Bart asks while looking around the shed.

"No." Liam shakes his head. "I found another box of ammunition that I'm pretty sure is for the handgun . . . the one from before. And I found a few slingshots."

"Slingshots?" I ask.

"Yeah, not the kid's kind either. Really fancy ones. There's one for each of us."

"Those could come in handy," Bart says. "So, my guess is we could fill at least three more bags and put them in the trunk. And let's take all the food in here and any in the house."

"Yeah, for sure." I nod and start working on two more bags.

"Liam, lets you and me start hauling things to the car while your mom packs the bags up."

"Sure, Grandpa." Liam grabs two of the filled bags. "Oh. They're too heavy."

"Need to fix them," Bart says. "A little heavy the first day or two might be expected with the extra food, but let's not go crazy."

We spend many minutes removing the excess items from the original three bags. The three extra bags, we'll stuff to the gills to have as backup items in case we need them during our car ride. I'm glad we'll be able to show up at Mollie's house with something. I don't want her to think we're only there for charity. We will be, of course, but it'll be better to have some goods to offer in exchange for the security of their home.

Once the packs we'll carry are a suitable weight for me and Liam, I ask Bart if he wants to try his.

"Yep, probably a good idea." Bart stands up, but as soon as he's upright, he sways slightly and grabs for the desk. I watch as he closes his eyes and wobbles again before plopping back into the chair. "Whoa. Guess I'm a little dizzy."

I'm quickly by his side, asking if he's okay.

"Yeah. Just woozy. Stood up too fast, I guess."

I put a hand to his forehead. "Bart," I gasp. "You're burning up."

He gives a slight nod. "Thought I was a little warm. I might be coming down with a cold or something."

"I picked up a thermometer from the Delgados' place. We'll check you when we get inside."

"Yep, okay. Let's wrap things up and call it an early night."

I glance to Liam, who's staring at us, and say, "Okay. Liam, can you start moving things to the car? Put the three packs in the back. I'll get the other three finished."

"He won't be able to open the trunk—those things are notorious for being difficult," Bart says.

"I'll help him. Go ahead, Liam. Um, actually, how about just take everything inside the house. I'd feel better about not having you in the driveway alone."

"All right, Mom." This time when he picks up the two packs, they're obviously much easier to carry.

As soon as he leaves the building, I turn to Bart. "When did you start feeling sick?"

"Not long ago. I thought maybe I was coming down with something this morning. It's been progressing throughout the day. Maybe you and Liam can take the first watches? If I can get some uninterrupted sleep, it might knock this thing on its head."

"Yeah, it might," I say, though I'm skeptical. "Where would you have caught a cold? We haven't been around anyone."

He shrugs. "Don't know."

"Is this like last winter? When you got so sick and it was bronchitis?" I'm suddenly scared. He had to be on antibiotics for weeks. The doctor treating him said he should have come in sooner;

the infection in his airways could've easily moved to his lungs and caused pneumonia. It was weeks before he was fully recovered.

"I don't have a cough. I'm just tired. And moving those folks, it took more out of me than it should've." He bends over and scratches at his leg. "And this leg is paining me some. Let's get me a fresh bandage and a good night's sleep. I'll be good as new tomorrow."

"I'll get you in the house, then finish packing the extra bags. No reason for you not to be resting while we're doing this stuff."

When Liam returns, I hand him the backpack we filled for Bart and I carry the pack we'll use as an offering for Mollie to house us. Just like the first three, it's way too heavy and I struggle with carrying it to the house. My slower pace works well to stay next to Bart. Once he's on his feet for a moment, he doesn't seem as woozy as when he was trying to stand up. He's right. It's probably just tiredness. Walking is different than the exertion of moving bodies.

Inside the house, Liam asks, "Should I go out and pack the other bags?"

"I'll feel better if you stick close to me. How about you see what we can use from the house. You said there's winter clothes?"

"Yeah. I'll grab them and the slingshots. There's some other stuff too. Having the car— " He breaks into a grin. "We could go a little crazy."

"Let's not go too crazy. It's not a very big car."

He gives me another cheeky grin before bouncing off. Bart's sitting at the kitchen table, looking like the walk from the shed wiped him out.

"Let me change your bandage. Do you want something to eat before you rest?"

"Not hungry. I'll nap and then eat. It must be, what, about five? There's still a few hours of daylight. When I wake up, I'll help our boy finish packing the bags we want to take and then we'll get the car loaded. We'll leave tomorrow morning at first light."

"Should we move the car now?"

"Best we don't. Starting it up could attract unwanted attention. We'll get it packed and then move it, but maybe inside the garage. Have you looked in there yet?"

"No, I haven't gone out there."

"It's a three-bay. They have two cars in there already, new enough to be nothing more than giant paperweights now. There are probably some other things we can use. Maybe you and Liam should check it out. If they have any more guns, they could've kept them out there."

"That's a good idea. Now roll up your pant leg." I unzip an outer pocket on my pack. I've stocked it with a few of the medical supplies we gathered at Levi and Amelia's house. I remove a couple of Band-Aids, antibiotic ointment, and hand sanitizer. I give my hands a squirt before turning back toward Bart. He's staring at his now exposed leg. I gasp before crying out, "Bart! What happened?"

Bart shakes his head. "It was just a scratch. I don't know how . . . " He continues to shake his head as his eyes meet mine.

What I expected to be a small cut is anything but. He's still wearing the original nonstick gauze pad with the wrap stuff that sticks to itself, likely the same one he had the day he got the scratch and bandaged it while I was working on Liam's ankle. Above and below the wrap, it's swollen and dark blue—maybe even black in some places. Leading from the discoloration are red streaks going toward his knee and down to his ankle. Tears sting my eyes as I take in the infected wound. I know computers, not medicine. But it's obvious this scratch is a serious concern.

"That might be why I'm feeling so poorly."

I close my eyes while I consider how to proceed. When a computer has a virus, I get to the source of the infection, find out what caused it so I can eradicate it. "We need to clean it."

Doing my best to keep calm, I put water on to boil. While it's heating, I grab a couple of washcloths from the downstairs bathroom and then check the drawers and medicine cabinet for additional supplies. I follow with checking the two full baths upstairs. While I do find a partial box of 4 X 4 gauze pads, an opened tube of ointment, hydrogen peroxide, and rubbing alcohol, there's no antibiotics—which is what I think he really needs. There are a couple bottles of over-the-counter painkillers. I give him two ibuprofen before getting started.

I put a portion of the now hot water in a bowl, adding tap water to cool it so I can soak a washcloth in it without scalding my hands. In a second bowl, I set up water for handwashing. I scrub them as best I can in hopes of not contaminating Bart any further. After scrubbing, I then bathe them in rubbing alcohol. Small cuts on my hands sting with the treatment.

Sitting in front of Bart, I get a whiff of an unpleasant odor coming off the leg. Thinking back, I might have caught a whiff of this before, but with his leg so close to my nose, it's quite strong and makes me feel a little sick to my stomach. Maybe I should put some of the vapor rub under my nose again.

"Why you making a face?" Bart asks.

"It smells. And it looks terrible."

He nods. "I should've kept a better eye on it. I think— " He lets out a sigh. "What's your plan?"

"Wash it with the hot water and soap. Then see how it looks?"

"Good enough."

"It might hurt."

"I expect it will. Let's get on with it."

Steeling myself, I peel off the bandage. The scratch I was expecting is a large, gaping wound. The edges are torn, and it's filled with pus. The bandage must have been holding in some of the odor because it increases substantially when I peel off the adhesive. A wave of nausea passes over me.

"Sorry, Clarice," Bart says. "It's bad."

I give a nod. Bad is an understatement. I dip the cloth in water, then gently dab at the wound. The skin surrounding it sloughs off. The more I dab, the more falls off. When I've cleaned as much as I think I should, the opening has more than doubled in size. The discolored skin surrounding it is hot to the touch. I use a little peroxide on it and then put on the antibiotic ointment. I probably only needed one or the other but decide today is the day to get it as clean as possible.

"Do you think I should cover it again?" I ask. "Or let the air get to it?"

"Not sure. What do you think is best?"

"The way it's wide open—I guess cover it. But maybe with the gauze roll? It'd help keep dirt out but still let air in, right?"

"You're asking me? Do whatever you think's best. I'm ready for a nap."

I wrap the gauze around it, trying to keep it somewhat tight but not too much, then secure the end with a piece of medical tape. After I'm done, I say, "I don't know, Bart. It's . . . it's pretty bad."

I'm still sitting on the floor as he places his hand on my shoulder. "I should've checked it. For not doing so, I'm truly sorry. But now, here we are. You've done what you can do."

"You need antibiotics."

"No doubt. But we don't have those. We'll keep it clean, I'll get some rest, and I'll pray. You could join me in that."

I shake my head, then immediately stop. "Okay." I give a reluctant nod. "I'll pray with you, but you have to talk. I wouldn't . . . I don't know what to say."

With his hand still on my shoulder, he bows his head. I look at his bandage. "Father God, I've been a fool. I should have— " He lets out a sigh. "I guess You know what I've done and what I should've done. So here we are. If it's Your will, I ask You to reach out with Your healing touch and make me whole. Please also help Clarice as she does what she feels is needed during this time. Help her feel Your loving arms wrapping around her. Let Liam come to know You also, Lord."

I feel myself stiffen as Bart continues, "I know Clarice has done what she feels is right. She has hurts that she feels You may be responsible for. Help her lay those hurts at the feet of Your Son, Jesus, and let her know You are the Lord. I ask these things in Jesus' Holy Name, amen."

I keep my eyes averted. I'm angry at Bart. I thought he'd only be praying for his healing, not whatever that mumbo jumbo was. And how dare he want Liam—or me—to . . . to . . . *argh*! I take a deep breath. I feel Bart's hand lift from my shoulder. Still without looking at him, I begin to gather my wound-cleaning supplies.

"I'm going to find a bed. Will you wake me up at least an hour before sunset?"

I respond with a nod. As angry as I am, I'm still scared—scared the infection in his leg is already so bad his leg needs to come off. I stop midmovement. The couple who owned this house took their daughter to the doctor when she was sick. That was over a month ago, but if there's a doctor in town, he can help Bart.

Chapter 22

September 8th

After working on Bart's leg, his limp is worse. I help him make his way to the downstairs bedroom. "Nice room," Bart tells me as we enter it. "Glad it's not done all frilly."

I glance around the space, obviously a guest room. It has two twin beds, each with a blue and white striped comforter. There's a nightstand between the beds and a window above the nightstand. A low-pile area rug in blue with a very vague pattern covers the hardwood floor between the beds.

"It is a good room," I say. "Not sure why they went with twin beds instead of a queen in here, though."

"I like it. Do you mind grabbing my pack for me? I should've thought of grabbing it on the way in."

When I return a minute later, Bart's sitting on a hardback chair untying his shoes. "Don't let yourself get into a dither," he says when I walk in the door.

"Hard not to. This is—your leg is bad."

"Yeah, it doesn't look good. I'm kicking myself for not paying attention to it. I've had cuts worse than this dozens of times. I never considered it could be a problem. I'm really sorry, Clarice."

"Try and get some rest. Do you need me to help you get into bed?"

He gives me a look I can only describe as horror, which almost makes me laugh. With a vigorous shake of his head, he says, "Nope. I've got it."

Back at the kitchen counter, I look over the note Isabel left in the car. The handwritten map shows their house and a town just beyond, with three miles written. I pull the map we got from the Delgados' out of my back pocket and spread it out on the counter, quickly finding the town. We'd found this town before, while we were camping and waiting for Liam's ankle to heal enough to begin our walk again. We'd planned to avoid it. With our plan of staying hidden, we had zero desire to enter the town. Instead, we planned to do our usual and check houses and cars on the outlying areas to restock our supplies. Now we have plenty of supplies—except the things Bart most desperately needs: a doctor and antibiotics.

Letting out a loud sigh, I leave the map where it is and slip out the back door, making my way to the garage. Opening the door slightly, I call out to Liam.

"I'm here, Mom. I found some good stuff. I just wish we had a bigger car so we could take more of it with us."

I glance around and find him standing by a table littered with items. Little Brown and Poof Head are happily exploring the room. He's sprinkled some grain of some sort—probably from one of the backpacking meals—on the concrete floor for them to nibble. There are two vehicles in the garage, an older SUV and a newish sedan.

"Look at these." He holds up a couple pieces of folded paper. "They've got these special maps—you know, the ones specific for different areas? Dad buys them when he wants a really in-depth look at an area he's hunting."

"Topographical—or topo—maps," I say. Even with GPS programs being his first choice for hunting, Ben still had a love of paper maps. "Are there maps showing the area between here and Bakerville?"

"I'm not sure. They have regular road maps and a road atlas of all fifty states too. I thought I could compare the road maps to the topo maps and see if I can find what we need."

"Do they have a road map of Montana? Wyoming?"

"Both." He nods.

"Those will be helpful, even if we can't get the topographical maps we need. Liam— " I shake my head. "I need to talk to you, tell you what's happening."

"Grandpa's sick." He says it matter-of-factly. "I thought he wasn't feeling well when we were shoveling the dirt on the grave. He tried to hide it. So we need to stay a couple of days so he can get over it? Or can we leave and get to Bakerville since we have the car, and he can rest while you drive? I could drive, too, maybe." His voice cracks a couple of times as he talks.

"It's worse than that," I say quietly. "He needs a doctor. I'm going into the town nearby— "

"No, Mom."

I hold up my hand. "The people who lost their daughter said they went to the doctor in town. It's only a few miles. I'll see if he'll come out here. If not, then I'll come back and get your grandpa and take him in. I need you to stay here. Grandpa's . . . you'll need to keep watch."

"Let me go into town," he says, standing tall.

I can't help but smile. "I'm taking the car most of the way. I'll leave it outside of town and then walk in. I don't know what I'll find, and I don't want to risk losing it. Come into the house with me. I want to show you what I found on the map and tell you my plan."

He shakes his head and starts to say something. I lift my hand before turning on my heel. He makes some sort of noise of disgust, which I choose to ignore.

At the kitchen counter, I point to the map. "Here's the town. We're right here." I point to the two places with my index fingers. "I'm going to take the car and leave it here." I point to a small road heading toward the creek. "I'll try and find a way to hide it. I'll walk into town from there. I'd walk the entire way, but it's getting close to dark and I want to save as much time as I can."

"You're sure this is necessary?"

I step closer to him and lower my voice. "Grandpa might lose his leg if we don't get him help."

Liam's eyes go wide. "What? How?"

"The scratch he got the day when we went through the fences, it's bad. He didn't think of checking it, and I didn't ask about it." I shake my head. "It's bad, Liam. Really bad."

"How— " Liam's voice catches. I watch as he swallows. "How'd it get so bad? It was just a scratch. He said it was just a scratch."

I shake my head. "There must have been something on the fence— bacteria or something got in afterward while we were camping. I don't know."

"What do you want me to do?"

"Just keep an eye out. Stay inside and keep the rifle handy. Um, why don't you do what you did before and put together an escape bag. Use one of the extra backpacks we're taking to Mollie's to build it. You'll have to help your grandpa get out if someone shows up while I'm gone. So just pack one you can easily carry with stuff for both of you. I'll take my pack with me. If you have to leave— " I scrunch up my face while I think. "Can you find the place we were earlier? Where we found the, uh, the car?"

He nods. "I can find it."

"Okay. Go there. If something is wrong here, I'll go there too. And, uh, if, um— " I let out a breath, trying to think of how I want to say what I need to say.

"If you don't come back, I should go after the car and head to Mollie's house?"

"Yes," I say, choking back a sob. "You take your grandpa to Mollie's house if I'm not back by morning." He nods unconvincingly. "I mean it, Liam. Getting him to Mollie's as quickly as possible will be his only chance. You'll have to do it."

I briefly wonder if that might be the best thing to do right now— just wake him up, pack up, and go. But the way this trip has gone, I can't count on anything. Finding him a doctor today seems smartest.

"I have to leave. I found a second set of car keys hanging on a hook. I'll take those. You keep this one." I plop the key onto the counter before hoisting the pack onto one shoulder. I then wrap Liam in a hug and tell him how much I love him. "I'll see you soon. Keep the doors locked."

"Should you wear a heavy coat? The wind's picking up."

I run my hand through my hair at the nape of my neck. "I think just the hoody is fine. It's been chilly all day. It shouldn't get too much worse before I'm back."

"Do you have the pistol?" he asks.

"On my ankle. The handgun we found is in the duffle. Maybe look around for a holster?"

"I found one in the bedroom, in the nightstand. I'll put it on and keep the rifle near me."

"Just keep the rifle with you. Until your grandpa can train you on the handgun, I don't want you wearing it."

"It's a revolver, like Dad's gun was—only not as big. I shot his last time we went out to the plinking spot."

"You did?"

He gives me a sheepish nod.

"Even so, just use the rifle until we can make sure you know what you're doing. Got it?"

"Yeah, Mom."

I give a stern nod and take a deep breath. "This will be fine. I'll be right back." I attempt a small smile before I step out the door.

My heart is crashing in my ears as I put the backpack on the passenger's seat. I take a moment to try and calm myself, letting out a breath before saying aloud, "Okay, if You really do exist, God, I could use some help here." I shake my head and turn the key. I'm off with a jerk.

As I pull out of the long driveway onto the pavement, I realize I've messed up the gravel again. I choose not to take the time to fix it as I turn toward town. It's only a couple of minutes until I reach the road I picked out on the map. I'm surprised at how perfect it is. It quickly turns a corner and I'm able to pull the Bug off the road and into the trees. I don't think it'll be at all visible from the main road. But if someone comes down this road—from wherever it goes—then it will be found. Nothing I can do about that.

I slide the straps of the backpack on before exiting the car. Making sure it's locked, I tuck the key in the pocket of my pants. I've decided to stay in the forest but near the road as I make my way into town. I move quickly and stay alert. What's the phrase they use in some of those movies Ben used to watch? *Head on rotate?* No, that's not quite right.

It's only a few minutes until the woods end and I'm suddenly at the edge of someone's yard. From the hedge, I look around. There's no one outside. A shiver runs through me. I should've worn a thicker jacket. The wind is much worse in town than at the house. I take a tentative step, moving in the direction of a road. I have no idea where the doctor's office might be. My loose plan was to find a friendly person and ask them. With a shake of my head, I move forward, attempting to look confident.

I'm soon on what appears to be the main road through town. My confidence fades as I walk down the empty street. This is the business district, but none are open. Not only are they not open, but they're obviously vacant—a few with broken windows and one completely missing the front door. We've been avoiding towns for many months. I wonder, do they all look like this?

It's several minutes until someone comes around a corner about a block farther down. A woman. Her long, black hair hangs across her face as she stares at her feet. Her arms are pulled around her middle as she holds her black coat closed. She has yet to see me. I clear my throat. She doesn't hear me, so in a way-too-loud voice, I say, "Excuse me."

Her head jerks up and she jumps back. Seeing her face, I decide she's probably around twenty. She's wearing heavy eye makeup in a Goth style, which matches the black coat and black skinny jeans. She has combat-style black boots on her feet. I can't help but admire her dedication to adhering to her desired fashion. All that fell by the wayside for me long ago. These days, if I comb my hair, it's a near miracle.

I lift my hands in a surrender motion. "Sorry, I didn't mean to scare you."

"What are you doing here?" she asks, backing up.

"Just passing through. I heard this town has a doctor. Can you tell me where his office is?"

She shakes her head. "He left. Lots of people did."

My shoulders sag. "Do you know where he went?"

"Someone came through here and said there's a FEMA camp set up in Coeur d'Alene."

I furrow my brow, trying to think of how far that is from here. Closer than Mollie's. "Why didn't you go?"

"My dad didn't think it was a good idea to go to a camp. We, uh . . . we stayed." She pauses, then in a rush says, "There's other families here too."

"Where is everyone?"

"We've moved to the far side of town, to the houses on the creek. Dad and the others say it's easier to defend that way."

"Do you know if there's any antibiotics? Maybe the doctor left some? Or is there a pharmacy?"

"No, no pharmacy. We don't have anything like that. Sorry." She turns to walk away.

"Do you think—maybe some of the houses might have antibiotics?"

She looks over her shoulder. "They've been stripped of anything useful. Sorry."

I bite my lip to keep from crying. "Wait! Is there another town nearby? I really need a doctor. My father-in-law is sick. He cut his leg, and it's infected."

She turns around and scrunches up her face. "That's not good. You could try herbs. My mom—she used to know about that stuff. She was a naturopathic physician."

"Your mom? Can I talk to her? Maybe she can help."

She shakes her head. "She died last year in a car wreck." She looks toward the sky, then looks back at me. "I think garlic might help. And oregano. She also used to put honey on cuts. But if it's really bad, it might be too late for that. It might be too late for any of it."

"Yes." I try to keep the anger out of my voice. "Yes, I know that. But I have to try something."

"Are you holed up someplace?"

"We have—uh, yes."

"Okay. Fresh garlic is best, but maybe you could use the granules or powder. I don't know. Oregano oil is what my mom used. I don't know if the leaves will work."

"Do I feed it to him?"

After a pause, she says, "Try a tea. My mom was big on teas. If you can find raw honey, use it on the wound. Is there livestock where you are?"

I shake my head.

"Too bad. Ranchers often keep animal medications on hand. They might have had antibiotics."

"Thank you." When she starts to turn once again, I ask, "Why are you out here alone? Aren't you worried about— " I finish with a shrug.

"We haven't had any trouble. I need to get out and walk or I start going crazy. I hope your father-in-law is okay."

She turns again; this time, I let her go. Garlic and oregano tea plus honey. Doesn't sound very promising. I waste no time as I hurry back to the car. We'll pack tonight and leave first thing in the morning. I'll check the map, but I think the FEMA camp in Coeur d'Alene is our best choice. If all goes well, we could be there within a few hours. I hold back a wry laugh. *If all goes well.* Nothing has gone as it should on this trip, from losing the semitruck, to losing my husband and then our dirt bikes. Now Bart's sick. It's been one terrible thing after the next.

It's dusk when I pull into the driveway of Isabel and Jeff's house. I move the car around back, deciding it'll be hidden well enough there but still close enough for us to get away if needed. I'm not even out of the car when Liam opens the door from the house. I shake my head.

"You couldn't find the doctor?" he asks.

"The doctor and most of the town has left. They heard about a FEMA camp, so they went there."

"Maybe we should go there."

"I think we should."

"Dad wouldn't like it, though."

I give a nod. In the early days of the attacks, Ben and I discussed what kind of services were being set up for people. We assumed there would be different types of government aid, including camps. He was adamant those wouldn't be a good choice for us. He was convinced FEMA camps and the like would be a hotbed of theft, abuse, and more. Not necessarily from those in charge but from those in the camp. But Ben is no longer with us, and Bart needs a doctor. If we don't find him help soon, he'll not only lose his leg but possibly his life.

"Yeah, but we're out of options," I say. "Let's get packed up. I'll talk with your grandpa, tell him what we're thinking. There are people still living in the town, that's how I found out about the doctor leaving. This girl, she said her mom was a natural medicine doctor. She suggested a few things to try. She also said it was too bad we weren't staying on a farm. They might have antibiotics for the livestock. I don't remember seeing anything like that at the Delgados' place, do you?"

Liam shakes his head. "No. But . . . let me show you something I found in the garage."

Inside the garage, he walks me to a large, empty fish tank. "They had fish. There's this big tank and a smaller one on the shelf." Liam points to it. "They've got things for the tanks too. Rocks and figurine things. And these." He plucks a plastic jar with a photo of a fish on the front of the shelf. "Look, fish mycin—antibacterial fish medication. Is this like the livestock antibiotics, only for fish?"

I take the jar and move it around. It says erythromycin on it. I'm sure that's a medicine my mom was given when she had bronchitis once. Will it work for Bart's infection?

"Great find, Liam. I think it might work." I open the jar and find individual packets of powder. "How many are in here?"

Liam answers with a shrug. "Not sure. But there's a second bottle that hasn't been opened." He grabs that off the shelf. "It says there's sixty individual packets, 250 milligrams each. How much will Grandpa need?"

I shake my head. "I have no idea. We'll just have to guess. Maybe he's taken this before and will know. Are there any more?"

"Not that I've found."

Chapter 23

September 9th

Though Liam and I agreed last night we would leave first thing this morning, when I wake Bart from his nap, he's in no condition to travel. His temperature is through the roof, and he can barely move.

I give him a couple acetaminophens to help with the fever, then ask him if he's ever taken erythromycin. He doesn't remember taking it, but he says the last time he had antibiotics he had to take them three times a day. So that's what we're doing. I put the powder in a small amount of water, and he takes it like a shot. From the little I know about antibiotics, they should work quickly. As soon as we see improvement, we'll head to the FEMA camp and get him proper care.

I'm also making him tea out of dried oregano and dried garlic granules. I even found some honey in the cabinet. It wasn't raw, so I haven't used it on his leg, adding it to the tea instead to make it more palatable. Bart has had three doses of the antibiotics and two cups of the tea. So far, he hasn't substantially improved.

Liam and I take turns staying with him. We're either sitting in the chair by his bed or, when it's time to sleep, we use the second twin bed. We're using a damp washcloth to help keep him comfortable. Whichever one of us is not in with Bart is keeping watch and organizing the gear. We have all the backpacks loaded and ready to go, but as Liam or I poke around the house, we find other things we want to take. Everything useful is piled on the breakfast bar in the kitchen.

Liam found a wagon in the garage and said it'd be smart to take in case we end up on foot again. I shudder to think of losing the car in some manner. Now, with the plan to go to Coeur d'Alene as soon as Bart can travel, Liam is mapping out the route there. Then, once Bart is well, we'll go on to Mollie's place. Liam found a TV tray he set up as a desk and is using the atlas book and colored pencils to shade in different routes.

"What are you doing, Clarice?" Bart asks in a gruff voice.

"Hey, I didn't know you were awake. Are you feeling better?"

"Hard telling. I could use some water."

I help him sip from a cup on the nightstand. After he's finished, he lies back and says, "I had a dream about Jessa. She looked the same as the day I married her. I wonder if that's how she looks now, in heaven."

"I'm sure she'd still be beautiful to you."

"God says we get new bodies in heaven—glorious bodies, like His."

"Is that right?" I think back to my attempts yesterday asking God for help. What a waste of my breath.

"Yup. I guess I'll be healed once I'm in heaven. This leg will stop hurting, and I'll be able to take my bride in my arms once again and we can dance the night away. We'll be able to hold our baby again. You think she'll still be a baby, or will she have grown up?"

"You're going to get better."

He gives me a small smile. "I'm not so sure. I think . . . I think it may have gone too far."

"You're not giving up," I say firmly.

"No, I'm not giving up. Keep giving me the medicine and herbs. I'm sure you told me last night, but things are a little foggy. Where'd you find the medicine?"

"In the garage."

"The garage? They kept antibiotics in there? You did say they're antibiotics, right?"

"Yes. For fish."

"Well, then! Will I start getting scales?"

"See? You *are* feeling better."

Bart gives me a wink. "Some, yes. Those fish drugs must be working. How'd you know what they were?"

"It does say it's erythromycin on the bottle. But I never would've thought of using them if the girl I found in town hadn't asked if we were staying someplace with livestock."

"You went into town?"

"Yes . . . I told you about this last night, remember?" He shrugs his answer. "When I got back, I told Liam about the conversation with her. He showed me the fish tank and supplies."

"See? God answers prayers."

"Humph. The girl in town is the one we should be thanking. I, uh, I tried talking to your God before I left, told him I needed some help. All the good it did. The doctor was gone. I'd think if God wanted to, He could've found me a doc."

"He put the girl there, right?"

"And?"

"And would you have told Liam about the livestock antibiotics if she hadn't told you about them?"

"How could I?"

"Exactly. And he wouldn't have thought to mention the fish antibiotics to you."

I lean back in my chair and cross my arms. "So, you're saying this is God's answer?"

"I don't know. And sometimes God's answer isn't the answer we want. It's highly possible this is it for me. Only God knows. He has already fixed the time of my death."

"And I suppose it was God who took Jessa from you at such a young age? Kept her from meeting her grandson? Took your own child from you?"

"Of course, if it were up to me," Bart says slowly, "I'd have preferred much more time with Jessa and Melissa. Jessa would've loved to fawn over Liam. But even when I lost her, God was right beside me, helping me through it. He promises he'll be there with us when things are rough. He can be there for You, too, Clarice. You just need to ask Him."

"No thanks."

He gives me a grim smile and a nod. "It's your choice, of course. God gives us the freedom of choice. He doesn't beat us with a stick until we submit. I'm going to sleep awhile longer."

With Bart sleeping, I stand up and stretch before stepping out of the room. I'm tired, exhausted even. Liam, who's watching out the window in the living room, asks me how Bart is. After telling him he's about the same, I ask him if he can keep an eye on things while I sleep. After he agrees, I crawl into the other twin bed in the guest room. If Bart needs me, I'll be able to hear him.

Sometime later, I wake to Liam's hand on my shoulder. My eyes dart open as I quickly sit up. "Is something wrong?"

"You were thrashing in your sleep. I heard you from the living room—thought it was Grandpa, but it was you."

I let out a breath. "I must . . . maybe I was dreaming. I don't know."

"You're okay?" His fear-filled eyes search mine. "You're not sick, right?"

"I'm okay. Is Grandpa still sleeping?"

"Not anymore," Bart's low timbre responds. "Our boy's right, you were making a ruckus. Thought about waking you myself."

"Sorry, Bart." I move to a sitting position, then ask Liam, "How long was I asleep?"

Liam twists his wrist to look at Bart's watch. We've been sharing the windup wristwatch, passing it from person to person as we relieve each other from sentry duty. "Not long. An hour or so."

"You ready to swap?"

"Yeah, that's fine. I'm done messing with the bags. They're as good as they're going to get."

"Do you plan to sleep?" I ask as I smooth out the covers.

"In a bit. Since Grandpa's awake, I'll talk with him. Okay, Gramps?"

"Gramps? Since when do you call me that?" Bart asks.

With a cheeky grin, Liam sits on the chair. "I was just trying it out. You look like you feel better."

"Some, yes."

As I leave the room, Liam starts talking about the backpacks and the things he's stuffed them with. It means a lot to him to take the extra things with us to Mollie and Jake's place. As much as I fear Mollie will make me crazy, I'm also excited to get there. When we were on foot, the distance was daunting. Even on the dirt bikes it seemed never ending with the stopping and backtracking, plus the limited amount of time we could ride at once due to the discomfort of the seats.

If we could go back and do it all over again, I'd tell Ben to take the biggest roads possible and not worry about staying out of view. Just drive right through any stalled cars with the big semitruck, pushing things out of the way.

That's my plan. While I won't have the power to push things out of the way with the tiny VW, maybe the size of it will allow me the ability to maneuver around any blocked areas. We'll get Bart well at the FEMA center, then make a beeline for Bakerville. Liam's routes and planning will help, but I truly want to take the easiest way. With

as many things that have gone wrong, our luck must change. I'm sure
of it.

Chapter 24

September 10th

The thermometer is beeping when I return from the kitchen with a fresh glass of water for Bart. His hand is moving to remove it from his mouth.

"I'll get it," I say.

He does a hurry up motion.

"Impatient this morning? You must be feeling better." I frown as I look at the thermometer. "It's down a little from last night—101.8. I guess that's an improvement since you were 102.6 when we started the antibiotics, but I'd hoped we'd see a quicker decrease."

"Too bad I'm not a fish. I'd probably be fully healed by now."

"No kidding. Are you getting hungry? Liam snared a rabbit last night and has it stewing. There's a can of oysters we found in the back of the cabinet you could have while we're waiting for the rabbit."

"Smoked oysters?"

"Yes. What do you think?"

"I could try one or two. Give our boy some, and you eat some too."

"We'll share them," I say with a nod. I hate oysters, but these days it no longer matters. We eat what's available. After those days of near starvation, I'm thankful for anything.

I divide the tin of oysters into thirds, making sure to drizzle the small amount of oil as close to equally as possible over each plate.

Liam, who's pouring over the atlas again, gladly accepts his portion. "How long do you think until the rabbit is ready?" he asks, glancing at Bart's watch.

"Give it a couple of hours at least. The meat should be falling off the bone."

"Okay. How's Grandpa?"

"Ornery. And maybe a little better."

"Do you think we can leave tomorrow?"

"His fever's down a little. If it continues to decrease, he should be up for traveling."

"The FEMA camp should only take a day to get to."

"Yes. He'll probably be well enough tomorrow."

In the bedroom, Bart's staring off into space.

"Here it is," I say. "Upscale cuisine from a tin."

He gives me a small smile. "Did you get enough for you and Liam?"

"Sure. It's fine. The rabbit will be ready in a bit, so think of this as an appetizer."

We eat in silence. I make a point of holding my breath each time I take a bite. It helps—barely. When we're finished, I quickly take the dishes out of the room—which already reeks of oily fish—and give them a rinse. I'll wash them better later when I take the time to heat up water.

Once I'm back in the bedroom and seated, Bart says, "We should come up with a plan."

"A plan for what?"

"How long I should take antibiotics that should be saved in case our boy needs them."

Tears instantly fill my eyes, and I swallow hard. "As long—until you're well . . . or until the doctors at the FEMA camp can treat you properly."

He gives a slight shake of his head. "I've had, what, three doses? Is that right?"

"Yes."

"Doesn't seem to be much change. How many more doses do you have?"

I think in my head. "There's an unopened container with sixty packets. I think there's around twenty remaining in the opened one."

He looks up at the ceiling. "You're giving me three packets a day. Let's finish out today and tomorrow. If the fever isn't gone and my leg's not looking better by the next day, we stop."

"Why would we do that?" I cringe as I remember the look of his leg this morning when I changed the dressing. The dark skin is spreading, and the putrid smell seems to have increased.

"Because at that point, I'd say it's a lost cause. There will be little doubt I have blood poisoning. You need to save the antibiotics in case Liam or you need them. If I would have paid attention— " He gives another shake of his head. "Remember this, Clarice. Any cut or wound is nothing to be trifled with."

"They're already working. Your fever is less than it was. And tomorrow, you should be well enough we can go and get you help."

He gives a slight tilt of his head. "Maybe so. I'm going to rest now. Wake me up when the rabbit's ready?"

While Bart sleeps, I have Liam switch with me. I need to spend some time out of the room, out of the house even. I make sure Liam knows I'll be outside and that I'm going to walk down to the road to see if anything has changed. This morning, as soon as it was light, I went down and swept the road to remove the tire marks. I only went as far as I thought was needed to keep anyone on the pavement from seeing the tracks. I should've done it last night, but with the excitement of finding the antibiotics, it slipped my mind. I really don't think there will be anything to see at the pavement, but it gives me an excuse to get out and about.

It's cooler today than it has been, and the hooded sweatshirt I picked up from Levi's closet feels a little light. I pull up the hood for extra warmth. I choose to walk in the trees instead of down the driveway. It just feels smarter to stay concealed.

I almost laugh at how I'm always so concerned about being seen. There was a time, which feels like years ago—decades even—when I sought out people. The girl from town probably thought I was strange, how I kept calling to her and not letting her leave. I'll admit, even though it was a risk, it felt good to hear another person's voice. On the days I worked at my office in Alto, I'd make a point of popping in on other friends at their offices or having lunch with Mark—that dirty rotten scoundrel. I can't believe I ever found him appealing. I sure wouldn't want to be stuck with him now. I can't imagine he has the wherewithal to make it through the things we've experienced.

I let out a long breath. What a fool I was. My eyes sting as I remember how my marriage was dissolving, the ways I went out of my way to be cruel to Ben. Oh, I know he wasn't always sunshine and roses toward me, but we were both at fault for the difficulties. Now, I'd give almost anything to have more time with my husband, to try and make amends and bring back what we had. There were a few times when we were on the dirt bikes when things started to feel like they used to, when the love seemed to be returning. But he was taken from me.

I miss Ben. I miss people in general. It's just Bart, Liam, and me. When we see others, they are something to fear. I think I'd even enjoy Leanne and her Bible-thumping family. Even Mollie, with her weird ways, will be a treat. At least I still have family and I'm not completely alone. I don't know if I could handle that.

After I reach the road, I carefully step out from the tree line and look up and down it. I'm just about to return to the house when something catches my eye—movement where the road dips and turns. I keep my eyes focused on the spot. After a few seconds, I decide it was either nothing or maybe a bird flitting around. Taking my time, I make my way back to the house.

Other than sitting by Bart's side or keeping watch, there's limited things to do here. At least at Amelia and Levi's house there was the dehydrating to keep me busy. My two little chickens are spending their time in the garage. Maybe I'll bring them outside for some fresh air.

After finding a second jacket in one of the closets, I check in with Liam, telling him I'll be outside with the hens. Isabel was shorter than me but wore the same general size. I've tried a few of her things, and as expected, the pants all fit wrong but the tops work. I add a thick winter sweater under the slightly oversized hoody.

As soon as I step into the garage, Little Brown Hen and Poof Head come running. Liam has set up a nice space for them, having brought in several evergreen boughs to make a bed. We've been feeding them weeds and greens from the forest and the spent garden, along with taking them outside several times a day to find their own nibbles. Liam and I were both disappointed to find there was nothing left of the garden. My guess is, when overwhelmed with the grief of losing their daughter, Isabel and Jeff shut down.

We've also found oatmeal and a few other whole grains for them in the kitchen that we're saving for when we start our trip again. I'm impressed with how tame my chickens are and their ability to stay close, even returning to us when we call them by name. Bart said his mom's chickens would do the same thing. They learned their names and knew when to come running. That may be, but I'm sure my two little chickens are the smartest of the species. Today, I'm going to take them into the garden and let my girls have a feast.

They follow behind me like little dogs, walking in their crazy, almost prehistorical way. I so wish I would've realized the pleasure of chickens sooner; Ben and I could've been raising them at home. While roosters weren't allowed in our new development because of HOA rules, we could've had up to six hens.

I'm halfway toward the garden, at the back side of the parking space, when I hear, "Hey there."

I immediately drop to a knee, fumbling to remove the pistol from the holster on my ankle.

"Whoa, whoa, whoa," the female voice says. "It's me—Destiny. We met yesterday."

With my heart pounding in my ears, I give a nod. I'm still on a knee and have the pistol in hand, but keep it pointed toward the ground. "What are you doing here?" I ask, then narrow my eyes. "Did you follow me?"

She answers with a one-shoulder shrug. "Only to the car. When I saw you driving the Frog, I figured I'd find you here. Where's Isabel and Jeff?"

I shake my head. "Dead."

"Dead? Did you kill them?" she calmly asks, not at all scared.

"Of course not. We . . . uh, we found them. They'd taken their own lives."

She gives a nod. "I heard Ava died. I guess I'm not surprised. Did you . . . did you bury them?" She glances around the area, possibly looking for a fresh grave.

"We found them up the road at a little picnic spot or something. They'd already dug the hole next to where they'd placed their daughter."

She gives a sad smile. "Sounds like them. They were always extremely helpful. How'd you find their house?"

"She left a note and a map."

"Really?" Destiny shakes her head.

I nod. "Why'd you follow me?"

"Oh. Well, at first, I was simply curious why you were in town. And why you didn't ask me for food. You only wanted medicine, but with as skinny as you are . . . you should have asked for food."

I look down at my body. With the layers on my upper half, I don't look that skinny. And I've put on a little weight from the worst of it, even though my legs still look like toothpicks. Yesterday, I was wearing these same pants with the hoody. I guess I can see how she might think I need food. "I needed to find help for my father-in-law. Are you . . . did you come here alone?"

"Yeah. I brought you a few things, stuff my mom had."

"You did? Why would you do that?"

She gives her standard shrug in response. "I couldn't sleep because I was thinking about how . . . you know, how you look." I widen my eyes at her. She hurries on with, "I figured your dad must be in pretty bad shape if you were only concerned about him. So . . . " She lifts her hands. "Here I am."

"Did you . . . what about the others? Do they know?" We need to leave here. Bart's in no shape to travel, but if she's here, then the rest of her town could easily show up.

"I didn't say anything. But I should hurry back. Honestly, I'm kind of surprised my dad or one of the others hasn't made a trip out here at least to check on Jeff and Isabel. So . . . do you want me to look at your dad? Or should I just give you the stuff I brought?"

"Do you have any medical experience?"

"Nope. Not for humans. But I had sheep and rabbits for 4H. It's over an hour to the nearest vet, so we did most of the stuff on our own."

"Your town had a doctor but not a veterinarian?"

"Yeah. Weird, huh? Dr. Jewell was over seventy. He'd retired from actual practice in some city. This was his retirement job. His office was just a room off his house. My mom used to say he was like the old country doc on *Little House on the Prairie*. She was surprised he didn't take chickens in exchange for treatment." She glances at my chickens as she says this.

I hope she isn't hinting she wants one of my girls in exchange for the things she's brought. I quickly think about what I can give her in trade. Nothing. I have nothing to offer except to tell her that as soon as we leave, she can get her people up here to clear out the rest of the goods.

"Before Dr. Jewell showed up, it was just my mom. She used to be a nurse before she switched to natural medicine. She really did help people in exchange for livestock sometimes. So, do you want me to take a look at him?"

I run through the trouble with that in my head. She could be a trojan horse, trying to get in our house and then the rest of her people will attack. But why bother? They could easily attack now. Unless she was sent as an advance scout to determine our numbers. Yeah, that would make sense. Or . . . maybe she's truly just being nice. A few months ago, that would've been the norm. Has society changed so much no one is helpful?

I give her a nod. "Yeah, if you don't mind."

"That's why I'm here."

I bend over to scoop up Little Brown. As I turn for Poof Head, I see Destiny already has her. My eyes go wide as fear overtakes me. Destiny pays no attention and starts walking toward the house.

"Um, the chickens stay in the garage," I say.

At the garage door, I gently set Little Brown down and reach for Poof. Destiny hands her over, then asks, "Will you stay the winter here?"

"No, we'll leave just as soon as my father-in-law can travel. We have friends in Wyoming."

She nods. "You'll take the Frog?" I give her a quizzical look. "The VW Bug. That's what Isabel called it, the Frog."

"The note we found said we could have it," I say defensively.

"That will help you get where you're going, if you can find fuel."

Chapter 25

September 10th

As we reach the door, I say, "We'll need to be quiet. My husband and his friends are all upstairs sleeping." A lie, of course. But if she was sent as a scout, it's best they think there's more of us than just a sick old man, a skinny woman, and a teenage boy.

Inside, I ask, "Have you been here before?"

"Yeah. But not since my mom died. She and Isabel were friends."

"He's in the downstairs bedroom. My son is in with him."

At the bedroom door, I say quietly, "Liam."

"Yeah, Mom?"

"Come out here, please."

At the doorway, he looks over my shoulder. I watch as he visibly stiffens.

"It's okay," I say, touching his arm. "This is Destiny. I met her in town the other day."

"What's she doing here, inside the house?"

"Shh. Keep your voice down. I don't want to wake your dad and the others."

He narrows his eyes as I turn to Destiny. "Night watch, you know?"

She answers with a noncommittal shrug.

"Liam, you go ahead and do your stuff in the living room." My eyes drill into his as I attempt to convey my desire for him to keep watch and keep quiet about Ben, or anyone else, not being here.

He gives me a solemn nod as he leaves the room.

I motion for Destiny to follow me in. As soon as she enters the room, she puts her hand to her nose. Is it that bad? I take a tentative sniff, not noticing anything different.

At Bart's bed, I give his shoulder a gentle shake. "Dad?"

He opens his eyes with a start. "Is something wrong?"

"I, uh . . . this is Destiny. I met her in town."

"The one who told you about the fish medicine?"

I give a nod before turning to her. "We found fish antibiotics. We wouldn't have known to look for them if you wouldn't have mentioned the livestock antibiotics."

"Okay, that's good. Can I see the problem?"

"Bart? She used to have sheep and rabbits. She thought she could maybe help with your leg."

"Ha! Isn't there a TV commercial about that?" he asks, his mustache twitching slightly. "Where a guy sleeps in some hotel and says he can deliver a baby?"

"Infection is infection," Destiny says. "And I already know you have a bad one. I can smell it. My rabbit lost a foot to infection, and it smelled better than yours."

Bart tugs at his beard as he gives her a wry smile. "C'mon in, then. I'm not a rabbit, but I suppose you might as well take a look."

She gives a nod and then walks to the dresser, having already spotted the pitcher of water and plastic tub we keep for washing up. Once her back is turned, Bart makes a motion to me, which I take as him asking, *What's she doing here?*

I give a slight shrug and shake of my head.

He mouths, "Be careful." To Destiny, he says, "Seems kind of strange of you to show this interest. How'd you get out here, anyway?"

"Walked," she answers with a shrug. After cleaning her hands, she squirts them with sanitizer. "This commercial stuff isn't very good for you. I should've thought to bring you some of my mom's sanitizer. Her recipe, anyway. I make it now. Of course, things like this won't be around much longer. Soon, we'll be back to using homemade lye soap."

"My grandma made her own soap," Bart says. "Made her own lye too. That stuff was caustic."

"My mom made soap too. I watched her a few times but have yet to try it on my own. I suppose that'll change at some point."

"Does your dad know how to make it?" I ask.

She gives me a strange look and tears fill her eyes, then a mask seems to fall over her face. "No. He never helped. I'm ready."

I meet Bart's eyes, and he gives a slight nod. As I lift back the blanket, the odor from the wound increases substantially. It's probably no stronger than the last time I looked at it, but with Destiny pointing it out, I'm more attune to it. The gauze wrap is yellow with a tinge of pink. It bleeds slightly but mainly releases pus.

"This skin is dying," Destiny says, pointing at the dark areas above and below the bandage. "Or . . . it's probably already dead. Do you usually cut the gauze off?"

"Yes," I reply, handing her the scissors. "We're running low on it. I think I have enough for one or two more bandages, then I'm going to use a sheet I found in the closet."

"When did you last change this?"

"Earlier, about four hours ago."

She nods as she cuts away the wound covering. As soon as it's clear, she lets out a sigh and looks at Bart. "It's not good."

"Yeah." He nods. "I don't think the antibiotics are cutting it."

"No," she agrees. "I think— " She bites her lip. "I think your leg needs to come off."

I gasp, but Bart gives a solemn nod. "That may have helped a day or two ago. But now, I think it's too late." Bart and Destiny share a look.

"The antibiotics are helping," I say. "His fever has dropped."

Bart gives a slight shake of his head. "Not enough."

"How's the pain," Destiny asks.

"Depends. Sometimes it burns like it's on fire."

"Are you having any trouble breathing?"

"I feel short of breath sometimes, even just laying here."

"I'll check some of my mom's books. Maybe there will be something useful. How often are you taking the antibiotics?" She motions to the jar on the table with the fish on it.

"Three times a day," I answer.

"Strength?"

"Two hundred fifty milligrams per dose."

"Okay, I'll figure out if it's the correct dose. Maybe that'll make a difference. It looks like you've already cleaned it. I can see the edges here, but . . . " She shakes her head. "Like I said, I think the infection has spread up the leg. It's probably systemic by now. I don't think topical treatments will work and probably not either of the oils I brought." She looks at Bart. "You need to be in a hospital on strong antibiotics."

He nods. "Yep. That's about the size of it."

"As soon as he's able to travel, we're taking him to the FEMA camp."

A look of horror crosses her face. "You don't want to go there," she says quietly.

"If your doctor is there, then we most certainly do. Bart needs a doctor. He needs real medicine—not oils and fish antibiotics."

She shakes her head. "It's not a place anyone should go."

"So what do you suggest?" I snap.

"The things I brought, I don't think they'll work. We'd just be wasting them. I'll go home and check my mom's books, see if the fish antibiotics at the right dose might help. I'll try to be back before dark. If I can, is it okay if I stay here tonight?"

"Won't your people have a problem with that?" I ask.

"No." She looks me in the eyes. "Will yours?"

I flare my eyes. She knows. She knows about my subterfuge. "As I said, they'll be on watch, spread out in the woods."

"Of course." She smirks.

"You can stay here," Bart says, waving his hand like he's swatting at a fly. I give him a hard look. "It's okay, Clarice. Don't you think if she meant us harm, it would've already happened?"

I shake my head as Destiny rebandages the leg, then says she'll be back as quickly as she can. After she leaves, I motion for Liam to go back into Bart's bedroom with me.

"Why did you let the emo in here?" Liam asks.

"What's an emo?" Bart asks.

"I'll tell you later." I shake my head. "I don't know why I let her in, but she's probably not a threat."

"*Probably*," Liam repeats. "But she might be."

"That little girl?" Bart asks with a scoff. "She's got good in her."

"What if she was sent here by the others? Mom said they have a small group of people still living in town."

"I thought of that," I say. "And my first instinct was we should leave. But after the way she was with Bart— " I lift my hands in surrender. "I think he's right. We should trust her. And she seems to have more knowledge than the rest of us. Though, I don't agree with her that the fish medicine isn't working."

"She's right about that," Bart says. As I start to argue, he stops me. "Let it go for now, Clarice. Let's see if she has any new information when she returns. How many people did she say are still in her town?"

"She didn't say, just that some of them stayed behind, and the rest went to the FEMA camp."

"Hmm. That's interesting."

"What do you mean, Grandpa?"

"Not sure. Just seems interesting. I'm ready to get some more sleep."

A few hours later, Liam calls out from where he's watching at the living room window. "Mom, here she comes. There's another one with her—another girl."

Rushing to the living room, I put my hand to my forehead. I should have known. It's another girl who looks several years younger than Destiny and not at all Goth—or emo, as Liam said. She's in blue jeans and a puffy pink coat. Both are wearing backpacks and carrying crossbody bags. Not a huge duffle like we have, but more like a large purse.

"You have the rifle?" I ask.

He points to where it's sitting on the coffee table next to him. "I'm not shooting them, Mom—not unless I have to."

"Obviously. I just want you to be ready. She may have brought more than just the one."

"I'll keep watching."

I'm at the door before Destiny reaches the porch. Opening it a crack, I say, "Who's your friend?"

"This is Leslie." Destiny jerks her thumb toward the girl who appears to be around Liam's age. "And this" —she turns so I can see her back— "is Wyatt."

"You have a baby?" The young infant, with a shock of black hair, is sound asleep in the backpack Destiny's wearing.

"Not mine."

I glance at the younger girl, who quickly says, "Not mine either. He belongs to a couple in town."

"Okay . . . so why'd you bring your friends?"

Leslie looks at her feet, but Destiny meets me in the eyes, almost challenging. "Our people have night watch too. So it just made sense for me to bring them along."

"Oh, really?"

"How's your dad? Any disorientation?"

"Disorientation?"

"You know, is he confused?"

"I know the word," I snap. "I'm just not sure what it has to do with his leg."

"May we come in?" Destiny asks.

Instead of stepping out of the way and ushering them inside, I stand steady. "Are your people a threat to us?"

Leslie's eyes dart up as she vigorously shakes her head.

Destiny puts a hand on Leslie's shoulder before saying, "No more of a threat than your people are to us."

I tilt my head and cross my arms. "What's that supposed to mean?"

"Nothing, just that there isn't anything for you to worry about. Other than your dad. I don't have good news."

"My father-in-law," I correct. "Though, I do call him Dad." I step completely outside and pull the door shut. In a low voice, I say, "After you left, he said he thought we should've amputated. He's said it before, then he follows with how it's too late now. And the confusion you asked about, it's happened a few times and seems to be getting worse."

"I think he has septicemia. The fish antibiotics probably aren't enough."

"We'll increase the dosage," I say firmly.

"I don't think it will help. Maybe if we had IV antibiotics and had already removed his leg."

"You read this in your mom's books?" I ask skeptically. "You think you can amputate after reading it in a book?"

"I may not have the training she had, but I know how to read. But no . . . we can't amputate. Spin around, Leslie." As soon as Leslie does, Destiny unzips the backpack and pulls out a large book. "You can read it for yourself if you don't believe me." She thrusts it in my direction. "It's starting to get chilly with the wind. May we come in?"

"Not a word about this," I say, as I lift the book up, "to Liam or Bart. Not until I read it. Then I'll talk to Bart and we'll decide how to proceed."

She nods. "The confusion will get worse. You should talk to him soon. I brought some medicine to keep him comfortable."

"No." I hold up my hand. "No talking like that."

Chapter 26

September 11th

With my eyes shining, I look up and say, "So, that's it. I've read everything about cellulitis, gangrene, and sepsis. Those are the things Destiny thinks we're dealing with. I think she's right, but— " I shrug. "I don't really know. If you're up to it, we need to leave today and find the FEMA camp."

Bart chews on the tip of his mustache before saying, "I don't think cellulitis is an issue now. I think it's gone beyond that. And the FEMA camp, I'm not at all interested in dying in a place like that." I start to object as he raises his hand. "And I'm even less interested in dying on the way there."

"It's not terribly far. We can get there within a day."

He gives a slight chuckle. "I doubt it. No, I'll stay here. It won't be too long now. I'm well into the second phase you mentioned. I'm having the abdominal pain and not going to the bathroom. I haven't urinated since yesterday and don't feel the need to. And there's some confusion, you know."

I give a small nod. It started innocently enough. Liam has been writing down some of the things Bart remembers from his childhood: the foraging and hunting his family used to do to keep from starving to death, the cheap meals his mom relied on, and any other tips. He'll often repeat himself or he'll wake up from sleeping and think Liam was Ben. Or he'll forget we've been on the road for months. He's asked for the light to be turned on several times. Nothing big, just little bits of confusion or loss of memory. But it's happening more often. I never even realized it was an issue until Destiny asked about it last night.

"Won't be long until I go into the shock phase," Bart says. "I like the girl's idea of trying to keep me comfortable. We need to stop with the antibiotics. Save them in case you need them."

"No. We stick with them for now."

He ignores me and says, "After I pass, you and Liam need to take those kids and get to Wyoming."

"Take those kids?" I ask, my tear-filled eyes drilling into him.

"They're all alone. She's been doing a good job caring for them, but they can't stay here. Take them with you to Mollie. She'll be happy to take them in too."

I shake my head. The confusion's returned. "They have their own families. They'll probably be going home shortly."

"How about you read to me for a bit?" Bart asks, changing the subject.

I clear my throat. "Sure." I put my wrist to my eye to stop the tears. I've been crying all night, since I read the chapter on gangrene and sepsis. I knew before then, but reading about it made it all clear. Bart's right. Keeping him comfortable in this bed is best for him. I hate it. I hate all of it. Losing my husband and now my father-in-law, who has been a dad to me for over twenty years, is heartbreaking. I reach for the fiction book on the TV tray.

"From the Bible," Bart says.

I close my eyes. "Okay, if that's what you want."

I open his Bible to the first page and read the inscription. *"To my beloved. You make my soul sing. You put a sparkle on everything. You fill my world with joy. I thank God for giving you to me. All my love, Jessa."*

The slight corniness of it causes me to smile. Jessa was exceedingly kind, a friend to everyone. She was also very quirky. She'd say and do things which were, to me, strange. Bart, who has his own weird ways, would often drive her crazy. The buying of the handguns was one thing, buying more shop tools also. Money was often a point of contention between them, but her love for him—even when she was chastising him—was always evident. As was her love for Ben, and even me too. She would've adored Liam.

"How about reading from the Gospel of John?" Bart says, interrupting my reminiscing. "It's in the second half of the Bible—the New Testament. It's a little more than halfway. Open it up and tell me where you are." Bart's had me read from the Bible a couple of times since we've been here. Even so, I'm terribly unfamiliar with it, so he has to give me guidance on where to find what it is he'd like me to read.

I try and gauge a little more than halfway through. "Jonah is on one side, Micah on the other," I say.

"Still Old Testament. Jonah's a good one. You should read it sometime. It's about a guy who's running from God and ends up in a whale."

"Yeah, sounds lovely," I say with a smirk.

Bart ignores my snark. "It's a good one. You're almost there. Flip through a few pages at a time until you see a page saying The New Testament or the book of Matthew."

"Okay, here it is."

"John is the fourth book in The New Testament, so keep going. Matthew, Mark, Luke and then the Gospel of John. Chapter 3 is where I'd like you to read."

Bart has settled back on his bed and now has his eyes closed. It takes me just a minute to find what he wants. I start reading about a pharisee named Nicodemus who is talking with Jesus. Jesus is telling the man about being born again. "The wind blows wherever it pleases. You hear its sound, but you cannot tell where it comes from or where it is going. So, it is with everyone born of the Spirit."

"That's an important part," Bart says, interrupting my reading.

"Oh?"

"Yes, we can't really see the wind, or predict everything about it. Just like the Spirit and His work isn't something we can completely understand. He's at work now, here in this room."

I give a slight shake of my head and then continue reading.

Shortly after, Bart interrupts again. "Read it again."

"Which part?"

"Start with, 'No one has gone to heaven,' then continue to where you are now."

I find the spot he wants. "No one has ever gone into heaven except the one who came from heaven—the Son of Man. Just as Moses lifted up the snake in the wilderness, so the Son of Man must be lifted up, that everyone who believes may have eternal life in Him."

"That's what Jesus would call himself—the Son of Man," Bart says. "It was one way He claimed He was the Messiah and would save the world. Now the next verse—you have to read it very slowly. It's one of the most important verses in the Bible."

I stifle a sigh and an eye roll. "For God so loved the world that He gave His one and only Son, that whoever believes in Him shall not perish but have eternal life. For God did not send His Son into the world to condemn the world, but to save the world through Him."

"You know this part, right?"

"Sure, Bart." Of course I've heard these verses before. The preacher who was trying to convert my mom said them. Even my mom would talk about it.

"I know you get hung up on thinking your dad didn't go to heaven."

"No," I say tersely. "I don't get hung up on that at all. I think it is . . . it's asinine to even consider my dad wouldn't be ushered into heaven—provided there even *is* a heaven. Heaven would be lucky to have a man like him. But instead, you Christians say since he didn't . . . didn't what? Since he didn't believe in God, he's perished? And according to you, perished means he's gone to hell, right?"

"Do you know he didn't believe?" Bart's no longer lying with his eyes closed but rather looking directly at me, his eyes boring into mine.

"I know my dad believed in things he could prove. He was a science teacher. He dealt with facts not fiction. And your thing before about the wind, they know a lot about the wind."

"That's true. But they don't know everything about it. I deal in facts too. As a machinist, we have tolerances and must be exact. We can't guess or estimate our math if we want to make our tolerances. I like facts and figures. I also know there's enough facts for me to believe Jesus was sent to earth to save us from ourselves. To save me. To save you and Liam. Did your dad choose to ignore these facts?" He gives a shrug. "I don't know. I wasn't with him when he passed. Neither were you. Do you know what his final thoughts were? Ben told me your mom said he'd made friends with a local pastor, right?"

"They were friendly, but I don't know if they were friends. He'd still . . . " I bite my lip. "He'd sometimes make fun of the things the pastor would say. Not in a mean way, but—well, he thought some of it was odd."

"Sure." Bart shrugs. "But you don't know if the things they'd spoken of may have got your dad thinking, may have had him considering things. Let's get back to reading. I want you to read something from the gospel of Luke."

"Bart," I say with considerable patience, "I'm happy to read to you, but I'm not interested in a sermon."

"Humor me," he says, twitching his mustache.

"Where's Luke?" I ask through gritted teeth.

"Right before John. I can't remember the exact chapter. It's toward the end of the book, during Jesus' crucifixion. My Bible has headings, so you should be able to find it."

Shaking my head, I turn back several pages. Seeing the heading *Jesus Arrested*, I scan down the page and over to the next until I find *The Crucifixion*. "Okay. I found the section."

"Go ahead. Start reading."

I read about how Jesus was led away and how the women followed and wailed. How He told them not to weep for Him, but for themselves and their children. Some of the stuff I'm reading doesn't even make much sense, but I keep going until I get to the part of Jesus and two criminals being crucified.

"Okay, this is the part," Bart says. "Jesus is going to say, 'Forgive them, Father, for they don't know what they are doing.'"

"Something like that," I say, then read the actual passage. "Do you want me to stop now?"

"Oh, no. Not yet."

As I read, a picture is painted of the horrific scene. People were watching and cheering for his death. They were mocking and teasing. They were celebrating his crucifixion. I feel tears brimming my eyes as I imagine the lack of humanity. "One of the criminals who hung there hurled insults at him: 'Aren't you the Messiah? Save yourself and us.' But the other criminal rebuked him— "

"Now we're getting to the good part," Bart says, his eyes shining. "This is important, Clarice. I want you to not only read it, but to hear it."

I give a nod before continuing, "'Don't you fear God,' he said, 'since you are under the same sentence? We are punished justly, for we are getting what our deeds deserve. But this man has done nothing wrong.' Then he said, 'Jesus, remember me when you come into your kingdom.' Jesus answered him, 'Truly I tell you, today you will be with Me in paradise.'"

"See?" Bart says excitedly.

I shake my head. "I'm not sure what I'm supposed to see."

"The thief. He didn't know the Christ. But hanging there, he called out to Him. And Jesus responded by saying you'll be with Me in paradise—in the kingdom of God."

"Okay . . . and this is important because?"

"Because of your dad. How do you know he wasn't like the thief? How do you know he didn't call out to Jesus in his final days—in his final moments. How do you know the things he and his pastor friend were talking about weren't working on his heart? How do you know he didn't believe Jesus was his Lord and Savior? You hold this . . . this grudge against Christians, believing we have sentenced your father to hell for eternity. But you fail to remember God gives each of us free will. We each have a choice to follow Jesus or not. And you may think you know what your dad's choice was, but you don't. Not really. And you hold a grudge against your mom because you think she made a choice your dad wouldn't have agreed with. When she accepted Christ before her death, you think she was unfaithful to her spouse."

"That's not true! I don't know for certain what she did. I just suspect it. And I think . . . I think she was weak. When faced with death, she looked to some fairytale savior."

"Or she looked at the facts presented to her and made a choice using those facts."

I take a deep breath. "I don't want to read any more of this rubbish. You can think whatever you want, Bart. But you don't get to try and strongarm me into following your fantasy."

"Free will, Clarice. I can't strongarm you into anything. You'll either come to Christ freely, on your own, or you won't. But one thing I do know: there's never any guarantees. There never was before, but in this new world . . . " He gives a shrug. "Life is fleeting. If your mom did accept Christ before she died, she's basking in the glory of heaven. Your dad may be there too."

"So now you're blackmailing me? Unless I accept Christ, I'll never see them again? I suppose Ben is there too?"

"I'm not blackmailing you. I'm stating a fact. There's one way to get to heaven, and that's by accepting Christ. But Ben—no, he'll be waiting for you in Wyoming when you get there."

I shake my head. "That's another fairytale you choose to believe. Ben's dead."

He returns my headshake with one of his own. "Think on what we've talked about, Clarice. Soon, I'll be with my beloved Jessa again, and I won't be here to share these truths with you, the truth of Jesus— how He is your Savior."

I slam the Bible onto the TV tray and stand up so quickly the chair topples over. I don't even bother to right it before storming out of the room.

Chapter 27

September 12th

Destiny, Leslie, and Wyatt are still here. Yesterday morning, when my "husband" and the rest of our supposed group didn't return from night watch, it was not addressed. I had a plan to tell her they were already in the master bedroom sleeping since she and her group took over Ava's room for the night, had they asked. They didn't. As the day went on and both of them took turns sitting with Bart, it became apparent they had no desire to go back to town.

I'm glad they took turns with Bart, allowing me to avoid my own turn. Instead, I played with baby Wyatt and spent time with my chickens, purposely avoiding thinking about the reading, the conversation, or Bart's dying.

Wyatt is around five months old. The girls don't know his exact date of birth, but he's at the age where he's smiling and trying to laugh. Like me, he loves watching the chickens. When Liam told Leslie we had baby formula, her eyes lit up and she asked if we could spare some for Wyatt. He greedily sucked down the small bottle she made. When I asked Leslie if his parents would be missing him, she gave a shake of her head followed by a shrug, saying, "You should talk to Destiny."

I corner Destiny when she's leaving Bart's room. She lifts a finger to her lips and ushers me down the hallway toward the half bath. Once we're safely away, she says, "His confusion is increasing, and so is his discomfort. The herbs aren't helping much for pain. I'll need to switch to the narcotics. I know you wanted to continue with the antibiotics, but at this point, you're just throwing them away."

"Bart and I agreed we'd continue them through today, then . . . then he wants to stop."

"Your choice, of course. But one more dose isn't going to help him, where it might make a difference if your son were to get sick."

"I'm sticking with the plan."

She gives me a solemn nod. "It's hard to let go."

I bite my lip, attempting to keep the tears at bay. "It's . . . it's not fair," I say quietly as the tears run down my face.

"No. It doesn't seem fair, not at all. You should go in and sit with him. He should be with people who love him. That's the best gift you can give him now."

I stay with Bart and keep watch from the bedroom while Liam sleeps. Instead of waking him at 2:00 am for his watch shift, as we agreed, I stay up the entire night. Bart's in and out. Sometimes, he's completely lucid and himself; other times, he's riddled with confusion.

As the sun rises on a new day, Bart turns to me and says, "No more fish pills. Liam or the baby might need them."

I slide into the chair next to him, reaching for his hand. "You're sure?"

"Yeah. They're not doing any good. I can feel myself fading away."

I pull his hand close to me, leaning into it as I cry.

"It's okay, Melissa. Don't cry, baby girl," he says. "Daddy's here."

His confusion and calling me Melissa causes me to cry harder. "I'm sorry, Bart. I'm so sorry we couldn't help you."

"The wallet—it has photos you might want. There's some money, but we know it's no good now. Maybe someday it'll be useful. Tell Ben, when you see him, tell him how proud I've always been."

Unable to speak, I give a nod.

After many minutes, Bart's asleep again. A noise at the door causes me to look up.

"Do you want me to sit with him so you can get some sleep?" Destiny asks me.

"Why are you here. Why did you bring Leslie and Wyatt here?"

"I wanted to bring you the information and the medicine to help with your dad's passing."

"He's my father-in-law. My husband's dad, not mine."

"Yes, but you love him like he's yours. And he loves you. He told me about Melissa and Jessa yesterday. He told me how Melissa would be a lot like you. Strong yet loving. He says sometimes you get too strong and come off wrong. But he knows your heart. He said you don't want to go to Wyoming, but you know it's best for Liam."

I answer with a nod. "There's no longer a time for caring about what I want or don't want. I know that now. But you didn't answer my question. Why are you here? And how is it your people are okay with you being here—being with strangers?"

"I think you know," she says quietly. "Just like I know your husband isn't sleeping upstairs during the daytime and watching in the woods at night."

"Your dad left you to go to the FEMA camp?"

"Of course not," she says, her face aghast. "They killed my dad—Leslie's and Wyatt's parents too—so they could take our vehicles."

"What?" I say in a gasp. "Why would they do that?"

She moves from the door to the second bed, sitting on the edge. "There was a community meeting. Someone had come through town and told us about the camp. Most of the town wanted to go. With the small convenience store emptied of food, everyone was scared. A few people were killing elk and deer, but many thought it wouldn't be enough. Dr. Jewell said we could make it through the winter on wild game and, if we grew gardens in the spring, we'd probably be okay. But the FEMA camp was a huge draw. So it was decided anyone who wanted to go would, and those who wanted to stay could stay."

"Okay. Sounds reasonable."

"Seemed like it would be. Until someone pointed out the need for running vehicles. There were a few—you know how small-town folks tend to hold on to things, so there's old cars and trucks city folk would never be caught dead driving. My dad had a pickup. Leslie's parents had a Ford Pinto—that thing was awful. Wyatt's parents had a beautiful 1966 Mustang. We were among the group of a dozen families who decided not to go. A lady, who used to be friends with my mom, said they should be forced to give up their cars for the good of the community. It got ugly after that. Wyatt's parents were killed first. We don't know who did it. They took the baby to Dr. Jewell's place, leaving him on the doorstep. My dad was shot but not killed—long range when he was outside of our house. Those cowards."

She pauses to make sure I'm following along. I give a nod, which she returns before saying, "Like Bart, he suffered for days. Dr. Jewell gave me the medicine to help relieve his pain. What I had left is what I've brought for Bart."

I feel my mouth hanging open and my head shaking. "You don't know who did it? There was no justice for killing Wyatt's parents and your dad?"

"None." She says with a shake of her head. She continues in a monotone voice, "Dr. Jewell came over one day with the baby and Leslie. She was a mess. Her parents were missing. My dad was in his final hours of life when Dr. Jewell made me take Leslie and Wyatt and go into hiding. I said my goodbyes, gathered up some clothes and things of my mom's that I didn't want to lose, and we left. We stayed in the woods in an old cabin. After several days, I snuck back into town. The town was empty. My dad was still in his bed—dead. All the families that planned to stay were dead—murdered. I found Leslie's folks too. They'd been tied up before being executed. Our neighbors did it."

I stare at her for many moments before saying, "I'm so sorry, Destiny."

"Yeah. Before they left, they cleaned out the town, taking things of value—or what they thought would have value. It was good they left my mom's books. I guess they figured since they had Dr. Jewell, an actual physician, they didn't need books and garbage from a former nurse and naturopath. So that's why we're here. We don't have any reason to stay in town. I'm kicking myself for not thinking of coming out here before seeing you in town. And I can't believe no one remembered the Frog or the business Jeff had. That's kind of a miracle."

"I guess it is," I say, nodding. "We'll leave what we can for you. There are some things we want to take along as a—I don't know the right thing to say, but to give to the people who will house us. We don't want to show up empty handed."

She furrows her brow. "I was hoping maybe you could at least take Wyatt with you. Leslie too. I can't . . . " She shakes her head. "I can't take care of them." She drops her eyes to the floor.

"Did you tell Bart about this?" I ask quietly. Many of the things he said now make sense.

"No, but he seemed to know. He told me we were smart to come here."

I leave the room, making my way to the living room where Liam is sitting on the couch, where he's started sleeping each night. "Hey, you're awake," I say, plopping down next to him.

"Yeah. I was going into Grandpa's room when I heard you and Destiny talking. They need to come with us."

"No, Liam," I say quietly.

"We can't leave them here. She's right—she can't take care of them. How would they get food?"

"We'll leave things for them. There's water here. They'll be fine."

"You can't be serious, Mom. They won't be fine."

"My responsibility is to you and you alone," I say in a low voice. "Do you not remember we were starving just a few short weeks ago? You could've died."

"They've lost everyone, Mom. And if we don't take them with us, they *will* die. Either we all go or . . . or I stay here with them."

"Fine. Then we spend the winter here. That works for me." I jump to my feet. "I'd much rather be here than go to Mollie Caldwell's house begging for a handout."

Open mouthed, he shakes his head and quickly averts his eyes. I stomp up the stairs to the master bedroom. I spend several minutes pacing the room, having a complete conversation with myself before I start getting ready for bed. After days of limited sleep and being up all night, I'm physically exhausted. I change into sweatpants and a T-shirt belonging to Isabel. The sweats are too short, but at least they aren't the awful elastic-around-the-ankle kind, so they're comfortable. I cinch in the waist using the drawstring so they don't fall off.

My hair—which I've been able to spend a little more time on here, thanks to a wide selection of haircare products in the bathroom—is no longer a rat's nest. I've been wearing it in braids to keep it tame. I take them out and give it a good brushing. I should re-braid it before I rest but decide to leave it loose.

I flip and flop in the bed, trying to get comfortable. I was cruel to Liam. What kind of mom talks like that to her son? Especially when her son was being kind and loving. Especially when her son is right. Destiny and the others can't stay here for the winter for the same reasons we can't stay here—or couldn't stay at Levi and Amelia's or even in our own home. It's too dangerous. Even with the addition of Destiny and Leslie to help keep watch, we can't do it. With losing Bart . . . I heave out a sigh.

Bart's been the one keeping us going. Not only has he been more devoted to night watch, but he's also the only one of us who can accurately shoot. If it would've been me shooting at those guys when Liam fell and hurt his ankle, I'm not sure it would've ended well for us. I'm not sure I could've kept Liam safe. How can I protect three more people?

And Bart knows things. The memories and knowledge from his childhood kept us from fully starving. Liam can do the traps and snares. He's taken them over while we've been here, and in addition to rabbits, he's caught squirrels and birds too. But foraging for the different berries was all Bart. Even though Liam has been writing down the things Bart shares about his childhood, it's not enough. No. Without Bart, I'm not sure even Liam and I can make it to Mollie's. No way we can take three more. Maybe we should go to the FEMA camp. I could leave them there; someone would take care of them.

At some point, I must have faded off. I wake slightly confused to my name being said—not Clarice, but Mom. "Mm-hmm," I say, turning toward the door.

"Mom," Liam has his head poking into the room. "Grandpa's asking for you. Destiny says . . . she thinks he's . . . " He scrunches up his face and shakes his head. He's crying.

"I'll be right there."

He gives me a nod and closes the door. I pile my hair on top of my head and secure it with a large tie. I close my eyes and suck in a deep breath. "Not yet," I say aloud. "I'm not ready to lose Bart. I need to tell him I'm sorry about storming out. Even though I may not believe the same as he does, I shouldn't have reacted the way I did."

Are you sure you don't believe?

I swivel my head toward the door. It's closed. My heart is pounding as I look for the voice. I give a small, nervous laugh and shake my head. It's nothing. My imagination. A shiver runs through my body. It sounded real.

Downstairs, Liam is in the chair by Bart's bed. A second chair has been brought in from the kitchen. I slide into it, reaching for Liam's hand. He's holding onto Bart, who is sleeping. His breathing sounds labored and irregular. I give Liam's hand a squeeze.

"He wakes up for short times, but he's more confused. We were talking earlier, and he wasn't too bad. But now . . . " Liam shakes his head.

"Has Destiny given him the painkillers?"

"He wouldn't take any, said he isn't in pain and we should keep it in case we need it. He did take more acetaminophen, though. But even with it, his fever has increased."

I give a nod. The acetaminophen hasn't helped with the fever much at all. The fish drugs were bringing it down slightly, but since we've stopped those, I expected it to increase.

Bart's eyes shoot open and he turns his head to look at us. "You have to keep going," he says. "Staying here isn't an option. Don't get any hairbrained ideas about the camp either. What those town people did—you don't want to be around them. Stick with the plan. Ben will be at Mollie's." He closes his eyes and lets out a loud, raspy breath.

Chapter 28

September 14th

"Let me take over for a little while."

"No, Mom. I want to do this for Grandpa. You can . . . you can make sure he's ready." Liam quickly drops his eyes and clears his throat.

Bart was a huge part of Liam's life. With the bond they had, I can see why my son wants to do this last thing for his grandpa. Digging his grave is his final show of respect and love.

"All right, Liam. Rest as often as you need to, and keep drinking water. I'll take care of everything else."

Back inside Isabel and Jeff's house, I find a sheet in the linen closet. I know I saw a spool of thread and a few needles somewhere when we first arrived and were poking around. Rummaging through a drawer in the master bedroom, I find the sewing supplies. As I'm walking down the stairs, I realize the best thing to do is to wrap the fitted sheet that's already underneath Bart around him and then stitch it closed. Liam will have to help me move him from the room to the grave. I wish Ben were here.

"Can I help you?" Leslie asks. "I know how to sew."

I give her a tight smile. "Thanks, but I want to do it."

She gives a nod. "Does Liam need help?"

"He's determined— " I close my eyes and give a small shake of my head.

"I understand," Leslie says. "Destiny thinks it's going to snow today."

"Really? It's already warm outside, warmer than it's been in days. I can't imagine it'll snow."

"The clouds look like snow. And sometimes it does that. It's warm in the morning and then the temperature plummets."

"It's only September."

She answers with a shrug. "Let me know if you need help. And then, when it's time, we'd like to be with you."

While getting Bart's body ready, I go through his wallet, the well-worn leather smooth from years of use. There's several hundred dollars in various denominations in the main section, his driver's license and a few credit cards, then a plastic photo holder—the old kind that lets the pictures flop out. I spend many minutes looking at each one. There's a very old photo from his and Jessa's wedding, along with a picture of the two of them holding a baby. Since the baby is in a dress, it must be Melissa rather than Ben. The three of them look so happy.

There's a later picture of them with Ben. While they still look happy, there's a sadness in Jessa's eyes that isn't there in the other picture. I find a school photo of Ben—he must be eight or nine and has the worst haircut ever, something resembling a bowl cut, but the back of his hair is standing up. I can't help but laugh and wonder why Bart kept this picture in his wallet. Then there's a wedding picture of me and Ben and a second one of us that includes Bart and Jessa. One of Liam's baby pictures is next, along with several of his school photos. There's a photograph of the three of them—Bart, Ben, and Liam when he was ten—that I took with my digital camera. Bart liked it so much he asked if I'd make a print for him.

Because he wanted wallet sized, I couldn't just get a single print because it came four to a sheet. I gave him the one and shoved the other three in a drawer at home. I'm fairly certain that was the last time I developed a physical print; all the rest of our photos are digital. Will we ever have access to them again? I pull the wallet close to my chest. This is all we have left of Ben and Bart.

After completing Bart's burial shroud, I go outside to check on Liam. Seeing me, he says, "Just finishing up. Do you think it's deep enough?"

Standing in the grave, only his nose and above is showing. Sprouting up over the last year, my son is now taller than my five-foot-ten and just shorter than his dad's height of six-one. "It's good," I say. "I have your grandpa ready."

"There's a short ladder in the garage. Can you grab it for me so I can get out? I didn't think of getting out until I couldn't."

While I'm retrieving the ladder, I also grab the utility cart to help move Bart to his final resting place. He died right at daylight this morning, with Liam and me each holding a hand. Yesterday he was barely lucid, but this morning when he woke up, his eyes were bright. He looked at Liam and gave him a smile that broke my heart. He turned to me and said, "Won't be long now. Can you open the curtains so I can see the new day?"

Destiny was quick to take care of that for him. He gave her a nod and said, "You're an asset. I'm glad Clarice will have help." He then turned to Liam, saying, "I want you to have my Bible. It was the last gift your grandma gave me, and I know she'd want you to have it. My watch, too, of course." He tapped the wristwatch Liam has taken to wearing. Liam answered with a nod.

"Clarice," Bart said, his voice catching. He put his hand to his heart before moving it to his mouth and kissing his fingers, then sent them in my direction. He turned his head toward the window. He was smiling when he died. The last few days he'd talked about seeing Jessa and Melissa again. I hope he got his wish.

Moving Bart isn't easy. He's tall, like his son and grandson, but has lost considerable weight in the time since we've left our homes. His death was about six hours ago, and he's started to stiffen. I wish again that Ben were here, not only to help us but to be able to say goodbye to his dad. Of course, Ben is also dead. And if there *is* an afterlife, he and his dad are once again together.

Destiny helps Liam and me get Bart into the grave. Leslie, holding Wyatt, is also there. Once he's positioned, Liam says, "Let me go get Grandpa's Bible. He told me what I should read."

Liam returns after a couple of minutes. "Grandpa said we should remember that, even though we're sad he died, he's happy and with my grandma and Aunt Melissa. He had me bookmark this verse so I could find it."

Liam clears his throat before starting. "There is a time for everything, and a season for every activity under the heavens: a time to be born and a time to die, a time to plant and a time to uproot, a time to kill and a time to heal, a time to tear down and a time to build, a time to weep and a time to laugh, a time to mourn and a time to dance."

He looks at me and says, "Grandpa is dancing. You know how he always talked about taking Grandma dancing. He said he thinks in heaven they are surrounded by happiness and laughter. There's no weeping or mourning. They'll dance for Jesus and bask in His glory. I think it sounds pretty amazing."

Tears stream down my face as I give a nod. I do hope Bart is right, that he is with Jessa and Melissa again and they're all healthy and whole.

"I've made a decision," Liam says, his voice increasing an octave on the final word. "Like Grandpa, I've chosen to accept Jesus as my Lord and Savior. Someday, I'll also join them in heaven."

I close my eyes at his pronouncement. Biting my lip, I give a nod.

"Amen," Leslie says.

"Does anyone else want to say anything?" Liam asks. "Mom?"

I shake my head and wipe my eyes. "I don't have much to say other than, thank you, Bart. Thank you for getting us this far. Thank you for keeping Liam and I safe more than once. I don't— " My voice squeaks as I try and talk through my tears. "I don't know how we'll make it without you, but we will. I will get Liam," I say as I take a deep breath and meet Destiny's eyes, "and the others to Wyoming."

Destiny gives me a solemn nod before mouthing, "Thank you."

Covering Bart with the dirt takes only a short while. This time, Liam allows Leslie and I to help while Destiny holds Wyatt. After we're finished, a shiver runs through me. I'm slightly damp from sweat, and the wind has picked up. There's a definite chill in the air. I turn to Destiny. "Leslie said you think it might snow?"

"I do," she says, cuddling Wyatt closer and kissing the top of his head.

"It's only September."

"Right. Late September."

"Late September?" I look to Liam.

"Um, we kind of lost track of time," he says to Destiny. "We think it's September 14th."

Destiny looks to Leslie, who shakes her head before saying, "It's the twenty-third. I have a small calendar in my pack so I can keep track."

I give a nod. "Liam, can you make sure to update our calendar? That means your birthday is the day after tomorrow."

He shakes his head.

I give him a small smile. "Almost fourteen."

The revelation of his birthday being so soon does little to affect him. I understand. It's not like we'll be having a party or doing anything overly special.

With a nod, he says, "I'll change the calendar. And Grandpa's Bible has a place to record his date of death. Grandma and Melissa are already in there. I'll put the correct date in for him."

We're eating lunch, rabbit stew, when it starts to snow. With a shake of his head and a small smile, Liam says, "I guess you were right, Destiny. How long do you think it'll keep snowing?"

"Today at least. Maybe overnight. I, uh . . . I'll need to go into town once it stops."

"Are there things you want to bring along?"

"If we have room. But I need to— " She looks at Leslie, then quietly says, "We weren't able to bury them. I moved everyone to a small house on the edge of town. With the snow, I think it will be safe to— " She clears her throat. "We need to burn the house."

Leslie has tears running down her cheeks as she says, "I want to go with you."

"I know." Destiny nods. "If it stops snowing overnight, we can take care of it first thing in the morning."

"How will you get it to burn?" Liam asks.

"Liam!" I say with a gasp.

"Well?" he answers. "With the snow, won't it be harder?"

"It's true," Destiny says. "We've already filled the inside of the house with dry twigs and wood, plus some furniture and clothing that seemed flammable. And we found a partial jug of kerosene, several containers of lighter fluid for grilling, and a couple partial bottles of rancid oil. I'll light it with road flares."

Liam nods. "That sounds like a solid plan."

"Maybe," Destiny answers. "We just want to do what we can for them. It's not right how they were just left."

As she says it, I realize my thoughts of dumping them off at the FEMA camp were very wrong. For her town to do what they did, there's no way I could put them through seeing any of them again. "Is there anything here that will help with your plan?"

"Not that I can think of. I know Jeff has the gas cans in the shed with the lawnmower, but we'll need them for the car."

I nod. "I've already emptied those into the Bug. We'll need to take the empties for finding fuel along the way."

"How difficult will it be?" Destiny asks.

"Easy," Liam says quickly. "We used to have dirt bikes and were able to keep them going. Just punch a hole in the gas tank of an abandoned car, and there you go."

"It might not be as easy now," I say, trying to keep any worry out of my voice. "It's been several months. Others may have started doing the same thing. We'll just have to see."

"Do you think we'll be walking again?" he asks me with wide eyes.

"I think there's a chance. Let's spend the afternoon figuring out the backpacks. We already had one packed for Bart. Let's check it and make sure it'll work for either Destiny or Leslie. And make sure they can carry both yours and mine. We'll take turns carrying Wyatt along with the duffle bag. Everyone else will carry a backpack."

Liam shakes his head. "I sure hope we don't have to walk again. No . . . no that's not right. I *pray* we don't have to walk again."

Chapter 29

September 24th

Even though it's later in September than Liam and I thought, it still seems much too early for snow. Especially almost twenty-four hours of snow. Big, fat flakes keep falling. It'll stop for a while and I'll think it's over, then it starts up again.

Finally, the sun comes out and Destiny declares the snow is finished. I nervously offer to drive Destiny and Leslie into town. With the snow on the ground, I'm not entirely convinced the little Bug will even make it out of the driveway.

"It probably won't be too bad once we reach the pavement," Destiny says. "The ground underneath might still be warm enough the snow didn't stick."

"You think?" I ask.

With a shrug, she says, "I'll walk down and check if you want. Also, they have good tires on the Frog. That'll help."

Destiny walks down to the road and returns shortly after, saying there's still a skiff of snow, but it's already starting to melt off the blacktop. With a nervous sigh, I agree we'll give it a go. Reluctantly, Liam stays with Wyatt. He tries to make a good argument for going along, but him keeping Wyatt while I attempt to navigate the roads is helpful to me. Destiny was right; once we get out of the yard and down the gravel driveway, there aren't any real issues.

The house they chose to use as their funeral pyre is well away from other homes and even has the vegetation cleared around it. "Did you do this?" I ask, motioning to the snow-covered yard.

Destiny nods. "We wanted to make sure the fire wouldn't spread. They didn't have any trees, just a few shrubs, so it was fairly easy. We added those to the inside of the house as part of the tinder. It's been a while, so it should all be dried out by now."

While Destiny is very matter of fact about the situation, Leslie has a much more difficult time. She is tearful and staring at the ground.

"Are you ready?" Destiny asks.

Leslie gives a small shrug. "I wish we could've buried them."

"I know. But there were too many. You saw how long it took Liam to dig Bart's grave. We'd still be digging."

"How many?" I ask quietly.

"Thirty-five."

I close my eyes. "I'm so sorry. I can't even—I'm sorry."

"So, you're ready?" Destiny asks Leslie again. "Do you want to say anything?"

Leslie starts to shake her head, then stops. "I like what Liam read for Bart. A season for everything. My parents liked to dance, and they loved being together. And I know they're happy I'm okay. I was with my friend when they went missing. I just wish—I wish when Dr. Jewell brought Wyatt and me to Destiny and told us to hide that we could've also got my friend and her little brother. Instead, they're here, too, along with their parents." She stops speaking as her tears overcome her. Destiny, who already has an arm around Leslie's shoulder, pulls her close.

I swallow hard. The thirty-five dead included children. I should've realized it, but I assumed since Wyatt had been spared, so would other children. What happened in this town to make them turn on each other in such a way they would murder children?

"Goodbye, Dad," Destiny says, her voice strong and clear. "I know you're with Mom and your friends you lost when you were in the service. Thanks for teaching me things. I know sometimes I thought it was stupid, but now I'll be able to help Clarice and the people we are going to stay with."

I wonder about the things her dad taught her. Will they help us reach Wyoming? Now, of course, is not the time to ask.

After a couple minutes of silence, Destiny asks Leslie if she wants to say anything else.

With a shake of her head, Leslie says, "I can't do the fire part."

"It's okay. Clarice, can you help me?"

I have a knot in my stomach as I agree I will.

"Okay, let me get the kerosene and stuff spread around."

"Did you want me to do it?" I ask.

"No," she answers harshly. She clears her throat and, in a much kinder voice, says, "Thank you, but this is something I must do on my own."

"Where is it? Can I help you carry it?"

"Inside the house. I figured, with the smell, no one would be going in there messing with things—you know, if someone happened upon our town."

She gives Leslie another squeeze before slipping away and going inside. Even from several feet away, the smell is intense when she opens the door. She moves to the front window, opening it a few inches. After a moment, she's at another window to the right of the door. It's several minutes before she returns. "The brush looks really dry. I think it should flame up well." She hands me three road flares, keeping three for herself. "I'll go around the back. Do you want to do the front? Toss one in the door and the two open windows. I'll toss one in the backdoor and a window on each end of the house. I wish we had a couple more, but this should do."

Not waiting for me to respond, she walks around the house, her boots crunching through the snow. As she leaves, Leslie says, "I'll take one—the one for the back room." She points to the small window to the right of the door. "My mom and dad are in this bedroom. I didn't help move them, Destiny did it all, but she told me where she put them."

"Do you know how to light the flare?" I ask.

She nods as I hand it to her, and she quickly moves to the window. I step to the front door, watching as she lights her flare. She mouths something that may be *I love you* and chucks it in. I fire up the door flare, toss it inside, then move to the living room window. As soon as it's in, I turn to see Destiny standing with Leslie several yards from the house, their arms around each other. I join them as the flames become visible in the back bedroom.

"Let's step back a little farther," I say.

It's only a few minutes until the house is fully engulfed. Even though we're well dressed for the cold and the fire is beginning to put off its own heat, I find myself shivering. There's a new, terrible smell filling the air. I pull the scarf wrapped around my neck up to cover my mouth and nose. I should have thought about this and brought the vapor rub for under our noses.

When it's obvious the fire will do its job, Destiny turns to me and says, "Should we grab the things Leslie and I have salvaged? We can take it all and decide what will fit in the car for the trip."

She directs me to her house. As we load the car, I'm shocked at the items they'd found. "The houses were pretty much emptied out," Leslie says. "But when we went through them again, we discovered they were kind of picky about some stuff. They didn't take partial bags or bottles of food or other items—like cooking oil. Some of the cooking oil was rancid, which we used for the fire, but we kept the stuff that still smelled fine."

"You should've said something about these a few days ago," I say, mildly chastising them as I practically drool over a partial bag of pinto beans. "Our meals would've been much more interesting. And we certainly could've used the fat."

"We didn't know what you'd decide," Destiny answers. "If you wouldn't take us with you, we'd need these things."

I stifle a sigh. I can't fault her. I wasn't overly kind to them while I was figuring out exactly what it was they wanted from us. "You should've been honest with me from the beginning."

"Like you were with us?"

"I was—I thought your people would attack."

"So did I," she says, standing tall.

"Okay, fine." I lift a hand in surrender. "Point taken. Let's get everything loaded. We might need to make a second trip. I have no idea how we'll get all of this in the little Bug."

"We could tie it on top," Leslie says. I stare at her for a moment, trying to think how that would work. "You know," she says, motioning to the roof with her hands, "put it all in a big bag or something and then just wrap some rope through the windows."

"Would it work?" Destiny asks me.

"Maybe? I don't know. But I like the idea. And there's several tarps in Jeff's garage."

"This is about it," Destiny says, exiting the house with a shotgun.

I'm beaming as I say, "That's a great find."

"This was my dad's. He had it hidden in our shed."

"Do you have ammo for it?"

"Of course. It wouldn't have done any good to hide the shotgun without hiding shells too."

She's right, and I feel kind of dumb for asking. "Did he hide any other guns?"

"He did, but not as well. I checked the other places I knew about, and they were all empty. I should've taken them when we fled."

"At least you have the pistol," Leslie says.

Destiny gives Leslie a dirty look, causing her to cower, before Destiny stomps off.

"What's this?" I ask.

Ignoring me, she calls back over her shoulder, "I'm going to take a look and make sure there's nothing else we can't live without." Okay, so Destiny has a gun.

She's back in a few minutes, saying, "That's it. Except for fuel. They took most of it, but my dad had a five-gallon can hidden with the shotgun."

"Let's put it in the car," I say. "Did the . . . the other people take the fuel from the cars the EMP wiped out?"

"Most of the cars were pretty low since we had a problem with getting gas, thanks to the cyberattacks and everything else."

"Let's see if we can get enough to fill the car. Remember how Liam mentioned we punched holes in the gas tanks to fill the dirt bikes?"

"We didn't know to try that," Leslie says. "There's plenty of dead cars."

It takes us about twenty minutes to empty enough gas tanks to fill up the Bug. We've crammed everything in the car, filling up the storage space under the hood and the backseat. Leslie and Destiny share the passenger's seat for the drive back.

As soon as we're out of town, I ask, "What's this about a gun?"

Leslie's head drops to look at her lap. I see Destiny elbow her lightly before saying, "I have a right to protect myself."

"Absolutely. I'm not trying to bust your chops about this. But if we're traveling together, it's something I should be aware of. Do you know how to use it?"

"Wouldn't do much good if I didn't," she scoffs.

I can't help but smile at her mild hostility. She puts on a tough front for sure. "So . . . that's a yes?"

"Of course it's a yes."

I choose to let it slide for the moment. When we're back at the house, I'll confirm her knowledge. The snow has completely melted from the pavement, allowing for a quick and easy drive. We quickly unload, piling everything in the living room. There are several things I'm sure we'll end up leaving behind, but it'll be good to sort it all and then decide based on our space. I look through the treasures and pick out things to make for a late lunch. There were partial containers of cornmeal, flour, and baking powder, which I turn into pancakes. The addition of an egg from Little Brown, along with a huge dollop of oil, help make them light and fluffy even though the liquid I use is water. They are so good!

After eating, I make a second, even larger batch so we can take them on the road. I also put beans in water to start cooking them, then we begin to attack the pile. We sort things into piles based on category. While the food pile is incredibly interesting, the small self-defense pile is where we start.

The shotgun has four boxes of shells, but two of the boxes, which are double-aught buck used for self-defense, have only five rounds per box. The third box is twenty-five rounds for hunting waterfowl, and the last is the same number for shooting clay pigeons or things like grouse. I didn't know any of this, but Destiny makes a point of showing us.

She also makes a point of teaching us how the shotgun works. It has a five-round magazine and is pump action. Before the sun sets, we take a few minutes in the backyard. Leslie, who was already trained on it before they found us, holds Wyatt. While we don't fire any shots, we load and unload it several times, making sure we know how to work the pump.

"This is a 12 gauge," Destiny says. "It has some kick to it when you shoot, so you want to make sure to pull it snug against your shoulder. Now, each of you get to reload it and work the pump again."

After she finally decides we could handle the gun, I say, "Liam and I have the rifle you've seen. I want to make sure both of you know how to work it. It's a lever action. Liam's really good with it. He'll show you how it works."

We go through the same process of loading and unloading, then move on to dry firing. When everyone is comfortable with the rifle, I say, "And we have two handguns. I have a subcompact 9-millimeter, and Liam's carrying a revolver. Destiny, what's your pistol?"

She flares her nostrils and gives me a side eye before muttering, "It's a Walther 380."

"So just a little one?" Liam asks.

She swings her head in his direction. "It was my mom's, and it'll do the job."

I rest my hand on Liam's shoulder before asking, "You said you know how to use it?"

"That's right. My dad was in the military. When he retired and we moved here, he made sure we knew how to handle weapons."

"What branch of the military was your dad in?" Liam asks.

"He's a Marine—I mean, he *was* a Marine."

"And he taught you Marine stuff?" Liam asks.

"He taught her lots of things," Leslie says. "And when the lights went out, he taught our entire town things so we could all survive. It wasn't right for them to turn on him—to turn on our families—like they did. If we would've all stuck together, Destiny's dad could've got us through this."

"They knew they had to kill him," Destiny says quietly.

"I know how to use her gun too," Leslie says. "Destiny showed me."

"How much ammo do you have?" I ask.

Destiny shakes her head. "Not enough. Two full magazines and a partial box. They took the rest when they found my dad's stashes."

"Okay. It's a short drive to Mollie's, so we'll be okay."

"Humph," Liam snorts.

I choose to ignore his response as I say, "Let me show you my pistol."

After familiarizing them with the Sig, we look at the revolver left behind by Jeff and Isabel. Then Destiny somewhat reluctantly shows us her pistol too. I'm not going to lie, it's a beauty. Almost too pretty to shoot. It has a strange trigger, though.

"It's a double-action, single-action," Destiny says. "Which means it has a longer, heavier trigger pull on the first shot. After the first shot, the hammer stays back in the cocked position, so when you squeeze the trigger again, it has a lighter single-action pull. Make sense?"

I shake my head while Liam shrugs.

"Yeah, it'll make sense if you use it. Just remember, the first shot is harder. After that, it gets easier. My dad said it was some fancy idea to help prevent negligent discharges."

We go through dry firing each of the pistols. Liam and I have each dry fired the Sig many times but never Jeff and Isabel's revolver. And Destiny was right about her pistol. It is hard to pull the trigger, but not much more difficult than the revolver. The nice thing about the revolver is we can pull the hammer back if needed.

As the sun sets, we go back inside the house. Liam brings two small tarps and a skein of rope from the garage to use for Leslie's idea of tying things to the roof. To keep things contained within the tarps, we use the rest of the backpacks from Jeff's business shed.

"What are these?" Liam asks, holding up two large metal platforms with cleats and laces.

They seem like something I should recognize, but I don't. I give a shake of my head as Leslie answers, "Snowshoes."

"Snowshoes," Liam repeats. "For walking in snow?"

"More like walking *on* snow," Destiny says. "They help keep you from sinking. We should stop in town and see about finding some for you two." She turns to Leslie. "How many pairs did we find?"

"I think there's some in the garage," Liam says, bouncing up from his seat on the ground. Leslie and Destiny discuss how they should've thought about grabbing snowshoes when we were in town. I play with baby Wyatt, making faces at him, trying to make him laugh. After a few minutes, Liam returns with similar-looking items, these made of plastic.

"Those will work," Destiny said. "They're not as good as these, but they'll do. I'm kind of surprised they don't have better ones. Isabel and Jeff did a lot of hiking—maybe they were only fair-weather hikers."

"Did you find winter clothes?" Leslie asks.

"We found coats and puffy pants. There was— " Liam swallows hard before continuing, "There were a pair of insulated bibs that would've fit my grandpa."

Leslie nods. "It's probably going to snow again." She looks to Destiny for confirmation.

"It may," Destiny agrees. "It's cool enough that we should plan on it. Winter clothes and boots take up lots of space, but they're needed."

"Mom and I each have a coat and pants in the duffle bag. I have snow boots too."

"Do you have snow boots?" Leslie asks me.

"I haven't found any in my size," I answer, shaking my head.

"I wish you would've said something earlier when we were in town," Destiny says. "Those hiking boots you're wearing might be fine for walking, but they won't keep your feet warm."

"I was fine today," I tell her. "I'm wearing two pairs of wool socks."

"It wasn't cold today," Leslie says.

I blink my eyes several times, thinking how to respond. While it wasn't freezing today, it *was* cold. Cold enough I needed my coat zipped up and my scarf pulled tight. "How much colder can it get?"

"In September?" Leslie asks.

I give a slight nod.

"Below freezing. In another month it'll be below zero."

My eyes go wide.

"*Could* be below zero," Destiny corrects. "Sometimes, it's nice into November. We just never know. Maybe your friends will have boots for you. Wyoming gets even colder than we do—parts of it, anyway."

"We each have two pairs of boots," Leslie says. "That way, you don't have to wear the same pair every day. They get wet and need to dry out."

Like Liam, I'm hoping—*almost* to the point of praying—we don't end up on foot again. With the car, we'll be able to make it to Mollie's place within a day or so. Destiny knows how to drive a standard, so she and I will switch off. Liam says he's more than happy to learn, and I'll likely take him up on it. With winter already giving us a teaser, I can't imagine what it may be like if we end up walking.

"You think you might know where I can find snow boots?" I ask Destiny.

"What size?"

"Women's ten."

"Yeah, I have a few ideas."

"Do you have warm clothes for Wyatt?" Liam asks.

"He has a snowsuit."

"Will it be enough? I found a box of baby clothes in the garage. There's some kind of quilted sack thing he'll probably fit into."

"That might be a good idea," I say.

It's well after dark before we finish loading the car, including tying the tarps on top. As we go back inside, Liam asks, "How do you want to arrange watch tonight?"

"I'll take the final watch," I say. "That way I can make sure we're ready to leave and can wake everyone up."

"You don't think it'll make it hard on you, with needing to drive?" Destiny asks. "The three of us can handle it tonight."

"You'll be driving too," I remind her. "It's almost nine. You take first watch until eleven, then Liam can have eleven to one. Leslie, one to three. I'll finish it off. I want to start waking everyone up before six."

Chapter 30

September 25th

I tossed and turned before falling asleep, making it exceedingly difficult to get out of bed when Leslie woke me. Since then, I've done my usual night watch of walking from window to window. In addition to walking, I turn more of the flour into flat, hard biscuits. Okay, probably not *actual* biscuits. I use water, flour, and salt to make a thick dough and then roll it out, cooking them in the skillet over low heat until they're dry and crispy.

Liam said one of the things Bart mentioned was hardtack, a cross between a cracker and biscuit. His mom would make them for his dad to take along when he was working away from home. Bart wasn't completely sure, but the recipe he remembered had only the three ingredients—his mom often substituting cornmeal or another milled grain for the flour. As I walk and cook, I think of several small items to tuck in with us—all things that will not only be helpful for us, but also to buy our way into Mollie's place.

I wake Liam up first, ruffling his hair and telling him happy birthday. While there won't be any real celebration, I do have something special planned foodwise. There are a few dehydrated desserts from Jeff's store; one is a just-add-cold-water cheesecake. When we stop for lunch today, we'll have that.

Now, it's almost sunrise, our designated time to leave. As Destiny finishes getting Wyatt ready, Liam and I take a final walk to Bart's grave to say our last goodbyes. There's still patches of snow from where the sun didn't reach it yesterday. I wonder how the roads will be today? Hopefully, the pavement will be warm enough it will have melted off, like it has here. Destiny says we'll have several higher elevations to travel through that may have snow.

Liam found a box of car chains with "Frog" written on them; we're bringing them along. Having lived in Oregon my entire life, I've never put chains on. The few times we've needed them, Ben took care of it. Destiny assures me she can help, that it'll be fine.

"Do you think, after this is over, we'll be able to visit his grave again?" Liam asks.

"I'm sure we'll be able to," I answer. "Destiny and Leslie might want to return to here too."

"When will it be over, Mom?"

"I wish I knew." I pull him close to me, spending several minutes like this before I ask, "You ready, birthday boy?"

Seeing the well-loaded car in the daylight almost makes me laugh. It's so jam-packed, it could be some kind of sad meme. In addition to the two knobby, bulging tarps, there's two small fuel cans between the two tarp packages, secured with several bungee cords to keep them upright. We'll stop in town and punch out a few more tanks to fill them. Destiny wants to add the larger can of her dad's, but I'm not sure adding more weight to the top of the car is smart. Instead, we'll stop whenever we see a car and get what we can.

One of the things brought from the stash of goods was a car seat for Wyatt. Destiny already has him buckled into the backseat. At some point, Isabel and Jeff must have retrofitted seatbelts in this car. In a vehicle this age, I expected only lap belts, if any. But both front seats and the two spots behind the front seats in the back all have shoulder belts. The middle back has a lap belt. Wyatt is in the middle, with Destiny behind the driver's seat and Leslie behind the passenger's, holding my little chickens in a box on her lap. Things we need easy access to are inside the car: daypacks for each of us with essentials in case of an emergency, along with other items. The loaded and ready-to-carry backpacks are under the hood.

While we had originally wanted to bring the wagon, with so many of us in the car, there was no way it'd fit. Liam found a red, plastic, three-person toboggan, which we tucked into the trunk first. Liam insists, if we end up on foot again, we'll be thankful we have it. Destiny thought it was a great idea and said she knows where there's a saucer-style sled in town. We left room for it under the hood.

"We ready?" I ask. Everyone agrees we are, and I pull out of the driveway. I can't help but look to the edge of the forest where we've left Bart. I try and ignore the tears as they escape.

Even though Liam and I had said we'd take the main roads and get to Mollie's as quick as possible, Destiny brought us back to our senses.

After she heard our story of losing Ben—it felt good to finally come clean about that lie—and then losing our dirt bikes, combined with what they experienced in their own town, she insisted we stick to back roads. Liam privately told me he thought she was right. It's just not worth the risk, especially since our car is so loaded and we might be a target.

After filling the fuel cans in town, Destiny again suggests taking the larger can of her dad's.

"I think, if we put it directly in the middle, it'll be fine," she says.

"Do we have any more bungee cords?" I ask Liam.

"No, that's it."

"I have a few zip ties," Destiny says. "They're still at my house. What if we zip tie it in place? I'll bring extras so we can reattach it. You said it might be hard to get fuel after this much time since the EMP. Five gallons will get us quite a ways farther."

I do some quick calculating in my head. I have no idea how many miles per gallon an older car like this will get. It's small, and I think they were marketed as commuter cars, but still . . . fifteen? Twenty? Five gallons could take us another seventy-five to a hundred miles. She's right. It's worth the risk.

Connected to the gas cans is an empty plastic coffee container with a small hole at the top to thread a bungee through, along with a plastic water jug with the top cut off. These are for collecting the fuel as it drips out.

We discovered early on in our fuel draining that one collection container wasn't enough. While most cars were stranded along the road after running out of fuel, occasionally they'd still have more than we expected. When we were on the dirt bikes, we used soda bottles with the tops cut down. With the larger fuel tank, more sizeable containers make sense.

Liam found these in the garage, along with a funnel. All of them seem to work well, but I can already see it's a pain having everything tied to the roof like this.

We tap four cars to fill the can to 80 percent—what Ben has told me in the past is a safe amount since gas expands. While the filling isn't difficult, attaching it to the center takes more time than I care to admit. That much fuel is heavy, and getting it up there takes all my strength. While Liam and I mess with it, Destiny goes in search of boots for me and the saucer sled she and Liam had discussed.

"Hey," she says when she returns. "There were two of the sleds—a green and a red. They fit inside each other, so they won't take up any more space."

"Good find. And you found boots?" I motion to the four boots she's balancing on the sleds like a platter.

"Yeah, here's two different options. These are a women's size ten, and these are a men's eight and a half."

The women's boots are an actual snow boot and incredibly warm with a zipper up the front. While they fit, they're slightly tight with my two pairs of thick socks. "They'll do, but let me check the other pair."

"Those look new," Liam says.

"They were still in the box," Destiny answers.

"Why would the owner leave them?" he asks.

"He, uh— " She tilts her head slightly and then lets out a sigh. "He's one of the ones they killed. I don't know why someone from town didn't take them. Maybe since it wasn't cold when they left, they weren't thinking about winter. Most of the winter stuff was left behind."

"They need camp shoes too," Leslie says.

"Good idea," Destiny replies.

"What are camp shoes?" Liam asks.

"When we hike, we wear our hiking shoes," Leslie says patiently. "Then, when we stop for the day, we change into something light and comfortable."

"We're not going to be hiking," Liam says firmly.

Leslie and Destiny look at each other and shrug. "True," Destiny says. "But it's still a good idea. Leslie and I each have warm slippers—the kind with thick soles. We even found Wyatt a pair of moccasins with lining. The cold is nothing to mess around with. Frostbite is real."

"Whatever you think is best," I say to Destiny. My experience with winter weather is limited to a few girls' weekends in Bend where we'd sit in the hot tub while it was snowing. I focus on the second pair of boots. These are more of an insulated high hiking boot, lacing up well past my ankle. They're lined and thick and a perfect fit. "These are good," I say, starting to take them off.

"You should take the second pair," Destiny says, reminding me how uncomfortable wet boots can be. "I'll try and find another pair for Liam too. What size do you need?"

After he gives her his size, she takes off on her salvage trip.

"You should wear your boots," Leslie says. "My parents always had us wear our winter boots when we were going on long car trips. In case we broke down, we'd stay warm."

"Us?" Liam asks.

Sadness overwhelms her face. "I had a brother. He died over the winter—before all of this."

"Oh . . . I'm sorry," Liam says.

"Me too," I say dumbly. This poor girl has been through way too much.

She gives a small nod, then says again, "You should wear them. Destiny and I have our boots on. So does Liam."

"Only because my feet are cold," he says. "I didn't know it was a smart thing to do."

"I guess I should switch over to the insulated hiking boots," I say. "I can just leave these behind." I motion to the boots on my feet. I've put many miles on them, and they're starting to break down.

After changing my boots, I pop open the hood to stash the second pair, along with the saucers. While we saved space for the saucers—which really take up little room anyway—finding a place for my boots isn't as easy.

"Do you want me to hold Wyatt?" I ask Leslie while we wait for Destiny to return.

She hands him to me, then does a few twists to loosen her back.

After many minutes of chitchat, Liam says, "Shouldn't she be back by now?"

I give a nod. "I was just thinking that."

"I'll go look for her," Leslie says, starting to walk away.

A weird feeling starts in my toes and travels up to my stomach. "No!" I say in a harsh whisper.

Leslie turns and gives me a strange look. I motion for her to come back to the car.

"You and Liam stay here," I say, handing her the baby. "I'll go find her. Do you know where she might have gone?"

"We moved everything we salvaged into three different houses, besides her dad's place. The first one is on the next street over."

"Do you think the snow boots were in that house?"

"Maybe? We tried to spread things out so not everything was in one home—you know, in case something happened."

"Okay. I'll start there. Liam, if anything goes wrong, take Leslie and Wyatt back to the house."

With wide eyes, he says, "I don't know how to drive the car."

"Then you walk—run. Just get out of here."

"No, Mom. We should stay together. All of us go and look for her. If I can't see you, I won't know if there's a problem."

I chew on my thumbnail while I consider what he says.

"I think he's right," Leslie says as she hands Wyatt to Liam. "Let me grab something." She reaches into the car and flips the passenger's seat forward, rummaging around. After a moment, she puts a sling across her body and then tucks Wyatt inside it. "Let's go."

Shaking my head, I start toward the next street. "You two stay back and behind me. I want you to be ready to run."

As soon as we near the house on the corner, I hear a noise—something like a scuffle. I quickly turn and put my finger to my lips. I point to the side of the house and then use two fingers to motion for Leslie and Liam to move against it. I do the same, then we carefully move toward the edge of the building.

When we're within a few feet, I turn and motion for them to be silent and to stay put. Liam nods. At some point, he took the revolver out of the holster and now has it by his leg. I quickly check to ensure his finger is not on the trigger. I give a nod when I see it properly indexed. Likewise, I'm holding my pistol in the same manner.

I put my mouth close to Liam's ear. "Do what you need to do to take care of Leslie and Wyatt."

He gives me a somber nod in response.

I stoop down and continue moving toward the edge of the house. I have no idea what I'm doing. Ben liked action movies, so we'd often watch those together, but that's the extent of my knowledge on maneuvering through a situation like this. I don't even know if there's anything wrong.

A guttural scream pierces the air just as I pop my head from behind the house. Less than twenty feet from me, Destiny is stomping on a man's foot. He's holding her from behind, and as he bends into the pain, she punches him where it hurts. His guttural sound returns as he releases her. She scrambles away, falling after a couple of steps.

I begin to quickly step toward them as he says, "You're going to pay for that." I immediately stop my forward motion when I see the gun in his hand, trained on her. "Stop moving or I'll shoot you in the back."

He's so focused on Destiny he has yet to see me, completely in the open, less than twenty feet from him.

I move my pistol into position, bracing my elbows and ensuring a strong grip with my left hand. With my heart pounding, I say, "Hey."

He starts to spin toward me as I squeeze the trigger. Without waiting to see the result, I squeeze again and again. He's holding his shoulder as he rotates toward me. I shoot again as I watch his gun bounce up, then I immediately hear the report. I shoot him again.

A shot from a gun other than my own, followed quickly by a second, sends him to the ground. With tunnel vision and blood swishing through my ears, I take several steps forward. When he twitches, I fire again.

"He's done for, Clarice."

"Huh? What?" I'm still staring at the man on the ground, his dead eyes staring back at me.

Destiny, her own weapon in hand, appears by my side. "You're empty, and he's not getting up again."

"I'm empty?" I echo, looking at the open slide. I reach in my pocket, where I've taken to carrying the extra magazine, then remove the spent ten-round mag, popping in the fresh twelve rounds. The action seems to jolt me out of my fog. "Destiny! Are you okay?"

She has blood dripping from her lip and a cut above her eyebrow. She gives me a nod and then looks at the dead man. "I'm not injured. I'm mad he grabbed me. I should've been paying better attention. Thanks for showing up when you did. I couldn't get to my gun with the way he had me held."

"Looked like you were putting up a good fight," I say woodenly, also staring at the man. "Do you know him?"

"No, must just be a drifter."

"You shot him too?" I ask, trying to make sense of what happened.

"Yeah," she says without emotion. "I need to get the things I found. I dropped them."

"Mom?" Liam calls from the edge of the house.

"Stay there. We're okay. You don't . . . no reason for you to come here." In a low voice, I ask Destiny, "You're sure he's alone?"

"I . . . yes. He's the only one I've seen, but we should get out of here."

I raise my voice, "You two stay against the house, keep an eye out for anyone else." In a quieter voice, I ask, "What should we do with him?"

"Leave him? Just let him rot."

I swallow hard before giving a nod. "I'll help you gather the things."

"I've got it. You make sure no one sneaks up on us."

I position myself so I can watch not only Destiny but in the direction of the other children. As soon as she has her load, we quickly move back to the hiding spot.

"Let's go," I say, urging everyone toward the car. When we're there, Liam goes to open the trunk. "Just get in. We're going back to the house."

Within a minute, we're on the main road. I drive much faster than necessary in my haste to get away from the killing place. My hands are shaking on the steering wheel, and I need to go to the bathroom something awful. Liam is in the backseat with Leslie and the baby, while Destiny is next to me. She's staring out the passenger window. In front of Isabel and Jeff's house, I'm not even at a complete stop when she jumps out. She makes it a few feet before vomiting.

"Wait a minute," I say to the others before I go to Destiny. I hold her hair as she continues to empty her stomach.

Chapter 31

September 25th

Inside the house, I clean the cut above Destiny's eye. "It probably needs a stitch."

"Yeah. Can you put one of those butterfly things on it? Or use superglue?"

"Let's try the butterfly. I put a couple of them in the first aid kit in my emergency bag. I'll be right back. Liam? I want you to stand watch on the porch while I go to the car. From now on, no one goes anywhere alone."

After Destiny is bandaged and cleaned up, I ask, "Should we stay here for the rest of the day and leave tomorrow?"

"Why?" Liam asks. "It's still early—oh, unless . . . are you and Destiny not okay to go?"

"I'm ready to go," Destiny says firmly.

I give her a long look. Physically, she's probably fine, even though she's pale. The cuts weren't much. She'll have some bruises on her arms, maybe her legs too, but he did little damage. If she wouldn't have fought him, I don't know how it would've turned out. If he would've still been holding her and pawing at her, I may not have had a shot. And when he let her go, she got to her gun so she could also fire. I'm utterly amazed she was able to keep her head so well. Her dad must have done a fine job with training. I'm still shaky, and probably equally as pale, but I'm ready to leave.

I have the girls stay inside with Wyatt as Liam and I go to the car. I stand watch while he puts things away. Destiny found him a second pair of boots and a pair of quilted camouflaged slippers with solid soles—his camp shoes. There's a pair of burnt orange moccasin looking things for me. There are a few other miscellaneous things, including several pairs of gloves and a pair of mittens. Once everything is tucked in and organized, Liam says, "I guess we're ready."

"Are you doing okay?" I ask.

"I'm really proud of you, Mom. I know you did something awful. But you did it and saved Destiny."

I bite my top lip as tears fill my eyes. "When your grandpa had to shoot the men that were after us, I was so glad it was him and not me who did it. And I truly wish this weren't something I ever had to do, but— " I lift my arms. "Sorry this isn't much of a birthday for you."

"It's okay. Let's get to Mollie's and then we can have a huge celebration." He gives me a cheeky grin.

I step over to him, wrapping him in a hug. "Deal."

As we once again load up and leave, Destiny acts as navigator, telling me which ways to turn to get us heading in the right direction but keeping us on small roads. While Liam and I were getting things ready, she fixed her makeup and changed her clothes, borrowing from Isabel's closet. The clothes she was wearing when attacked were left in a heap in the bathtub. While she's not exactly chipper, she's much better than I'd expect.

After less than an hour of driving, Leslie says, "Can we stop? Wyatt needs to be changed."

We have a handful of disposable diapers but not all in the size Wyatt needs. Destiny and Leslie had been using cloth diapers, dish towels, and anything else they could find for the last several weeks. Washing wasn't a problem, with the creek nearby and the ability to heat water, plus many partial bottles of detergent left behind.

I laugh every time I think of the snooty townspeople only taking full containers of stuff. What is up with that? Maybe they thought the FEMA camp would only accept them if they brought proper goods? Who knows? Now that we're on the road, we're using the disposable diapers. We'll go back to washables when we get to Mollie's.

"Mom? How about you teach me how to drive?" Liam asks as we're ready to get started again.

"You sure you're ready?" I ask.

"Now's a good time," Destiny says. "It's quiet through here, and the road isn't too bad. The road we'll take next isn't paved."

Teaching Liam to drive a standard transmission takes every ounce of my limited patience. I try and remember it's not his fault—I even struggled with it those first few days. But it'd be so much easier for me to just keep driving, then we'd be making better time at least. After he finally gets going, he's fine, but the sheen of sweat on his upper lip tells me he's a nervous wreck. I look closer at his lip. Does he need a shave?

With Liam seeming to do fine, I sit back in the seat and close my eyes, not intending to sleep but to relax. The day has taken its toll on me. Closing my eyes, I see the dead man—the man I killed—lying on the ground bleeding. I do my best to blank my mind. It feels like I've only just shut my eyes when Liam touches my arm. "Mom, we'll need to take a different road soon."

"Mm-hmm," I answer, wiping a bit of drool from my mouth. I sit up straight and look around. "Where are we?"

"A couple of miles from the turn off to the dirt road," Destiny says.

"This is a road you know?" I ask, turning to look at her.

"There's several good places to camp. My dad took us there. The road goes over the mountain and then back down. It comes out near a little town. It's pretty bumpy but should be fine."

"As long as there's not too much snow," I say, looking around. What had been patchy snow when we left Isabel and Jeff's place is now more consistent.

"Oh, there's going to be snow," Leslie says, her voice very matter of fact.

Destiny nods her agreement. "We'll put the chains on if we need them. They're right here, on the floor beneath Wyatt."

I look to where she points. They've stacked up every inch of the back floor with things we need to get to quickly. Destiny and Leslie each have their crossbody bags at their feet. On top of the plastic box holding the chains is Wyatt's diaper bag, which includes the fabric carrier Leslie had him in earlier. The larger, more comfortable baby backpack is under the hood with the other fully loaded multiday backpacks.

We're not only using the floor but also the seat backs. Both the sedan and SUV at the house had little fabric bags that hung around the back headrests. We grabbed those to use in the Frog, filling them with snacks—a partial bag of raisins Leslie and Destiny salvaged, along with the meal replacement bars and drinks from Jeff's store—and other things we wanted easy access to. The shotgun is next to Destiny, already loaded. Liam and I each have a small bag in the front, along with the rifle. If we need to leave the car in a hurry, these bags have our absolute essentials.

I reloaded the empty magazine and have it in my pocket, with Bart's 9-millimeter back on my ankle. Finding a waist holster is at the top of my list for salvaging. I'm suddenly kicking myself for not asking Destiny if she knew where one was in her town. Liam has the .357 of Jeff's on his hip. He also made sure both Destiny and Leslie have two of the three slingshots and steel balls he found. While we were at Jeff and Isabel's, he did quite a bit of practicing with one he deemed his favorite; that one's in his daypack.

"You need to downshift," I tell Liam. He's already easing off the gas. "Hear how it sounds? That's an indicator to move to a lower gear."

"Okay," he says as he grinds down to third. "Oops."

"Just keep decelerating and downshift again." After a moment, I say, "There's a wide spot up ahead. Pull off there."

He gets us off the road, killing the engine in the process.

"Good enough. You'll get better at it."

"How about I drive?" Destiny asks. "I'm probably more comfortable if we encounter snow."

"You haven't driven in snow either," Leslie says.

"Not true. I drove some last year."

I look to Destiny again before asking, "How long have you been driving?"

"Almost a year."

"Humph," Leslie scoffs. "She got her license in March."

"Why'd you wait so long?" Liam asks.

"I didn't wait that long. My birthday was in February."

"You're only sixteen?" Liam asks. "Or do you have to be older than that to drive in Idaho?"

"I'm sixteen," she answers reluctantly.

Discovering she's several years younger than I thought, still a child, I'm extremely glad I listened to Bart and brought them with us. I can't imagine a sixteen-year-old trying to keep them all alive in today's world. When I thought she was in her early twenties, that was different. She would've at least had some life experiences to lean on. Of course, with the way she kept her head today, she's definitely well beyond her years.

"Leslie, how old are you?" I ask.

"Twelve. I'll be thirteen on Christmas."

At least she's around the same age I thought she was.

"Your birthday is Christmas day?" Liam asks. "That must have been a huge bummer."

She shrugs and quietly says, "My mom and dad always tried to make it special."

I quickly change the subject. "I'll drive. But maybe Destiny should sit up front. Just in case I need guidance on what to do, you'll be able to see the road better than from the back."

After we swap seats and are on the road again, it's only around the next curve when we take the side road. The road is considerably better than I expected—graveled like the driveway up to Isabel and Jeff's.

When I tell Destiny this isn't too bad, she says, "Just wait."

I don't have to wait for very long before the road narrows. As we climb higher and higher up the mountain, the snow on the side of the road increases and then fresh snow begins falling. We've just finished climbing a hill, and the road has flattened out. I loosen my grip on the wheel to relieve the cramping in my hands.

"I think this was a bad choice," Liam says. "Mom, you should turn around. There's room here. Go back to the other road."

"That road runs into a town that's bigger than ours," Destiny says.

Leslie nods. "What if those people are—what if they . . . " Her voice fades away.

"Is there any other way around the town?" I ask. I've slowed the car so we're still moving but barely creeping along.

"Not that I can think of," Destiny says. "Do you want to put the tire chains on?"

"I guess we'd better," I answer with a sigh. "I'm not slipping, but it's . . . it's scaring me."

"This is a good place," Destiny says.

After putting on gloves and hats and then zipping up our coats, Destiny, Liam, and I work at getting the chains on. Because the Bug is rear-wheel drive, the instructions tell us to put the chains on the back. We debated for several minutes on whether the car is front- or rear-wheel drive. I finally made a judgement call based on the age of it, determining it should be rear wheel. I'm not entirely sure, and we may end up having to put them on the front. I hope I'll know right away if we've done it right. With the instructions, and Destiny, getting the chains on is less of an ordeal than I anticipated.

"Don't go too fast," Liam says when we're back in the car and starting to move. "The instructions said no faster than twenty-five."

Twenty-five would've been lightning fast compared to the ten I drive for the next three hours as we wind our way up the curvy road. Several times, Destiny says it's probably good there's snow because it helped even out the road. The road is a bumpy, bouncy mess, even with the gradually increasing snow. And not only is there snow on the ground, but it's also starting to fall from the sky again.

When we finally reach a level spot, I breathe a sigh of relief and let out a small laugh. "It's all downhill from here."

Chapter 32

September 25th

I let out a breath and grimace as I look at the fuel gauge. "Let's take a break and fill up. Leslie, how's the chickens?"

"Okay, I guess. They didn't like a few of the bumps you hit, but since it's pretty dark in the box, they're probably sleeping."

With the snow still falling, we each get out and stretch. I take Wyatt out of his car seat and put on a fresh diaper. After he's clean and bundled in a blanket, Destiny walks with him so he, too, can stretch a bit. I peek in the chicken box and see Little Brown Hen staring back at me. The bottom of the box, lined with newspaper and topped with a few branches, is lightly soiled. It'll be fine, but it'll need a cleaning at the end of the day. Hopefully, by then, we'll be out of the snow and the chickens can stretch their legs too. I drop a portion of oatmeal from Isabel's kitchen into the box.

I make each of us sandwiches using the final bits of a jar of peanut butter—also from Isabel's—spread between two pancakes. Destiny also has a partial jar of peanut butter that we can use for a future meal. I've already decided, tonight, we're firing up one of the camp stoves and having the rest of the beans from yesterday. We each had a small bowl last night, and they were amazing.

Since we don't plan to camp, but rather to drive through the night, we won't be able to set up any snares or traps. With the things I've cooked and the assorted camping meals from Jeff, we'll be more than fine on food in the time it takes to reach Bakerville.

Even with the lightly falling snow, the weather isn't terrible. I make Wyatt a bottle, then follow it with a pancake broken into small pieces and soaked with water to resemble something like baby cereal. With his mom, who was nursing him, murdered and the town cleared of most foods, they've struggled to feed him. In their salvaging, they'd found a few partial containers of powdered baby formula and even powdered milk. They'd used it sparingly while combining it with solid foods.

Leslie said, when they found us, they were down to the last of the milk products. According to her, our single container of formula was an answer to their prayers. We've also tried giving him the milkshake packages from Jeff's store. While Liam and I both thought the convenience of those would be wonderful, the texture leaves a lot to be desired. But Wyatt doesn't seem to mind and happily gobbles it down.

After lunch and filling up the car, then reattaching the now empty fuel cans to the top using only the bungee cords, Destiny asks, "You want me to drive down the hill?"

"What's the next road like?"

"When we get off this forest service road, we'll connect with a county road. There's a town not far. I think I know the way around it, using farm roads."

"Farm roads?"

"You know, roads that people live on."

"Oh, okay. So we'll need to stay alert? Those could be good places for ambushes."

"Could be," she agrees with a shrug.

I think about it for a minute. As the only adult in the group, I should be the one ready to protect them if something happens. But the truth is, Destiny has considerably more experience with the shotgun—and has already proven she keeps her head under pressure—and Liam is more comfortable with the rifle than I am. My greatest strength is my driving experience. Mario Andretti I am not, but I should be able to drive well enough to get us out of a jam.

"How about you drive now," I say. "I'll rest a bit, then I'll drive when we're back in civilization. You or Liam will ride shotgun."

She nods. "It's probably a good idea."

Destiny is almost as white-knuckled driving down the mountain as I was driving up. Thankfully, it's not long until the snow stops falling. And according to Destiny, we're still a ways from the bottom when the road begins to clear up. The eastern-facing slope must have received a dose of warm sun since they last had snow. Taking off the chains is much easier than putting them on. Getting them to properly fit back into the container—not so much. As soon as we reach the bottom of the hill, we take another short break.

As agreed, I'm behind the wheel when we resume our travels. Even though there's no snow and the road is smooth and easy, knowing we're entering civilization has me, once again, strongly gripping the steering wheel. I've decided a steady speed, keeping it around forty-five, is safest. I don't know the area and want to be able to react as needed, plus I can always speed up if necessary.

Destiny gives directions from the passenger's seat while also paying attention to our surroundings. Liam and Leslie do their part from the back, watching for people. When Leslie says she sees someone near a house, my grip tightens, and my heart goes into overdrive. Luckily, nothing happens. Once we're beyond the town, Destiny guides me back toward the main road.

"I don't really know the area beyond here," she says. "We'll need to use the maps. Do you want to find a spot to pull over so we can look at what's ahead?"

"I'm ready for a stretch anyway," Liam says.

"And Wyatt is starting to fidget," Leslie adds.

"It's almost five." I point to the little digital clock stuck on the dash. "Let's warm up the beans and eat while we're stopped. This has been a long, stressful day, and we still need to find fuel before it's too dark." I try to keep the disappointment out of my voice. With Destiny's attack and the snow, we've made terrible time. My hopes of reaching Mollie's place sometime tomorrow is fading.

Our break lasts until six, giving us all a chance to rest and the chickens a chance to be out of the box and peck around. During that time, Destiny has mapped out the next bit of our route, again avoiding state highways in favor of small county roads and forest service roads when possible.

"We're going to have a problem around here," she says, pointing to the map. "There aren't any good options to avoid Interstate 15. We'll need to cross it."

I look at where she's pointing. It's a long way from where we are and not a problem for today, not even tonight, but we will have to deal with it. She's found a smaller state road, which looks like it goes under the interstate. "That should work. Do you have a plan for getting us there?"

"Not a good one. I don't see any obvious ways around these towns." She points to another section of the map. "I'll study the wilderness maps. Maybe something will show up on those. These driving maps don't give the best details."

"I'll drive first," Liam says. "Do you want to sit in the back and try to rest?"

"What's the population density on these roads?" I ask Destiny.

"No towns for a while, but I'm not sure about houses. I think there's some vacation cabins in this area. There could be cars stalled on the roads to get gas from."

"I'd better drive," I tell Liam, then turn to Destiny and ask, "How far have we gone?"

"I'm not sure, but we still have a long distance to go—like over five hundred miles at least."

And that's assuming we don't run into trouble, I think to myself. Destiny was right about the scattered houses; we see several before the sun goes down, but thankfully no people.

It's dusk when I spy a car along the side of the road. I stiffen and say, "Be alert. There's a car up ahead."

"Abandoned?" Liam asks.

Destiny pulls up a small pair of binoculars as I slow the Bug to a near crawl. I almost forget to shift and catch my mistake before the engine dies.

"Yeah. I think it's just sitting there," Destiny says. I glance over at her as she's scanning the area. "There's no houses or anything around."

I pull around the car, stopping about thirty feet in front of it. "Liam, get in the driver's seat. Be ready to take off if anything happens. Destiny, you keep an eye out while I get the fuel."

The wind has picked up and almost takes my breath away when I step out. What felt like a warm, comfortable temperature when we stopped to eat is now chilly as the sun drops. With a hammer and a roll of duct tape in my right hand, I reach in my left pants pocket for the brass punch. I've been carrying this since we left the semitruck. Ben made sure each of us had one so we could easily take turns getting fuel. Liam had a punch also, but instead of keeping it in his pocket, it was in his backpack when those guys stole all our stuff. Out of fear of losing my punch, I've added a small toolbox to the car that includes assorted screwdrivers.

While I've done this a couple of times, it still makes me nervous. There's a very real chance of causing an explosion. When we were on the bikes, we had a couple of small hammers to use with the punch.

The hammer I have now is larger, and even though it worked yesterday when getting gas in town, it's still awkward. I should've thought to have Destiny find me one that's smaller, more suited for the job.

Liam is standing by the car, ready to climb into the driver's seat, when he says, "What if I have to leave?"

"I don't think you'll need to. If something happens, Destiny and I will try and jump in. But be ready just in case. We'll leave the passenger's door open."

"I'll get the collection container, then you can get started while I grab down a fuel can," Destiny says.

"No," I say, looking around. "I'll get everything ready and you keep watch. I don't want you doing anything but looking for bad guys while I'm under there."

She holds the shotgun and looks around while I get the coffee can, water jug, and funnel. Not knowing how much fuel is in the tank is a hindrance. Do I only need one gas can or all three? It's likely I need only the one and we'll get a small amount. I let out a sigh and walk around to grab the other small can. If there's more than that, I'll have Liam hurry and get the big one off the roof. We really need to figure out a better way. I feel like a sitting duck here.

"Okay, we're ready," I tell Destiny as I walk back to the car with all my gear. After arranging everything, I get down on my knees in front of the rear axle on the gas flap side. Ben laughed at me once when I went to the driver's side, automatically assuming that was the side with the tank. In that car, the tank was on the passenger's side. Now I make sure to look where they actually add the fuel. I undo two strips of duct tape, attaching one to the frame where I can reach it— just in case I need to stop the flow. It won't completely stop it for any length of time, but it buys me a minute or so until the fuel begins to seep around the tape.

Crawling under the car, it takes only a second for me to locate the tank and put the strip of tape in place. With the brass punch and the strip of tape, I hope to avoid a spark. Everything works as it should, and fuel is flowing freely and quickly from the hole. As soon as the coffee can is full, I move the water jug into place. The funnel is already in the gas can spout, and I quickly fill from the one can to the other. The jug is almost full, so I swap them out and continue. The second can is almost full when the flow begins to slow. When it finally stops,

I have both cans and the water jug full, and the coffee can is more than half full.

"How'd it go?" Destiny asks as I stand up.

"It's good." I carefully carry the water jug and funnel toward the Bug. When I'm close to it, I say, "Can you have Liam get out? I'll need his help."

Liam holds the jug of gas while I climb up and undo the cap on the large fuel can. I have the brilliant idea of leaving it all hooked up and pouring it in—brilliant if the wind wasn't blowing. Though most of the fuel does end up in the can, some of it blows onto me. I even get a mouthful, causing me to cough and sputter. While I'm filling it up, Liam grabs the second collection container. I climb down when done, deciding I'll never try that shortcut again, as I spit gasoline from my mouth. It takes only a couple of minutes to attach the smaller cans, then we're once again on the road.

We've only driven a mile or so when Leslie says, "It stinks like gas in here."

She's not wrong. It's terrible. I pull over at the next wide spot to remove my sodden gloves.

"You should rinse them with water," Destiny says. "Then put them in a plastic bag." She reaches into her bag that's sitting by her feet and pulls out both a bottle of water and a plastic zipper bag.

After taking care of removing and cleaning the gloves, Destiny hands me a fresh pair from her pack and we start again. The gasoline aroma's still evident, but not as strong.

It's fully dark when Destiny says, "Okay, time to go back into the woods. The road is only a couple of miles ahead." She's had the map on her lap for the last half hour, making sure we don't miss our turn.

I grimace at the thought of driving on bumpy, snow-covered roads again. "Can you tell if we'll be going up in elevation?"

"Yeah, I think so, but not like the last one. This road skirts around a mountain instead of going over it."

Unlike the previous dirt road, which started off as a smooth gravel drive, this one's tiny and bumpy from the beginning. We've gone less than a mile when I say, "I don't like this. What are our other options?"

"Drive through a town."

"Can we get around it?"

"I couldn't find any roads that look like they go far enough around to not have a good number of houses on them."

"How big is the town?"

"I'm not sure . . . I've heard of it, though, and it's larger than our town." She turns to Leslie and asks if she's been there before; she doesn't think she has.

"Okay . . . I just don't think it's safe to take this road in the dark," I say. "We're going to have to change plans and camp for the night."

"You're sure, Mom?" Liam asks, his voice dripping with disappointment.

"I'm sure," I answer, my own voice defeated.

I find a spot wide enough to pull off and set up camp. With the car parked next to the road, there's a strip of bare ground before the forest begins. Opening the hood, I pull out two of the two-man tents—left out of the packs specifically for this use. I again stare in awe at the storage area. It's unbelievable how much stuff we've crammed in here. While I'm confident Mollie won't turn us away, I feel better about bringing things.

We have a snack of pancakes and peanut butter, then crawl into bed. Tonight's watch will be held from the Bug. It's too cold to not have some sort of shelter. Following the same schedule as last night, I'll have the final watch before we leave.

"Take your emergency bags in the tent with you," I say. "If you need to get out in a hurry, grab the bags. If we can't get to the car, head for the woods. Keep hidden until daylight and then— " I shake my head. "Then we'll do what we can."

"We'll take Wyatt in with us," Destiny says.

"I guess we'll take the chickens," Liam adds, looking at me. I give him a nod.

I let Liam go inside the tent to get ready for bed. He pops back out in sweatpants, a jacket, and his new slippers, allowing me to go inside. "Just let me know when you're in your sleeping bag and I'll come in," he says.

I can't stop shivering as I change. I, too, brought my new slippers into the tent. Wanting to get my cold feet warmed up, I put them on and then slide into my bag. I let Liam know I'm ready.

"I can't believe how cold it is," he says, zipping up the tent.

It's only a few minutes after he crawls into his bag when I hear his rhythmic breathing. I'm exhausted, too, and expect to fall asleep immediately. Instead, the dead man staring at me with his dead eyes makes sleep difficult. I must have dozed off at some point because I awaken with a start when Destiny ruffles the edge of the tent to wake up Liam for his turn. With my heart pounding, I think I'll have trouble falling back to sleep, but the next thing I know, Leslie is waking me for my watch. I didn't even hear Liam return to the tent.

Chapter 33

September 26th

Even with my coat on and blanket spread over my legs, I'm still freezing during watch. I'm glad Destiny found me the boots; at least my feet are warm. Instead of the hiking ones, I'm wearing the second pair. In some ways, I'm thankful for the cold. It makes staying awake easier. Even so, we'll need to make sure the person on watch is warmer dressed if we have to do the same thing tonight. I let out a sigh. We need to keep driving tonight. If we can do that, we could be at Mollie's tomorrow.

I use a small flashlight to follow the paths in the atlas that Liam added while he sat with Bart. Thinking of Bart causes my heart to ache. I shake my head and try to focus on the map. The paved road we were driving on earlier was one Liam had marked. This crazy bumpy road was also. Looking at the atlas, it seems it should be a better road than it is. Usually, goat trails aren't mapped out.

Using the map key, I gauge the distance guide to estimate the miles from here to Bakerville as the crow flies. My best guess is around three hundred. Its twice as far by road, probably farther with all the small side routes we'll need to take. I can't help but feel we're making a mistake. We've made mistakes from the beginning. We should've taken main roads all along. Our plan of staying out of sight hasn't worked very well. My husband and father-in-law are both dead, and we're still a long way from Mollie's.

I let out a snort. While I've hated the fact we were going there, now I can hardly wait to arrive. Where all I could think about was how crazy she makes me, I no longer care. I'll milk her goats, shovel her stalls, do whatever it takes to keep her farm going.

My guard time passes slowly, with my mind often drifting back to the man who tried to take Destiny. I know we did what we had to do, but it still makes me feel a little sick when I think of him, when I think of the deadness in his eyes.

When Bart killed those men who were after us, it took several days before he seemed to come to terms with what he'd done. At the time, I thought it odd. They were trying to kill us; Bart did what he had to do. It's the same with the drifter. He had Destiny and planned to . . . I don't know, but whatever he planned, it wasn't good. I don't know if it was one of my bullets that ended his life or one of Destiny's, and it doesn't matter. Like with Bart, we did what we had to do. And like Bart, I'm having a hard time with it.

When the sky begins to lighten, I climb out of the cold car and fire up the camp stove to start warming water for oatmeal. As the sun rises, I'm amazed at the beauty surrounding me. We're in a well-forested area with a combination of evergreen and deciduous. The broad-leaf trees are all in full color, sporting varying shades of yellow leaves. I breathe deeply, taking in the fresh scents of the crisp morning. Breakfast is almost ready when Liam crawls out of his tent.

"Hey, Mom," he says, chicken box in hand. "Can they roam around for a little bit?"

"Sure, yes. Did you stay warm enough?"

"Inside the sleeping bag was fine," he says, as he opens the box and lifts Little Brown out. She gives a squawk before ruffling her feathers. She's starting to lose some of her feathers. Destiny and Leslie both say it's common, that chickens molt every fall and she may completely stop laying eggs too. Poof Head's feathers look fine. Destiny says it's because she's still a pullet and they don't always molt their first year. She hasn't started laying eggs yet either, but my hope is she'll start around the time Little Brown stops. Poof doesn't seem any happier about being woken up than Little Brown did. Both sit in the grass while they wait for more light.

"Destiny says we have all-weather tents, designed to be warm even in the winter, and that the sleeping bags are good ones too. But taking watch in the car was sure cold," Liam says. "Was it cold when you were in it?"

"Yes, very. Come over here by the cook stove. It's giving off a little heat."

"Should I wake the girls up first?"

"Please. Breakfast is just about ready."

Bundled well against the cold, the girls and Wyatt soon join us by the stump I've chosen as a cooking table. Breakfast and packing up take the better part of an hour. It's fully light by the time we're ready to leave. Little Brown Hen and Poof Head both voice their displeasure of being returned to their box. Though we had them in the duffle before finding Isabel and Jeff, we decided to return them to a box. They seem more comfortable with the solidness of cardboard, plus it's easier to keep tidy. Liam takes the time to clean it out and put fresh foliage in. I must admit, I had no idea chickens pooped so much.

I'm driving and Liam's in the passenger's seat. Destiny's behind me, her map already spread out—not an easy task in the backseat of a VW Bug with a baby in the middle. In the daylight, the road has zero improvement. At least I can see the largest pits and boulders before I drive over them. While the road itself is clear of snow, the potholes are often full of water from where it's melted. And there's still snow in patches on the hillsides. The road quickly narrows, and we have a cliff on one side and a rock wall on the other. Who ever thought it was a good idea to add a road like this?

We've gone a few miles when Destiny says, "I think I may have made a mistake."

"What do you mean?" I ask, glancing in the rearview mirror.

"This is the wrong road," she says. "At least, I think it is. We should've gone a little farther."

"How do you know?" Liam asks.

"I don't—not for sure. But this road seems too rough to be on this map. And it isn't curving like the road should, like the road I thought we took should."

"Okay," I say. "As soon as the road widens again, I'll turn around. We'll drive back down this awful thing and find the right road."

Five minutes later, with no improvement to the road or a place to turn around, Liam asks, "Can you just back down?"

I let out a snort. "No way. I can barely drive this road going forward. I wouldn't want to do it backwards."

A few minutes later, we go around another curve. Liam yells, "Watch out!" just as the car bottoms out where the road has sloughed away, leaving a deep ditch.

"No, no, no!" I cry as the engine ceases.

Wyatt is screaming, apparently startled by the sudden bump. Liam and Leslie are both saying something, but I can't focus on what it is. *Please don't let the car be messed up*, I think as I open the door and carefully step out. One look at the tire, flat and leaning out slightly from the body of the car, and I know it's bad. Destiny is out of the car too.

"I'm so sorry, Clarice. I don't know how I made such a big mistake with the road."

I give a solemn nod. "Maybe it's just a flat and something we can fix." The road is so narrow, there's only about two feet between the car and the cliff. "Stay inside," I say to Liam and Leslie. "Try and comfort Wyatt." I shut the door so I can get around.

Destiny shuts her door and gets her first good look at the tire. "Oh no."

I can't help but cry at the damage. The entire front end is down in the ditch, and the passenger's tire is also flat and wonky looking. I suspect, if I crawled underneath of it, I'd find the axel broken. I glance at Destiny, who is also in tears.

"I'm so sorry," she says again.

I lift a hand. "It is what it is. We'll just— " I let out a loud breath. "We'll be on foot." With that, I let my tears overwhelm me as sobs wrack my body.

Liam is immediately by my side, arms around me.

"I . . . told you . . . stay in the . . . car," I say between sobs.

"We'll be okay, Mom. We'll be okay."

Liam and I stay with our arms around each other for several minutes. When I finally pull away, I see he's also crying. At some point, Destiny returned to the backseat of the car with Leslie. Both have their heads down.

"We can't fix it," I say.

"I know. We were smart, Mom. We have stuff to make our walk easier. And maybe we'll find another car as we go."

"You think another car will be waiting for us in the woods?" I scoff.

He gives a partial shrug. "Grandpa said God is full of miracles. He did it once, maybe He'll do it again."

"Don't you think God could've kept this from happening?" I snap. "If He's truly full of miracles, He could've just made it easy for us to get to Mollie's."

Liam shrugs again. "I don't know. Maybe . . . maybe He's testing our faith."

I give him a hard look. Through clenched teeth, I say, "I have no faith."

"Then maybe He wants to give you faith."

I lift a hand in a halt signal. "I can't deal with this right now. Unless *your God* miraculously transports us from here to Mollie's, I'm calling fake. God is fake news."

Liam's face falls as he drops his head. "I don't think He's fake, Mom. He feels completely real to me." He walks back to the passenger's side of the car, opens it, and in a too cheery voice to those inside says, "We're on foot. We'd better get organized."

As the girls spill out of the car, I admonish them to be careful of the ledge, my tone irritable and snappy.

Carefully, probably for fear I'll lash out at her, Destiny asks, "Should we go back down the hill and then use the other road?"

"I think we're close to the top," Liam says, looking up at the wall of packed dirt on the passenger's side. "If we are, it'd make sense just to finish going up and then head back down."

"We don't know where this comes out," I say, modulating my voice so it's matter of fact and not cruel. As I look from Destiny to Leslie to Wyatt and finally Liam, I realize I need to pull myself together. This is no place for my whining and crying about how unfair things are. That may have been my normal reaction before—before our world fell apart—but now everything is about survival.

"Does it matter?" he asks. "As long as we head in the general direction, we can correct our course as we go. And now, since we aren't limited to roads, we have more options."

I bite my lip, remembering not long ago when we were going across a field and were suddenly under fire. More options aren't always safer. Of course, roads aren't safe either. We were on a road when our dirt bikes were stolen. It's a no-win all the way around. *Survival, Clarice. Focus on survival and getting to Bakerville.*

"We need our things," I say. "Then let's try and get some miles in today." I reach over to squeeze Liam's arm. He gives me a nod before pulling me into a hug.

Getting the hood open, where most of our gear is stored, is near impossible. Liam and I work on it while the girls start unloading things from the roof. I'm just about ready to give up when Liam, with a long screwdriver in one hand and a hammer in the other, is able to undo the latch. He lets out a whoop as it releases.

"Good job!" I exclaim, hugging him close. "I didn't think it was going to open."

He nods and says, "Should we move everything from under the hood to behind the car? Leslie and Destiny already have all the roof stuff there. Then it'll all be in one place and we can see what we have."

"That'll work."

Once it's in one big, overwhelming pile, Liam says, "Let's move the multiday backpacks out—you know, the ones we've already filled and know we're wearing. And we'll need the smaller daypacks, Wyatt's baby bag, plus the big duffle too. We know those have to come with us."

After we do that, the pile is still mindboggling. How in the world did we get so much stuff in this little car?

"Okay," Liam says, motioning to the smaller pile of bags we know we're taking. "These are the things we must take."

"Should we put them on one of the sleds?" Leslie asks.

"We know we'll each wear one of the multiday backpacks—well, three of us anyway, since one person will carry Wyatt in his backpack," Liam says.

"The one not carrying Wyatt can carry one of the crossbody bags," Destiny says.

"Right." Liam nods. "Can everyone handle the large duffle in addition to Wyatt? I think the person carrying Wyatt should not have to pull a sled." He looks around for our thoughts. After we all agree, he says, "Okay, let's see what we're taking from the extras pile."

"I'm not sure we should think of any of it as extra," Destiny says. "I know you thought it'd be a nice gift for your friend, but we'll need these things if we're walking."

My tears again threaten to make their appearance. My throat feels raw as I say, "We'll take what we can."

"This large black backpack is full of food," Liam says, pulling it from the pile. "We definitely want to take it."

"We should take extra sleeping bags too," Leslie says. "When it's cold, we can double them up."

"Were you all warm enough last night?" I ask.

"Not in the car," Leslie says. "But I was fine inside the tent and the sleeping bag. Wyatt seemed warm enough too. He's like a little heater tucked inside the bag."

"I think we'll put the bag of food on the bottom of the toboggan," Liam says. "Mom, does that sound good?"

"It sounds smart."

I catch his beaming smile before he drops his head to examine the pile. We spend several more minutes organizing and choosing before we start loading the sleds. We put one of the tarps on the bottom of the toboggan, then add the food backpack, topped with the snowshoes, and then smaller items on top.

One of the things he adds surprises me: the crowbar from the car. I ask him about it, and he says he thinks it might be useful for getting into houses and cars. I give a nod of agreement. Bart usually used a rock or a stick he found on location. We've popped trunks open with screwdrivers, which we also have on the toboggan, but the crowbar makes sense.

When Liam thinks it's as full as it should be, he gives the sled a slight tug to check the weight. "It should be okay," he says.

We then fold the tarp around and attach everything to the sled with a couple of bungee cords. We do the same thing on the small green saucer. Unfortunately, the huge tarp has lots of excess fabric, making it not fold neatly. We decide to cut the tarp in half so we can use a portion on each saucer. To keep the edges from fraying, we seal them with the duct tape. Little Brown Hen and Poof Head are riding on top of the red saucer, with their box well secured. We decided the edge of this cliff wasn't a good place to let them stretch their legs, so we'll take a nice break once we reach the top. Hopefully, there will be space for them to peck around.

"It looks good," Leslie says. "We just pull the string on the sled?"

"We'll add some twine and tie them around our waist. I helped my dad haul a deer out that way, just put it on the game sled and used this string with a special belt attached to get it out."

"Good plan," Destiny says. "My dad has done something similar."

I look to these children. All have had so much heartache and are now forced into doing what we must do to get through each day. What will life for Wyatt be like? Will he ever be able to simply be a child, or is his future full of a day-to-day struggle? I can only hope things are better in Bakerville. While we may have to work hard, at least we won't constantly be looking over our shoulders for fear of others.

"Is that everything we need?" Leslie asks.

Liam shakes his head. "Probably not. It's still a long way to Bakerville. We'll have to salvage along the way. But this is everything we can take with us."

There's several moments of silence as each of us look at the pile still on the ground. We've taken all the food, fuel for the three backpacker-sized cookstoves, extra sleeping bags, three two-man tents along with the small bivy tent, and several other miscellaneous items. As Liam said, it's not all that we need, but there's no way we can haul any more.

"What should we do with what's left?" Leslie asks.

"Put it in the car," I say. "It'll be protected from the elements and animals. Maybe, if someone else ends up this way, it'll be useful to them."

After we reload everything, I set the car keys on the dash. While I doubt anyone can get this thing moved from here, they'll still be able to start it up. The small digital clock, the one we were so surprised to find still working, catches my eye.

"Liam, do you have something we can pry the clock off with? It should just be stuck on with some sort of adhesive."

After releasing the clock, I shove it in the pocket of my snow pants. Liam asks if I can carry Wyatt first. He thinks dragging the sleds up the hill will be best done by them—they can work together and not worry about the baby. I agree with the plan. With Wyatt, who's fresh from a nap in his car seat while we did all the arranging, in place and the large duffle resting on my hip, it's less than comfortable. Liam drags the toboggan, and each girl has a sled.

While it's not as cold as it was early this morning, there's still a chill in the air and a breeze making it feel even colder. Even so, an hour and a half later, when we reach the crest of the road, I've shed my heavy coat and am only in a hoody, the children having done the same. We even stopped and undid Wyatt's snow suit so he could get a little extra air. We're all thoroughly exhausted after our uphill climb.

"It's pretty here," Leslie says, looking around. While the mountain reaches high into the sky, the road starts down the eastern slope. The valley below really is breathtaking.

Destiny lifts the small binoculars and scans the space. "I think I can see the town—well, maybe. These aren't very powerful, but I'm pretty sure it's over there."

With my naked eye, I can't make out anything, which tells me it's a long way to town. That's both good and bad. Good because hopefully we won't run into anyone else. Bad because . . . well, it's a long walk still. At least each step will get us closer to our destination.

Chapter 34

October 26th

It's been a month since we lost the car. A month of walking. Some days, thanks to the weather, we walk very little or not at all. Two days after we crashed the Bug, it started snowing. It snowed steadily for several days, causing us to stay holed up in our tents until the storm passed. With the tents next to each other, as long as the wind wasn't roaring, we'd talk through the thin walls. I decided to take Wyatt in with Liam and me so the girls, especially Destiny who was still shook up, could rest. Holding the baby and caring for him helped me come to terms with the killing I did. While I hate that it was necessary, I know I'd do it again if it was needed to keep any of my group safe.

Unlike before, the snow hasn't melted away. The temps have dropped to below freezing, and it continues to snow off and on. Some days, the snow is light and the weather—though cold—is relatively mild with the sun shining, allowing us to walk. Other days, the wind blows, lowering the temperatures to something unbearable. Out of fear of frostbite, we're incredibly careful to not be out on those blistery days. While I know little about frostbite, I do understand it's something we don't want to risk.

When there's adequate cover, we walk parallel to roads. Many times, that's not possible, and we again take the forest service two-tracks or other rarely used routes. To help with our continued scheme of staying hidden—or as Bart called it, *evade and escape*—we have what Destiny calls ghillie suits. One is really just a white coverall set like painters use that we found in the garage of a house we were salvaging. Liam wears that one. A white pillowcase covers Wyatt's backpack, and the second pillowcase was turned into a cover to go over his snow suit. We were able to find a larger insulated suit, so he's still wearing two and seems plenty warm.

The girls and I made our ghillie suits out of white sheets we've found. We even wear white hoods, which way too much resemble a certain well-known hate group. Even though we've cut out the faces instead of just the eyes, I still balked at the idea at first. Then I realized we really need to do all we can to remain unseen. After covering our bodies, we found sheeting to cover our sleds and backpacks. It won't fool anyone closeup—and maybe not even from a distance, considering we're moving across the landscape—but we like to think it helps.

The snowshoes have been amazing. Like Destiny said, they keep us above the snow. In the areas where there are bare patches, thanks to sunshine or the wind blowing the snow into drifts, we'll often encounter mud. The snowshoes even help with keeping us from being sucked in completely, though Liam and I do need to be careful. Our snowshoes don't hook on nearly as well as the pairs Destiny and Leslie have, and we've lost one or both on several occasions. As much as we wish we could make huge miles each day, we're averaging less than ten on the days we hike. The snow and cold slow everything down.

Walking has taken a toll on not only our bodies but our gear. The saucer sleds were not made for the kind of abuse we've given them. Thankfully, we found a heavy-duty game sled, allowing us to double up the saucers—making them sturdier—and still have three sleds. And the game sled is much larger, giving us the ability to carry more. Finding extra tarps has been no problem, so our load is well covered to protect from the elements. We're still looking for two additional, thicker sleds to replace the saucers and toboggan.

Most nights, we're camping in our tents. Liam was smart to add the third tent, which we use to stow the extra gear and as a place we can all gather to get out of the weather. We brought the little bivy tent also but have yet to put it up. Cooking in the snow and wind is a huge challenge, but we make it work most nights. Liam sets up his snares every time we stop, but we rarely catch anything. Surprisingly, he and Leslie have each provided a meal using their slingshots. She got a rabbit, and he got a tree squirrel.

Poof Head gave us an egg when we were stopped to wait out the snow; we'd found a shed to stay in during the storm. Since then, she's given us an egg every few days, even when traveling. We get a sporadic egg from Little Brown. We've long been out of formula, so the eggs are for Wyatt. I'm starting to worry about him. While most of the time he's good natured, occasionally he'll start screaming and won't stop. Destiny has some herbal tonic she's been using for him, but we're running low on it. It does seem to help when he starts screaming. She says the ingredients are to help soothe a stomachache or colic. He's a little old for colic, but I can understand the stomachache.

We've gone through most of our food. We're salvaging empty houses when we can, with Liam often taking the role of salvager. I clear the houses while he keeps watch. Occasionally, what we find inside will be too gruesome for him to see. Those times, I stay in and salvage what I can. But most of the time, he salvages and I stand watch. Leslie and Destiny keep Wyatt away in a safe place.

We have a list of things we're always looking for. Food, of course, is at the top of the list. It's also the hardest thing to find since we're rarely the first ones to search a place. Diapers and other things for Wyatt are also something we're always looking for, as are socks, gloves, and other warm items for each of us. And underwear. We all need underwear and other clothing. We don't do laundry while trekking; it'd be too much work. Our clothes are disposable. But the outerwear isn't that big of a deal to keep wearing day in and out.

Some other things we're on the lookout for are vitamins, herbs, and any type of medicine. Anything Liam finds in the medical category, he brings out. Sometimes we can't use what he finds, as it'll be heart medicine or something similar. We have a small book from Destiny's mom's things that helps us figure out medicines. If we're not sure of something, we get rid of it. We've also all found sunglasses, which helps cut down on the continual glare from the snow. Even Wyatt has tiny ones.

Last night, we found a house to stay the night in. It was completely empty—meaning there were no bodies inside—and well hidden. We hadn't seen any houses for quite some time, and according to our map, we're many miles from the nearest town. It was nice to be out of the elements, but still cold inside. Though the propane cookstove still worked, enabling us to heat water and food and provide a small amount of heat, there wasn't a woodstove or fireplace. We set up the tents to give us little cocoons of warmth. The house had already been looted, so there wasn't much in the way of food or supplies we could use. Still, it was a welcome refuge.

This morning, I have the last watch. The sun has yet to rise, but the moon is full and bright when a herd of mule deer walk into the yard. After only a moment's hesitation, I slip into my coat and slide on my zip-front boots, then grab the rifle and move to the door. After quietly letting myself out, I crouch-walk to the side of the house where I saw the deer.

I'm half shocked they're still there, snacking on bushes and trees. One small spike buck is even pawing at the ground, trying to move enough snow to get to the grass underneath. He's not even thirty feet from me, and he's my target. I lean against the house, using it and my knee as a brace. While I'm somewhat steady, my heart is pounding so hard it's throwing me off. I take a deep breath to sooth myself. I have him in my sights, with the front pin on him. I take another deep breath as he lifts his head. Now or never.

I squeeze the trigger and watch him jump. I work the lever to rack in another cartridge. He spins around, takes a few steps, and falls. The rest of the deer run like the wind into the night. I'm breathing hard and trying to get control when the door opens slightly.

"Mom?" Liam says in a hiss. "Mom?"

"I'm here. I, uh . . . I shot a deer."

"Really? Is it dead?"

"I think so. It's on the ground. Will you let Destiny and Leslie know what's happening so they don't worry? I didn't think. I'm sorry." With the rifle at the ready, I start walking toward the deer. I remember reading about a guy who was elk hunting and thought his elk was dead, but he wasn't. The elk jumped up and gored the guy. Then, the elk ran away and the guy died. As I get closer, I can see the deer is obviously dead. A mix of emotions runs through me. This deer will give us food for weeks. In this weather, it may even stay frozen as we walk.

Seconds later, Liam and Destiny are both by my side. "Good job," Destiny says. "Do you think the shot—will someone have heard it?"

"Uh . . . I don't know," I admit. "Do you think we can use the pulley set up in the shed?" I ask Liam. He and I briefly checked the outbuildings to make sure they were empty.

"Yeah, I think that might be what they set it up for."

"Let's take it to the shed then. Destiny, have Leslie get Wyatt ready. We'll all go to the shed. Bring the gear, too, in case we need to leave in a hurry."

"It'll take me just a minute to get everything together," she says, quickly walking away.

"He's going to be heavy, Mom, and we'll leave a blood trail and drag marks."

"There's nothing we can do about it," I say. "I should've thought about that. I was just— " I shrug.

"Hungry?"

"Yeah."

Liam and I have the deer about halfway to the shed when Destiny comes out towing the toboggan and a pack on her back. She hustles past us, saying, "I'll help you when I'm finished with this." She runs back to the house and quickly reappears with Leslie by her side, carrying Wyatt. They stay in the shed while Destiny makes another trip to the house.

"Hold the door open," I say. "I'll get it the rest of the way." Once he's inside, I'm exhausted.

"We should've gutted it," Liam says.

"Yeah. I'm going to do that other thing. The one your dad was watching videos about." Liam gives me a blank look. "You know, where they just cut the legs off."

"Do you know how?" he asks skeptically.

"No. But I don't really know how to do the regular gutting and cutting up either."

"I know how to do it," Leslie says. "At least, I've seen it done. I can help."

Destiny pops back in with the final bit of gear and looks at the deer. "He's a great one, Clarice. I'm going to see if I can make the trail to the shed a little less obvious, then I'll stand watch over there. I'll be able to see you guys and see if anyone comes up the driveway. Um . . . do you know what to do with the deer?"

I shake my head. "We'll figure it out. Leslie says she thinks she knows what to do."

"Maybe Leslie and I should take care of the deer? You and Liam can stand watch."

"I can help," Liam bristles.

"Okay. Help me scuff up the trail and then we'll get started. Clarice, do you want the shotgun or the rifle?"

"Rifle. Did you bring my snow pants out?"

"Yes, on top of the toboggan." Destiny motions to them. "Thought you might need them." Eyes shining, she gives me a brilliant smile. The second morning we found ourselves on foot, she gave up her Goth look. Since then, her face has been bare of makeup, letting her natural beauty shine. Her black hair, courtesy of a bottle, now sports a good inch of dark blond roots. I'm also showing roots—gray ones at my temple. That's something new.

After getting my snow pants on, I turn to Leslie. "Make sure someone is always looking out the window. Keep eyes on me. I'll signal if needed."

"How long do you think we need to stay out here?"

"I don't know. If someone heard the shot, they may or may not come to investigate. Let's get the deer done and then go from there."

After an hour at my perch, Liam comes to relieve me. "The deer is about half done," he says. "We're not very good at it, so it's a pretty slow process."

"Are they taking the hide off too?"

"Yeah, as they work on each quarter. There are places to hang them in there, a rack at the back, but I don't think we should leave it out here. It'll freeze—unless that's what we want?"

"Maybe we should move it into the house? It's cold in there, but probably not as cold. I think I'm going to go through the woods, see if there's any nearby houses farther up the road."

"You sure, Mom?"

"It'd give me some peace of mind to know the likelihood of someone coming here after hearing the shot. Besides, a walk will do me good. Let me go tell the girls."

Wyatt is stretched out on a blanket bed they made him, sound asleep. He looks adorable. "The deer looks good," I say.

"Thanks," Destiny says. "Both Leslie and I have watched this done many times, and I've helped, but doing it on our own is something else. We have both the front and back legs off the one side, plus the backstrap and the tenderloin are out. There's quite a bit of meat on his neck, so we're taking it too. We still have the other side to do."

"I'm going to walk through the woods a bit, toward the east, to see if there's any houses nearby. Might help us know if there's an impending threat."

"Good idea," Destiny says, wiping her hand across her nose and leaving a streak of blood.

I walk what I judge to be a mile without seeing any sign of civilization. Feeling somewhat relieved, I hustle back to the children. When I'm close to Liam, I softly say his name.

He answers with, "I'm here, Mom." As I walk closer to him, he says, "They've got it done. They're taking the pieces inside and hanging them in the bathroom."

"Good plan. I'll start getting us some snow to melt." Unlike the running water we had at Isabel and Jeff's, or the solar-powered stock tank at the Delgados', there's no water here. As we've been doing for the last several weeks, when we can't find a stream or river, we melt snow. Melting snow is awful. It takes a large amount of snow to melt into a small amount of water. This snow seems particularly dry and doesn't produce much water at all. It's definitely not my idea of a good time.

"They found a game sled in the shed," Liam says. "It was tucked in a corner behind some other stuff. I don't know how I didn't see it yesterday."

"We only did a cursory inspection yesterday since it was getting dark. You would've found it in the daylight. It'll be good to have. The toboggan wouldn't have made it much farther."

Chapter 35

November 16th

We stayed at the house several days, never having any trouble with people showing up. We cut, cleaned, and cooked the venison. What we didn't immediately eat, we put in the shed so it would freeze solid. We ate like queens and kings those days. Wyatt was happy, and the chickens couldn't get enough of the scraps we'd give them. The backstrap steaks were amazing, as was the tenderloin medallions. We even cooked a couple of the bones down to make broth. That was put in zipper sandwich bags we found in the cabinet and then set outside to freeze.

We've been back on the road for two weeks now, and I think we're making much better time than before the deer. We all seem to have more energy and can hike farther each day. We're certainly not setting any records, but if we can keep up this pace, we think we'll be at Mollie's house before Christmas. I dare to even hope we can make it by then. What a Christmas gift it would be.

As we discussed this, Liam brought up what he believes is the greatest Christmas gift: the birth of Jesus. Then he recited a section from the Bible Bart had me read in those final days: *"For God so loved the world that He gave His one and only Son, that whoever believes in Him shall not perish but have eternal life. For God did not send His Son into the world to condemn the world, but to save the world through Him."*

Each night when we stop, Liam talks a lot about what he's reading in the Bible. Both Destiny and Leslie participate in the conversations, but I'm more hesitant. I've decided it doesn't really bother me that Liam has chosen this path, but it's not something I'm interested in.

Could Bart be right, though? Could my dad have made a different decision right before his death? Did my mom truly accept Christ before she passed away? In a way, that feels wrong. Why would God or Jesus—whoever it is that makes the decisions about who goes to heaven or hell—allow someone to say they'll follow them at the last minute, in their last dying breath? Shouldn't they be expected to decide when they're young, like Liam, and can really make a difference? Not just as they are dying?

Then I think about the story of the guy on the cross next to Jesus. Not just a guy—a thief. He even said he deserved to be up there. That doesn't sound like he was a good man. My dad, though, he was a good man. He was always helping people and would go out of his way to be a good neighbor and friend. But Jesus told the thief they'd be in heaven together. It's all very confusing.

"Don't you think, Mom?" Liam asks in a low voice while touching my arm. It's obvious he's tried to get my attention before now. We make a point of walking in silence since the area we're going through is more populated than most. I'm surprised I didn't hear him the first time.

"Sorry?" I ask, looking around to get my bearings. We're reaching the top of a hill.

"We think there's a town down in the valley. Don't you think we should go around it?"

"Oh, yes, of course. Sorry, I was woolgathering. Are we on the right track to miss it?"

We're only a few feet from the top of the hill when Liam grabs my arm and pulls me down. He turns behind him and motions for the girls to get down and be quiet. They're several feet behind us, staying well back from the game sled Liam has and the toboggan I'm pulling—a new blue one we've salvaged along the way that's smaller than our old red one. With the addition of the new toboggan, we're now each pulling a sled. Destiny has the baby and the doubled-up saucer sleds, while Leslie has the other heavy-duty game sled.

"What do you see?" I ask in a low voice, right next to Liam's ear.

"People."

One of our greatest fears. I give a nod and say, "Let's go back down and then go around."

"Let me see exactly where they are," he says.

"No. Stay down. There's no need to risk being seen."

"If we don't know where they are, we won't know which way to go around."

I motion him to hold still while I try and think. Finally, I lean toward him and say, "I'll look."

He offers me a tight nod. I quickly release my snowshoes and untie the toboggan, then take the pistol out of my new hip holster I found just a few days ago. The dead lady was still wearing it when I cleared a house; the weapon itself was gone. With a deep breath, I slowly move up the hill toward a scrawny bush near the top.

As soon as I can see, I stop moving. Not bothering with the binoculars, I look over the expanse of white. Far down the other side of the hill, almost at the bottom, is a line of people. They're walking across the space instead of coming uphill and toward us. I squint slightly, trying to make out what I'm seeing, and then decide to pull out my field glasses.

As soon as I have them in place, it's obvious things are not right. The people in the line are flanked by others walking on the sides and behind. The ones in line aren't dressed for the weather: no coats, hats, or scarves. Their clothes are ratty and well-worn. I don't even think they're wearing shoes. The ones flanking them are fully dressed and carrying guns, directed at the barely dressed people.

I look ahead to see where they're going. I don't need to look too far to see a drop off. Suddenly, it all becomes clear. The undressed are prisoners. As they reach the drop off, the ones with the guns start motioning to the others to line up with their backs to the cliff. I shake my head in disbelief. They're going to shoot them—shoot them and let them fall off. They'll be murdered as I watch, and there's nothing I can do about it.

Our weapons don't have the range needed to stop them. And how could we? We'd make ourselves sitting ducks. I give a small shake of my head. Whatever's happening there, it's none of our business. Not only is it not our business, but I don't want to see this. And I don't want the children to know what's happening. But I must watch— watch so we know what the ones with the guns do next.

I scoot back down slightly so my head is below the crest. I motion for the others to cover their ears. Liam gives me a quizzical look. "Just do it," I mouth. He nods. I look to the girls. With wide eyes, Leslie nods several times, her hands in place. Destiny has taken Wyatt from the backpack and is cradling him; thankfully, he's asleep. She has one hand over his ear with his other ear pressed against her chest. She shakes her head slightly, telling me she'll only be able to take care of him. I nod my understanding and then carefully move back to where

I can see, keeping behind the bush and appreciating my white covering and ugly white hood.

The prisoners are lined up, and the shooters are in position. I put my hands over my own ears. Even though I'll see it, I don't want to hear it. From our distance, and with my earmuffs, I still jump as the shots go off. What I expect to last only seconds seems to go on an eternity as the shooters keep firing. One person finally raises his hand, getting everyone to stop.

I'm surprised when I wonder if any of the people who were shot have accepted Jesus. *Are they now on their way to heaven? Would I know?* Bart had a serene smile as he passed. He looked peaceful and almost joyous. I look intently at the bodies on the ground. I'm too far away to see their faces, only puddles of red staining the snow.

The man who stopped the massacre walks from prisoner to prisoner with his handgun at the ready. I jump again when he fires. After he's done, I take my hands down and strain to hear. He's turned slightly away from me. With him in profile, I can see his mouth moving and hear the slight rumble of his voice in the wind, but I can't make out anything he says. After a moment, the others sling their rifles and walk over to him, chucking the people they just murdered off the cliff.

With my gloved hand covering my mouth, I watch as the dead are disposed of. As soon as the gruesome job is completed, they turn and start walking back to the south, using the same general trail they arrived on. While there's little chance of being seen, since they're now walking across the field and slightly away from us, I make sure I'm as low as possible, keeping my head down so only my eyes are showing. Hopefully, my white cap will make me look like nothing but a snow-covered rock, should one of them turn this direction and scan the hillside. I let out a small sigh of relief when they're finally out of my view. I scoot back down to where the children are.

"What happened?" Liam immediately asks.

"Nothing good. I'll tell you about it later. Right now, I'm going over to that small knob." I point to a place in the general direction where I think the shooters may have gone. "I want to see if I can tell where they're going." I start putting my snowshoes back on.

"What are you going to do?" Destiny asks in a quiet yet fierce voice.

I shake my head. "Just watch, see which way they went and make sure we go a different way."

"We need to make them pay."

I close my eyes and take a deep breath. "I don't really know what . . . what I witnessed." She starts to speak, but I hold up my hand. "I know what happened, but not *why* it happened. Maybe those people were the aggressors, and this was punishment or something for attacking them. I can't make anyone pay when I don't know what happened. Besides, *you guys* are my focus."

"It's not right," she mutters.

"I know. Stay behind the hill. I'll be right back." I move quickly across the hillside. Well, not overly quick since the angle and snow makes movement difficult.

Once I reach the spot, I glass the area with the binoculars. It takes only a moment to find the people, still heading in a southerly direction. Scanning ahead, I see houses. Taking the glasses down, I look over the entire area and decide it's a small town. There are strings of smoke making their way from the homes. With the binoculars back in place, I give everything another good look, then look to the north for any obvious threats.

After deciding I have the information I need, I make my way back to the children. Like Destiny, I feel like the murderers should pay. Tears sting my eyes as I remember the massacre. Watching that is something I'll never forget. It also gives me more determination to continue being stealthy and avoid all people.

When I reach the children, Destiny gives me a hard look.

Liam hands me a piece of hardtack and says, "We should eat something before we move on. Have some water too." The hardtack's made from flour, part of a huge score we found a few days ago, and doesn't provide much nutrition, but it helps keep our bellies full.

"They're gone?" Leslie asks after finishing a long drink of water.

"Yes, there's a town not far from here. Looks like they're going there."

"They shot people?"

I give a slow nod. "They did."

"Could you tell if the shooters were the bad guys?" Liam asks. "If they are, we should do what Destiny said and make them pay."

"I don't know." I shake my head. "It doesn't matter. We're not going anywhere near that town. Even if we did know, we couldn't do anything about it."

We sit in silence for several minutes before Destiny says, "It's not right."

"No," I agree. "It's not right."

"But there's nothing we can do, right?" Leslie asks, but it sounds more of a statement. "I mean, we don't have the right kind of guns for going after people. And how many of them were there? I didn't see."

"Too many," I say. "And no, we don't have the right kind of guns. We'll go north for a bit and then start east again." I take out the water I have tucked inside my jacket against my chest to keep from freezing. After I have a long drink, Leslie asks if I want another piece of the hardtack. We still have venison, but we've been making it last as long as possible by eating it only when we stop for the night. While our food is still never enough, we're doing better than we were at one point, especially after a good salvage a few days ago. The flour we found was in a car, along with bags of other groceries.

The car appeared to have been in an accident—which must have happened in the early days of the attacks—and was abandoned. We made up our own story as to why it was still there, since we'll never know the truth. They were making a trip to town for groceries after the airplane or bridge attacks. On the way home, a deer darted in front of them and caused them to swerve and go into the ditch. Leslie says it was a woman driving since the seat was slid forward. They called someone to pick them up and planned to go back for the groceries. Why they didn't, we don't know.

When we popped the trunk open and found all the food, I started to cry. The produce was long passed spoiled, now only frozen bags of slimy liquid. Some of the cans had burst or were bulging from freezing, but we were able to salvage several cans of stewed tomatoes, baked beans, and dozens of cans of soup. All the dry goods were fine—flour, pasta, rice, pinto beans, oatmeal, tea bags, and even coffee—along with a large jug of cooking oil and a slightly smaller jar of olive oil. There were even several tins of tuna in oil that escaped any issues. Currently, tucked in my jacket next to my water bottle, I have a zipper bag—also found in the car—filled with pasta and water.

Our cooking is now done sparingly. We've already used all the fuel canisters for the small backpacking stoves we found at Isabel and Jeff's place. We're now using a larger one-burner propane stove with the green one-pound propane containers found in a garage. We do anything we can to cut down our fuel usage. The pasta will soften throughout the day, and we'll give it a quick warmup so we can have a hot meal. The last can of tuna will go in the pasta; it'll almost be a delicacy.

"Ready?" I ask when my biscuit is halfway gone.

Destiny's still angry at me and refuses to meet my eyes as we get ready to go. Once we're on our way, she softens slightly and gives me a slight tilt of her head.

As we travel across the side of the hill, I make sure we'll avoid the gully used as a burial ground. About an hour before sundown, we stop and set up our camp.

We're sitting in our supply tent, eating our supper, when Liam asks, "Do you think it'd be safer for us to walk at night? I know we've discussed it before and decided not to, but we're getting to an area with more towns."

"I've thought about it, but I just don't think we'll be able to see well enough. And even though it's cold during the day, its miserably cold at night."

"What about during the full moon?"

"Still cold," Leslie says, giving a shiver.

"Let's wait until we're closer to the full moon and then decide. Maybe we'll get a warming streak. Destiny and Leslie both say that's common during winters around here."

"I thought we'd have one already," Destiny says. "To have snow on the ground continuously isn't normal."

"We do have cold winters sometimes," Leslie says. "My parents were always talking about the snow they used to get when they were children."

"And last year was really cold," Destiny says with a nod. "But this snow . . . " She gives a shrug. "I don't know. Maybe, when we get to a lower elevation, it'll decrease."

"I thought we've been in lower elevations," Liam says with a shrug. The girls both nod their agreement.

After several minutes, Destiny asks, "You saw the nuclear bombs? Isn't there a thing about those causing bad winters?"

I search my memory, trying to find any recollection of what she's talking about. "I don't know," I finally say. "I've never thought much about nuclear attacks."

"Seems my dad mentioned it at some point. We didn't know about actual bombs—just the EMP wiping everything out—but he was talking to Dr. Jewell once and said, 'At least we shouldn't have nuclear winter—if that's really a thing.' I meant to ask him about it but never did."

"Nuclear winter . . . " I say slowly. "That does sound familiar. I think I remember talk about it after Chernobyl. But that wasn't an actual nuclear detonation, like bombs. It was a nuclear reactor and didn't do anything to the weather. At least, I don't think it did. I don't know." I shake my head.

"The internet would sure come in handy right now," Liam says. "We'd have our answer in a matter of seconds."

Chapter 36

November 27th
The Day After Thanksgiving

Two days after the massacre, Wyatt started coughing. At first, I didn't think much of it; we all cough from hiking in the cold. We also always have runny noses. None of us seem at all sick. It's just a part of being in the elements. Within twenty-four hours, he was running a fever and crying almost constantly. We were in a more populated area and decided to find a house to stay in while we tried to sort out what was wrong with him.

When Liam was a baby, he was extremely sick with respiratory syncytial virus, commonly known as RSV. While for most babies and young children the virus is nothing more than a cold, for Liam it resulted in him being hospitalized for three days. But RSV is a virus spread through the air and direct contact. We're never around anyone but each other. How would he get a virus?

We were nearing Yellowstone Park and would likely not be able to find a good place to stay, other than our tents, once we were inside the boundaries, so I started to look for a house. The first one had a body. While I didn't want us staying there, Liam was able to do a little salvaging and added to our supplies.

The second place, which we could see from a distance, had smoke billowing from the chimney—obviously occupied. It wasn't far to the next house. With no smoke, I crept up to it and peered in a window. The room was a bedroom, and it took only a quick glance to see two bodies in the bed. It was a death house. We almost skipped salvaging or anything, but I desperately wanted to get Wyatt inside. I thought maybe, if we could get him out of the elements and give him a little extra nourishment, he'd be fine.

I decided on a quick trip through the house, having Liam stand guard this time while I did the salvaging. With the cold permeating every inch of the home, there wasn't much of a lingering odor. As I looked through the empty cabinets, I came up with an idea.

If we kept the bedroom door shut, we could stay there for at least a night. There was a woodstove in the corner, and it would be dark in a few hours. We could light up a fire and warm the house overnight. Maybe a night out of the cold would be enough to rid Wyatt of his cough. I checked all the rooms, except the one I'd seen from outside, to make sure they were clear. I didn't want to open the tomb but knew there was no choice. While unlikely, there could've been a living person in there, someone who meant us harm. It was empty except the bodies in the bed.

We ended up staying there until this morning, shattering any chance of making it to Bakerville in time for Christmas. While it was too risky to have fires during the day, for fear of people seeing our smoke in a house that had clearly already been looted, we had a fire each night, boiling pots of water to make extra humidity. We also gave Wyatt multivitamins and extra vitamin C crystals—a find from several weeks ago that Destiny called *a lifesaver*. By the third day, I was starting to wonder if Wyatt needed to be given some of the fish antibiotics.

"Why's he drooling so much?" Leslie asked.

I took a good look at him and realized she was right. He'd been coughing and gagging incessantly. I wondered, was it from the drool? I reached inside his mouth and rubbed my finger along his gum. Liam never had any trouble with teething and didn't even get his first tooth until he was almost ten months old. I remember the doctor telling me not to worry at our six-month checkup; while six months was a common age for a baby's first tooth, some get them earlier and some even much later. He went into a long, drawn out story about one of his patients not getting a tooth until he was over a year. Wyatt is somewhere around seven months old, so a tooth would make sense.

While I didn't feel an actual tooth, there was a hard lump on the bottom. Was all of this over a new tooth? Maybe, or maybe he was really sick. Erring on the side of caution, when we had our nightly fire, I made a hot pot of water and used a blanket to hold in the steam. The two of us sat in the steam tent for hours. When the steam would begin to lessen, one of the other children would give us a new hot pot. His coughing began to ease off afterward, and he even slept through the night. After that night, his sickness began to improve. Now he's once again happy, smiling and sporting a new tooth.

While at the house, we got two eggs from Poof Head and one from Little Brown, and Liam supplied us with three rabbits and two squirrels—through a combination of snares and his slingshot—along with catching a wild pigeon in a box trap. We almost ate like royalty.

Yesterday, according to the calendars Liam and Leslie keep, was Thanksgiving. Liam surprised us with a second pigeon he'd caught a couple of days before. He cleaned it and kept it frozen until the morning before Thanksgiving. When we started our nighttime fire, he brought it out. We all oohed and awed over it. I left it whole and dredged it in a small amount of flour, then browned it in a dollop of our precious cooking oil before adding previously boiled snow water to simmer the bird.

We've been using the olive oil found in the trunk of the car as a tonic, each taking a portion daily to add an extra hundred calories to our meager rations. Once it's gone, we'll use the cooking oil in the same manner. While this house had been well-scoured for supplies before we arrived, we still managed to find a few things that were missed. As we've found out during our looting from house to house, people put things in strange places—places easy to miss.

This couple used the tops of their cabinets for storing things out of sight—or at least one of them did, and my guess is it was the husband. We found two boxes of individually packaged brownies made famous by a certain little girl. One box had only two packages left; the other was unopened. He had a second stash of fun-size peanut-filled candies underneath the top drawer of a desk in the office. Finding those treats led Leslie and Liam to spend many hours each day looking for other hidey holes, to no avail.

Once our pigeon was thoroughly cooked, we removed the meat from the bone and added our final can of stewed tomatoes. We kept it cool all day, then warmed it up once the sun went down and we started our evening fire. Pigeon stew for Thanksgiving. While it's never a meal I would've considered in the past, it was amazing. We had the last of our carefully rationed sweets for dessert. The pigeon bones were cooked overnight, giving us broth for future meals.

Today's a beautiful day for walking through the snow. There's no wind, and the sun's shining. There's even a bit of melt going on—not so much the snow-packed ground risks clearing, but the *drip, drip,*

drip of water falling from the trees provides a nice background noise. Little Brown Hen and Poof Head were less than excited to return to their box. While we were still at the house, Leslie suggested we may want to look for a cage for them. If they can get some light during the day, they may give us eggs more regularly.

Destiny said she didn't think it'd matter much because they need a certain amount of daylight to lay regularly, and that just doesn't happen during the winter. She suggested we put one of our battery-operated lanterns in the box with them to provide artificial light. The exchange was rather spirited for a few minutes while Leslie attempted to make her case, stating they gave more eggs while we were staying in one place than when we traveled.

I agreed, but I know nothing about chickens since I've never been around them before staying at the Delgados' place and only brought these two with me to save them from the people who showed up. While I do love getting the eggs, I've come to think of Little Brown and Poof Head as pets—friends, even. And I'm not sure an open cage is a good idea. The box keeps them warm. And since it's dark, they sleep, which also keeps them fairly quiet—a definite plus. I've considered the lantern idea, but I'm not sure we should be using our batteries like that.

Wyatt's feeling much better and is jabbering as we walk. It's not a problem with no one around, but if we were to find ourselves in a dangerous situation where we needed to be completely silent, we may have difficulty. And we've been in a more highly populated area for too long as we make our way from Idaho well into Montana. It won't be long now until we reach the edge of Yellowstone National Park.

As we walk, I think about the part of the Bible Liam was reading last night. I've stopped fussing about his desire to share what he reads. I often have something else to do during the time and barely pay attention. Last night, I found myself tuning in to what he was saying. I don't know what he was reading about, but the phrase *be strong and courageous* kept being repeated.

As I walk, strong and courageous echoes through my head, combining with the dripping from the snow melt to create a cadence. Am I strong and courageous? Months ago, I was teetering on the edge. Starvation was consuming not only my body but my mind. I wanted nothing more than to stay at the Delgados' place to try and create the semblance of a normal life. Liam told me I needed to pull myself together, to be fierce.

Now, rather than fierce, I think strong and courageous is what I need. Not only did he say to be strong and courageous, but he also said to not be frightened or dismayed because God would be with me. Strong and courageous . . . is that something I can be on my own? Or if I choose to follow God, to accept Jesus, will I have help? As the cadence continues to beat in my head, I realize I need help. No matter how fierce I try to be, I'm still weak.

Destiny sidles up next to me, interrupting my thoughts. In a quiet voice, she says, "I think we're being followed."

I whip my ahead around, looking in all directions, seeing nothing. "Why's that?"

"There's just—we are. I've caught a glimpse of movement several times."

"Maybe it's a deer?" I ask as we keep trudging through the snow. We spied a town in the distance and have been making a large loop around it, keeping talk to a minimum as we walk, especially after seeing human footprints. The prints were several days old, possibly someone traveling through like us, or maybe one of the townsfolk out hunting. Could that be who's following us?

She gives me a look I interpret as me being daft. "Deer don't usually follow people. They run away. Or at the very least, stand still until we pass them. This has been going on for several minutes."

I give a nod. "I'll drop back. You and the children go on ahead." Destiny was walking at the back of our group, towing one of the game sleds, with me directly in front of her with the blue toboggan. Leslie is pulling the saucer ahead of me with Wyatt on her back, and Liam's in the lead with the other heavy-duty sled.

"Should I tell them?" she asks.

"Let me see what's going on. Just keep the usual pace." She tilts her head at me. As she opens her mouth to say more, I lift a hand. "I'll see what's going on."

She gives me a reluctant nod before moving ahead of me. As we walk, I keep glancing around, as does Destiny. I begin to relax after about ten minutes, having decided everything is fine.

The sound of a twig breaking causes me to turn quickly. I let out a yelp as I'm shoved to the ground.

Before I even know what's happening, a wave of pain goes through my shoulder. I'm smacked in the head, knocking me farther into the snow. The pressure on my shoulder lessens as huge teeth quickly come toward me, aiming for my throat. My attacker lets out a short, high cry as his head suddenly springs back and a black blur connects with it. He lets out another yelp as he's hit again and again. I struggle to make sense of what's happening, the pain in my shoulder engulfing my senses.

"Mom, Mom," Liam says as he grabs me near the collar of my coat and yanks me away. I cry out as the pain overwhelms me. I've slid several feet across the snow when the shotgun roars. I'm looking at Liam's face when everything starts to spin.

"Go, go!" a faraway voice says.

Something's cutting into my hip as the voice says we need some distance. I'm on my stomach and bounce up, letting out a shriek as my left hip and right shoulder scream in pain. "You're okay, Clarice. We're going to stop in a few minutes."

I lift my head to try and see her so I can respond. The pain in my shoulder's intense, and everything goes black.

"Mom, I'm going to roll you off the sled and onto your back. Okay? Are you ready?"

"Watch her shoulder," one of the girls say.

There are hands on my hips, at my knees, on top of my head, and at my elbow. Someone's crying. A baby. The baby is crying.

"On three," the girl says. She starts to count, and I wonder what's going to happen on three. Suddenly, I'm moving, being rolled from my stomach.

"Oh! Stop! Stop," I pant before everything goes dark again.

The next time I wake, I'm in a tent with Liam sitting next to me.

"What happened?" I ask in a croak.

"Oh! You're awake!"

"Mm-hmm," I say, closing my eyes.

"Are you . . . going to tell . . . me?"

"What's that, Clarice?" she asks.

"Where's Liam? I was talking to him," I answer as I try to focus on her face. What's her name?

"He's getting some rest."

"I was— " I feel my forehead wrinkle. "We were just talking."

She nods her head. "I think you might have a concussion. There's a knot on the back of your head. Does it hurt?"

I start to shake my head. Just the simple movement sends pain from my head down through my neck and into my shoulder. I let out a gasp.

"I guess it does. We gave you ibuprofen and one of the pain pills. You can have more in an hour or so," she says, looking at Bart's watch.

Bart's . . . he's dead. I close my eyes as memories of the last several months wash over me. "Destiny?" I ask.

"Yes?"

"Where is . . . where's my son?"

"Sleeping. He has Wyatt with him."

Wyatt. "The baby?"

"Right. Leslie is on watch."

"What happened to me?"

"Mountain lion. It must have . . . I thought we were being followed. Do you remember that?"

I start to shake my head, then decide against it. "No," I whisper.

"I didn't see her until you cried out. I think she might have been teaching her kittens how to hunt."

"Her kittens . . . " I let out a breath. "I need . . . to . . . "

Chapter 37

November 28th

"I brought you a cup of coffee, babe."

The smell is tantalizing, rich and nutty. He's put the French vanilla cream in it—my favorite. I reach my arms lazily above my head to stretch. *Argh!* My breath is suddenly taken away by pain in my head, shoulder, and various other places. What's wrong with me?

"You're okay, Mom. You're okay."

"I'm not. No, something's wrong, Liam. I hurt." Opening my eyes, I look around. I'm in a tent. Where's Ben? Where's the special coffee? I meet Liam's eyes. I was dreaming, dreaming of my dead husband. I scrunch up my face. What did the girl—Destiny—what did she tell me happened? "A cougar attacked me?"

"Yes, a mountain lion—I don't know if a cougar is the same thing. Is it?" He scrunches up his face while he searches his memory.

"When?"

"Yesterday. Do you need some more pain medicine?"

"I . . . I hurt."

He helps me take two little reddish pills, then says, "We have the stronger stuff, too, but it's not time for those yet. You can have one in two hours if you need it."

"I'm . . . things don't make sense."

"You hit your head. When she knocked you down, she smacked you with her paw and slammed your head into the ground. It's a good thing there was snow on the ground. It was mostly covering the rock you landed on."

"And my shoulder?"

"She bit you."

"Oh. Is it bad?" Bart cut his leg and ended up dying from it. Wouldn't a mountain lion bite be worse than a cut from barbed wire?

"It's pretty bad. We think a bone might be cracked. But—and this is good, Mom—you were wearing so many layers her teeth didn't cut into you. And she couldn't get to your neck. Destiny thinks that's what she was aiming for—that's how they kill, by breaking the neck. But when she knocked you down, you must have fallen funny and she clamped onto your shoulder instead. She had just released and was going in again when Destiny hit her."

"You killed her?"

"Destiny did. We didn't see the kittens until afterward. They should—we think they'll be okay."

I bite my top lip as I close my eyes. As Liam gives me details of the attack, things start to come back to me in fuzzy pictures. "Was she teaching them how to hunt?"

"Maybe. Leslie and Destiny think so. It makes sense."

I close my eyes. "I need to sleep some more."

When I wake again, Leslie is in the tent with me. I move slightly to become more comfortable, and she looks up from the book she's reading.

"Hey, Clarice."

"It's too dark in here to read," I say, my voice hoarse.

"Yeah, I was just getting ready to stop. It wasn't too bad until a few minutes ago."

"The sun's going down?"

"It's going to snow. It's only midafternoon, but it's definitely getting darker."

"Where are we?"

"About a quarter mile from—you know, where it happened."

"Are we far enough from the town?"

With a sigh, she says, "Probably not. We were worried someone would show up yesterday after we fired the shots, but they haven't. We're keeping watch."

I close my eyes to try and alleviate the pounding in my head before I ask, "How's Wyatt? His cough still gone?"

"He's fine. Liam's on watch right now and has Wyatt with him. Destiny is sleeping."

A wave of emotion washes over me as I think of these children and the things they've had to do. "The tents are good and secure for the storm?"

"Should be fine. We have all three tents up, plus the bivy sack thing. The gear's in the bivy."

"Did it fit?"

"Mostly. We put a few things in the tents, but it's not too bad. Liam will take Wyatt to Destiny when the snow starts."

"He can bring him in here. I can hold him—on this side." I motion with the arm the mountain lion didn't try and eat.

"The noise won't bother you?"

"I don't think so. My head isn't pounding like it was. Can you help me get a drink of water? Then go ahead and get him. I'd like them inside before the storm."

When Leslie returns with Wyatt, Liam pops his head in. "Hey, Mom. You look a lot better."

I give him as large of a smile as I can muster. "I feel better, not nearly as foggy and my head isn't too bad."

"How's your shoulder?"

"It hurts. Does everything look good out there?"

"Seems okay. This storm's probably going to be a bad one. We'll have to keep watch from inside the tents. Destiny's relieving me in two hours. Leslie is going to stay with you and Wyatt until the storm subsides. She'll help you with anything you need. Right, Les?"

She gives him a look. "Of course. But don't call me that."

With a cheeky grin, he says, "Oh, yeah. Guess I forgot. Our tents are close together, Mom. Even with the storm, I'll be able to hear you. I'm right there." He points to his left. "Destiny is on the other side of me."

"Okay, good."

"Do you want me to help you go to the bathroom again before the snow starts?"

"Again?" I search my mind, trying to remember when I've gone to the bathroom recently. As I focus on it, I have a vague recollection of Liam walking with me earlier this morning and then Destiny having to help me get my pants down. As I remember this, I wonder when they took my mass number of layers I was wearing off. Right now, I'm wearing flannel pajama bottoms and a tank top. My shoulder is wrapped up with a fabric bandage and held tight to my chest with a triangle sling.

Leslie and Liam help me up and I slip into my easy-on snow boots, tucking the pant legs inside so I don't get them wet. They drape my parka over my shoulders. Liam walks with me, but I make sure he knows I can handle things on my own. I'm partially right. I enlist the aid of a tree to keep from falling over, and getting myself back together takes longer than it should. Once I'm back inside my sleeping bag, Liam goes on to his tent while Leslie and I play with Wyatt. It's not long before the wind kicks up and the snow starts. As the tent flutters, Leslie asks if I'm hungry.

"Do you want some of the broth you had earlier?"

Like going out to the bathroom, I don't have a ready memory of having broth, but now that she mentions it, I can remember Liam patiently feeding me spoonful after spoonful. "Is it still hot?"

"Yeah, we put it in the small thermos we found. It should at least be warm."

"Where'd we get broth? Did Liam snare a rabbit?"

She drops her eyes, but not before I see something in them. Guilt? Instead of answering, she grabs the thermos and removes the lid. Using it as a cup, she pours in a small amount. I watch as the steam escapes. My stomach responds with a rumble; Wyatt, who must also be hungry, lets out a whoop and a giggle.

Leslie laughs and says, "There's enough for you, too, little man. We'll each have some. And we've got meat too. Can you sit up a little?" she asks me. "I can help."

Once I'm up, she hands me the thermos top and then pours more broth in one of our mugs, telling Wyatt, "We'll let this cool a minute for you while we start on the meat."

I take a sip of the broth. It's salty and has a flavor I can't quite place. Maybe one of the herbs or spices we've found in our salvaging? I sip on the broth while Leslie takes a small piece of meat and chews it slightly before placing it in Wyatt's mouth. Even with his new tooth, he's far from ready for actual chunks of meat. "Do you want some meat?" Leslie asks me, handing me a piece. "Will you be able to eat it?"

"I'll be okay with it," I say. "I have a few more teeth than Wyatt, so you don't need to chew mine first."

Leslie laughs. "I didn't mean that."

Like the broth, the meat has a strange flavor. "Is this rabbit?"

"Uh, no," she answers, giving Wyatt another pulverized piece.

I feel the color drain from my face. "Not my chickens?"

"Oh, no! Of course not. They're in with Destiny. They're fine, Clarice." I let out a slow breath as she says, "It's . . . it's the mountain lion. We didn't want to waste it. And we need the food. Destiny says some people used to eat them before. It's just—well, it doesn't seem right since it's a cat."

I swallow the piece of meat, which seems to have doubled in size. "She's right. My husband knows people who hunt and eat them too."

"Destiny said we had to. It wouldn't be right to leave it when we're . . . since it's so hard to find food. They went back for it as soon as we knew you were . . . as soon as we knew you weren't going to die. We set up just this one tent, and Wyatt and I stayed with you. It was so scary. You were so out of it. But I knew, I still know, we need the food. And it made sense I was the one to stay with you while they took care of the meat."

She pauses for a moment before quickly saying, "I didn't want to eat it, but being picky doesn't help us. I do still feel bad, and I feel really bad about her cubs. Or kittens. Destiny said both things are right to call them. Do you think they'll be okay on their own?"

"I don't know," I answer honestly. Just like the time for being picky with our food has passed, so is the time for platitudes. "How'd you cook the meat?"

"Open fire. We made the really small double-hole kind. We had to clear out a lot of snow and then we waited until dark, not just because of smoke but in hopes it might help prevent people from investigating if they caught the smell of food cooking. Destiny and Liam stayed up all night, cooking and keeping watch. We still have some raw meat left to cook."

"That was smart. Leslie, I'll tell Liam and Destiny this also, but I'm proud of you. I know this has all been a lot. Not just me getting hurt, but the entire trip. And you and Destiny taking care of Wyatt."

She gives a partial shrug as she feeds Wyatt another bite. "I just hope your friends won't mind us being with you."

"Oh, you don't need to worry about that. They'll most certainly welcome you."

"Liam says they have a small farm."

"They do. Speaking of, have the chickens given any eggs?"

"Not yet. I had them out earlier today when Liam was in with you. Where we cleared the snow for the fire is a good spot for them. There were even some grass shoots. They loved those. Will you put your chickens in with your friend's?"

"Put them in with their chickens? I don't know. We'll have to see. I don't know how their farm works." I let out a small laugh. "I don't know anything about farms. I lived in Portland until my dad died, and then my mom and I moved to Alto. We didn't have livestock."

"Will you miss living near the ocean?"

"I might. But with the way things are, I don't know if I'll have time for missing it."

"Do you think— " She pauses as she bites her lip. "Can you ask Liam to call me my full name."

"Oh, yes, of course," I answer, trying to keep a straight face. "Nicknames can be annoying."

"Did you have a nickname?"

"I did. My friends called me CC. Clarice Cervelli. I actually really liked it."

"Did your husband call you CC?"

"No. He usually called me babe." I feel my cheeks redden as I say it. I also feel my heart break a little. The dream from earlier when he was giving me coffee, it seemed so real.

"He must have really loved you."

I allow the tears to build in my eyes. "Marriage isn't always easy. And sometimes, well, the truth is, I wasn't always as loving as I should've been. My husband, Ben, always wanted the best for us. We both worked hard to have a nice house and the things we thought we needed and wanted. But now I see that, in some ways, we were caught up in it all. I wish we would've concentrated more on being a family than the material stuff."

"Having a nice house is good. We lived in a very small house, but it was still nice. My mom and dad were always happy and laughing. They made things fun. Even after my brother died, they made sure I knew I was loved, and they showed me they still loved each other."

My heart aches as she talks about her family. Did Liam have that kind of loving household? I know the answer: no. He didn't usually see the best in me, as I was continually nagging on Ben.

"I like how Bart talked about dancing with his wife," Leslie says. "My parents danced, right in the kitchen or the living room sometimes. Did you dance?"

"No. Never. I wish we would have."

Chapter 38

January 9th

The storm raged for days and dumped over a foot of snow on us. The blizzard was quickly followed by a second one. Between the weather and my injuries, it was nearly two weeks before we started walking again. While we were hunkered down, Wyatt cut a second tooth, this time with much less difficulty than the first. He also learned how to scoot along on his belly while dragging his legs behind him. While not exactly a crawl, it was impressive. Unfortunately, the size of the tent meant he was going in circles.

I'm terribly impressed with his scooting. I've worried, with our diet and life on the road, he might be developmentally behind. But at his age, of somewhere around eight and a half months, scooting seems on target.

Our pace is still terribly slow, but at least we put in several miles each day as we walked through the eastern part of Yellowstone National Park. We'd hoped to find cars abandoned in the park, but it seems most people left while they could. However, things changed when we reached Roosevelt Lodge. Surprisingly, the place was full of food, supplies, and various goods.

We stayed there for over three weeks, thanks to a couple of storms, the holidays, and the plethora of food. We celebrated Christmas, Leslie's birthday, and New Year's at the lodge. During the time we were there, Destiny killed a spike elk and Liam killed a buck deer. The abundance was wonderful.

Giving Christmas gifts was something we made a game of. The general store at Roosevelt Lodge still held its wares. Wyatt was given small stuffed animals and a couple of balls. Liam gave me and each of the other ladies a beautiful blanket scarf. Destiny handed out Yellowstone logo sweatshirts, and Leslie gave new T-shirts. I gave card games and small pocket games to the older children and an amber necklace that's supposed to help with teething issues to Wyatt. I can't tell you how excited I was to find a stash of those on the shelf. I pocketed two more just in case.

The gift shop, lodge, kitchen, multiple cabins, and lodge-owned vehicles gave us ample salvaging opportunities. There were even large bags and cans of food still in the kitchen. Like other cans we've found previously, several were bulged or had burst due to the weather, but many were still good, including several canisters of coffee. We indulged on the large containers while stopped and then opened and repacked it into zipper bags—which were abundant at the store—then froze them so we'd have them as we trekked.

There was plenty of flour, allowing us to make the flavorless but good-for-traveling hardtack biscuits. A hardtack biscuit dunked in hot coffee isn't bad. There was even powdered creamer and plenty of sugar to dress up the coffee.

We left Roosevelt Lodge six days ago and have just started today's walk. We expect to see the exit from Yellowstone anytime. Last night, we wanted to keep going until the gate came into view, but it didn't happen. Once the sun starts setting, it gets dark fast. Traveling through this section of Yellowstone, in the middle of winter, on foot, has been nothing short of amazing. The buffalo and other wildlife are still out. Although it's amazing, it's also nerve-wracking since we're extremely aware of predators.

I'm a bit of a wreck after the mountain lion attack and jump at any sound. It's been around six weeks since the attack. I'm doing fine physically, though my shoulder still hurts some.

And I'm not only concerned about mountain lions but bears and wolves too. We're taking extra precautions when we set up our camp by wrapping our food in the smaller tarps and hanging them in trees well away from where we sleep. We don't even cook at our camp, choosing to stop and eat and then walk farther before stopping for the night. As I've said, it's nerve-wracking. And these precautions will need to continue for the duration of our journey. Mollie's shared many stories of seeing grizzly bear and wolves where they live.

One advantage to this section we've been walking is a creek. Yesterday, when we stopped, we found a fast-moving spot void of ice and used a small fishing pole and tackle we picked up at the lodge. Using marshmallow bait, we only caught one fish, but it cooked up wonderfully. What a treat!

"There it is," Liam says, pointing to the gate in the distance. With the excitement of a goal soon to be reached, we all pick up our pace as we veer off the road. While we've found using the main road to be much easier walking, we've decided our efforts to remain stealthy are smart. We walk between Soda Butte Creek and the road as we exit the park and make our way to the small enclave of Silver Gate.

Liam and I have been here before, on a trip to Yellowstone a couple of years ago, and I seem to remember houses scattered along the roadway for many miles. With several feet of snow on the ground, a creek on one side of the road and tall mountains on the other, it's going to be a challenge to avoid people. On the flip side, we're hoping to be able to do some salvaging. We're currently good on food, but we know we have a long journey ahead of us.

The walk along the mostly frozen creek is amazing. As the snow crunches and the ice groans, I'm engulfed in the beauty of my surroundings. And it's not much more strenuous than walking the road. We take turns leading since the first person does the trail breaking, which is the hardest work.

The snowshoes do a fine job of keeping us on top of the snow. One of my straps broke when the mountain lion pounced on me. Destiny, wise beyond her years, had made a plea for us to look for more snowshoes at each house we'd salvaged. We were only able to find one pair, and they aren't even as good as the ones I had, but I'm now wearing those. We've kept the other pair and have rigged them to use with shoestring—also something we've been on the lookout for, along with replacement snow boots—but I haven't tested them yet.

Liam's snowshoes aren't looking too good either. The buckle broke on one, and now he tapes it together. Both duct tape and electrical tape are on our salvage lists. Right now, we have a decent supply of both, hopefully enough to last until we reach Mollie's place.

If we can continue this pace we've set the last several days, we should reach Bakerville in around two weeks. I'm doing my best to tamp down on my excitement, and the children's too. We all know how our plans can easily go awry.

We take a small break while switching leaders. "I don't think the houses will be much farther," Liam says. "We're well past the entrance gate."

"I think you're right," I say. "I'll take Leslie's turn of breaking trail. We'll keep a slow pace and stop as soon as we see anything, then we'll make a better plan for getting around the houses. Maybe we'll be able to find a high spot where we can see what our options are."

"They're going to see us," Liam says with a shake of his head. "Even with our ghillie suits, there's no way they won't see us. Snow doesn't walk."

I give him a shake of my head, knowing what he's going to say next.

As expected, he says, "I still think going through here at night would make the most sense." For the last several days, he's made a strong argument for taking this section at night. While I agree that it'd help us stay hidden, the moon isn't putting out enough illumination for us to be safe.

"Let's just see what we're dealing with. Maybe we can stick next to the creek."

"There's houses along the creek," he says. "There isn't any way for us to get around. We need to go at night."

I give him a patient smile before asking, "Everyone ready?"

I haven't gone far when a house comes into view—or I should say, the *remains* of a house. At some point in recent history, the house burned down. My guess is, it was after the attacks but before the winter. It's well covered in snow, with only the chimney and a section that didn't collapse poking above the snow cover.

"Guess we don't need to worry about this one," Liam says quietly.

I give a nod as we keep walking. When we see the next house is in similar shape, Liam says, "This doesn't seem right."

I agree it doesn't. We discuss it for a few minutes before deciding there doesn't seem to be an imminent threat. These fires are months old. A terrible feeling settles over me at the third burned-down house. What happened here?

As we approach the town of Silver Gate, we have yet to see any evidence of people—only destroyed structures. The town itself also has burned-out buildings. Liam points to a place slightly up the hill that's still standing. There's no smoke from the chimney, but we know from our own experiences that isn't a sure indicator of it being empty.

"I'm going to go check it out," I say. "Maybe we can get some answers as to what's happened here."

"We don't need answers," Destiny says. "Whatever happened doesn't concern us. We need to get through this section. We still have the next town, right?"

"True."

"Okay, so let's just stay on target. And be alert."

I give a nod and start walking. We stay close to the creek as we make our way toward Cooke City.

Along the way, we see more of the same burned buildings. I suspect, if we didn't have several feet of snow on the ground, we might be seeing bodies too. And at this point, I have little hope of Cooke City being any different. Something terrible has happened here.

A short while later, Liam says, "Mom, we should start looking for a place to camp."

"There's a building still standing," Leslie says, pointing to a place near the road.

"I think we're at the edge of the town," I say.

"I agree," Destiny says. "The rubble's getting closer together."

"Let me check it out," I say.

"Let me go," Destiny says. "I'll take Liam. With your shoulder . . . " She tilts her head.

"Okay," I agree. "Take it slow and easy."

She passes Wyatt, who's sleeping in his backpack, off to me. He barely stirs as I put him in place. She starts to put on the pack I was carrying, when I say, "Leave it. We'll bring it up with us."

"You ready, Liam?" she asks.

"Make sure you stay out of sight," I say. "If you see anyone, come right back down. We'll go back and camp near one of the destroyed homes."

"We'll be fine, Mom." Liam gives me a thumbs up before turning to leave.

As they cautiously and carefully make their way up the incline from the creek to the road, Leslie and I take cover behind trees. Even though all have long ago lost their leaves, the trunks give us a modicum of concealment. I take in a breath when Destiny reaches the top and disappears. Liam is lying prone on the edge of the hill. It's many harrowing and tense minutes before she returns to view. She says something to Liam, and as he stands, she motions for us to join her.

It takes Leslie and me many minutes to make our way to the top of the hill. Once we're there, we get a full view of the town, showing most of the houses and buildings as little more than rubble. There are parked cars covered in so many feet of snow only the tops of them stick out, and some of the smaller vehicles are nothing more than a mound of white.

The building Destiny and Liam were sent to check out, while still standing, has all the windows shattered and the door is hanging by a single hinge.

"The animals have moved in," she says. "We won't want to stay in there."

"What do you think happened here?" Liam asks, his arm motioning to take in the entire town.

"They were attacked?" I suggest.

"Or they turned on each other," Destiny says bitterly. Leslie agrees with a nod.

"Why did they burn everything down?" Liam asks. "I think even the cars were torched—some of them, anyway. That doesn't make sense."

"I agree," I say. "And think about how much fuel you used, Destiny, and that was just for one house."

She shakes her head. "It doesn't make sense. But something happened, and there doesn't seem to be anyone left in this town."

I look around at the destruction and agree. There's zero indication anyone is here or has been here recently. Other than the tracks Destiny's snowshoes made as she walked in front of the building and into the road, even the snow is undisturbed.

"There's a house up on the hillside," Destiny says as she points to it. "I scoped it with the binoculars, and the door is still intact. One of the windows has a hole, but it might be livable, at least for tonight."

"Should we all go up together?" Leslie asks.

"I think we should," Destiny says. "Clarice?"

I use my own binoculars to check the cabin and surrounding area. There are trees between us and them, preventing some of my view but also giving us concealment as we make our way there. "We'll stay together and get closer, then we'll see." I take the lead this time. Halfway to the house, I stop when I see tracks in the snow. I motion for the children to take cover while I move forward with my pistol at the ready. I let out a loud breath of relief when I realize its animal tracks—specifically, a lone buffalo. We've seen so many buffalo tracks in the snow the last several days, so I'm positive that's what I'm looking at. I motion the children to come on ahead.

Nearing the cabin, I check an outbuilding first. Once it's proven to be safe, Destiny, Leslie, and Wyatt wait there while Liam and I check the rest of the buildings. The cabin isn't very large, with one big room functioning as the living room, dining room, and kitchen, plus a small bathroom. There's a pile of snow near the window with the hole and wet soggy leaves at the edges of the snow. The place smells damp and maybe a little moldy. Upstairs is a loft covering half the main space. I take a deep breath before mounting the stairs. Will the bed be empty?

My fear of finding a body or two on the bed is unfounded. I take a quick look around the seemingly undisturbed room. My eyes land on the nightstand. There's a picture of a couple; he's huge with an unruly beard and long hair, and she's tiny in comparison to him. She looks remarkably familiar. Is she someone famous? I'm not sure, but I'm struck by how happy they look—incredibly happy.

Back outside, I tell Liam, "Go get the girls. Everything's fine."

Inside the cabin, Leslie slides Wyatt and his carrier off, placing it upright on the floor. He's beginning to wake up and will need a diaper change and food. We were able to refill our supply of disposable diapers at the lodge's store, thanks to several packages on the shelves. Before that, we salvaged diapers here and there, but it was never much. We've even used adult diapers and our trusty duct tape to make them fit. But we've mostly been using towels, blankets, even clothing. Washing diapers, like doing any laundry while on the trail, is nearly impossible.

While we're still okay on disposables for now, we'll need more before we reach Bakerville. Maybe we'll find some here in Cooke City, though I hold out little hope of finding many salvageable goods, based on what the town looks like.

"Are you ready for a bottle?" I ask Wyatt in a sing-song voice. There were also two containers of baby formula at the lodge store, which he's happily enjoyed as a supplement to our regular meals. He rewards me with a smile while waving a fist at me.

"I'll use one of our grocery sacks and duct tape to cover the hole in the window," Liam says.

"Good idea," I agree, moving Wyatt from his carrier to a blanket on the floor.

After I take care of changing the baby, Liam has the window patched and says, "I'll try to find some dry wood to start a fire. The sun will go down shortly. I want to check the garage too."

I give him a nod. "Destiny, can you go with him?"

She's opening cabinets in the kitchen. "No food. Maybe we can shoot a deer while we're here."

"Or a buffalo," Liam says.

"A deer or small elk," I say. "A buffalo would be too much. I can't even imagine we'd be able to handle skinning it."

"The stovetop doesn't work," Leslie says. "There's no gas . . . I mean, propane."

"Liam, can you check the propane tank while you're out there and see if it's empty?" I ask.

While they go outside, Leslie continues checking cabinets and drawers. Now redressed, Wyatt promptly rolls over and begins to scoot away. Giving him a minute to move around, I take my chickens from their box.

"Look, Wyatt," I say, "chick chicks."

Stopping his movement, he spins his body to look at me before saying, "Mama."

My heart melts as he reaches for me. "That's right, Wyatt. Come to Mama."

Chapter 39

February 9th

"What do you see?" I ask. Hidden behind a group of boulders, we each have our binoculars as we scope the area ahead.

"The house at the top of the hill is empty," Destiny says.

"What are their names?" Liam turns to me. "They were nice when we met them at Jake and Mollie's barbecue."

"They were nice," I say. "His name is Evan . . . hers is Daisy or something."

Liam nods. "I hope they're okay. Some of the windows have been covered with plywood or cardboard. I think something bad happened."

"I think you're right," I agree.

"I'm pretty sure their house is empty," Liam says. "And there's no smoke coming out of Mollie's house either—or the other houses in this neighborhood. I can see the pens they keep their goats in, but they look empty. Same with the chicken coop."

We've been scoping the area from the top of this hill for many minutes. Our pace the last several days has been nearly grueling, knowing we were on the final leg of our long journey. We stayed over a week at the cabin in Cooke City and were never able to determine exactly what happened there, other than nothing good.

While the house we were staying in was free of bodies, we found several in a partially standing restaurant. There were a dozen or so other homes that were not completely destroyed, and we went through all the buildings I felt were safe to enter—based on their degree of destruction—plus cleared all the cars. Notable finds included disposable diapers in assorted sizes, winter gear, a single snowshoe, and both Montana and Wyoming gazetteers—a wonderful find. There wasn't any food to speak of.

Fortunately, Liam was up early the first morning after we arrived at the cabin and shot a forked horn deer, allowing us to replenish our meat supply. He got us a second deer the following day. We're now well stocked on meat, but cooking them took some time, which was the main reason we stayed in Cooke City as long as we did.

We were not able to get the propane working to fire up the stove. There wasn't a tank! We think the homeowners—Sandy and Stella Jean Carmichael, according to some mail we found in the desk—had a smaller tank and someone picked it up and took it with them. Maybe the homeowners themselves. Perhaps they were able to leave before whatever happened, happened. I hope so.

Just like at the Delgados' and Isabel's house, I felt like I got to know the Carmichaels through photos. Not only did they have the framed picture on the nightstand, but there were several photo albums in a storage chest. While I couldn't figure out who Stella Jean looked like, right after seeing her picture, Leslie said, "She looks like Dolly Parton." Definitely from years back, but that's who she resembles.

We used the woodstove to cook the meat, also drying a good portion of it by hanging it on wire we strung behind the woodstove. Nearly three weeks later, we're beginning to run low on meat, and Wyatt has only a dozen or so diapers left. As we stare at the empty houses in front of us, a terrible feeling fills my stomach.

"At least the houses are still standing," Leslie says. "Maybe . . . maybe your friends are just doing what we do and not lighting fires during the day."

"That's a good point," Destiny says with fake confidence in her voice.

"I don't see anyone around," Liam says, not even bothering to hide his disappointment.

I swallow hard, trying to keep my tears at bay. It's taken us over seven months to travel halfway across the country, with the hopes of security at the end of our journey. When Ben, Bart, Liam, and I left our home, the last thing I wanted was to go to Bakerville. No . . . that's not true. Staying with Ben was the last thing I wanted. Asking Mollie for help and safety was a close second. To go to her, groveling, seemed beneath me.

But now, with the things we've seen, the things that have happened to us—Ben's abduction, Bart's death, then gaining Destiny, Leslie, and Wyatt—and knowing the dangers of this new world, I'll happily beg Mollie for protection. Whatever is needed to keep my new family safe, I'll do it.

I think about the reading Liam did last night from the Bible. While I don't remember the exact words, the gist was how the Lord watches over foreigners while taking care of the widows and those without fathers, but He doesn't help the wicked. My own wickedness almost overwhelmed me as he read. I'd never thought of myself in that way, but the more I learn about God's ways, the more I understand my failings. My son, Destiny, Leslie, and Wyatt are all fatherless, and God's proven time and time again how He cares for them and helps them.

I'm a widow, but I can see how my wicked ways have been part of my downfall. My conceitedness of being so sure I'm always right has led to many poor choices and so many over reactions. The way I treated Ben—not only since we left our house, but in the days, months, even years prior—caused us to no longer have a loving husband and wife relationship. We were mere roommates, just going through the motions, with me always critical and ready to berate him at each opportunity and vice versa. We hadn't been happy for years.

And me planning to leave Ben for Mark leaves me with much guilt. While I hadn't yet been unfaithful in a physical sense, I was certainly having an emotional affair. It was so nice to have someone who listened to me, who was interested in what I had to say, who made me feel special. It'd been a long time since I'd felt that way with Ben. One of those days on the road, after the EMP, I felt an unfamiliar spark. Had we had more time, I think we could've made our way back to each other. No . . . I didn't deserve God taking care of me as a widow; I was among the wicked. Until recently, anyway.

I'm not sure when it happened, but the seeds were planted somewhere along the way as Liam would read to us and lead us in prayer. Perhaps even back to when Bart would do the same thing. Maybe it was the time he had me read to him from his Bible. But at some time during all of that, I started listening and hearing. Somewhere along the way, I realized my need to turn from my wickedness, a wickedness the Bible says we all have, and turn toward God by way of His Son, Jesus.

I don't know if I've actually done that, if I'm truly a Christian. But even today, with the disappointment of arriving in Bakerville to seemingly empty homes, I'm not distraught. I'm sad and don't know what will happen next, but I feel—no, *I believe*—God has a plan for us. It may not be the plan I'd choose, but He's placed a feeling of peace and comfort in my heart.

"Liam, will you lead us in prayer before we continue on?" I ask.

With a small smile, he gives me a nod. He knows I've changed. We don't talk about it, but he knows I listen when he reads and prays. This is the first time I've verbally requested he pray, but other times, he's seemed to know when we need it, when I want him to.

"Heavenly Father, we're thankful for Your help and protection as we've made our way to Mollie and Jake's. We ask You to continue these blessings. Right now— " He sucks in a deep breath. "I don't know what we'll find. I'll admit, I'm scared, scared the safety we've been after won't exist. Please help us with whatever comes next. Amen."

"Thank you, Liam," I say, wiping a tear from my eye. When I look at his fallen face, I pull him close, whispering how much I love him and how proud I am of him. After hugging Liam, I move on to Leslie and then Destiny. "Help me get Wyatt off my back, please. I'm going to take the lead, and I want Leslie to carry him."

Destiny helps me get Wyatt off before we pass him on to Leslie. I play with him for a minute and elicit a quiet laugh from him. I tell him how much I love him before getting him ready to go.

"Okay," I say. "Whatever we find, we'll figure this out. With God's help, we'll come up with our next plans. Everyone be alert. We're not home yet."

It's about half a mile down the hill to the first home where Evan and his wife live. The closer we get, the more obvious it is that the house is abandoned. The snow, which has decreased in quantity since we've reached a lower elevation, has been disturbed recently, but only by deer tracks. At least that's a good sign; we'll be able to replenish our meat supply. From their house, it's almost another mile to Mollie's, but at least it's mostly downhill and not strenuous.

While I'm still underweight, I've developed some serious leg muscles from walking through the deep snow. With less snow, walking is almost easy. Liam has sprouted up a good inch in height and is lean and sinewy. Leslie, who by her own admission was plump before the attacks, has the body of an athlete, as does Destiny. Wyatt isn't as chubby as I think he should be at close to ten months old, but he still seems on target developmentally. He sits on his own and can pull himself to a standing position with help—a new trick he learned while we were in Cooke City. I don't think he's ready to walk, and with the tight quarters of our tents, he doesn't really have the space to learn.

The beauty of the area is amazing. When we've visited Mollie and Jake before, it was during the summer months, when the aridness of the land left much to be desired as far as beauty. The mountains were nice, but covered in snow, they're breathtaking. Of course, I've had enough of snow and mountains after walking through them for the last several months. Even so, I can see the appeal of living here. We cross a bridge over a small creek. Even though it's mostly frozen, there are a few spots where the water's still moving.

"Maybe we can catch a fish again," Liam says.

"Maybe so," I agree. "And remember, they have ponds. At least one of them is stocked with fish. Remember Mollie talking about it when she was at our place?"

"That's right! Can we fish those in the winter?" He wrinkles his face. "Won't they be frozen over? And wouldn't the fish die?"

"I asked Mollie that once. She said the pond is very deep, so it doesn't freeze all the way. And they have some kind of . . . something, I don't remember what, but *something* that keeps the water moving. But I don't really know. We'll have to see." I don't say that I suspect, with no one there to take care of things, which is how it looks from a distance, the pond is probably frozen solid and the fish are all dead.

Past the creek, we're starting to get a good view of the Caldwells' homestead. As Liam already pointed out, there's no livestock. We would see or hear them by now, and the silence of the area is almost deafening. Continuing past the other homes, also showing snow undisturbed by humans, I find myself continuing Liam's prayer.

Please, Lord, please guide us. Give me strength to endure whatever we find. While I've made a point of declaring my dislike for Mollie the last several years, I don't—please don't let me find her dead.

As we begin the final slight incline to reach their house, I glance up the gully and locate the bunkhouse we stayed in last time we were here. Like all the other houses around, it appears vacant. "Why don't you guys stay here," I say. "I'll go ahead and check things out."

"I think we should go together," Liam says.

I give him a slight shake of my head. "I don't—we don't know what we'll find. Mollie is someone you've known your entire life. I'd rather . . . " I give a shrug.

He nods. "And Malcolm, even though he can be annoying, is a friend. I understand what you're saying, Mom. But how about we wait at the edge of their shop?"

"I'll go in with you," Destiny says. "Just like always, no one goes anywhere alone."

Reaching Mollie and Jake's driveway, I'm surprised to find the driveway gate open. I would've expected it to be locked to help discourage people entering the yard. The fence along the road is still fully intact, and the thorny berry bushes, which Mollie told Ben are not only for food but for a layer of security, are wilted with the winter. Again, there's no sign of humans in the snow, but plenty evidence of deer and rabbits.

From here, a second bunkhouse, which Mollie and Jake had purchased shortly before our last visit, and a third much smaller cabin I've never seen before are both fully visible and empty. I know the large shop has a studio apartment attached to it, and as we walk closer, I see it's also undisturbed. With no sign of people, the feeling of dread in the pit of my stomach increases.

Another Bible verse Liam read at some time in the past comes to me: "*Do not fear, for I am with you.*" I give a visible nod. "Let's go, Destiny. Liam, Leslie, we'll be back shortly."

We walk around to the south side of the house. There's a gate into the yard with rock columns on either side. On previous visits, hanging above the gate was a wooden sign that read *Welcome*. It's not there. I cautiously open the gate and peek into the backyard. Empty.

I'm surprised to see a new sunroom added to the house. It spans most of the south side and leaves just the large window in their living room visible, which looks out over the mountains in the distance. The new entrance is now via the sunroom.

"Should we knock?" Destiny asks.

I almost laugh. We've broken into dozens of houses in the past few months and have never once considered knocking. Even so, I give a firm rap on the sunroom door. When there's no response, I try again. "Let's go around and check the windows and other doors. This room is new since I was last here. We can't really see in very well."

There's an entrance at the back of the house, which goes into the master bedroom. The decking stretches across the room, which has a large window. Mollie made a point of telling me before how the west-facing window helps warm the room up on a winter evening. Right now, the heavy curtains are in place, preventing me from looking in. I try the door. It's locked. I knock before we move on.

"There's a patio door on the west side." Like the other window, this door is curtained and locked, and my banging receives no response. On the east side of the house is the final door that goes into a mudroom. There's only a small window there, also curtained, and the door is locked.

"I guess it's empty," Destiny says.

I knock at this door, just to make sure, before saying, "I think this is the best window to break for entry. I don't know if I can get in it all the way, but I should be able to reach in and unlock the door. Let's find a rock. They should have plenty of them since this is a rocky area."

"We should've been practicing lockpicking skills," Destiny says. "I don't like ruining your friends' window."

"Yeah. You know what? Let me go get the crowbar. It'll be easier than searching for something."

Liam and Leslie, still on the other side of the shop with Wyatt, both ask what's happening as soon as they see me.

"No one's home. We haven't made it inside yet. I should've taken the crowbar with me to begin with." I undo the top of the tarp on the blue toboggan to retrieve it.

"Look over there, Mom." Liam points to the tree line in the distance. "Someone has a fire going."

I narrow my eyes slightly, trying to make things out in the white of the snow. I end up having to remove my sunglasses and put the binoculars to my eyes to see what he sees. "Not just one," I finally say. "It looks like several houses have smoke coming from the chimneys. But I can't see the actual homes from here, just the curls of smoke."

"What do you think that means?" Liam asks.

I bite my lip before shaking my head. "I'm not sure. Let me get inside and see if we can figure out where Mollie and her family have gone. I'll be back shortly."

I tell Destiny about the smoke, and she takes a minute to scan the tree line too. "Is that a river?" she asks.

"Maybe? Yes, I remember a river over there somewhere. But I can't make out any houses, can you?"

"No, they're too low and are behind the hill. Maybe if we went to the edge of the butte, we could see them."

"We can do that later. Let's check the house first." It takes only a minute to break out the window and clear it enough for me to reach in and unlock the door somewhat safely. It's a long stretch, and I need to have Destiny give me a boost. Entering the mudroom, we find it cleared out and empty of coats, boots, and everything else. A small room off the mudroom, which they use as a pantry, is also empty. Even their freezer's gone.

The door entering the main house turns easily, having been left unlocked. I step in and cautiously sniff the air. It's stale but doesn't give any indication of death. Of course, with the freezing temps, we've rarely been alerted by the odor lately. Like the mudroom, the main house is void of most things. The dining room to the right still has the table and chairs, and the living room on the left has a couch but no easy chairs.

"Not much furniture," Destiny says.

"No. Definitely less than last time I was here. Let's check the bedroom."

Separating the living space from the master bedroom is a woodstove with a brick surround. It's some kind of special set up that's supposed to help heat the house by warming the brick. I reach out and touch the cold brick on my way by. Behind the brick wall is an office, which still has a desk but none of the furniture I remember. We're then led into the master bedroom. I take a deep breath before pushing the door open. It's empty. Even the bed's gone.

"What's that?" Destiny asks, pointing to a metal drum molded inside a section of plaster and attached to a long bench.

"Another woodstove. It's ugly, but Mollie says it gives off amazing heat."

The closet has a few clothing items that, on first glance, all appear to be summer wear. The master bath is cleared of any personal items. We continue through the house, checking the guest room and bath on the main floor. We then go upstairs and find Malcolm's room. Like the master bedroom, his room is missing everything but a few clothes in the closet. The upstairs bathroom has a few motel-size bottles of shampoo under the sink, but nothing else. And what used to be an open-to-the-downstairs loft is now closed off but bare.

"What about the basement?" Destiny asks.

"Oh. I think it's just storage, but we should check it. Good idea."

"Where's the stairs?"

"In a weird place—off the master bedroom."

She nods, apparently not thinking that's an odd place to have stairs going to the basement. Destiny turns on her flashlight as we make our way down the stairs. Expecting to find a narrow, almost rustic staircase, I'm surprised to find it extra wide and covered in finished wood. At the bottom of the stairs, instead of a storage room, is a game room with a coffee table and a bar-height table and chairs.

Destiny moves the light around while we get a good view of the space. The polished concrete floor has tape on it, likely used to hold area rugs in place to keep them from moving around.

"Fun coffee table," she says, pointing with the flashlight to the table with a foosball game built into it.

A door on the left leads to a bedroom, with the only bed in the house still in place and another one of the ugly woodstove contraptions. A second door off the family room opens to a half bath.

Destiny steps in and opens the door leading out of the bathroom and into a room with just a tub/shower combination. "Huh," she says, opening yet another door into a second half bath. "Good idea. Two half baths sharing a shower space."

Leading out of the bathroom, we finally find the storage area I expected. Yet, it's not what I'd anticipated. There's empty shelving and cabinets covering every wall. There are also two rooms with hasp locks on them missing the padlocks. I open the first room on the right to find more shelves filling the entire space—all empty. Standing in the back corner, nestled where two shelving units meet, are several rugs wrapped in plastic.

"Guess we found the rugs from the family room," Destiny says.

"Guess so," I agree as we move to the second room.

"Check this out," Destiny says. "I think it's a reloading room. They probably had guns over here too." She gestures to the racks on the wall.

The room is quite like Ben's gunroom at home. Mollie never said anything about this. "I've never been down here . . . but it seems it might be something like that."

"They didn't leave much behind," she says. "Where do you think they went?"

"I have no idea. They never really said anything, but I always got the impression the things they were doing were so they could live here forever. At least . . . at least we didn't find them here."

"Yeah. Should we get the others?"

"Yes. Then we'll figure out what our next plans are." I don't mention the wave of disappointment coursing through me. Not only because Jake, Mollie, and Malcolm are gone, but because Ben's not here. Even though I'm positive he's dead, there must have been a small piece of me holding out hope he'd be here when we got here.

Chapter 40

February 11th

"What is it?" I ask, jolting up from my bed on the floor.

"I'm not sure," Liam says. "It sounds like gunfire. I can't really see much, but I think it's coming from the houses."

The houses with the chimneys belching out smoke. After not finding Mollie or Jake here, and the rest of their neighborhood also seemingly gone, we talked about those living on the river. Are they friendly? Or are they responsible for the disappearances?

Destiny and Leslie are also awake now, sitting on the bed in the toasty warm basement bedroom.

"We'll be right up. Wait for us at the door at the top of the stairs," I say, clicking on a lantern. "Leslie, you stay with Wyatt. We'll be right back."

"Should we get dressed? In case we need to leave?"

Destiny and I meet each other's eyes, and she gives a slight nod.

"Good idea," I say. "Get everything ready."

Destiny and I struggle into our multiple layers of warm clothing as Leslie starts shoving things in bags. We've left our emergency packs intact, but there's miscellaneous things lying around.

"Move upstairs as soon as you're ready," I tell Leslie. "Wait in the master bedroom for us. The snowshoes are at the top of the stairs. If you have to get out— " I bite my lip, thinking about what to tell her. "If you have to get out, take Wyatt to the trees at the back of the property."

Biting her lip and visibly shaking, she nods her head.

"We're going to be okay." I give her a small smile. *Please, God, make it so. Keep my children safe from harm.*

Liam, looking nervous at the top of the stairs, asks, "You ready?"

"Where's your snowshoes?"

"Outside. They were wet."

"Okay. I'll put mine on outside too. Destiny, you stay here. I'll go with Liam to see what we can figure out."

"Take your binoculars," Destiny says. "They might be useful, even with the limited light."

As soon as we step outside, I hear a far-off shot.

"See?" Liam asks. "What do you think is happening?"

I shake my head as I work on my snowshoe. Liam's no longer wearing the one with the broken strap. He now has the single snowshoe we found in Cooke City on one foot and his original, unbroken one on the other. They aren't the same style, or even the same size, but he makes it work.

With my light aiming low to the ground, I say, "Let's move to the edge of the hilltop, that way we're closer to the houses." We spent a lot of time yesterday exploring Mollie and Jake's land. Liam and I even went to the edge of the butte, but we made sure to stay hidden. From the edge, we could see at least half a dozen homes spread along the river.

The shooting continues as we walk, coming in long strings and then pausing before there's more. There must be dozens of people shooting.

Once we reach approximately the same spot we were at yesterday, Liam says, "I wish we could see something." The words are no sooner out of his mouth when I see a flash of light, almost like a quick fire, then two more immediately following. The sound of the shots reaches my ears in three rapid sequences. A second or so later, there's another flash, this time seeming to come from inside a house.

"Do you think we're safe here?" Liam asks.

"I don't know what's happening there. I don't know. But as far as we *do* know, they have no idea we're here."

We stay for many minutes as the shooting continues. I try to blank my mind and not think about what's happening down there, about the number of people being killed.

Liam reaches for my hand. "Pray with me, Mom."

I give his hand a squeeze as he begins his petitions, asking God to bring His people to Him and ease their suffering. When Liam's finished, I tell him to go back to the house. I'll stay here. I want him to keep watch from the upstairs, focusing on the east and north directions, especially watching the way we approached the house from the wilderness area. Destiny should stay at the back, watching the western hillside. My view is southernly.

"Can you see the road okay from here?" he asks, motioning to the gravel road leading up the hill to Jake and Mollie's.

"Good enough," I answer. "I should be able to see if anyone is coming up it."

Even though I'm bundled well against the cold, I shiver as I sit alone in the frigidness of the early morning. The shooting soon becomes sporadic. As the sun begins to rise, the gunfire slows to a rare discharge.

With the increased visibility, I realize I'm not in the same spot as yesterday where we spied on the houses. Where I'm at now isn't as hidden. I carefully move closer to the mountain, snuggling in next to a boulder. Once in place, I scope the houses with my binoculars. From this distance, things aren't crisp, but I can see people moving around. They seem to be rounding up cattle and horses.

I stay nestled against the boulder until midmorning when the last of the raiders—that's how I've come to think of them as I watch them take everything from the community—start to leave. As the sun comes up, it's easier to see what's happening. I expected to see bodies strewn about, but there's very few.

There were a few late shots—finishing the job, I guess—and some of those seemed to be outside. But I think the people were slaughtered while in their homes, even in their beds. I know we should go down and look for survivors, but I just don't know if I can—if I can see people so freshly murdered. I let out a breath as the last of them move out, taking the livestock with them.

While I watch them leave, I think about yesterday. As we spent the day exploring, we were trying to determine where Jake and Mollie might have gone. Was it like Cooke City? I don't think so, since there were people living just fine on the river—at least until a short while ago. Unless it was a similar event to what happened to Destiny and Leslie where the townspeople turned on each other. Could that have happened?

As we went through the Caldwells' house and then each of the outbuildings, we didn't find any answers. It wasn't until we found keys to the bunkhouse and other guest homes in a basement drawer that we found a slight clue. In the studio apartment attached to the shop was a note, written simply to *Son*.

It started with how happy the parents were the son and his family had made it, and then it went on to say they should make themselves at home until spring. Most of the community has gone to a place to ride out the winter, but they'd be back in time to start the planting.

There's plenty of wild game, the note went on to say, and necessary items have been stashed for their use. Then it gave a clue as to where to find these necessary items. The clue made little sense to me, but the next section piqued my interest. Those in the community who didn't want to go to the hiding place are living along the river. The son was encouraged to contact them in a safe manner. They have lookouts stationed in a variety of places, and he should go down waving a bandana or other flag to get their attention. Once he tells them who his brother is, there should be no problem.

"Who do you think wrote the letter?" Liam asked.

"I don't know," I answered. "My guess would be the brother is Jake—that makes sense, anyway. But I don't know anything about his family or if his parents even lived nearby."

We decided the recommendation was good and we, too, should introduce ourselves to the people living along the river. Our plan was for me to leave this morning at daylight. Of course, that's no longer an option.

I let out a long breath. Where would Jake and Mollie go? Why not stay here? They worked so hard putting this place together and seemed to have everything they needed to be self-sufficient.

Obviously, they took the goats, chickens, and other livestock with them. The pond, which I expected to be a frozen-over mess, wasn't at all bad. Something using solar power, based on the small panel we found, is keeping the water moving in the middle of the pond during the daylight. There are several little white balls, possibly ping-pong balls, floating in the clear area. The water is moving enough so the ice is completely gone in places and thin in others.

We're going to see if we can figure out a way to melt some of the ice along the edge to help with getting water. Making water from snow is a long process, so something easier will be welcome.

Yesterday, Liam and I took a garden wagon we found in an outbuilding to the creek we crossed over on the way here and filled two five-gallon buckets. It was wonderful to be able to heat the water to boiling and end up with almost the same amount we started with. While the stream is fine, having water closer will be much better.

When the raiders are out of sight, I wait another ten minutes and then start my walk back toward the house. Destiny, who's waiting on the back deck, gives a small wave as I walk toward her.

When I'm close enough, she asks, "Is it over?"

"They're gone. I want to get something to eat and rest a bit, then I'm going down there."

"I'll go with you," she says without hesitation.

"We'll talk about it later," I say, knowing I won't have her with me. While I might let her go along and keep watch, I don't want her seeing that. "How's everything here?"

"Okay. Liam is sleeping. Leslie took over his watch from upstairs. We have everything packed to go except the chickens. They're in the master bathroom. I thought I'd put them in the pen for a while, if you think it's okay?"

"Should be. We'll need to keep watch, of course. Is Wyatt good?"

"He's with Leslie, probably about ready for a nap. You could take him with you when you rest. We have the south-facing curtains open to let in the sunshine. It really warms the house up nicely. And did you know, if we open the window that opens into the sunroom, heat comes in from there?"

"Really? I didn't realize that."

She's right about the large window. Plenty of heat comes in—enough to warm the house while the sun is up. Not so warm we can go without our layers or our stocking hats, but it's definitely comfortable.

"Is the master bedroom staying warm?" I ask Destiny.

"Yeah, I've let the fires go out, but both bedrooms are fine."

The day we arrived, we fired up the weird woodstove in the basement and the main one in the living room as soon as the sun went down. Surprisingly, both not only warmed the rooms while they were lit, but the heat was retained long after the sun came up and we let the fires go out. The brick surrounding the main stove and the rock bench around the basement one were both warm all day and radiated heat. Last night, we lit the stove in Mollie's room to increase the main-floor's warmth during the day.

After lunch, I wake Liam and let him know I'm going to nap. He groggily gets to his feet so he can keep watch with the girls.

I realize we've been incredibly lucky. No, not lucky—blessed. We've been blessed only the four of us have been able to keep watch for all these months. Admittedly, there were times when our watch was done from the tent. And it truthfully wasn't an actual watch, just one person awake and listening for anything out of the ordinary.

Last night was the first time we've been in near danger at night. And even during the day, we've managed to use our motto of staying hidden to keep safe.

Now we're finally where we've been trying to reach, and I feel the danger more than ever. Will the raiders stay away now that they've murdered and stolen? Or will we be targeted next? As much as I don't want to do it, I realize I need to go down there now. Not after a nap, but immediately in case someone is injured. Do I leave the children here? Or should I bring them along and find someplace safe for them to stay?

Deciding to go, I start to scoot out of the sleeping bag when Leslie appears at the door.

"Hurry! There's people coming up the road on horses."

"Where are they," I ask, grabbing a sleepy Wyatt. "And how many?"

"I only saw two. They were just coming over the hill when I saw them. Liam is outside. Destiny went after him, and I came for you."

"No one is watching them now?"

"I came to get you," she says again as I hand off Wyatt. "We need to hurry."

My outerwear, wet from sitting in the snow for hours, is hanging in the bathroom. I quickly move into the small room, leaving the door open, as I tell Leslie to see where they are but to stay hidden and get ready to leave the house. With a nod, she grabs the diaper bag and Wyatt's snowsuit. Pulse pounding and hands shaking, I struggle to get into my wet snow pants. As she makes it to the top of the stairs, I call out, "Stay out of sight."

With my fumbling, it seems to take forever before I'm somewhat dressed. I grab my heavy, damp jacket and bound up the stairs, stopping near the door where I left my boots. The snowshoes are also there, but I leave them for now.

Leslie is peering out the east window, her body behind the wall. Wyatt is on a blanket next to her, sound asleep. *Thank you, Lord, for that.*

"Where are they?" I ask, also keeping my body behind the wall while I look out. Since I've been in the basement, it's started to lightly snow but our visibility is still good.

"At the driveway. I think they're trying to say they're friendly. They have a white flag."

She doesn't point out how they are armed. Everyone is in this world; it'd be stupid not to be. I take quick notice of the leather scabbards holding rifles, and I'm sure they have sidearms also. "Liam and Destiny?"

"I think they're next to the shop. I saw movement there right before you came in here." Just then, the French door by the dining area opens, and Liam and Destiny step in.

I look to Leslie. She shrugs and says, "I guess I was wrong. I . . . I really did think I saw someone."

"Where did you come from?" I ask Liam.

"I was back by the chicken coop playing with our hens when Destiny came out. I didn't see the people, but we can hear them talking."

"The chickens?" I ask.

"We locked them in," Destiny says. "We didn't have their box with us and didn't want them to squawk. What are we doing?"

"They have a white flag up. Look!" Leslie cries. "There *is* movement by the shop. See?"

I look to where she's pointing but see nothing. At that same moment, I hear a very faint *"Hello, in the house!"* called out from one of the guys on horseback.

"What should we do?" Liam asks.

"Go to the upstairs window. Take the rifle and keep them covered. Give Leslie your handgun." As Liam does my bidding, I turn to Destiny. "You have the shotgun. I'm going to talk to them. I want you to be ready at the window we broke out yesterday." We covered it with plastic and duct tape from our supplies, which will be fine for her to see out of and can easily be ripped down as needed.

"Can't we just . . . ignore them?" Leslie asks.

"They know we're here," I say. "We've left tracks everywhere. I want you to be ready to go to the trees with Wyatt. But in the meantime, you're watching for anyone else to appear, okay?"

The cowboy repeats his plea, calling out to us in the house.

"If I see someone?" Leslie asks.

"Let us know. Liam?" I holler so he can hear me from upstairs.

"Yeah, I'm here. I can see the two guys. I don't see anyone else coming up the hill."

"You're going to need to check all the windows, make sure there isn't anyone coming from a different direction." As I talk, I fully realize the concerns Bart and Ben had with us trying to provide our own security. It's too hard with such a small group. We can't be in all places at once.

In barely a whisper, I say, "Please, God, please help us through this."

"Amen," Destiny says.

I turn to her and nod. "Let's go. Leslie, Liam, if things go bad, take Wyatt and get out."

I slip into the mudroom with Destiny right behind me, closing the door to the main house.

Destiny quickly gets into position, ripping a hole into the plastic. "Ready," she says.

"Okay. I'm going to open the door, but I'll keep my body back." I have my handgun at the ready but know both the shotgun and handgun have limited range. Liam, with the rifle, has a farther range, but with open sights, his accuracy may suffer.

With the door barely open, I lower my voice as much as I'm able to and yell out, "Go away!"

"We're not a threat," the cowboy yells back. "We saw— " He clears his throat loud enough for me to hear him. "We saw what happened. Our friends are supposed to be here in Bakerville. We're trying to find them."

A second voice says, "We know Pete Fairbanks, your neighbor. We're going up there next but wanted to check in with you."

"Go on to Pete's then," I say, forgetting to lower my voice this time. I clamp my hands over my mouth as soon as I realize what I've done.

"Sure, we will," cowboy number one yells back. "We were just checking to make sure you folks were okay. After what happened down by the river— "

"And we'd like to find our friends," cowboy number two interjects.

"How about instead of moving on to Pete's," a new commanding voice calls out, "you get down off those horses and move on over here."

"Who is that?" Destiny asks, fear filling her question.

"I don't— " I start to answer and then shake my head.

"Are they . . . are they trying to help us?"

"Shh," I caution, as one of the cowboys says, "Hey, we don't want any trouble. We've had a rough few months and are just looking for our friends."

"We've all had a rough few months, buddy," the new voice says. "Get off the horses one at a time. I want to see your hands while you do it."

I strain to look over Destiny and out the plastic window, trying to see the speaker. I can't control the tears welling up in my eyes.

The cowboys look at each other. One of them gives a shake of his head as he says, "We're doing what you ask. We really don't want any trouble." He slides down off his horse. Once on the ground, he keeps the horse's rein in one hand and the other out to his side, well away from his body. "Go ahead, Donnie," he says to the other guy.

"Fine," Donnie huffs, then joins the first cowboy on the ground.

As soon as they're both down, the voice says, "Toss your sidearms. Be smart about it."

Seconds after the rifles are on the ground, Destiny says, "There!" She points to a person stepping out from the far side of the garage. It's a woman, holding a rifle of her own as she walks toward the cowboys. She kicks the handguns farther from their reach.

The man with her, still out of our view, says, "She'll take your horses so we can get a better look at you."

"We're not here to cause you trouble," not-Donnie says. I've decided he's the nicer of the two.

"Either way, you've got a whole load of guns pointing at you, so be smart."

She takes the reins without trouble, moving both horses far to the side. I'm straining to get a better look at her but can only see a slight glimpse of her profile.

"All right. Now lift your coats and turn so we can see all the way around your belt. You know what? How about you just take those coats off."

"It's cold out here, man," Donnie says gruffly.

"No kidding. Let's get this done and we can all go inside, maybe even have a nice hot cup of coffee."

"You've got coffee?" Donnie asks, perking up considerably.

"Take your coats off," the man orders.

I jump when the door into the main house opens.

"Mom," Liam says in a hiss.

"Liam! You need to be on watch."

"Did you see who that is? The lady? It's Leanne!"

Is it? How could it be? Leanne and her family were taken with Ben. I bite my lip to try and keep my emotions under control. "Doesn't matter. Right now, you have to stay on watch."

"But, Mom, if she's here, Dad has to be here too. I think that's him talking. It doesn't sound like her brother."

Destiny looks to each of us before saying, "I'll go. You two stay here." She hands Liam the shotgun and grabs the rifle. She reaches out and squeezes my hand before leaving. With my pounding heart and overwrought emotions, I'm having trouble focusing. I give her a weak nod as she goes.

Liam and I watch as the men in the yard first remove their coats and then are instructed to take off their boots and show their ankles. There's plenty of grumbling. He doesn't stop there, having them remove their insulated pants and twirl around. If it wasn't such a serious situation, I might almost find it comical.

Finally satisfied, the man—who I'm now almost certain *is* my husband—tells them to sit down and put their hands over their head. With the snow falling slightly harder, I wait to see what will happen next.

"Okay, guys," he says. "Now tell me again why you're here?"

Donnie says something I don't quite catch, but the other puts a hand on his shoulder and says, "We made a plan with our friends to meet in Bakerville. It took us longer to get here than we expected, but here we are. We barely missed being butchered along with the rest of the people."

"And why are you here, at this house? *That* is what I want to know."

"I know Pete Fairbanks," Donnie says. "He's your neighbor right up the road there. We came to make sure he's okay and to make contact with . . . *anyone* who might know where our friends are. We found a few people we knew among the dead, but several were missing. Do you know Sheriff Jason Spieth? Or Harry English?"

"Why are you looking for them?"

"Because we agreed to meet here," Donnie says, clearly exasperated. "Look, man. It's snowing and cold. How about you send someone to Pete's place? He'll vouch for us."

At that moment, the man steps out where I can see him. He's walking with a limp, and his scraggly hair is skimming his shoulders. He's in profile, but even so, there's no doubt. Ben.

"Mom," Liam says, his voice barely a whisper. "He's alive."

I wrap my arm around my son. "He's alive."

Chapter 41

February 11th

"Jake? Mollie?" Ben hollers toward the house. "It's Ben Ferguson. Send out your army. I could use a hand with these guys. And bring something to tie them up with."

"Ah, c'mon, man," Donnie grumbles. "That's not necessary."

Liam starts to move. "Wait," I say, my heart pounding in my ears. "We need to be smart about this. Those guys need to think there's a whole house full of people here—guns trained on them."

I quickly move back to the door leading inside and, loud enough for both girls to hear, say, "Leslie, grab some of those zip ties out of the backpack. Is everything good upstairs?"

"No changes," Destiny says. "Still just those guys and whoever is at the side of the house."

"Okay," I say, accepting the stack of nylon cables from Leslie and shoving them into my coat pocket. "We're going out. Be ready for anything. Destiny, yell out the window if you see anyone approaching." Back beside Liam, I say, "Let's go. Walk purposefully. I'll do the talking."

He nods, eyes with a sheen of tears and a happy smile on his face.

Touching his hand, I say, "I'm happy, too, but we still have to be serious. Anything could happen."

He clears his throat and straightens his shoulders. "I'm ready," he says, his voice cracking between youthhood and adult.

I yell out the door, "Jake has everyone in their stations, Ben. He's sending two of us out to assist you. The others will fire if I give the signal."

Ben turns slightly toward me; I suck in a breath at my first full look of his face. He has a scar running from his left eye down toward his chin and his features—round and healthy before—are now angular and skeletal. But the look on his face melts me to the core. A smile covers his face, reminding me of the man I married. His eyes glance from me to Liam, and he gives a slight nod. He coughs before saying, "Good enough."

Liam's face again cracks into a smile before he catches himself, once again turning serious. He handles the shotgun like an expert, keeping it in the low, ready position. I have my handgun by my thigh.

As I step off the porch, Ben says, "You have something to secure them with?"

"Zip ties."

"Perfect. Let's take care of their hands but leave their feet free until we get them moved."

"Man . . . " Donnie whines.

"One at a time, stand up and put your hands behind your back," Ben says. "You go first." He points to not-Donnie, who responds with a nod.

"Step over here," I say, not wanting to get too close to the two of them together. "Liam, you shoot the other one if he moves." In a louder voice, I say, "Jake, shoot the whiney one if he moves."

"Hey," Donnie says, "I'm not whiney."

"Yes, you are," not-Donnie says in a low voice. "You're making this harder than it needs to be."

"Yeah," Liam says. "Listen to your friend."

"He's not my friend," Donnie spits out. "He's my brother."

I holster my sidearm and secure the brother's arms behind his back, then move on to take care of Donnie. "Let's bring them into the shop," I say.

"Good idea," Ben agrees.

Turning to Liam, I ask, "Do you have the keys?"

He nods his answer as the brother asks, "Can you put our horses up?"

"Bring them inside too," I say, not really knowing what we should do with them, but it's as good a choice as anything.

"Open the garage doors to take them in," the brother says. "That will be fine for now, but I'd rather not have them on cement for too long."

"Liam, go ahead and do as he suggests," I say. "Then grab a couple of those kitchen chairs from the loft space."

Within a few minutes, horses and humans are inside the garage. Leanne called her children to come from around the building, and they're also inside. Sadie is pushing a utility cart; under the wheels are skis. That has to be Ben's handiwork. I give them a small wave. Sebastian enthusiastically waves back, but Sadie lowers her eyes.

The gauntness of their features almost breaks my heart. Is this what my children also look like? If possible, Leanne looks even worse than the children or Ben. Leanne's brother didn't come in; he must be keeping watch outside. That's good.

I use more of the zip ties and secure their legs together. "Should we connect them to the chair?" Liam asks Ben.

"Let's just finish our chat and then we'll see," Ben says. "But first— " With a crooked smile, thanks to his new scar, he opens his arms wide. Liam sets down his shotgun and moves into them. I give them time alone. I want to be in his arms, too, but it's been so long and things were so rough between us. And . . . and I thought he was dead.

When he releases Liam, he looks at me with a slight tilt of his head. I give a nod and step into his embrace, feeling myself melt as he holds me. When he finally releases me, he asks in a husky voice, "Where's Dad?"

"I— " I swallow hard, then in a rush say, "We lost him. He got an infection. I'm so sorry, Ben."

Ben's smile evaporates and his shoulders sag. "When?" he asks, his voice cracking.

"September," Liam whispers.

I glance to Leanne. "You're all still together."

Ben nods. "Yeah, there was some trouble."

"How'd you know?" I ask.

"Know what?"

"Know we needed you? You got here right at the perfect time."

"Just—I don't know. Providence, I guess. We were coming up the road when I heard them call out to the house. I took off toward here. Leanne and the children followed. Where's Jake? Maybe he knows where the guys these two are looking for might be."

I motion with my head that we should move farther from the captives. "Liam?" I say.

"Yeah, I'll keep my gun on them."

In the corner of the garage, eyes still on the brothers, I quietly say, "Jake's not here. They're all gone. We found a note someone wrote saying they were hiding out for the winter."

"Hiding where?"

"I don't know," I answer, shaking my head.

"What's this about dead people?" he asks in a normal tone.

"You don't know, man?" Donnie calls out. "Could you not hear the shooting?"

"We heard it," I say, then turn back to Ben. "Something happened shortly before daylight this morning. I don't know exactly what, but I think the people living on the river were killed."

"Murdered," Donnie says. "It was Richard Majors and his crew. They killed them all."

"Who's Richard Majors?" Ben asks as we step back toward the others.

"I don't know," I answer, while not-Donnie says, "He took over Prospect. Didn't you hear about it?"

"Look," Ben says, impatience brimming to the top. "I'm not from around here. So how about you start at the beginning and tell me what's going on. Start with your name." He points to not-Donnie.

"Jerry McCullough." He tilts his head. "And this is my brother, Donnie."

"I'd shake your hand," Donnie says, "but I'm a little tied up at the moment."

"Cool it, Donnie," Jerry says. "We'd probably do the same thing."

"Humph."

"And why are you here?" Ben asks.

Jerry takes his time telling us about the terrible things that happened during the summer in nearby Prospect. When Ben and I visited before, we went into Prospect for dinner, and it seemed like a nice town. Jerry paints a picture of a community pulling together after the attacks. And when the EMP hit, changing life forever for all of us, the town's mayor did all he could to save lives.

But a few weeks later, the mayor and many others were killed in what sounds like a coup. The person responsible declared himself the new mayor and was executing anyone in opposition. Jerry and Donnie, along with the county sheriff and a handful of others, barely escaped the town alive.

They were holed up at a ranch outside of town and made plans to conquer Richard Majors, the self-appointed mayor who sounds more like a dictator, and his minions. Jerry and Donnie went south to Cody to try and find help, agreeing Bakerville—where the owner of the ranch had a friend living—would be the fall back in case it was needed.

"Unfortunately, Cody's in the middle of their own troubles," Jerry says.

"Ha! They're just scared," Donnie scoffs. "They made a big deal about how sending people to Prospect and trying to defeat Majors would leave them shorthanded if trouble happened in Cody. Even people we thought we could count on didn't want to leave their families."

"Which does make sense," Jerry says. "They're under threat from Meeteetse."

"Or they think they are," Donnie says. "I don't think it's near the threat we've got in Prospect. We tried to convince them that Richard Majors won't stop with Prospector County. He intends to rule over the entire region."

"Like a warlord?" Liam asks.

Donnie shrugs while Jerry says, "Maybe. He's . . . I don't think he's quite right in the head, hasn't been for years. Nothing would surprise me about him. Anyway, we couldn't get the help we needed in Cody. We went down to Powell, where we have a few friends— "

"Turns out they're just as yellow-bellied as the others," Donnie says. "None of them had heard about the things Majors is doing, but they had heard about the trouble in Meeteetse and said they couldn't risk it."

"What's going on in Meeteetse?" Ben asks, looking as confused as I feel.

"Some derelicts took over the town," Donnie shrugs. "There's only a handful of them, though. Not the group Majors has. And he's adding to his . . . his . . . "

"Army?" I offer.

"Sure, yeah. That works. He's adding to his army every day. He's starving the people, so they think they have no choice but to join him or die. And he's not just starving the adults, but the kids too. He's even adding young ones—like your boy there—to his legions. Mark my words, Cody is going to be sorry they didn't help us nip this in the bud."

"We think they've combined forces with an entity that infested Wesley too," Jerry says.

"Who's Wesley?" I ask.

"Not who, what," Jerry says. "It's a little town east of here. Early in the attacks—even before the EMP—a bunch of criminals were causing trouble."

"Really bad guys," Donnie says. "The sheriff thought he had it nipped in the bud, but it seems he didn't end it all. It was a mess—still is a mess."

Jerry nods. "We finally realized we're on our own. We went back to our hideout ranch, but everyone was gone."

"Not just gone," Donnie adds. "The place was leveled. The ranches around it too."

"We saw something like that," Liam says.

"What do you mean?" Ben asks.

"Cooke City. Someone burned the town down—there were only a few houses not destroyed."

"Really?" Jerry asks with a shake of his head. "Cooke City?"

"Well, I'll be," Donnie says. "They tell you what happened?"

"There was no one there," I say. "We found bodies, but no one living. We don't know what happened."

Jerry and Donnie are both quiet for several moments before Donnie says, "I never would've expected it. This kind of stuff shouldn't be happening here. Big cities have these kind of troubles, not places like this. Places where you know your neighbors should be safe."

"It doesn't surprise me," Leanne says quietly. "You wouldn't believe some of the things we've seen. The entire country has gone mad."

I look to Ben, who gives a small nod before saying, "We can talk about that later." He looks to the brothers. "What I want to know is, why are you two here today?"

"After we found the ranch destroyed, we came here to meet up with everyone, just like we'd agreed," Jerry says. "We camped out of town last night in the foothills, heard the shooting and started watching to see what was going on. After Majors's people left— "

"Wait," I say, holding up my hand. "This Majors guy that took over, you're saying he killed the people here?"

"That's right," Donnie says.

"How do you know?"

"We recognized a few of the people," Jerry says. "We grew up in Prospect, so we know who lives there—the good and the bad."

"Hey, how about you go and ask Pete Fairbanks about me?" Donnie says. "Then you can untie us, and we can get that cup of coffee you promised."

"Do you really have coffee?" Jerry asks. I can almost see his mouth watering.

"Sorry, no." Ben shakes his head. He reaches for my hand before asking Donnie, "Where's Pete live?"

"Next house up the way. On the left."

Ben shakes his head. "Their house is empty. All the houses in this neighborhood are. Leanne and I checked each on our way here."

"They're probably with Jake and Mollie," Liam says.

"Tell me more about the note you mentioned," Ben says.

"Not much to tell," I say. "It was cryptic, written from a father to a son, telling him to make himself at home and that he's left some things he'll need. They'll be back in the spring. I think it may have been written by Jake's dad."

"Why didn't it just tell him where to go to find them?" Donnie asks.

I shrug my shoulders and shake my head, while Ben says, "Smart not too. If the wrong people got the note, it could be bad."

The wrong people. I swallow the lump in my throat. "How did you escape your capture?"

He holds up a hand. "Later. I want to hear about how you got here, too, but let's figure things out with old Donnie and Jerry first."

"Good idea," Donnie says gruffly.

"Are you two related?" Jerry asks.

"She's my wife," Ben says.

Jerry nods. "I'm glad you two found each other again. Sorry about your dad."

"We've all lost people," Donnie says roughly, though I don't think he means it as a dig, especially when he continues with, "Never thought I'd see the kind of death and destruction we've experienced in the last several months."

"It's true," Jerry says. "While Cody seemed to be almost holding its head above water, we know it's a struggle. I can't really blame them, especially when we heard about the troubles in surrounding towns. It's a mess out there for sure. Where did you folks come from?"

"Oregon," Liam says.

"Oregon?" Donnie's eyes go wide. "Didn't they get nuked?"

"Yeah . . . " Ben says slowly. "There was a detonation. We don't really know much about it. We weren't near it and only saw it from a distance."

"You didn't get radiation poisoning?"

"Not that I know of." Ben shrugs. "My hair was already falling out before all this, and I haven't noticed it being any worse."

Leanne lets out a coarse laugh.

"So, about the note," Ben says to me. "Did it say anything helpful?"

"No, just they were going someplace safe for the winter and they'll be back in the spring. Oh, and to make contact with the community members who didn't want to leave. I guess those are the ones living on the river that— " I finish with a tilt of my head.

"The ones Majors's people murdered," Donnie says. "Yeah. Gabe Griffin was among the dead. Several others that I know from here too. Didn't see Pete, though, or Sheriff Spieth, Harry English— "

"Milena wasn't there either," Jerry says quietly.

"I don't know any of those people," I say. "Do you know Jake and Mollie Caldwell?"

"Nope, sorry," Donnie says.

"Wait a minute," Jerry says, looking thoughtful. "Who was the guy that helped stop Bill Vanderberg's pawn shop from being robbed? You remember his story about it? How Glen was so nervous he peed himself? Wasn't his name Jake Caldwell?"

"Got me," Donnie says. "Bill was a good guy. Too bad Majors murdered him."

After another ten minutes of getting nowhere with talking to Donnie and Jerry, and both beginning to shiver regularly, Ben says, "What should we do with them?"

"We can't let them freeze to death," I say. "Better let them get dressed."

"We should take them inside," Liam says. "Keep them tied up but at least keep them warm."

"Even if you don't have coffee," Donnie says, "maybe we can have a different warm drink?"

"Can we take care of our horses first?" Jerry asks.

"I'll handle them," Leanne says. "Sadie, Sebastian, each of you hold a rein." She turns to Donnie. "Do you have what we need in your saddlebags?"

"Yeah, everything is there. There're a few hay cubes they can have. Usually, we're scraping snow so they can eat. It's been pretty slim pickings, but Majors's people did leave a few bales of hay behind. We should go back for those."

"There's hay in the chicken coop," Liam says.

"Grass hay?" Leanne asks.

"I don't know . . . just hay." He shrugs.

"I'll look at it. Ben, can Liam help me?" she asks, after hefting the saddle off one of the horses.

I bristle when she asks Ben instead of me. Ben, however, looks to me and says, "If Liam helps us get them inside, can you and I handle them from there?"

My heart does a flipflop at him including me in this. Several months ago, before we were separated, he would've made the decision on his own. And I would've internally—or possibly externally—raged about it for hours. "Leslie and Destiny can help us too. It won't be a problem for Liam to give Leanne a hand."

"Who?" Ben asks.

"You'll see," I say with a smile.

"Liam, grab Little Brown and Poof Head, please. They've been out there long enough."

"Who?" Ben asks again.

"My chickens." I shrug.

"Your chickens . . . okay. That's new."

I giggle like a schoolgirl before saying, "Wait until you see what else is new."

Chapter 42

February 11th

Liam and I keep our guns trained on the brothers while Ben helps them back into their jackets and boots. When we're ready to go inside the house, Liam says to Leanne, "I'll be right back to help you. Do you want me to bring a bale of the hay I found?"

"Can you carry it?" she asks.

"I think so. There's a garden wagon in the shed. I could use that."

"Be careful with what you feed my horse," Donnie growls.

"I'm not an idiot," Leanne says in response, as she continues to use a brush on the horse, patting it as she goes.

"Good to know," Donnie sneers.

"Enough," Jerry says. "You've watched her with Gordie. She knows what she's doing. Thank you, miss. Thank you for caring for our horses."

Leanne gives Jerry a nod before turning her eyes to Donnie. If she's expecting an apology from him, she's mistaken. All she gets is a harumph.

The snow is coming down even harder as I lead the way into the house, making sure to look up to the window where I expect to see Destiny. When I do, I give her a nod and motion for her to go downstairs. At the interior door leading to the main house from the mudroom, I open it slightly and say, "Leslie, Destiny, it's me. Everything's okay."

Destiny is within view of the door, handgun by her thigh, as she says, "We're ready."

I step in and quickly look for Leslie and Wyatt. Destiny motions with her head to tell me they're beyond the brick wall of the woodstove. I give a nod. Once everyone is inside, I say, "Ben, this is Destiny. Destiny, my husband—Liam's dad."

"Good to meet you," she says. "Bart was sure you'd be here waiting for us. You're only a couple of days late."

"Is that right?" Ben asks, keeping his voice even. I know he's brokenhearted over losing Bart, but he'll put on a false front for now. Ben's always been able to compartmentalize things until the right time for letting loose. "Where should we put these gentlemen?"

"I'll grab chairs from the dining room," Liam says.

After we have Jerry and Donnie once again secured, this time in the middle of the kitchen, Liam goes out the door by the dining room. He pops back in a couple of minutes later with my little chickens. "Where do you want them?" he asks.

"Master bathroom," I answer.

I catch a small smile crossing Ben's face. "Chickens, huh? Did Mollie and Jake leave them behind?"

"No, I found them in Idaho."

"Idaho?" Donnie asks. "You brought them from Idaho? You do know we have chickens in Wyoming, right?"

"Yes, thanks for that," I say. "Are you always so unpleasant?"

"Only when I'm forced to strip in a snowstorm." He gives an exaggerated shiver.

I shake my head and start to remove my boots. "It's warm enough in here that we usually take our jackets and boots off but leave our sweaters and hats on." I give Ben an awkward smile. "Did you want to take off your boots?" I ask him.

"Better not," he says. "They've been on for days. It wouldn't be pleasant."

"Couldn't be any worse than Jerry's," Donnie says with a laugh. "Every night when we bed down, I'm looking for a gas mask."

"Right back at you, brother," Jerry says.

Destiny gives a small laugh. I roll my eyes, but I admit, it was funny. I'm feeling confident these guys are exactly who they say they are. Well, mostly confident. Not enough to untie them.

Although Ben leaves his boots on, he does take off his jacket. It's then I can see he's little more than skin and bones. The middle-aged gut he'd been working on is long gone, and even though he's still wearing several layers, it's obvious he's emaciated. He looks like I did those many months ago when I was such a wreck.

As I remove my own jacket, I calmly say, "Leslie, you and Wyatt can come out."

Ben raises his eyebrows at me. "More new friends?"

As Leslie comes into view carrying Wyatt, I reach for Wyatt as he calls for me. Smiling, I say, "Destiny, Leslie, and Wyatt are more than friends. We're family."

Ben's eyebrows shoot fully up to the edge of his stocking cap. "A baby? And he calls you Mama?"

I lift one shoulder in response. "Like I said, we're a family."

At my request, Destiny puts on some water to boil. "Ben may not have any coffee, but we do."

"You do?" three excited voices ask at once.

I want to ask Ben about his journey, but not in front of the children. There's no reason to remind them of their own terrible days in the past. From the little Leanne said, they had a much more difficult time reaching Bakerville than we did. Instead of talking about either of our trips, Ben moves over to where I'm holding Wyatt and says, "He's a cute one. How old?"

"Around ten months. We don't know his exact birthdate, but Destiny and Leslie think he was born in April."

"We're going to celebrate on April 15," Leslie says quietly. "That was my brother's birthday."

I can't keep the silly grin off my face. Even though I'm overwhelmed and even slightly nervous about being with Ben again, I can't help but smile. He's alive. He's here.

The water has yet to boil when Liam, Leanne, and her children come in. Her brother's still not with them. At this point, I'm wondering if he's keeping watch or, like Bart, if he's not with them because he died.

"It's getting pretty cold out there, and it's snowing harder," Sebastian says, giving me a shy smile. "Nice to see you again, Mrs. Ferguson. Ben said you'd be here."

"Nice to see you, too, Sebastian," I say. "You too, Sadie."

Sadie gives a solemn nod as Donnie asks, "My horse okay?"

"The horses are fine," Leanne says. "We can leave them in the garage tonight. We'll just want to make sure and get them off the concrete for several hours tomorrow. It looks like there's some pens out back that'll work—no loafing sheds or anything I can see, though. I guess they didn't have horses."

"They had goats," Liam says, taking off his boots. He motions for Sebastian and Sadie to do the same. They look to their mom, who gives a small nod.

"The hay was okay," Leanne says. "Grass hay. I need to take some water out to them."

Liam stops mid boot and slides his foot back in. "I'll help you. We have boiled water we got out of the creek yesterday. How much do they need?"

"Not much," Jerry says, "just a small amount now and more later."

Liam grabs a big pot we found in the garage that's already filled with water.

I half expected the water to work here since Mollie and Jake have a solar system that runs their well. When it didn't, we quickly discovered why. The solar system is gone. We assume they took it with them wherever they went.

The coffee is ready when Liam and Leanne return. "We have sugar and powdered cream," I say.

"Almost like a restaurant," Jerry says with a smile that twitches his mustache and lights up his eyes. Ben unbinds their hands from behind their backs and attaches one of their hands to their chairs. I'm glad zip ties are something we have an abundance of since we've already used several just in the last hour.

"How is it you have coffee?" Donnie asks, slurping from his cup.

"We stayed at Roosevelt Lodge in Yellowstone," I say. "It was like they just locked up and left. The kitchen was still full, the general store was full—it was crazy."

"We had coffee before that too," Liam says. "We found a wrecked car with groceries in the trunk."

"Sounds like you had some better experiences than we did," Leanne says quietly. "Do you have food? The children haven't eaten today."

"Oh!" I raise my hand to my mouth. "I'm so sorry. I should've asked that first. Yes, of course."

"We'll take care of it," Destiny says, motioning to Leslie.

"I snared a rabbit this morning," Liam says. "Let me finish cleaning it and we can put it on the stovetop."

"Ought to use that fancy shotgun of yours and kill some of the chukars," Donnie says. "They're all over the field down the way. Tasty little birds."

"Geese too," Jerry says. "We planned on trying for a couple after talking to Pete."

"We might do that," I say. "We were trying to stay quiet until we were able to properly meet the people living on the river. I guess that's no longer necessary. You're sure there were no survivors? I planned to go down and see— "

"You don't want to go down there, ma'am," Jerry says solemnly. "It's not— " He shakes his head.

"Should we move to the table?" Destiny asks, holding a cutting board in her hands with chunks of meat from one of the deer we harvested in Cooke City and the hardtack biscuits made out of a combination of flour and cornmeal we found in Roosevelt Lodge.

Finding those supplies at Roosevelt was most definitely a blessing, but none of it will last forever. We loaded up as much as we could bring with us, but we've also consumed a good amount. In fact, what we have more of than anything is coffee. While it seems a luxury, it's not something that will provide much nutrition. Maybe my chickens will give us the occasional egg now that we've stopped. And like the brothers said, we can hunt more than just deer and elk.

"What about us?" Donnie asks.

"We'll help you move—chair and all," Ben says. "You can eat with one hand just like you had your coffee."

As everyone gathers around the table, Liam says, "I'd like to pray before we eat."

"You would?" Ben asks, looking to me.

I give a nod of agreement and say, "Ben, would you like to thank God for not only the food but . . . everything?"

Leanne gives a snort as Ben says, "I, uh . . . I'll let Liam do it, if he'd like."

Before I bow my head, I notice Leanne and Sadie both stare off into space. Leanne, who I found so terribly annoying in those days we were together with her Christian rhetoric, seems to have had a change of heart. Of course, in these past few months, so have I. I wonder if her change came on suddenly or, like me, developed slowly over time. I'm so lost in my thoughts of Leanne I barely listen as Liam fervently thanks God for bringing his dad and Leanne's family safely to Bakerville. Leanne snorts again and Ben clears his throat.

After Liam's amen, Jerry says, "It's good to hear a young man like you so on fire for God."

Liam smiles as he says, "My grandpa told me about Him, even gave me the Bible my grandma gave him before she died. We've been reading while we made our way here."

"You have?" Ben asks Liam but looks to me.

"We have," I say with a light shrug.

"And you think that has helped you get here?" Leanne asks skeptically. "Because my guess is, the only way you got here—looking as healthy as you do—is luck. Pure and simple luck. But let me tell you, not all of us were as lucky as you. We certainly didn't find coffee, not even flour." She holds up her biscuit.

I glance from Leanne to Sebastian. He's keeping his eyes down while he works on his meat, taking tiny bites. Sadie's doing the same thing.

"I thought you were a Christian?" Liam asks Leanne.

She rolls her eyes before shaking her head.

"I'm a Christian," Sebastian says. "Mom's not now. Not after Uncle Wes died when we tried to escape."

Ah. Well, that explains why her brother isn't here.

"Sadie's like mom now," Sebastian continues. "But me, I remember when my dad left us, and Grandma said we can't always know what God's plans are. I think it's like that now too."

"Your grandma is dead too," Leanne says harshly. "Murdered. The neighbors here, too, right? With everything we've seen and experienced . . . no thanks."

The room is silent for several minutes as everyone eats. I'm not hungry, having just eaten before I laid down, but I do give Wyatt a couple bites while I sip on my coffee.

I choose not to bring up the difficulties we had getting here. No matter what Liam and I went through, I won't even attempt to one-up Leanne. More than anything, I feel bad for her. When we first met her, she was determined and at peace. She was adamant God would help them get home. To see her now—not only as a physical shell of her former self, but also a spiritual shell—is sad.

Could this happen to me? Will I turn my back on God when things get tough? Bart did in some ways. After Jessa died, he stopped going to church and, like Leanne, seemed a shell of his former self. The months before he died, he gained a new intensity. A fire. Right now, I don't have a fire. It's more of a smolder. But it's there and I want it to stay there, to increase even. I wish Mollie were here. She'd help me fan the flames.

After an uncomfortable lunch, Ben asks how we pass the time without needing to walk all day.

"We've only been here two days," Liam says. "We spent yesterday exploring."

"Anything exciting?"

"No food, if that's what you mean," Destiny says. "They must have taken everything with them."

"Hmm. That doesn't sound like Mollie," Ben says, scratching at his beard. "Seems she would've left something behind in case it was needed. Like the hay. I don't know much about chickens—anything, really—but is it normal to have bales of hay in chicken coops?"

"Maybe if you were trying to hide them," Jerry offers.

"Exactly. Like the note said, there's things stashed somewhere."

"They probably buried it," Donnie says. "You know, like an underground cache."

"Could be," Ben agrees with a nod. "How would we find it?"

"We wouldn't. Not with all this snow. Maybe if the ground were bare, we could see where the soil had been disturbed."

"If there's nothing pressing to do," Leanne says, "I'd like to take the kids and lie down."

"Of course," I say. "We've been using the downstairs bedroom. Do you— " I hesitate a moment before pressing on, for fear of upsetting her again. "Do you have sleeping bags?"

She gives me a look I interpret as *duh* before saying, "We were able to get camping gear and winter clothes from our home. My mom and stepdad were murdered, and all the food and most everything else was stolen, but they didn't touch those things. Probably because it was still summer. Finding things to use now is almost impossible. For us at least."

I nod my agreement. "We found a single snowshoe. We took it because one of Liam's was about done for. We ended up needing it."

"Are your things still in the cart?" Ben asks, as she stands from the table.

Leanne gives him a warm smile, warmer than I think she should be sharing with my husband, before saying, "Yes, I only brought in the bags."

He gives her a nod. "I'll grab them. Liam, is there water for washing up?"

"Sure, Dad. We'll need to get more, but there's enough to use a washcloth. There's already some in the downstairs bathroom."

"I'll show you," I say.

One of the things we did yesterday was put the area rugs back in the family room to give us a cushion for more sleeping space. We've been sharing the bed in the basement—or as Destiny says her dad would call it, *hot racking*—but when more than one person is sleeping, the floor is needed. I offer them the bedroom, which Leanne gratefully accepts.

"And you can use the bathroom. The water isn't hot, but it won't be too bad. And the toilet flushes if you send a little water down the bowl. We try and go as long between flushes as we can since getting water is a hassle."

"Thank you," Leanne says. "I, um . . . I'm sorry I've been so cross. It's a disappointment not to have" —she gives a shrug— "more. Ben said your friends would be here and that they were prepared for anything. I guess they weren't as prepared as he thought since they had to leave."

Nodding, I say, "I'm not sure why they chose to leave, but like Ben, I thought we'd be . . . rescued. I guess that's the right word."

"Rescued from what?" she scoffs. "You don't seem the worse for wear. You aren't even any skinnier than when I first met you. And the children look healthy."

"We've been blessed for the later part of our trip. That's true."

"Has Ben told you he lost a couple of toes?" She gives me a look I can't quite interpret.

"No. We haven't discussed much." I feel like a heel for not asking him about his health. Is that why he's limping?

"Yep," she says, almost gloating. "He found the children and me a safe place to stay while he went looking for food. A storm came in and he got lost. He had a hole in his boot and frost bit his three toes. They never healed. Someone with a little medical training and a big heart removed them."

"I'm sure he and I will talk about things later," I say, attempting to give her a smile. "Do you have everything you need for now?"

"Humph. Not even close," she says, before turning her back on me.

Chapter 43

February 14th

The last several days have been stressful. Leanne alternates between pleasant and disagreeable—almost to the point of hateful. Sadly, I see much of myself in her with the uptightness and reacting, even overreacting, to every little thing. She seems to snap at me most of all but also her children and my children. Even little Wyatt hasn't fully escaped her wrath. Ben, however, is apparently immune. Instead of harsh words, she speaks calmly and gives him shy smiles. To his credit, Ben seems completely oblivious to her attention, treating her more like a sister than anything.

He and I being together again is different. We're taking our time and getting to know each other again. Our marriage was in dire straits before the world fell apart. At the time, I didn't care. I was more than happy to be done with it and start anew, ready to run away with my business partner Mark.

Those few days we were on the road, making our way to Wyoming, we started to connect again. But then he was taken from me, and I was sure he was dead. Bart, though, Bart knew all along Ben was alive, and he insisted we'd be together again. And we are.

The love I feel for Ben is there, but the months have changed both of us in many ways. Ben's had many physical changes but also internal. He suffers from nightmares every time he sleeps, which isn't often. Insomnia plagues him.

I asked about the frostbite and the scar on his face. While he shared pretty much the same story as Leanne regarding losing his toes, he was very vague about the scar, saying he was in the wrong place at the wrong time. He's not the same as he was, but his love for Liam—and for me—is still evident. And I notice he treats Sebastian and Sadie as his own too. I imagine what he feels for them is like the love I have for Destiny, Leslie, and Wyatt.

Even though he's not comfortable giving details about some of the things he went through while we were apart, there's other things he's comfortable sharing. Where I thought Ben was dead, he said he knew Liam and I would be here when he got to Bakerville. Admittedly, he expected us to have arrived many months ago since we still had the dirt bikes when he was kidnapped.

The kidnapping made little sense. Why the people even took them—other than to raid our camp for the few provisions we had—was never clear. And it soon became evident they were planning to kill them. Ben, Leanne, and her brother, Wes, devised a plan for escape. Wes was shot in the process. He was still with them when they escaped but died later. With her brother dead, Ben didn't feel he could leave Leanne on her own to get home, especially with two children.

It took them over a month before they got to her mom and stepdad's home to find them murdered and the house pillaged. The nearby neighbors suffered the same fate. With nowhere for Leanne and her children to go, Ben convinced them to come to Bakerville. I'd already heard a few of the details about their terrible trip from Leanne, but Ben filled in the blanks, often glossing over the worst parts. I don't know if he'll ever be ready to share those worst parts—or if I'll ever be ready to hear about them.

Brothers Jerry and Donnie are still with us. They're essentially our prisoners. At night, we lock them in the basement room with all the shelves. With the bundle of keys we found were a couple of padlocks to use on the hasp. Donnie grumbled a lot about being locked in, saying they'd be dead if the house caught on fire. During the day, we keep them secured to a chair, now using rope instead of wasting the zip ties. I half suspect they'd have little trouble getting loose if they put their minds to it.

Donnie, always gruff and annoying, puts up a continual fuss. Jerry keeps reminding him they'd do the same thing. He also tells us they're not a threat and would be happy to lend a hand toward hunting, gathering water, and security. In fact, at this very moment, they're in the kitchen—strapped to their chairs—as Donnie talks about geese.

"C'mon, man. Now that you've figured out how to work the oven, can you imagine how tasty a roasted goose would be?"

Figuring out how to work the oven part of the range was exciting. While the children and I had been able to use the stovetop without any trouble, we figured the oven wouldn't work. None of the other places we'd stayed at had a functioning oven, even with the gas working. Ben was the one who said he was certain Mollie made a big deal about their range being battery-operated with an oven that works, even without the batteries installed, simply by striking a match. The batteries had been removed, but as Ben expected, he was still able to light the pilot and fire it up.

I'm surprised Mollie and Jake didn't take the range with them. They took most of the furniture; the solar systems from the house, garage, and bunkhouse; and even the hot water heater. Why not the range? I'm truly thankful they left it, but it is a bit of a mystery.

Ben lets out a sigh. "I did hear the geese go over earlier. Maybe Clarice and I will go try to find them."

I give him a smile, liking the sounds of that. All the children, except the baby who's napping, are outside right now. Liam spent some time clearing paths around the house, and the kids are using them for playing. They took my chickens with them. While playing is a rather loose term, since they've been cautioned to stay quiet, they seem to be having fun. I checked on them a few minutes ago, and all five, plus Little Brown and Poof Head, are in the chicken pen. Leanne is upstairs on watch. Soon, Liam will take her place, so I'm glad he's having a little fun and almost acting like a kid for the moment.

"Humph," Donnie exclaims. "Have you ever hunted geese before?"

Ben shakes his head. "Not really. I've gone duck hunting a few times but didn't enjoy it. I'm a big game hunter."

"The deer you got the day before yesterday was great," Jerry says with a nod. "Much appreciated. But I'm with Donnie on this. Let us help you. We'll go down to the field and see what we can come home with. Have you ever had goose jerky? The deer version pales in comparison."

"Which field?" I ask, walking toward the large south-facing window.

"That one right down there," Donnie says. "There were geese in it when we came up here. Should've taken the time to whack a couple. Then, maybe if we'd come bearing gifts, things would be different."

Ben lets out a laugh as I grab the binoculars we've placed on a shelf. Even though the kids and I had made a point of always being ready to leave at a moment's notice, with Ben here, we're a little laxer. We still have our smaller packs with essentials ready to go, but we've taken many things out to use. It's much easier than packing and unpacking multiple times a day.

Watch is still a challenge, but adding Leanne and Ben to the rotation helps. I thought Sadie should be old enough to take a turn since she's the same age as Leslie, but both Leanne and Ben have asked that she be given more days to rest from their journey. Admittedly, she needs it. All of them are looking better just from being off the trail and having regular food—even if it isn't exciting food since it's mainly just meat with small amounts of grains and veggies we have left.

Unfortunately, we only have a few more days' worth of the staples we found at Roosevelt, then we'll be existing completely on the meat we hunt. Liam and Ben tried fishing the creek yesterday but didn't even get a bite. Rabbits, though abundant, are terribly lean. Geese are a good idea.

"Where are they?" I ask, looking through the binoculars over the field.

"Should be there," Donnie answers. "Do you see dark specks?"

I take the binoculars down and catch a glimpse of movement when I do. Was it a goose? I put the glasses back up, looking more toward the tree line where the river is. Scanning the entire area, I decide I do see birds flying. Maybe they're geese.

I look back toward the field and this time see the dark specks, some of them are even moving. I'm smiling when I take the field glasses from my eyes. Again, I see movement. I look out over the yard to where Mollie and Jake's fence begins. That's when my heart skips several beats, and I quickly move from the window.

"Ben!" I cry. "Someone's here."

"Your kids are outside," Jerry says. "Let me go after them."

Ben puts up a hand. "Leanne, what do you see?" he calls upstairs as he squat-walks to the window, staying out of view. "Leanne?" he calls again as he reaches the window.

"What? Huh?" she asks groggily.

"People," I say, none too calmly. "They're at the edge of the property by the road."

"Wait a minute," Ben says slowly. "Hand me the binoculars, Clarice."

As Ben takes the binoculars and quickly puts them into position, Leanne calls out, "I see them. One's waving a bandana."

"Hot diggity," Ben cries out, sounding exactly like his dad. "Take a look, Clarice. It's Jake!"

"Jake?" I ask, squinting as I try to see. "Are you sure?"

"I think so, yes. He has a beard but . . . you look."

He thrusts the binoculars toward me. I focus on the one waving the bandana. It could be Jake. Next to him, with binoculars trained on us, is another guy. Maybe it's one of the neighbors we met during our last visit, but I can't be sure. Mollie isn't with them. If I saw her, I'd know for sure. "I don't know . . . it could be."

"Leanne, you see anyone else?" Ben asks.

"I thought I saw movement, but I don't have a good view. If they're farther down the hill, I wouldn't be able to see them. No one else is within view."

"I'm going after the children," I say.

"Untie us so we can help," Donnie says.

"Not yet," Ben answers, still looking out the window as I move toward the door off the dining room. I'm halfway there when it opens and the children come falling in.

"Someone's here," Liam says hurriedly. "Where do you want me?"

"You saw them?" Ben asks, not taking his eyes from the window. "Sebastian did."

"I saw them," Sebastian says, nodding vigorously.

"Liam, come over here," Ben says. "Stay low, but I want you to look out the window and tell me what you see."

"Destiny," I say, "go to the back door. Leslie, wake Wyatt and get him ready to go. All the emergency packs are still loaded, right?"

"Right," Leslie says, as they both run to do my bidding. Wyatt is on a blanket bed on the floor of Mollie's former office. We've been keeping the emergency bags in the office, so letting him nap there makes sense.

"Sadie, Sebastian, it might be best if you stay with Leslie," I say loud enough for Leanne to hear so she can contradict me if she wishes.

"Is that . . . " Liam starts and then stops. "Dad, I think it's Jake. Do you think it's him? Mom? Did you see?"

I stop moving as Donnie says, "Great. Your friend is here. Maybe he'll let us go."

"You're sure?" I ask. Wyatt lets out a cry from his room. Leslie is shushing him.

"Pretty sure . . . yeah," Liam says. "I think so."

So, no. He's not sure. "Ben, what should we do?"

"Leanne, do you see them from upstairs?"

"I have them," she answers.

"Liam, you go to the side of the house with your rifle. Clarice, we'll go out the sunroom and to the fence. The rock column is where I want you, okay?"

I nod my agreement as I slip into my coat.

"You've already sent Destiny to the back porch. Will she know what to do?"

"She'll know," I say. "Leslie?"

"We're hurrying," she answers.

"What are you doing?" I ask Ben.

"I'm going to talk to them. We'll go out together. Hurry, Liam. Leanne, be ready."

"You're just going to leave us here?" Donnie asks. "If the shooting starts, we'll be sitting ducks."

"Leslie, if things go bad, untie the brothers," I say.

Ben meets my eyes and says, "We're going to be okay." He squeezes my hand, then hands me the binoculars. I slip them over my neck before we open the door from the main house into the sunroom. Instead of flinging it wide, Ben moves it just enough for us to slip through.

Once we're down the few steps and on the paver-lined ground, Ben says, "Keep low. If it's not Jake but someone hostile, I don't think they'd have a shot at us with the fence in the way, but let's not risk it."

"You really think it's Jake?"

"I hope so." Within a few seconds, we're out of the sunroom and at the fence. "Stay against this," Ben reminds me, touching the rock column part of the fence. "Can you see any better from here?" he asks, motioning to the binoculars.

Putting them up, I scan the men. "No improvement."

He's next to me, also hugging the rocks, as he shakes his head. "Okay, here goes nothing." He opens the gate and yells in a very loud, very commanding voice, "State your business!"

There's a faint reply, but I can't quite make it out.

"Did you get that?" Ben asks me.

"No." I lift my stocking hat slightly to free an ear. "Ask again."

He clears his throat, then says, "Repeat why you are here."

A smile spreads across my face as the faint voice this time reaches my exposed ear. "It's him. At least he says it is."

"What did he say?" Ben asks.

"He said, 'This is Jake Caldwell.' That's all."

Ben lets out a breath. "Run to the door, yell in, and tell Leanne not to shoot them. I'm going to ask them to come closer."

"You think she'd shoot first?"

"Hard telling."

I shake my head but quickly move back to the house, continuing to keep myself low. At the door, I open it enough to yell in. When Leanne responds, I deliver the message. She answers with a snort.

Donnie again suggests he and Jerry be untied. I shut the door without response. We're going to have to do something with those two, but not until this is over.

Please, Lord, please let it be Jake.

When I'm back by the column, Ben says, "Here we go." He raises his voice and says, "Jake, you and only you start walking up the road."

I lean out slightly so I can get a glimpse of what's happening. Jake—if it really is him—is talking with the guy next to him. The other guy has his binoculars down and is shaking his head. Jake moves out of sight for a moment, then quickly reappears on the road. He's holding his hands near his side but away from his body.

He's about halfway up the road when Ben says, "It's him, right?"

I train the binoculars on him. "I just don't know." He's the right height, but he's thin—we're all thin, though. Just then, Jake turns his bearded face in my direction. He lifts his hand and gives a smile. I put the glasses down and yell, "What's your wife's favorite food?"

"Umm . . . " He pauses. "She likes everything—almost everything, anyway."

Okay, that didn't go so well. I try again. "What does she eat every time she goes to the coast."

"Oh! That. She eats oysters."

"It's him," Ben says.

"Yeah," I say, tears running down my face.

Chapter 44

February 14th

There are many more minutes of confusion as it becomes obvious Jake has not only one friend with him but several. And horses too. Jake leads his horse, as do the rest of the adults. Some of the horses have children in the saddles. As the entourage approaches, Ben keeps watch as I touch base with my children and let Leanne know what's happening.

Her response is, "It's not like I'm blind."

"We don't think anything is awry, but Ben asked if you could stay where you are for the time being. Should I send Sadie and Sebastian up with you?"

"Keep them with you," she answers. "I don't need the distraction."

"Ready to let us loose?" Donnie asks.

Ignoring him, I go into the office where Leslie and Leanne's children are sitting, patiently waiting.

"What do you want us to do?" Leslie asks.

"I think everything is okay, but just hang tight for now. I'm going to have Destiny move to a different spot."

Destiny, on the far southern side of the back deck, looks toward me when I open the door. She gives me a smile and asks, "So that's your friend?"

"Yes, and we think everything is fine, but I'd like you to stay out of sight until we're sure. Let's move you to the far side of the garage where Ben was when Jerry and Donnie arrived the other day."

She narrows her eyes before nodding.

"I know," I say. "I'm sure we're fine, but things are not always what they seem these days."

"Where's Liam?" she asks as we step inside the house.

"Up front."

We go through the kitchen, where Donnie again makes his plea for release, and out the dining room door. Liam, as expected, is on the front corner of the house.

"Everything's good now," he says with a smile.

I let out a loud breath. "I think you're right."

"Do you think they're back already? You know, from wherever the note said they were spending the winter?"

"I don't know why they're here today. I guess we'll find out soon enough. Your dad wants you to stay ready, just in case. I'm going to go out and meet them. Destiny and Leanne, along with your dad and you, will back me up."

"Why you?"

"It makes sense." I don't tell him Ben and I had a brief discussion about it, in which he wanted to be the one to go meet them, but I put my foot down. I'm in better health and am able to move quickly if needed. With his limp from losing his toes, he's not nearly as agile.

Turns out, our precautions were unnecessary. Jake greets me not only with a huge smile but opening his arms for a hug. I hesitate a few beats before accepting.

"I can't believe you're here," Jake says. "Your family?" he asks cautiously.

"Ben and Liam are here. We were . . ." I shrug. "Just being cautious." I raise my voice and say, "Ben? Liam? Come over. You too, Destiny."

"Always smart." Jake doesn't ask me about Bart, and I don't volunteer the info yet. Every time I say the words out loud—say he's dead—the pain opens anew.

"You remember my neighbor Evan?" Jake pats him on the shoulder.

"Evan, hi," I greet him with a smile.

"And you met Noah Hammer at the barbecue we had last time you visited." He hooks his thumb in the direction of a young man. "Boy, that seems like a lifetime ago."

"Ma'am," Noah says, tilting his hat.

"Hello. I do remember the barbecue and meeting your friends. And it was a lifetime ago."

"This is Pete, Dusty, and Dax. And the children—well, we'll get proper introductions later. They've had a tough couple of days."

I start to ask why, but with the way Jake shakes his head, I decide to leave it for now.

When Ben and Liam appear, Jake says his hellos and then repeats the introductions. Destiny is hanging back slightly; I introduce her but don't take the time to share everyone else's names. "We have more people inside," I say.

"Well, let's head on in," Evan answers.

"We'll take care of the horses if you want to take the kids inside," one of the men I've just met says, taking the rein from Evan while another takes Jake's horse. "Noah, Pete, can you help?"

"There's two horses in the garage," I say, as Noah and Pete agree to help. "We had them out earlier, and they'll go out again shortly."

"We'll put them in there to unsaddle them, then put them out in one of the pens in the back. Sound good, Jake?" the man asks.

"Yep. Same as last time—whatever you need to do with them."

"One of the people with us, Leanne, she loves horses. She can help with Jerry's and Donnie's," I say. I turn and look up at the window where I expect to see Leanne. She's there, with a determined look covering her face. I motion to her to come down.

While she's been less than friendly with me, she does enjoy spending time with the horses. Maybe she'll want to help with these. She doesn't give a wave, or anything, but does disappear from the window.

As we walk toward the mudroom entrance, Leanne comes out. "Did you need me?" she asks.

"This is Leanne," I say to Jake and Evan.

After they give their greetings, I say, "I thought you might want to be with the horses when they take care of the ones they brought."

"Yeah, good idea. The children are still in the back room. You can send mine out to help."

Once we're inside the house, Evan looks at Jerry and Donnie. With his hand on his sidearm, he asks, "What do we have here?"

"A kidnapping," Donnie says gruffly.

"Is that right?"

"Not exactly," Jerry answers.

"We're being held against our will!" Donnie cries. "What else would you call it?"

"I'm Jerry McCullough. This is my brother, Donnie. We were in the wrong place at the wrong time. They're just being cautious."

"Ha! They know we're not a threat. They're just wielding power while they can."

"And *that* is why we're still tied up," Jerry says. "My brother doesn't know when to keep his mouth shut."

Ben lets out a laugh, then says, "Truth be told, they'd just convinced me to let them loose so we could go goose hunting."

"We did?" Donnie acts shocked.

"That's why we're here, to goose hunt," Jake says. "But then we— " His eyes dart to the children. "We found some trouble."

"We saw the trouble," Jerry says.

"Not a place to take your kids," Donnie says. "Hey, Ben, how about undoing us?"

"These aren't our children," Evan says evenly. "And let's hold off on anything until you explain what you know about the trouble."

"Um, Clarice," Jake says. "Would it be possible for the children to get a bath?"

"Yes, uh, sure."

"I'll take care of it," Destiny says, returning from the office with the others. "Leslie, I'll take Wyatt if you can warm some water. Liam, can you help her? Bring it downstairs when you have it." She smiles brightly at the oldest boy. "I'm Destiny. You want to come with me?"

"Can I play with your baby?" the tallest girl asks.

"Sure. Wyatt loves to be played with."

"Sadie, Sebastian, your mom said you could go out and help with the new horses." While Sadie's face lights up, Sebastian seems disappointed. He nods anyway as they go for their coats and boots. We wait until all the children, including Leslie and Liam with pots of warm water, leave the room.

"Now tell us what you know," Evan demands.

The brothers share the same story Ben and I have heard dozens of times. Jake and Evan share a look when they tell how they were sent to Cody for help.

"So I suppose the people who lived at the ranch outside of Prospect would know you? They'd vouch for you?" Evan asks.

"Of course they would," Donnie says. "So would Pete Fairbanks. We were heading to his place when we stopped here to make sure everyone was okay."

Evan and Jake share a look before Jake asks, "How do you know Pete?"

"Met him at a trapper thing he did. He had me and my girlfriend at the time over for dinner."

Pete, I think to myself. Isn't one of the guys with the horses named Pete? Ben catches my eye and gives a slight nod. We've no sooner exchanged our silent communication when I hear boots at the door and a knock. It pops open slightly, and one of the cowboys walks in.

"We're getting the horses tended. Leanne said you have water?"

"Some," I say. "We just sent the children down to clean up. We might have to get more."

He steps farther into the house and glances into the kitchen, where his eyes briefly rest on Jerry and Donnie.

"Hey, Dax," Jerry says.

"What's going on here?" Dax asks.

"You know them?" Evan asks.

"Of course. They escaped from Prospect with Grant and Shelby. They went to Cody for help, but then— "

"See!" Donnie says triumphantly. "I told you."

After clearing up that Donnie and Jerry are who they've been saying they are, they're let loose. Jake and his group planned to spend a few days goose hunting on the river and fields, but finding the massacre changed their plans.

The children with them are the only survivors of the slaughter, having survived by being in an unexpected place for a rare sleepover. The oldest, Chandler, hid the younger children and kept watch with only a BB gun for protection. They've been alone since then. Jerry felt terrible they hadn't done a better search and found the children when they went through the houses.

Now, instead of hunting, Jake and his friends are heading back to their winter refuge to warn those there about what Evan believes to be an imminent attack. With Donnie and Jerry confirming the belief that the murders were the work of the bad guys from Prospect, Evan is adamant they get home and make plans for defense.

"Why'd you leave here?" I ask Jake. "You and Mollie, you've done so much over the years."

"That's a long story. There's plenty of time for those details."

"You planning on leaving tonight?" Donnie asks. "Because if not, we really ought to go after those geese."

As they're discussing whether they should still goose hunt or not, those caring for the horses come in. Leanne, her cheeks rosy from the cold, has a smile on her face. Pete and Dusty, surprised to see the brothers whom they know, get caught up on the story of how they are here, with Donnie making plenty of cutting remarks about being held captive.

I notice a small smile pass between Donnie and Leanne, when she says, "I'm glad to see you untied. You're taller than you seem while sitting."

Chapter 45

February 15th

This morning has been a whirlwind. They did end up goose hunting last night, deciding there was no reason to go home empty handed. I stayed with the children while Leanne and Ben went with Jake's group and the brothers. They returned at dark with over two dozen geese. Most went again this morning, right at daylight, bagging a dozen more.

While they were hunting yesterday evening, the children and I packed up. Jake briefly explained that, to join the Bakerville community, we had to know residents. When he said he'd sponsor us, Ben made sure that would include Leanne and her children, plus my new children—Destiny, Leslie, and Wyatt. Jake said absolutely, and that there'd be other things—like all of us would be expected to join the work groups to help the community succeed.

Our biggest challenge now will be getting to the ski lodge they're staying at. With Jake's group and the brothers on horseback, it's only a short half-day trip. But the rest of us are on foot, with Ben's group not yet recovered from their harrowing journey. My children and I are feeling strong, and even though it'll take us at least two days to make the uphill trip, I'm confident we can do it.

After discussing my concerns with Jake, he and Evan come up with a plan. Jake will walk with us and let Leanne and her daughter have his horse. Evan, who is concerned about the marauders, wants to get back as quickly as possible to start planning defense, but he'll send more horses back for us. When Jerry hears the plans, he offers to walk with us so Ben and Sebastian can have the second horse.

In the end, Ben insisted on walking. Leanne and Sebastian are on Jerry's horse while Sadie rides the old horse Jake was on. The horse riders are all well prepared and brought along backpacks with snowshoes strapped to them, allowing Jake and Jerry to join us without issue.

Wyatt is on my back as we start our trek. He's playing with my hair and singing a song only he knows the words to. Every once in a while, his favorite word, *Mama*, comes through loud and clear. Destiny, Leslie, and Liam have their packs. Liam is pushing the ski cart Ben made. Jake and Jerry are pulling our black sleds.

We left the toboggan and saucer sleds behind, along with a few things Jake said we wouldn't need. Little Brown Hen and Poof Head are in their box, riding on the sled Jerry is pulling.

Before leaving, Jake pulls us all into a circle and asks for God's blessing on our trip to the winter refuge.

"Are you ready?" Ben asks, giving me a grin that takes me back twenty years and melts my heart.

"I'm ready," I answer, as he reaches for my hand.

New to the Havoc in Wyoming series? The adventure begins with Caldwell's Homestead: Havoc in Wyoming, Part 1.

Thank you for spending your time with the people of
Bakerville, Wyoming.

If you have five minutes, you'd make this writer very happy if
you could write a short Amazon review.

I appreciate you!

Join my reader's club!

Receive a complimentary copy of *Wyoming Refuge: A Havoc
in Wyoming Prequel.* As part of my reader's club, you'll be the
first to know about new releases and specials. I also share info on
books I'm reading, preparedness tips, and more.

Please sign up on my website:

MillieCopper.com

Now Available

Havoc in Wyoming

Part 1: Caldwell's Homestead

Jake and Mollie Caldwell started their small farm and homestead to be able to provide for an uncertain future for their family, friends, and community. They have tried to plan for everything, but they never imagined this would happen.

Part 2: Katie's Journey

Katie loves living on her own while finishing up her college degree, working her part-time jobs, and building a relationship with her boyfriend, Leo. When disaster strikes, being away from family isn't quite so nice, and home is over a thousand miles away. Will she make it home before the United States falls apart?

Part 3: Mollie's Quest

Two or three times a year, Mollie Caldwell travels for business. Being away from her Wyoming farmstead is both a fun time and a challenge. They started their farm to be able to provide for an uncertain future for their family, friends, and community. The farm keeps the entire family busy, meaning extra work for her husband while she's away. This time, while on her business trip, terrorists attack. Her weeklong business trip becomes much longer as she tries to make her way home.

Part 4: Shields and Ramparts

The United States, and the community of Bakerville, face a new threat . . . a threat that could change America forever. As the neighbors band together, all worry about friends and family members. Have they found safety from this latest danger?

Part 5: Fowler's Snare

Welcome to Bakerville, the sleepy Wyoming community Mollie and Jake Caldwell have chosen as their family retreat. At the edge of the wilderness, far away from the big city, they were so sure nothing bad could ever happen in such a protected place. They were wrong. Now, with the entire nation in peril, coming together as a community is the only way they can survive. But not everyone in the community has the people of Bakerville's best interest at heart.

Part 6: Pestilence in the Darkness

Surrounded by danger, they band together with the community of Bakerville to move to a new defensible location. But they weren't prepared to have to give up so much for the security they so desperately need. And they quickly learn trust must be earned, not freely given.

Part 7: My Refuge and Fortress

When Jake and a group of hunters return to Bakerville and find their former neighbors slaughtered, they realize there is a new, even more deadly threat. Will their reinforced location be secure enough? And what about the radio announcement from the president? Will his promise of help arrive in time?

Acknowledgments

Thanks to:

Ameryn Tucker, my editor, beta reader, and daughter wrapped in one. I had a story I wanted to tell, and Ameryn encouraged me and helped me bring it to life.

Dauntless Cover Design for the amazing cover.

Sheri at Light Hand Proofreading for not only looking for those pesky typos but also sharing in the creative process.

My husband, who gave me the time and space I needed to complete this dream and was very patient as I'd tell him the same plot ideas over and over and over.

Two more daughters and a young son, who willingly listen to me drone on and on about story lines and ideas while encouraging me to "keep going."

My amazing Beta Readers! Thanks to Ginger, Barbara, Dianna, and Tammy for your help in creating the final story. Your insights and abilities to see the things I miss are very much appreciated!

And to you, my readers, for spending your time with the people of Bakerville, Wyoming. If you have five minutes, you'd make this writer very happy if you could leave a review. I appreciate you!